The Blacksmith's Daughter

A Novel of the American Revolution

by

Suzanne Adair

Whittler's
Bench
Press
A Dram Tree Books Imprint

First Edition 2007
Published in the United States of America by Whittler's Bench Press, an imprint of Dram Tree Books.

Publisher's Cataloging-in-Publication Data
(Provided by DRT Press)

Adair, Suzanne.
    The blacksmith's daughter / by Suzanne Adair.
    p. cm.
    Includes bibliographical references.
    ISBN 978-0-9785265-3-5
1. Camden, Battle of, Camden, S.C., 1780--Fiction. 2. United States--History--Revolution, 1775-1783--Fiction. 3. South Carolina--History--Revolution, 1775-1783--Fiction. 4. Historical fiction. I. Title.

PS3501.D175 B43 2007
813.54--dc22

10 9 8 7 6 5 4 3 21

Whittler's Bench Press
P.O. Box 7183
Wilmington, N.C. 28406
(910) 538-4076
www.dramtreebooks.com
Potential authors: visit our website or email us for submission guidelines

Volume discounts available.
Call or e-mail for terms.

ACKNOWLEDGEMENTS

I receive help from some wonderful and unique people while conducting research for novels. Here are a few who assisted me with *The Blacksmith's Daughter*:

The 33rd Light Company of Foot, especially
Ernie and Linda Stewart
Carl Barnett
Lonnie Cruse
Bonnie Bajorek Daneker
Marg Baskin
Howard Burnham
Dr. Ed Cashin
Larry Cywin
Mike Everette
Jack E. Fryar, Jr.
Nolin and Neil Jones
Marja McGraw
John Robertson
Dr. Tony Scotti

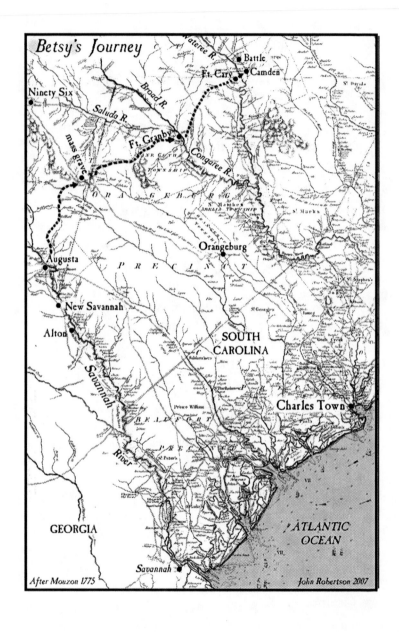

Betsy's Journey

Battle
Ft. Cary
Camden
Ninety Six
Broad R.
Saluda R.
mass grave
Ft. Granby
Congaree R.
Orangeburg
Augusta
New Savannah
Alton
Savannah
SOUTH CAROLINA
Charles Town
ATLANTIC OCEAN
GEORGIA
Savannah

After Mouzon 1775
John Robertson 2007

CHAPTER ONE

S erenaded by predawn cricket chirp and frog song on July 11,
Betsy Sheridan paced in the dining room, already dressed in her
shift, short jacket, and petticoat. Her stomach uneasily
negotiated the collision of oily pork odor from Monday night's supper
with leather's rich pungency from Clark's shop, but she knew better
than to blame the queasiness on being four months along with child.

News delivered at suppertime had driven nettles of anxiety into
her soul. Her mother and uncle captured by Lower Creek Indians in
East Florida — good gods. The Lower Creek didn't treat their
prisoners to tea parties. Imagining her mother Sophie and her Uncle
David tortured in creative, native ways made her gut feel like a blazing
spew of grapeshot.

At the window, she breathed in familiar morning scents wafting
from the back yard on a cool breeze: sandy soil entwined with red
veins of Georgia clay, wood smoke, pine resin. "Pregnant nose," the
midwife had called her heightened sense of smell. Out back, King
Lear the rooster crowed. With Clark's apprentices arriving at seven,
Betsy had best fetch the eggs and start breakfast soon. Perhaps the
morning routine would ease some of her anxiety.

A lit candle aloft, she padded for the cobbler's shop before pausing to peer up the stairway. Annoyance rifted her anxiety at the soft snores issuing from their bedroom. Clark wouldn't have overslept had he not stayed up for that midnight delivery of Cordovan leather from Sooty Johns. Betsy had never liked Johns, a greasy little peddler. Because she, curious, had tiptoed downstairs to watch the two men unload the leather, and they thought her asleep the whole time, the delivery had felt illegal.

In the shop, she lit and hung two Betty lamps. Her gaze skimmed over the counter where she kept the ledger and lodged on the workbench piled with Cordovan leather. Magenta by lamplight, it almost assumed the hue of coagulated blood. *Spain.* Why should Spanish leather be delivered early Tuesday morning to John Clark Sheridan, a British sympathizer, ostensibly one of Spain's enemies? A shudder rose in her, and she wondered whether she should hide the leather.

Not that she needed more to worry about. Shaking off her concerns over the delivery, she walked to the workbench and pushed aside an awl and two cowhide boots to make room for her candle beside a small mirror. The action of settling her mobcap atop her braided dark hair eased her stomach. After a final inspection to ensure a trim appearance, she stood.

One of the cowhide boots slid off the bench, so she leaned over and snagged it. When she propped it beside its mate, she spied a sliver of paper between heel and sole. Curious, she pried it out and read *Mrs. Filbert's daughter is Sally* in her husband's handwriting.

Odd. Who was Mrs. Filbert?

Betsy tilted the paper closer to the candle. Here, now — what was that? Writing appeared on the edge of the paper nearest the heat.

Amazed, she passed the rest of the paper above the flame. Bluish script gibberish and three-digit numbers filled in the page — some sort of cipher. She waved the paper around. It cooled, and the writing vanished.

A chill brushed her neck. Clark had planted a secret message in the boot. Should she tell him she'd found it?

More annoyance and anxiety wound through her. Bad enough that her family on the St. James side was in so much trouble lately — but now her own husband was dabbling in questionable deals. When they'd married in January, she'd dreamed of leading a normal, uneventful life: helping him with his business, raising children, tending the garden and house. By the lamplight of that Tuesday morning, though, her optimism looked as naive as that displayed by fifty-six Congressional delegates who'd signed their names to a declaration of independence from George the Third's rule; four years later, thousands of redcoats still occupied the thirteen North American colonies.

Another crow from King Lear prompted Betsy's attempt to wedge the paper back in the heel. Unsuccessful and exasperated, she shoved the note into her pocket, lit a lantern, and bustled from the shop with it. The back door squeaked when she exited from dining room into garden, and Hamlet and Horatio loped around from the front yard, tails awag in greeting. She paused to scratch behind the hounds' ears, and memory caught up with her.

Almost two months earlier, during her mother's last visit to Augusta, they'd sat in the dining room sipping herbal tea, and Betsy told her the news: *You shall be a grandmother before Yule.* They'd laughed and embraced through tears of joy, and for the first time ever, Sophie had talked with her as one mother to another, dissolving the physical distance between them that seven years of living apart had imposed. But now, captive of the Lower Creek…Betsy blinked away the salty mist of misery, her stomach afire again with apprehension.

She stumbled a few steps before righting herself and continued down the path to the henhouse. The dogs bounded away to the front of the house. A sparrow began his reveille. The earth smelled cool, damp, and ripe. Inside the henhouse, she hung the lantern on a hook and grabbed a basket. The hens welcomed her with soft clucks, the acrid odor of their droppings magnified by her nose.

"Well, Titania, have you an egg for me this morning?" The hen shifted to allow Betsy's groping fingers access to straw only. She proceeded to the next hen. "You, Desdemona? Alas, no egg." She straightened. "Strange. Perchance you need a change in diet. Well, I'm sure to get something from Portia. No? Oh, very well, you did lay two eggs yesterday." She fumbled beneath more hens without success, and an eerie sense of familiarity spread through her. The only other time this had happened was when all the eggs had been collected as a *prank* just prior to her arrival.

She lowered her voice, not daring to believe. "Uncle David?"

She heard amusement in his voice outside the henhouse. "I cannot play that trick on you twice, can I?"

She raced out and flung her arms around him — dark-haired, lanky, handsome David St. James who'd no doubt passed the night in the arms of a certain wealthy, lovely widow in town before dropping in on his niece. Small wonder the hounds hadn't alerted her to his familiar presence. "Great thunder, it *is* you, and you're all right!" She smacked his cheek with a kiss. "Oh, gods, when I heard the news yesterday, I could scarcely believe it." She tugged him toward the house. "Clark has been so worried, too, but you've escaped the Indians!"

David braked their progress toward the house. "Don't tell your husband or anyone else that you've seen me."

"Why not?" She noticed her uncle's hunting shirt and trousers and checked herself. "You're running, aren't you? Mother, too."

"Yes."

"Just like Grandpapa Will."

She watched David's stare home on her. "What do you mean?"

"*He* was hiding in the henhouse yesterday morning."

David darted a look around. "Where is the old man?"

"Probably in South Carolina — at least that's where he seemed to think he could lay low with rebel friends because —" Betsy couldn't contain her sarcasm. " — he landed himself in all that trouble with the redcoats last month. Running a spy ring from Alton, printing incendiary broadsides, escaping to Havana to intrigue with the Gálvez family. The *Gálvez* family. Zounds. How did someone like my grandfather, a printer from a frontier town, ever catch the eye of people so high up in the Spanish court? And what did he expect from all that intrigue? Surely not a pardon — but I don't suppose he'll ever learn, will he? So I fed him breakfast and sent him on his way before it grew light. And where's my mother?"

"On her way to a Cherokee village in South Carolina." He glanced at the sky. "And since I don't want to be recognized on the road, I must away to Williamsburg before it gets much lighter." His tone became shrewd. "I'm here only to assure you your mother is safe and well, and she sends you her love."

The unreality of the situation descended on Betsy, and for a moment she felt as though cotton stuffed her head. "A redcoat from our garrison came by last night to relate a fantastical report. You and Mother had been arrested as rebel spies after chasing Grandpapa to

Havana, and then you were captured by Indians north of St. Augustine while the redcoats were escorting you back to Georgia. You and Mother, rebel spies? Hah. Perchance if men bore children, yes, but why don't you tell me what really happened."

David ejected a soft laugh. "Well, we did go after the old man, but it was for his own good. We aren't rebel spies, and it's a great misunderstanding that would take me too long to explain. Rest assured, though, that your mother is safe for now."

Betsy frowned. Of course it was a misunderstanding, and no one could dance a reel around the truth like her uncle. "When shall I have the full story?"

"When someone has the time to explain it."

Ah, no. He wasn't going to escape without explaining the greatest mystery of all. "But surely you can tarry long enough to clarify *one* detail. Wait here while I fetch what arrived by post yesterday and show it to you."

"Very well, but hurry."

She bustled up the path, flung open the back door, seized the package from within a cupboard, and trotted back out to David. "See here, this was addressed as follows: 'To Mrs. Betsy Sheridan in Augusta, Georgia.' Well, go ahead and see what's inside."

Stupefaction and recognition flooded his voice when he examined the parasol and lace veil within. "I don't believe it."

She set the box and its contents down next to the basket of eggs David had collected. "There's a brief letter here somewhere. Who is Miguel de Arriaga, author of the letter?"

"Captain of a Portuguese merchant brig, the *Gloria Maria*."

"So you and Mother had quite an adventure!" Awed and envious, Betsy straightened and handed him the letter. Then she leaned inside the henhouse, unhooked the lantern, and held it to illuminate Captain Arriaga's script on the page.

David skimmed the letter, and she followed the path his eyes took over it, having already memorized the contents:

MADAM:

> *Your Uncle and Parents were Passengers*
> *aboard my Ship, the* Gloria Maria. *I gave this*
> *Parasol and Veil to your Mother, a remarkable*

> *Woman, and she lost them in Havana when British*
> *Soldiers captured her. If you see her again, please*
> *give them to her and tell her I tried to help.*
>
> > *I am Madam*
> >
> > *Your humble Servant*
> >
> > *Miguel de Arriaga*

"How did Captain Arriaga find me?"

"Your mother told him about you." Her uncle folded the letter with haste and handed it back to her. "Here you go. Now I must away."

She'd once seen a large-mouthed bass wiggle off a hook with greater finesse. "Oh, no you don't." After tossing the letter into the box, she seized her uncle's arm. "You tell me what the captain meant by my 'parents,' and no more pretense. Look at me. Dark hair and eyes, olive skin. And these cheekbones! Both my mother's husbands had blond hair and blue eyes. I couldn't be the daughter of either of them. So who was — *is* — my father?"

David squirmed, trying his best to get off that hook. "Your mother's the one who must have this conversation with you."

"But she's on her way to South Carolina, and you're here." Betsy released him and set the lantern down. "She's with my father, isn't she? I shall go looking for *both* of them so I may have a proper explanation."

"Come now, you've more sense than to travel into a war-torn colony."

She jutted her chin forward. "You tell me, then."

He sighed. "Your father is Mathias Hale, a blacksmith from Alton."

Astonishment shot through her. "Hale?" She had a vague recollection of the Hale family as blacksmiths in her hometown of Alton, south of Augusta. The wonder of discovery began arranging perplexing pieces of her past into a logical picture. "*That's* why Mother sent me here to be fostered with Lucas and Sarah seven years ago. I must resemble my father or someone in his family, and she wanted me out of Alton —" Confusion trailed off her words, and she blinked at her uncle "Why didn't Mother marry Mr. Hale? Was shame or hardship involved?"

David held up his hands. "Another long story which I've no place or leisure to explain. Forgive me, but I must begone." He strode to the back of the henhouse and unhitched his horse.

She tracked him, her thirst unquenched. "Is he a good man?"

"Yes, a very good man."

"Well, then, I truly don't understand why she didn't —"

"Betsy." He turned to her and seized her shoulders. "You must leave it for now."

"But can you not imagine what it's been like for me, Uncle David, to never have had a father? In all my seventeen years, I've had uncles, a stepfather, and grandfathers, but they haven't been my *father*."

"You shall meet him someday, I know it. He's that kind of man. But now isn't the time to look for him." David pressed a kiss to her forehead, released her, and climbed into the saddle with his fowler. "*Don't* go to South Carolina."

Betsy stepped back, certain she exuded defiance in her stance. "Why not?"

He wagged his finger at her. "I mean it, Betsy. *Don't* go to South Carolina. And, for that matter, stay clear of Alton for awhile — especially a lieutenant by the name of Fairfax."

Oh, faugh. Her uncle's "enemies" were all cuckolded courtiers of wealthy widows. She sweetened her smile. "Not to worry."

The paling sky outlined perplexity in her uncle's posture. As much as he enjoyed women, he'd never figured out what to do with those who were headstrong. "I cannot command you to anything, can I?"

"Good luck in Williamsburg, Uncle David." She blew a kiss.

He shook his head, reined his horse around, and trotted it from the yard with a final wave. Betsy watched until the gloom of dawn swallowed him before retrieving the lantern, eggs, and box. Then she ambled back to the house escorted by the aria of a mockingbird.

So. Her kinfolk had evaded British "justice" upon the gallows and torture at the hands of Indians and were *en route* to sanctuaries in other colonies. And for the first time in her life, she had a father — a blacksmith, a "very good man." At the back step, she paused to address the sky, her shoulders back, her face aglow. "Mathias Hale," she whispered, "expect me soon."

CHAPTER TWO

T he stairs groaned liked a gouty old man, testament to Clark's descent, but Betsy continued dusting the counter, her back to the door, pondering exile imposed on her uncle and mother, her husband's note hidden in the cowhide boot, and a blacksmith named Mathias Hale. Clark entered the shop sniffing the air, and she could hear his grin. "Coffee — and mmm, biscuits with your blackberry jam. What's the occasion?"

She tried not to sound peeved or nervous. "No occasion." The apprentices hadn't arrived yet. Perhaps now was the time to talk with him about the secret message. "Clark, I —"

"Ah, sweetheart." He embraced her from behind and nuzzled her neck through her tucker. "I'd have been up early, too, if my kin were prisoners of the Indians. I'm surprised you slept at all last night."

Some of Betsy's tension diffused, and she turned to face him. Thank the heavens her husband wasn't an insensitive lout. A tremble not entirely feigned caught her lower lip.

"Hush, now, let's have none of that." He gathered her in his arms and held her, and she cuddled against him, the fine, navy wool of his coat warm on her cheek. Never mind that his nose was crooked and his face too narrow — to her, that twinkle in Clark's blue eyes made him handsome. Besides, few were impervious to his boyish charm. She slid her hands beneath his coat to his breeches, tan wool like that of his waistcoat.

"Madam, know that if you don't stop squeezing my arse, those biscuits will harden."

Biscuits, right. She kept her hands on his buttocks and indulged in his good morning kiss, letting the citrusy scent of his soap on his skin drain more tension from her. Some women lost interest in their husbands after becoming pregnant, but she'd never felt more lustful.

"I hope you baked enough biscuits for the boys."

"*Boys*? In case you hadn't noticed, Tom is my age."

"Yes, I had noticed. And speaking of Tom —" They heard shoes scrape the front porch. Clark released her with a wink, grabbed a biscuit, and headed for the front door. She followed with the entire basket of biscuits.

When Clark opened the door, she smiled at the entrance of tall, gangly Tom Alexander, who was always one size larger than the coat, waistcoat, and breeches he wore, no matter how quickly his mother sewed. "Good morning! Bless me if you aren't the only one who's always here a little early. Have a biscuit?" But sandy-haired Tom didn't lunge for several biscuits; nor did he flush and shyly return her smile as usual. He didn't even gawk at all that Cordovan leather, set aflame by a beam of sunlight.

Instead, he fidgeted his cocked hat in his hands, a crease of concern between his gray eyes. "You folks haven't been out front yet this morning, have you? Better come take a look."

The three walked out and turned to face the front of the house. Daylight illuminated the message *TORY SCUM* painted red across the gray wood siding on the first floor.

Shock rammed through Betsy. Augusta was full of Whigs, but she never believed they'd vandalize a neighbor's home. Clark wasn't outspoken in his political beliefs.

The dogs trotted from around back, and Tom patted Hamlet's side. "Clark, did you hear any suspicious noises last night?"

"No."

"Dogs bark?"

"No."

Betsy's jaw slackened with more shock. The vandal was
someone familiar to the hounds; otherwise they'd have bayed up a
storm. Her uncle wouldn't deface the home of kin; plus a man on the
run had no time to dally with paint. A more likely culprit was Sooty
— but why would he do that to a client?

Clark touched the lettering and shook his head. "Dry."

Tom stripped off his coat. "I'll help scrub it off."

"Thanks, Tom."

Betsy recovered her mettle and cleared her throat. "Since the
paint's already dry, gentlemen, cleaning it off can wait fifteen minutes.
I've a pot of coffee inside, and I don't make biscuits every day."

***

Neighbors and their children pitched in with cleanup, even the
Sweeneys and the Cochranes, Whigs. Sarah and Lucas O'Neal, first
cousins to Betsy's mother, lent a hand. Sarah removed a second batch
of biscuits, burned, from the beehive oven out back before guiding a
fretting Betsy inside. "Off your feet. I shall manage." When Betsy
protested, her foster-mother shushed her with a St. James expression
she'd seen her mother wear. "The day will only get longer, and you
want the baby's cooperation."

Clark's friend, Lieutenant Adam Neville, who had arrived to
investigate the crime, popped inside wearing a smile and his Loyalist
Rangers' hunting shirt and trousers. Twenty-five years old, like Clark,
Adam removed his hat and bowed to Betsy and Sarah, manners
impeccable despite having fought rebels in the East Florida swamps
beside Colonel Thomas Brown. "Morning, ladies." He assessed
Sarah's competence at replenishing biscuits, ale, and molasses
switchel, and nodded his approval to Betsy, his brown eyes merry.
"Listen to Mrs. O'Neal, now, and stay off your feet. That's a hot sun
out there."

"Yes, sir." With humor, Betsy saluted him from her chair.

Several off-duty British soldiers and Rangers — friends with
whom Clark shared ale at the White Swan — arrived with brushes and
buckets. Shoulder to shoulder they worked: Whig and Loyalist,
soldier and civilian. They discussed the weather, crops, midsummer
fair, and new babies. Nobody talked politics.

Late morning, amid children playing Thread the Needle and

Prisoner's Base, potluck appeared on blankets in the front yard —
ham, squash cooked with apples, fruit pastries, molasses bread —
along with grandmothers who shooed away inquisitive dogs and flies.
By mid-afternoon, the Sheridans sported the cleanest house north of
town center. Everyone shook hands and congratulated themselves on
an event no less festive than a barn raising — one that had, as a bonus,
worn excess energy out of several dozen little boys and girls.

In the dining room, Betsy pondered what to do with the leftover
food, when she heard Hamlet and Horatio baying in the front yard.
Strangers.

From the window, she spied Clark striding around front with his
axe. After grabbing his fowler and cartridge box, she headed for the
front door and peered out the window.

Their coats blazed scarlet by patchy afternoon sunlight, their
muskets resting across their thighs, six unfamiliar British soldiers sat
on horseback in the yard gazing down at the hounds. Dust and sweat
lined the men's faces. Betsy watched Clark round the corner of the
house and heard him whistle. The dogs quieted and ambled over to
him. "Afternoon, gentlemen. May I help you?"

A young lieutenant with dark hair removed his cocked hat.
"Good afternoon, sir. I'm Lieutenant Michael Stoddard, sent out of
Alton by Captain John Sheffield. I've business with Elizabeth
Sheridan. They've told me this is her home. Do you know where I
may find her?"

"Ah." Clark gestured for the soldiers to dismount, propped his
axe against the side of the house, and shook the lieutenant's hand.
"How do you do. I'm John Clark Sheridan, her husband. Betsy?
Hallo, Betsy! You've visitors."

A diminutive chill drifted up her spine. What did the soldiers
want with *her* when they should be tracking her wily, old Grandpapa
Will St. James, the rebel who dared collaborate with enemy Spaniards?
Had they sniffed her mother or uncle's escape? She set down the
fowler and ammunition, walked out to Stoddard, and curtsied. "Good
afternoon. I'm Betsy Sheridan."

Reins in his hand, the officer stood at attention and inclined his
head. Her first impression, that he was but twenty years old, arose
when she spotted a few pimples on his chin, but she realized from the
responsibility in his dark eyes that he was probably three or four years
older — of average height and slight build, not at all an uncomely

fellow. "Lieutenant Michael Stoddard out of Alton." From inside his coat he removed a sealed letter, which he presented to her.

She broke the seal, opened the letter and read:

10 July 1780, Town of Alton

MADAM:

For the Purposes of Formality, I am desirous of tying up a few loose Threads regarding this disturbing Business of your Grandfather, Mother, and Uncle. Therefore I beg leave that you grant me an Audience. You and Mr Sheridan are welcome to join me for afternoon Tea on Wednesday 12 July. Please accept Lieut Stoddard and his Soldiers as Escort. I shall see that you are given a suitable Escort for your Return to Augusta following our Audience.

I am Madam

Your obedient Servant

Captn John Sheffield

Mrs Elizabeth Sheridan nee Neely

Betsy reread the letter, noting Sheffield's wording. She wasn't under arrest or being commanded. This was a social event, and her husband was invited. Except for the presence of the soldiers, she sensed no pressure in the arrangement. Considering that highwaymen often roamed postal roads, the soldiers represented a generous gesture from Captain Sheffield. She'd wanted an excuse to go to Alton anyway and begin her search for Mathias Hale, and here was that excuse.

So why the twinge of foreboding from her instincts?

She folded the letter. "Clark, shall we have afternoon tea on the morrow with Captain Sheffield?"

"Must we stay overnight with your Aunt Susana?"

"It's just for one night. Come now. For that time, you can nod your head at her gabbing and bite your tongue."

"Oh, very well. I shall make arrangements with the neighbors to look after the animals while we're gone."

Betsy smiled at Stoddard, who relaxed for the first time in her presence. "I shall be delighted to take tea with Captain Sheffield. What time shall we away in the morning, Lieutenant?"

"Look for our escort at seven o'clock. Thank you, madam, sir." Stoddard signaled his men to remount and climbed into his horse's saddle.

Clark's smile was all charm. "You're a man after my heart, Mr. Stoddard. Nothing like an early start to escape the heat, eh? And things must be blessedly slow for you fellows in Alton if Captain Sheffield could afford to send his lieutenant."

"Er, no, sir. We've some cattle thieves about." Stoddard paused, and his voice flattened with discretion. "However, the lieutenant formerly stationed in Alton is there through this Thursday, so Captain Sheffield felt he could spare me to assure you of his good intentions."

Stay clear of Alton for awhile — especially a lieutenant by the name of Fairfax David had said. Was the officer to whom Stoddard referred Lieutenant Fairfax? From Stoddard's reserve, she assumed the two of them had had a tiff. After all, one too many lieutenants in a garrison of only forty was bound to generate some epaulet crowding, and officers rubbing each other the wrong way was nothing new in the British Army. But as she watched the redcoats ride away, foreboding prodded her that she shouldn't have accepted Sheffield's invitation. Alas, with the recent actions of her family, she couldn't back out of the trip without generating suspicion.

***

She awakened deep in the humid well of summer night and found the bed empty of Clark except for the scent of his soap. Recognizing the faint sounds of her husband puttering around in the shop, she wondered why he couldn't sleep. Her stomach growled. Maybe they could both use a snack. She climbed from bed and eased open the door.

A conversation in the shop halted her descent. What business had anyone with Clark so late at night? Had Sooty Johns returned? Clark said something indistinguishable. Then she discerned a man's voice, Spanish-accented: "To Camden?"

"Yes, Basilio." That was Clark's voice.

Wide-awake, Betsy sneaked down a few steps where she could remain in shadow but observe. Her eyes bulged at the sight of two Spaniards headed for the front door, one carrying the cowhide boots. "Luck to you, Clark."

Clark ushered them out. "And to you."

Baffled and disquieted by the visit, Betsy retreated upstairs and crept into the tiny front room, soon to become the nursery. The window overlooked the yard and let her observe the Spaniards mounting horses while the dogs circled, their tails wagging in recognition. After the Spaniards headed their steeds to the road, the dogs trotted back to the porch.

Clark shut the door, and she sneaked back to bed. In another minute, he shuffled in, shucked his clothing, and sank into bed with a sigh of exhaustion.

She considered what question to ask him first. Did Sooty vandalize the house? How many times had the Spaniards visited? Did they give Sooty the Cordovan leather? Where were they taking the boots? Why was a Loyalist secretly meeting men from a country at war with Britain? And to whom was he sending secret messages in the heels of boots?

While she debated, he fell asleep. She lay awake staring at the ceiling, instincts screaming that her husband had plunged into something very ugly. She wouldn't be able to address it with him on the morrow, not surrounded as they'd be all day by British soldiers. But she must confront him soon afterward and find out what was going on. She laid her right palm on her belly, where she'd imagined flutters in the past few days. No venture was just about Clark and Betsy Sheridan anymore.

CHAPTER THREE

I n the cool of a morning mist, apprentice Tom Alexander showed up
to ready the horses. When Betsy unloaded potluck on him — "For
you and your mama" — he gazed at her, astonished, and blushed.
Clark never seemed to notice how he got clumsy or blushed when she
was around, maybe because Tom wasn't offensive about it. She'd
considered fixing him up with a good wife, but alas, there just didn't
seem to be any suitable candidates in town.

The soldiers arrived at seven, and the hounds howled and dashed
about, frustrating Clark's attempts to control them. Tom chased down
one scampering, barking dog with rope and lassoed him. The redcoats
guffawed and applauded, and Tom bowed — entertainment at its finest
on the Georgia frontier.

Before Clark mounted his gelding and received his fowler from
Tom, he assisted Betsy onto her mare, Lady May. He'd strapped the
package sent by Miguel de Arriaga behind her saddle, not at all
curious about the contents. The night before, she'd removed
identification from the box, hidden the letter in her pocket along with
the cipher, and told him, "Just some of my mother's things. I'll drop
them off at the house in Alton."

They walked their horses out to the street behind the soldiers, and the party of eight headed south at an easy pace on the sandy postal road. Nevertheless, Betsy noticed tautness in the shoulders of Stoddard and the privates. Mid-morning, just north of the Indian settlement of New Savannah, Stoddard rode back and paced his horse beside those of the Sheridans. Tension pinched at the corners of his mouth. "We aren't far north of New Savannah. We shall pause for dinner around noon."

"Is something amiss this morning?" said Clark.

"No cause for your concern. Our party skirmished with some bandits yesterday near here and sent them running."

"Ah, so I need keep my fowler ready?"

"As you wish, Mr. Sheridan — however, it appears they've not the stomachs for a rematch."

He touched the brim of his hat in courtesy and rode forward, but Betsy sensed he wasn't convinced of the bandits' cowardice. Not a one of the soldiers discarded his road wariness.

Between New Savannah and Alton, they stopped to eat. The privates took turns standing guard during the meal. Heat rippled the rolling hills, cicadas buzzed in the brush, and the raucous calls of crows punctuated the noon air. Betsy sweated in the shade of an oak, thankful to have a broad-brimmed straw hat and linen tucker to keep off the sun.

She noted the soldiers' less-than-appetizing rations and shared pastries with them, after which Stoddard pointed out a red-tailed hawk circling a thousand feet high. The Sheridans observed the hawk's glorious, parabolic dive toward the earth. When the gleam-eyed raptor soared away with a field rat, Stoddard's preoccupation with bandits thawed long enough for him to exclaim, "Got it!"

At Clark's prodding, the lieutenant admitted that the benefactor in Yorkshire who'd helped purchase his ensign's commission raised peregrines, and he'd often swept out the mews and cared for the raptors. Soon Clark had him and the men chatting about hunting and fishing. By the time they got back on the road, Stoddard — still keeping an eye on the surrounding terrain — had lowered his reserve enough to offer to buy Clark ale that night in the Red Rock Tavern.

Betsy had seen her husband's sociability at work so often she'd almost ceased thinking about it, but this time her instincts vibrated. He made friends everywhere, perhaps because he'd been orphaned and hadn't many friends from youth, and could charm the gab out of just about anyone. At the Red Rock that night, he'd buy enough rounds to cheer his new friends. A good listener, he'd be treated to a great deal of information from the soldiers — not all of it bluster. She wondered again who was privy to the cipher written with invisible ink.

They arrived in Alton just after two and walked the horses down the street lined with a couple dozen drab wooden buildings — businesses on the ground floor, residences upstairs — past Will St. James's print shop and post office at the north end of town. Heat pulsated the ground. Limp-leafed oak and fruit trees shaded the buildings. From the concentrated smell of dust, wood smoke, dung, and rotting fruit, she surmised that rain hadn't fallen in Alton for several weeks. Chickens, goats, and hogs ranging free scuttled out of the way of the horses. The residents they passed paused to regard them with curiosity.

About a hundred yards to the east of the street wound the Savannah River, and across it, Alton's garrison had pitched their tents amidst the haze of campfires; but Captain Sheffield occupied a house south of town center. In June, its former occupant, Major Hunt, had set off in pursuit of Will, Sophie, and David with eleven soldiers from Alton's garrison. Stoddard, Betsy, and Clark dismounted, secured their horses in the shade, and entered the house.

Inside, Betsy's eyes adjusted to the gloom of the entranceway, and her gaze wandered up the staircase. A servant in his fifties emerged from the rear of the house, gray frosting his bronze-colored hair. "Ah, Finnegan." Stoddard gestured to the Sheridans. "The captain's guests have arrived. Where is he?"

"In the study, sir." The man nodded his head toward a closed door opposite the front parlor.

"Very good. See that the Sheridans have the opportunity to refresh themselves, and I shall fetch him." The lieutenant bowed to Betsy and Clark before knocking on the study door.

Finnegan ushered the guests into the parlor and seated them in ladder-backed chairs around a circular tea table. Over the clink of china as he set up the tea service, Betsy heard the study door open, and Stoddard's voice, low and urgent: "*I* was the target, sir. Had the men not performed commendably, I'd have been murdered yesterday. You must *do* something about him!"

Clark raised his eyebrows at her, having also overheard. Betsy

rubbed clammy palms on her apron and swallowed. "The devil,"
Clark muttered. The devil, indeed. Small wonder Stoddard had been
nervous all day. No random target of "bandits," he'd been singled out
by an assassin.

The front door creaked open, and a deep, hushed voice consoled
Stoddard. The thump of the lieutenant's boots down the front steps
preceded Betsy's view of him striding out to his horse and the five
privates, who'd remained mounted. Then the swarthy commander of
Alton's garrison stomped into the parlor. Betsy doubted he could have
tiptoed anywhere — taller than her uncle and outweighing him by
forty pounds. Omitting a shave for several days, he'd be mistaken for
Blackbeard. Fifteen years earlier, Captain Sheffield must have been
the terror of everyone's china collection, but in his early thirties, he
and some semblance of poise had made peace with each other.

While the servant slipped from the room, the captain pivoted to
his guests, dust clinging to his uniform, dulling the scarlet. "John
Sheffield at your service." Clark introduced them. The captain wrung
his extended hand, and Betsy smirked at Clark's wince of pain.
"Pleased to make your acquaintance. Thank you for coming." He
directed a cordial smile at Betsy and bowed. "After tea, your aunt
awaits your arrival in your mother's home."

"Thank you, sir."

Sheffield assumed his seat and measured leaves from the canister
into the pot. Finnegan entered with a kettle of steaming water, added
water to the pot, and left to reheat the kettle. Small talk ensued while
the captain passed around cups of steeped tea and offered sugar and
milk. All Betsy wanted at first was to inhale the bouquet of the
beverage, and she noticed Clark doing the same. They'd made do for
so long with coffee and hot chocolate for afternoon "tea." Rebels in
several colonies had been out of their minds to dump such nectar into
the ocean.

She balanced her cup and saucer in her lap. "Captain, I'd not met
your predecessor, Major Hunt. I understand the Creek Indians injured
him. How does he?"

"He took a ball in the leg. A surgeon in Cow Ford removed it
cleanly. It's a matter of waiting for the infection to clear. Kind of you
to ask. Your mother and uncle were captured by those same Indians.
You must be ill with concern."

Betsy dropped her gaze to hide her knowledge otherwise. "Yes, I can hardly sleep. What news do you have of them?"

"A delegate from Cow Ford met the Creek's mico — their leader — to ask the terms for their release. The mico refused to talk. Negotiations are at a standstill this moment, and I'm sorry for it, but those Indians can be capricious. They decide daily whether they'll honor treaties and alliances."

Betsy let out a slow breath of relief. Thank the heavens the redcoats didn't know Sophie and David had escaped.

Sheffield cleared his throat. "We've interviewed residents from Alton, and I expect Major Hunt's account of the events culminating in Havana within a week. Everyone we've spoken with insists that neither your mother nor uncle were rebels. Frankly I'm puzzled as to their motive for taking up with the rebels."

She considered the rationale David had implied the day before. "Perhaps, sir, they didn't take up with the rebels but were simply concerned for my grandfather's well-being. They followed him to Cuba and became entangled in his schemes."

Sheffield scratched his chin. "Your aunt advanced a similar theory, but she's known for supporting rebel viewpoints."

Betsy smiled. "Aunt Susana talks a great deal, but I doubt she'd throw herself wholeheartedly into the rebel cause."

"Why is that?"

"Promise you won't repeat this."

"You have my word."

"She has a dramatic flair that obscures a lack of backbone."

"Ah. But your mother and uncle *do* possess backbone?"

"Yes, sir."

Sheffield nodded. "Mr. Sheridan's support of His Majesty is known in Augusta. But tell me, madam, where are your loyalties?"

She held his gaze. "I won't take sides. Parliament and the Congress are doing a shabby job of listening to each other."

Sheffield pursed his lips. "Neutrals. The townsfolk claim your mother and uncle are neutrals."

"I've heard them remark on the pig-headedness of both sides, yes." She maintained a cool eye on the captain. "In my mother's recent letters to me, she mentioned that Major Hunt had begun spending time with her."

Shrewdness twitched Sheffield's eyebrows. "Gossip says they were courting. Hardly the actions of a woman dedicated to the rebel cause." He studied her reaction.

At first she expected him to explain away Major Hunt's actions with a statement such as, "Your mother must have been a spy who set out to dazzle and deceive him." But he remained quiet. If he felt the major's reputation tarnished by the liaison, he didn't hasten to polish away the smudge. He must have concluded that Sophie Barton was a decent woman and Edward Hunt was in full command of his faculties. She respected Sheffield for that.

After a moment, he stirred. "Neutrality is a difficult and often dangerous position to maintain."

"There are plenty of neutrals out there, sir."

"Yes, I'm aware of it — and so is Parliament. A grievously untapped resource for His Majesty." He inspected their teacups. "More tea?" Betsy and Clark extended cups at the same time, their eager expressions eliciting a chuckle from the captain. "Could I win over a neutral simply by serving tea, I'd give my next month's pay for a crate of the stuff."

Finnegan reappeared with hot water, and Sheffield replenished their tea. Conversation turned apolitical. Betsy watched Clark manipulate anecdotes from the captain about his boyhood in Yorkshire, Sheffield's hearty laugh filling the room. Not in his wildest dreams did the captain suspect her husband stuck secret messages in boots or dealt with enemy Spaniards. No, indeed, there were *two* John Clark Sheridans, and Betsy, with growing unease, wondered which she'd married.

At the conclusion of tea, Sheffield crushed Clark's hand in another handshake, kissed Betsy's hand with a gentleness that surprised her, and held up his forefinger. "Before I forget — about your escort back to Augusta on the morrow."

"Stoddard heading it up again?" Clark grinned. "An excellent officer, and good company on the road."

"Er, no. The lieutenant serving beneath Major Hunt has been wrapping up business in Alton since his return from Havana. He leaves on the morrow for an assignment in South Carolina."

The flat, diplomatic smile on Sheffield's face said that he disliked Major Hunt's lieutenant every bit as much as Stoddard did. Betsy's foreboding escalated. If she wanted to keep David's visit secret, she saw no way she could discuss her misgivings, even with her husband.

The captain broadened his smile. "And since you're traveling in the same direction, it's sensible for him to head your escort. I assure you he's quite capable of handling any problems that might arise on the road. In fact, I have him out investigating livestock theft this afternoon because I know he'll get to the bottom of it, if anyone can." He turned to Clark. "Shall I send him over to the house tonight to meet you?"

Clark shook his head. "I'll likely run into him in the Red Rock this evening."

"Very well. I shall have your escort at the house on the morrow at seven to return you to Augusta."

"Thank you, sir. But we didn't catch his name."

"Oh, of course. Fairfax is the name — Dunstan Fairfax."

CHAPTER FOUR

Betsy plopped her tote on the counter beside Arriaga's package and surveyed the shop. Upstairs, her aunt hollered, "I'll be right down!" Betsy sneezed, dismayed at clutter neither Sophie nor Will would have permitted in the print shop. Susana may have kept the newspaper going, but in what state was the ledger?

The back door whammed open, and a flame-haired girl trudged in. She bobbed a curtsy at Betsy, the sullen tug to her mouth vanishing. "I'll tell Mrs. Greeley you're here, Miss — ?"

"I'm Betsy Sheridan, Sophie Barton's daughter."

Her scrutiny of Betsy deepened. "Ain't I met you before?"

And so it started, recognition of Betsy's features. "I don't think so. I've not been to Alton in a number of years."

Susana hollered again: "Mary, get up here this instant!" The servant hurried upstairs. Shaking her head, Betsy picked her way around a shop smelling of dust and mildew. Within a minute, Susana clomped downstairs, a harried twenty-nine-year-old mother of six, dark-haired and gray-eyed like her two older siblings. Delight softened her scowl, and she blazed a trail through stacks of newspaper for an embrace. "Betsy, what a pleasure to have you here! You've been away much too long. Let me have a look at you. My goodness, not showing at all. How far along are you?"

"Just over four months."

"How do you stay so tiny? Just like your mama, heaven help her." Susana sighed, pulled a handkerchief from her pocket, and dabbed her eyes. "Your poor mama and uncle, captured by those Indians. I'm so worried, I can scarcely eat or sleep." She blew her nose and crammed the handkerchief back in her pocket. "I hope this nightmare ends soon and everyone comes home. I've kept the press going, but I'm not the business manager your mama is."

Betsy squinted at Susana's earlobes. "Aren't those my mother's garnet earrings?"

Susana snaked lampblack-and-varnish stained fingers to her ears and flushed. "Oh, my. I was dusting her room this morning and tried them on. I was just fancying that I was somewhere else, somewhere *exciting*. No harm done, eh?" She tittered, removed the earrings, stuck them in her pocket, and craned her neck about the shop. "Where's Clark?"

"Visiting the tanner on business. He'll come for supper."

"Good." Susana seized her hand and towed her toward the pressroom. "I've had such trouble with the newspaper." Composing sticks full of type and galleys full of composing sticks cluttered the workbenches in the pressroom, dominated by Will's big, hand-pulled press. Betsy smelled lampblack and varnish, ink for the type. She stepped around a bucket of filthy rags and pushed drawers of type into their cabinets so she could squeeze past. "Your mama arranged so much copy on just one page and squeezed in advertisements, too. I'm not that talented. Do you think I should add a second page?"

Betsy blinked at her. "It's been seven years since I helped with a print run." And she hadn't missed it at all. Printing was filthy, grueling work. "A few calculations should show whether the increase in your expenses is worth adding a second page." Her back to the window, she glanced at the workbench near her elbow, where Susana had composed an article, letters arranged backwards. Her brain inverted type. Someone named Reverend Gunn had authored the article.

"I'm not good at numbers. Might you help me after supper?" At Betsy's gesture of acquiescence, Susana smiled and squeezed her hand. In her peripheral vision, Betsy saw a flash of scarlet uniform on the porch. The relief on her aunt's face converted to a snarl, and she lowered her voice at the sound of the shop bell jingling. "Wait here while I get rid of that *ghoul*."

After she huffed from the pressroom, Betsy read a line from the article: *Only then shall man be at peace with his god.*

In the shop, Susana snapped, "We're *closed* for the day."

The soldier responded, "I think not, else you'd have changed the sign in the front window. I shall have a look around. You're acting culpable, as if you've something to hide."

Susana's voice rose to a whine. "I have family visiting. That's why I've closed early today. I've nothing to hide — very well, look around. I lost a scissors in that rat's clutter last week. Do let me know if you find them."

With the soldier and Susana occupied in the shop, an impish smile seized Betsy's lips. She inverted a "g" and "d" on the stick and inspected Reverend Gunn's revised message: *Only then shall man be at peace with his dog.* Animal worship. Now Alton was the exciting "somewhere" Susana longed to be.

While wiping ink off her fingers, Betsy heard anxiety rise in Susana's voice: "Begone! You've *no right* to snoop about."

"To the contrary, madam, I've heard you express seditious sympathies. My superiors are loath to imagine women acting as spies, but I'm not handicapped by such views. In light of your family's recent activities, you'd make a perfect rebel courier."

Well, he certainly was yanking Susana around — not that her annoying aunt didn't deserve a little yanking around. Betsy meandered to the doorway of the pressroom, crossed arms over her chest, and leaned against the doorjamb to watch the show.

The soldier scoured shelves, piles, and boxes with his gaze, aware that Susana fidgeted behind him when he'd poke in a shelf or box. He'd laid his cocked hat on the counter next to the package. A plait of russet hair extended over his collar, and he sported a tan on his hands and face. Approximately Stoddard's age and height, he moved with the confidence and solid musculature of a man at home in his body — not like the striplings she knew in Augusta. And not at all like Stoddard, either.

"How rude of you to come in just to heckle me!"

"Just to heckle you? Hardly. I've a letter to post." He whipped it from his waistcoat pocket. Betsy's gaze snagged on braid ornamenting his left shoulder. Lieutenant. So this was Fairfax, so disliked by his peers and her uncle. Maybe it was his arrogance. Her gaze roved his profile, and she recalled the pimples on Stoddard's chin. Not a pimple in sight on Fairfax.

"We're closed. Return at nine on the morrow for the post."

"My dear Mrs. Greeley, I'm charmed. You've enjoyed my company enough to detain me in Alton another day."

Betsy could almost hear her aunt's teeth grinding. She stifled a snort while Susana rose to the bait again and snatched his letter. "Fine. I shall post it for you." She marched around the counter, dragged the ledger out from the shelf, and slapped it down before her, pluming a cloud of dust into the air.

While she readied quill and inkwell and flipped open the ledger, Fairfax laid coins on the counter. His gaze strayed to the package. He opened it, reached in, and seized a fistful of the veil. Betsy watched his eyes widen with an emotion she couldn't quite fathom. His lips parted, and his fingers fondled the lace like it was an old friend — or at least an ally. Cold gripped her stomach.

Susana completed the ledger entry and scooped the coins into a pouch. "Your letter is posted. Now begone." She spied the veil in Fairfax's hands and reached for the box. "And I shall thank you to keep your hands off more of my property."

He flung down the lace, all expression gone from his face, and seized her wrist so hard she gasped. "You've exhausted my patience with your rebel games. Shall I arrest you for treason?"

"T - treason? What have I done but record the post for your blasted letter? How is that treason?"

He squeezed her wrist, and she winced. "The items in that box belong to your sister. She left them in Havana. How did you obtain her property from the Spaniards?"

"I — I've never seen that package before in my life!"

"I want the names, code names, and nationalities of agents who made the transfer. When and where is your next meeting? What did they send with the parasol and veil? Maps? Ciphers? Quickly, or I shall haul you to jail and clap you in irons."

Choking noises issued from Susana's throat, and Betsy frowned. Fairfax might be a handsome enough fellow, but he was overbearing and obnoxious. She uncrossed her arms and straightened in the doorway. "I'm the one who can tell you about the package. My aunt knows nothing of it."

He released Susana and swung around to meet her gaze with eyes the temperature of gray-green rime on the shore of the North Sea during the Midwinter Solstice. Betsy had to restrain herself from gulping and cowering as he advanced on her. Ugh. The sentiments of Stoddard, Sheffield, and her aunt and uncle weren't a mystery anymore. Over his shoulder, she saw that Susana had collapsed on a stool and begun fanning herself. Betsy lifted her chin. "You must be Lieutenant Fairfax."

"And you must be Betsy."

What impudence. She flared her nostrils. "Mrs. John Clark Sheridan."

"Mrs. John Clark Sheridan." No emotion touched his voice. "Well? The package."

"It arrived Monday, sent by someone named Arriaga. His letter said that he'd given the items to my mother, and she'd lost them in Havana, so he was sending them to me. I didn't know what to do with the items, and since my mother's property is upstairs, I brought them along when I came for my interview."

"What did Captain Sheffield think of the package and letter?"

"I didn't show them to him."

"Why not?"

"Why should I have?"

"Don't trifle with me. Your mother, a rebel spy, sent you communication. That warrants a full investigation."

Betsy felt she should have laughed at his insinuation, but she was unable to retrieve any humor — not with those icy eyes on her. "For goodness sakes, it's just a parasol and a veil —"

"The letter must be examined for hidden messages. I hold you responsible for delivering it and the package to Captain Sheffield, and I shall alert him to expect all of it from you."

Her lips tightened. Arriaga's letter, stashed in her pocket, burned against her thigh. Fairfax wasn't a person in whom she wanted to confide the secrets of her paternity, and he might ask after reading Arriaga's reference to her "parents." "There were no 'hidden messages' in the letter. I've given you accurate account of its straightforward content."

"Rebels write between the lines of innocuous sounding missives using a combination of cobalt chloride, glycerin, and water. When the ink dries, it becomes invisible. Exposure to heat then reveals the message."

Great thunder, that cipher she'd found in the heel of the boot the previous morning — both sides in the war might employ such ink. She felt her face pale, and in the next second realized that Fairfax had read her expression. His hand shot out. "Give it to me."

"It's at my house in Augusta."

He withdrew his hand. "Perhaps you prefer to be strip-searched."

Did he presume to perform such a search himself? Ye gods. Clark's cipher was also in her pocket. Betsy thrashed down panic and steadied her gaze on him, polluted as it made her feel. "I shall turn it over to you on the morrow, if you so desire."

He said nothing, drilling his stare through her brain, watching her the way a panther observes a deer. No doubt about it — he knew she lied. After too many seconds of silence, he took a step closer. "We've met before."

For a moment, she resisted her body's flight response. Damned if he was going to intimidate her like Susana. Above the smells of horse and leather on him she detected the scents of his skin and hair — dark, humid, savage — a combination her pregnant nose routed out and found fascinating. Reasoning and senses collided, and she retreated a step at last. For no reason on earth should a ghoul with a glacier for a soul look and smell so superlative. "No, we've not met."

"I'm certain of it. Your features are familiar."

Her features must be represented in half the populace of Alton. "I've never met you before this day."

"Have you heard from your mother or uncle?"

"They were captured by Creek Indians —"

"I didn't ask if you'd heard *of* them. I asked if you'd heard *from* them."

Her pulse stammered before finding rhythm again. Sweat beaded to her forehead, and she swallowed, recalling David's visit just the day before. She plastered a hopeful smile to her lips. "Have they escaped the Indians, then?"

"Answer the question." She felt the very ether between them convulse, flogged by his tone. "Is it not true that you've recently had contact with your mother or uncle?"

Her smile withered. "No. I've not." She heard how her voice croaked and knew he'd read her second lie, too. Her flight response got the better of her then, and she attempted to rush past him into the shop.

His hand braced on the doorjamb, his arm imprisoning her. "If they escaped and contacted you, what action would you take?"

"Are you telling me they've escaped?" Horror spiraled through Betsy. Fairfax suspected her mother and uncle were free.

"I asked what you'd do if your kin escaped and contacted you. Cease evading me and answer the question."

From somewhere in her soul, she found the strength to glare at him. "Sir, how dare you ask of me a hypothetical question and demand a definitive answer?"

The gray-green ice in his eyes pinioned her, and she felt herself smothered, desperate to escape him. "A non-hypothetical interrogatory — very well. State your loyalties."

"I'm neutral."

"There are no neutrals in this war."

"Captain Sheffield doesn't agree with you."

"Captain Sheffield's opinion on this point doesn't concern me. Your grandfather, mother, and uncle are rebel spies. Your aunt is a rebel sympathizer. The apple seldom falls far from the tree, madam."

She continued to radiate indignation and outrage to mask her fear of him. The thought of being in his company seven hours on the morrow for the return trip to Augusta appalled her.

After what felt like hours, he softened his voice, but ice clung to his gaze. "Rising to challenges, wretched at lying — how like your mother. It took me little time to dismantle her lies. I'm intrigued to imagine what set of stimuli might loosen *your* tongue."

Intuition dragged Betsy's gaze to the black veil peeking from the package on the counter, and her stomach churned again. Without knowing how, she sensed that Fairfax had used the veil to degrade her mother. If she didn't get free of him soon, the scream compressed in the back of her throat would explode.

He shifted his gaze, too, verifying the object of her attention. A smile dallied on his lips, gruesome when employed with that midwinter stare, and he removed the hand blocking her escape. "I appreciate our spirited and informative conversation and look forward to more of it." After a bow, he retrieved his hat from the counter. "I shall return at seven on the morrow to escort you to Augusta. Good day, Mrs. Greeley. And good day, Mrs. John Clark Sheridan."

CHAPTER FIVE

The bell over the shop door jingled again, and a dark-haired man Susana's age entered carrying a hoe. "Afternoon, Susana." He brushed soot from his apron. "I apologize for taking so long with your hoe. Father and I had to let that new apprentice go." He granted Fairfax a nod of minimal civility. "Lieutenant."

Fairfax nodded and strode for the door. "Mr. Hale."

Hale. A relation to Betsy's father, perhaps? She perked up and stepped into the shop, in clear view of the man with the hoe.

He spied her. "Oh, you've company —" His eyes widened, and recognition sliced his expression. "Susana, who's this?"

"You remember my niece, don't you, Joshua? Sophie's daughter, Betsy. It's been years since she last visited Alton."

Fairfax lingered by the door, privy to their conversation. Joshua, still staring, said, "How peculiar!"

Mary thumped down the stairs. "Mrs. Greeley, I've finished the floors —" Her jaw dangled at the sight of Betsy and Joshua in proximity. "Why, Mr. Hale, don't Mrs. Sheridan look a bit like your uncle, Jacques le Coeuvre?"

"Le Coeuvre, yes!" A laugh full of dark humor exploded from Fairfax. "Jacques le Coeuvre and Sophie Barton — oh, that's rich, indeed. No doubt such a revelation will vibrate Major Hunt's sense of humor, too." With another laugh, he strutted for the door, yanked it open, and exited.

Silence seized the shop after the bell tinkle faded. Betsy fidgeted. Of Jacques le Coeuvre, to whom she was now linked, memory furnished her only with the image of a wandering, old storyteller fond of brandy. Her heart sank. Could that be correct? Not a pedigree to boast of.

Mary looked around. "Did I say something wrong?"

Susana snatched the hoe from Joshua and thrust it at the servant. "Put this in the shed outside and weed the bean plot, you lazy wench."

Mary fumbled with the hoe, curtsied, and scurried out while Betsy, Joshua, and Susana studied each other. "Betsy looks more like my mother." His face long, Joshua gazed in the direction Fairfax had taken. "But I don't suppose that matters now."

Susana fanned herself with vigor. "Well, Betsy, I see why Sophie hid you in Augusta all these years. What do you know — Uncle Jacques, that sly, old dog."

Betsy cleared her throat. "Uh, Mr. Hale —"

"Call me Joshua —" He smiled. " — cousin."

"May I have a word with you — alone?"

"Go ahead, dear." Susana gestured to the package on the counter beside Betsy's tote bag. "What shall I do with *this*?"

"Put it all in my mother's room." Betsy motioned Joshua toward the door. "Shall we go for a walk?"

He followed her outdoors around the corner of the house between trees laden with peaches, where they paused to regard each other. Insects hummed in the air sultry with honeyed fruit. She managed a tentative smile. "You've a brother named Mathias?"

"He's my half-brother. His father was a Creek warrior who died of smallpox." Creek warrior? Betsy touched her cheekbones, understanding where they came from at last, dazed, not certain how to deal with the idea of being one-quarter Creek Indian. She wasn't as ambivalent about her new-found French ancestry. "Our mother married Jacob Hale and had Mathias four months later, and in a few years, Jonah and I came along." He frowned. "Here, now, let me look at you more closely." His gaze enlarged. "Ah. You're Mathias's daughter, aren't you?"

She nodded. "*Uncle* Joshua."

He grinned. "Well, what a surprise. Here's a hug. Watch the grime." He brushed at his apron again. "Blacksmithing's dirty work." They embraced and laughed, and Joshua held her a long time. It felt the closest she'd ever felt to hugging a father, and she didn't want to let go.

Her voice sounded muffled against his shoulder. "You're going to be a great-uncle come Yule."

"Congratulations. Hmm, great-uncle. That takes some getting used to." He considered. "Do you suppose your father knows about all this — you, the baby?"

"Yes."

He set her out at arms' length. "You sound certain of that. Alas, we've no way of communicating with him." Worry pinched his face. "Prisoner of the Lower Creek — god's teeth."

She glanced around and whispered, "Can you keep a secret?" His eyebrows lifted, and he nodded. "My parents are in South Carolina with the Cherokee."

"Jove's arse — how did they — you —"

"Uncle David hid in my henhouse yesterday —"

"The three of them escaped the Lower Creek?" Joshua gaped.

"I got the impression the Lower Creek helped them escape the redcoats. Uncle David couldn't stay to explain. He was on the run. Do you know where my parents went among the Cherokee?"

"No. I'm not familiar with the Cherokee."

"But there's a Creek village near here."

"A few miles to the southwest. It's where Toókóhee Nókúse — Mathias's father — and my mother lived."

"So his relatives might live there. Take me there."

"Today?" Joshua studied the angle of the sun. "Very well. We've a good five hours daylight left. But the Creek won't tell you anything."

"I'm Mathias's daughter. You're his brother. Don't you think the two of us can persuade someone to talk with us?"

"Betsy, with this war, it comforts me greatly to know that my one living brother is alive and not captive. He and Sophie have a damned good reason to stay hidden, and I respect that."

She bit back frustration. "I want to know my blood father before my baby is born, and I want him to see this grandchild. Walk in my shoes, Uncle. Think what it would be like to wake up one morning and have a father when all your life you've never had one. Would you wait for a war to wind down before you sought him out? I won't let two armies of pig-headed men come between me and my own blood."

The corners of Joshua's eyes creased in a smile. "I don't suppose you would, standing there, looking so obstinate, just like your mother. All right, I'll introduce you to the village's Beloved Woman. Her family adopted my mother. But don't say I didn't warn you if she won't tell you what you want to know."

***

Cool and moist after the swelter of afternoon sun, the forest embraced them. Ahead on the Indian trail, Joshua swiveled in his saddle. "Are you a good rider? If we pick up the pace, we'll be home in time for supper."

Betsy signaled her agreement and sent Lady May cantering after him. Verdant foliaged branches of oak, maple, hickory, and dogwood whizzed past, and the earth beneath their horses' hooves mingled with the smells of sandy soil and horse sweat. Their passage silenced the sizzle of cicadas, but undaunted mockingbirds, redheaded woodpeckers, blue jays, and cardinals cavorted in the yellow-green air around them. After a few minutes, Betsy called ahead. "Joshua, where is your Uncle Jacques?"

"He took off after Will with Sophie, David, and Mathias. The official word was that the British executed him in Havana for resisting arrest."

She recoiled. "From what little I know of Major Hunt —"

"I don't think *Hunt* executed him." The sting in his voice made his meaning clear. No wonder Fairfax had found the thought of Sophie as Jacques le Coeuvre's mistress amusing. "Alton is well rid of Fairfax. You cannot spend a minute in his company without realizing that something is broken inside his head."

And she'd be treated to seven hours of his company on the morrow — how naïve she'd been to dismiss David's warning. "Clark and I wondered why Lieutenant Stoddard and Captain Sheffield were so eager to see him gone."

"They're decent men. So is Major Hunt. But it doesn't surprise me a bit that those murders back in early June occurred while Fairfax was here. That's when my brother Jonah's throat was slit. And the same night, a Spaniard was skinned alive."

"Gods," whispered Betsy, following Joshua's implication. "Was Fairfax responsible?" Panic leaped about in her gut.

"Stoddard's 'official' finding, that the murders were the work of a Spanish assassin, placated everyone and came just in time. The Creek had been implicated in the murders, and they were incensed, while the Whites were itching to butcher Indians."

"You think Stoddard and Sheffield covered for Fairfax."

"Wouldn't surprise me. The redcoats cannot afford to let a story leak about one of their officers torturing a prisoner to death."

"He's heading our escort back to Augusta on the morrow."

Joshua pulled back on the horse's reins. "Whoa. Steady there, lad." He patted the gelding's neck, and when Betsy drew even with him, caught her hand and held it. "Whatever you do, stay out of his way. Don't give him cause to suspect you of anything. That hound from Hades will tear you to pieces."

She swallowed, her throat dry. She'd been worse than naïve to dismiss David's warning. She'd been a fool.

***

A half-dozen dogs issued from lengthening shadows at the outskirts of the village. Each barked to alert the Creek of their visitors and circled Betsy and Joshua. Indians tagged along after them smiling with recognition, curiosity, and welcome. Joshua returned their greetings.

Betsy followed Joshua in dismounting and leading her horse. She had little exposure to large groups of Indians and tried not to gape at the villagers, but she knew she wasn't doing a good job of it. The truth was that she felt overdressed.

Four naked little boys, gripping branches whittled like spears, chased a rolling hoop in the dirt street between household compounds, and one boy sent his weapon through the center of the hoop, earning cheers from his companions. A young woman scraped flesh from deerskin stretched on a wooden frame. Strands of shells adorned her naked, bronzed upper torso, flowers diademed her black, braided hair, and a skirt of floral print covered her from waist to knee. Dressed in like fashion, women bearing baskets of corn strolled toward the *talwa*, the town center, laughter from their gossip jiggling their naked breasts. Two warriors in breechcloths hauled a catch of bass and trout, their earrings and nose-rings shining in the sunlight. Charcoal-colored tattoos whorled over their bronze skin from their ankles to their shaved heads and circled their topknots of black hair.

Almost everyone Betsy and Joshua encountered in the street or sitting before wattle-and-daub huts waved to Joshua, and he waved back. A warrior about ten years older than Betsy jogged over with a grin of amiability and, stinking of rancid bear grease, clasped arms with Joshua. He and Joshua spoke Creek — salutations and what Betsy presumed to be polite inquiries after family members. Among the tattoos, Betsy noticed a scar on the warrior's thigh still pink with healing — a sharp knife cut, from the smooth line of the wound.

His hand on her shoulder, Joshua pulled her a step closer to the Creek. "Betsy, this is my cousin, Sehoyee Yahuh. That's 'Standing Wolf' in English. He's a son of Laughing Eyes, the Beloved Woman. She's talking with the medicine man right now, but we can wait for her in her *huti*'s pavilion."

"Thank you." Betsy inclined her head to the warrior.

"Sehoyee Yahuh and his brother traveled with Mathias, Sophie, David, and Uncle Jacques as far as St. Augustine."

Betsy studied Standing Wolf. "You didn't go to Havana?"

The warrior grunted. "Spaniards." She was reminded of the two sneaky Spaniards and all that Cordovan leather in Clark's shop. "Bandits. Ambush. Wolves. Assassins. Escaped slaves." His upper lip curled. "Always the redcoats."

With such an itinerary, the trip to St. Augustine must have been sheer nightmare. Perhaps the wound on the warrior's thigh was acquired in the adventure. She wondered how her parents, uncle, and great-uncle had survived to reach St. Augustine.

Standing Wolf escorted them past the town plaza and square ground to the pavilion of his mother's *huti* and trotted off. Beneath the shade house, Joshua offered the deer hide hammock to Betsy, who settled into it, gazed at flies on the thatch ceiling, and yawned. Summer's heat and the needs of the baby growing inside her had made the trip more wearying than usual.

"Uncle Jacques used to bring Jonah and me to the village when we were boys."

"That's how you learned the language." She yawned again. The hammock creaked and swayed, and she sank further into it, comfortable for the first time that day, realizing how tired she felt.

"Yes. The Creek named your father Ayukapeta Hokolen Econa. It means 'Walk in Two Worlds' because Laughing Eyes took him with her when she talked with settlers. He spent enough time among colonists and Indians to be considered White by most Whites and Indian by most Indians. On top of that he learned blacksmithing from my father."

The family history lesson wavered in and out as sleep overtook her. "Maybe my father didn't go to South Carolina just to hide." She yawned a final time. "Maybe he went there as an ambassador."

She'd just nodded off when Joshua cleared his throat. "Hssst, Betsy, they're coming."

The smell of corn cakes being fried by two women in the *huti*'s cooking area adjacent to the pavilion roused a grumble from Betsy's stomach. She rolled from the hammock, groggy, and smoothed her petticoat. "How do I look? Oh, dear, all the dust and wrinkles —"

She straightened. Too late for grooming. Standing Wolf stepped beneath the shade of the pavilion, behind him a Creek matron whose gaze flicked over Betsy once before focusing on Joshua and softening.

CHAPTER SIX

The matron, her upper torso adorned with strands of shells and wooden beads, her black hair braided with flowers, smiled at Joshua. He bowed, and she coughed with disapproval. "A bow is all you have for your mother's sister?" They hugged, and she patted his back with a hand gentle enough to burp babies and firm enough to steer negotiations. "How long has it been since you visited us? Late spring?" Sheepishness slid over his face. "Bring your children next time." She fluttered her hand. "But leave that quarrelsome wife of yours at home."

Joshua continued to look chagrined but extended his hand in Betsy's direction. "Betsy, I have the pleasure of introducing you to Uhbeleduh Duthlwuh, sister to your grandmother. I'm proud to claim Betsy as the true daughter of my brother, your sister's son, Ayukapeta Hokolen Econa, and Nagchoguh Hogdee."

Nagchoguh Hogdee: Paper Woman, the name given Sophie by the Creek for all those years of printing newspapers. Betsy fumbled her petticoat in both hands, and her curtsy felt clumsy. "Madam."

Laughing Eyes turned a gaze full of kindness and humor on Joshua. "She has indeed been raised among Whites."

Hardly a compliment — Betsy tensed even more. But Joshua smiled. "Hear what she has to say, Grandmother."

Laughing Eyes regarded Betsy, her expression calm, and Betsy understood herself the object of the matron's undivided attention. She recalled reading somewhere that Queen Elizabeth of England had focused on valued visitors the same way, making them feel of merit to earn her audience.

Humbled, she took a deep breath. "Yesterday morning, my uncle, David St. James, was hiding in my henhouse." Tiny movement in the matron's lips told her Laughing Eyes read the depth of the field, and there would be no subterfuge. "He implied that the Lower Creek in East Florida rescued him and my parents from the redcoats. He was headed to Williamsburg to hide and said my parents had sought refuge with Cherokee in South Carolina, also to hide."

"He spoke the truth. Have you told anyone of this encounter besides Joshua?"

Betsy shook her head.

"Tell no one else."

"Yes, madam." Betsy's heart ached against her ribcage. Laughing Eyes must know how nervous she was. "Until my uncle's visit yesterday morning, I didn't know that Mathias Hale — Ayukapeta Hokolen Econa — was my father. I haven't spoken with my mother about him. I've been raised with grandfathers, stepfathers, and uncles, but I've always known they weren't my father. I've never had a father."

Kindness suffused the matron's brown eyes. "We believe the mother more important than the father, and the brother and sister of the mother also. You have been raised with all three."

"I want to meet my father."

"I have no doubt the future holds a meeting for you, but ill shall come if you force it before your father can arrange it."

Betsy lowered her voice. "I've waited so long. Please tell me where they went."

"You know enough to destroy them. Hear the timing of Creator, the all-wise one who urges us to guard our secrets."

Betsy pressed her open palm to her chest above her heart. "Never knowing my father gives me great emptiness and sadness. If he's half the man I hear him to be, he feels empty and sad from never knowing me. Tell me where they've gone, I beg of you, so I may follow them. I won't tell anyone. I swear it."

"How will you gain your husband's permission to travel?"
Anxiety leaked into Betsy's voice. "I shall find a way."

Laughing Eyes caught up Betsy's hands in her own rough, warm, wise-woman hands, and scrutinized her with an unsmiling face and a gaze that bored into her soul. "Daughter, I sense a great restlessness in you, a fear. Beyond acquainting yourself with your father, what is your reason for seeking him?"

An answer rose to Betsy's lips, although she suspected it wasn't quite what the matron had sought. "I carry the first grandchild. I would find a way to unite us before I bear this baby, even if I have to search the entire South Carolina colony. Please. You understand how important family is."

"A baby." Resolve in Laughing Eyes's face softened. Her gaze sought Joshua, who nodded in confirmation. Then she studied Betsy again. "I assumed you ripe for the lesson of patience, Daughter, and I thought I saw something else — something demanding that you answer to yourself." She sighed. "The pull of blood is strong. It can be a noble pull, but it can also be senseless. Even my judgment is affected by it.

"The life within you is the most precious gift of Creator. I do not wish you be blinded by the blood pull." Still holding Betsy's hand in one of hers, she extended her other hand to Joshua, who grasped it, and then swept her gaze around to ensure that only Betsy, Joshua, and Standing Wolf were within hearing. "In the name of the all-powerful Mother of the earth, I charge both of you to use this forthcoming knowledge wisely, or you will invite suffering upon us all."

Joshua's face sobered. "Yes, Grandmother."

The inside of Betsy's mouth felt dry as cotton, but she managed to swallow. "Yes, Grandmother."

"Keowee," said Laughing Eyes, her eyes not at all laughing. "They have gone to a place near Keowee. It lies north-northwest of here by some seventy miles. Now may the wisdom of the old ones guide your lips and feet with this knowledge."

***

Leaves resonated with nocturnes of birds, and fireflies lilted in the twilight. Joshua dismounted before the print shop and helped Betsy off her horse. From inside, she heard her six cousins hollering and thumping about. Joshua, who'd kept quiet most of the trip back except for sharing a few anecdotes about Mathias, took her hand in his and said low, "Will you go to South Carolina in search of them?"

"Yes, somehow." She studied the longing on Joshua's face. "Mathias is your only living brother. Will *you* go?"

"I have four children and a — uh — quarrelsome wife. But she understands about family. If my niece, daughter to my missing brother, must undertake a journey to South Carolina —" He smiled and dropped her hand. " — I consider it a matter of honor and duty to accompany her." He bowed. "Likely even with my wife's blessings."

"Ah, Joshua. Thank you."

"Huzzah! It's Cousin Betsy!" Children spewed from the house and pounded down the steps to encircle Betsy and Joshua. After they'd taken turns hugging her, they turned on him.

"Mr. Joshua, Mama says you and Betsy are cousins!"

"That makes us your cousins, too, doesn't it?"

"Hug me!"

"Hug me, too!"

Betsy watched, amused, while her youngest cousins attempted to leap on Joshua and the eldest boys stood off to the side grinning, having decided they were too grown up for such a display. Joshua laughed, at ease with children swinging off him like monkeys. "Ho, there, one at a time, will you?"

From the front porch came the deep voice of Susana's giant-of-a-husband, John. "Well, Joshua old boy, welcome to *our* family." The boards on the porch squawked beneath his weight as he lumbered down the steps. "Looks like Will had a good basis for his long-term friendship with the le Coeuvres, ho ho ho." The children hanging on Joshua scattered. John pumped his hand and slapped his back as if Joshua were Betsy's father. "Stay for supper, hey? We've plenty of food."

"No, thank you. I must get on home for supper."

"Join me at the Red Rock later, then. I'll buy a round."

Joshua tipped his hat. "Excellent. I shall see you there." With a wink for Betsy, he mounted his horse and rode off, several of the children waving after him.

"Say, woman, how about a hug for your uncle?" John reached for Betsy and hugged her, restraining his usual spine-popping pressure because of her pregnancy. "You sure you're expecting? Susana was out to here by four months." His meaty hand snagged the shoulder of his eldest son. "Take your cousin's mare back to the stable and rub her down."

"Yes, sir." The youth led Lady May around back.

Betsy spotted Clark trotting his horse toward them on the dusty street, and she waved. John seized the next older boy. "And you rub down Clark's horse when he gets here."

Clark alighted, pecked Betsy's cheek, shook John's hand, and submitted to a round of hugs from cousins. After a vague response to her query about his visit with the tanner, Mr. Givens, that afternoon, Clark followed Betsy up the porch steps, preceded by John and four children while the second eldest boy trudged to the stable with his horse. At the threshold, Clark murmured to Betsy, "What's this about you being the daughter of an old French spy?"

Gossip in Alton flowed as free as September ale. Betsy wondered whose tongue had wagged the most. No sense in trying to straighten out the truth with her husband until they had some privacy. She fluttered eyelashes at him. "*Mais oui!*"

He sneaked a moist kiss to her neck. "Mmm. I cannot wait to hear the details." He released her and groaned. "Oh, gods."

Susana had emerged from the dining room and was bearing down on him with arms flung wide. "Dear, dear, Clark! What an absolute delight to see you again! Do come here give your auntie a hug! We have so much to talk about, don't we? Next time you visit, you *will* stay an entire week!"

***

Yawning, Betsy elbowed the stable door open wider, her lantern pushing back the night inside. "Evening, my lady." Lady May perked up her head with pleasure. Betsy hung the lantern, set down Captain Arriaga's box, and patted Clark's gelding before reaching for the mare's saddle blanket. "I'll catch the devil from Mr. Fairfax on the morrow if I don't show the captain what's in this box." After a day on the road and an evening calculating business expenses for Susana, she was too tired to walk.

She'd wished for Clark's company, but he'd been impatient to seek the tavern after supper — escape Susana's futile attempts at justifying a second page of the newspaper, and buy his promised drinks for Stoddard's patrol. Through her disappointment, she realized she'd have to explain first why she hadn't told him the entire truth about the veil and parasol. The business of half-truths had become convoluted, and she wanted to be done with it, even though the thought of facing Sheffield alone with the veil and parasol felt ominous. Lady May, at least, didn't seem to mind accompanying her on the short trip to the other end of town, so she stroked her horse. "That's my good lass."

Minutes later, she dismounted before Sheffield's house and secured the mare beside a gelding she recognized as the one Stoddard had ridden. The door opened when she stepped onto the front porch, and Finnegan lifted a lantern to illumine her and the box she carried. "Mrs. Sheridan." Avian screeches and human cheers from a cockfight behind the Red Rock Tavern reached their ears, and fastidious concern furrowed the servant's brow. "What might ye be doing out alone tonight?"

"Lieutenant Fairfax ordered me to show the contents of this box to Captain Sheffield before I left town."

The Irishman's concern descended into distaste. "Fairfax — hrumph. Come inside, then, while I fetch the captain."

Prompted by Finnegan's knock on the study door and murmured message, Sheffield opened the door, eyebrow cocked with piqued interest, and invited Betsy in. What if the captain found something in the package that made her suspect of colluding with the rebels? Throat clenched, she entered, her posture demure. Near the study's side window, Stoddard set aside a glass one quarter full of amber brandy and bowed. With both officers present, perhaps one was guaranteed to find *something* amiss in the box. Fairfax had seemed certain of it. Finnegan lit more candles, conferring a warm glow upon the room with its plain, sturdy furniture, but Betsy fidgeted.

Without preamble, she explained how she'd come by the veil and parasol. The officers examined everything and within two minutes decided that the box and its contents weren't hiding any secret messages. Holding to her story about leaving the letter in Augusta, Betsy recounted Arriaga's message. Her instincts, or perhaps Laughing Eyes's warning about the safety of her parents, told her not to repair the misunderstanding just yet that Jacques le Coeuvre, not Mathias Hale, was her father. Fortunately the letter was vague on the point of her paternity.

Sheffield handed her back the box with the veil and parasol. "The letter sounds innocuous enough, and we've no intelligence that Miguel de Arriaga is an agent for the rebels. However, the rebels have been known to intercept the missives of neutral parties and implant seditious messages within. Therefore, I think it prudent that, upon your return to Augusta, you surrender the letter to Colonel Thomas Brown for his expert examination."

Colonel Thomas Brown: Adam Neville's superior officer, His Majesty's Ranger. Could Lieutenant Fairfax be right about the letter containing a cipher from the rebels? Not liking the thought of it, Betsy moistened her lips with the tip of her tongue. "Sir, if Colonel Brown finds a hidden message, whom do you suppose was the intended recipient?"

Sheffield and Stoddard regarded her, their expressions revealing nothing, and didn't answer. The clock in the study ticked. She swallowed, and sweat trickled between her breasts. "Oh, see here, you must know by now that *I* am not an agent of —"

"Madam." Sheffield smiled. "I assure you that if you've been forthright with us, you've nothing to fear."

They did indeed suspect a rebel cipher in Arriaga's letter, but they weren't certain it had been intended for *her*. Cordovan leather. Sooty Johns and two Spaniards in the middle of the night. Dear heavens. *Clark.*

"I shall direct Lieutenant Fairfax to confiscate the letter immediately upon your return to Augusta and present it to Colonel Brown. Mr. Stoddard, please escort Mrs. Sheridan back to the house for the night. Thank you for your diligence, madam."

Lieutenant Fairfax. Oh, gods. "Captain." Stoddard at her elbow, Betsy turned back to Sheffield in the doorway. "Sir, it would put me at great ease if Lieutenant Stoddard accompanied us back to Augusta on the morrow, rather than Lieutenant Fairfax."

"Ah." The diplomatic neutrality slid over Sheffield's face again. "I'm honored by the confidence you've gained in my officer. Alas, I need him here in Alton. Believe me when I say that if I didn't trust Mr. Fairfax to see you safely back to Augusta, I'd most certainly send Mr. Stoddard in his stead. Again, I thank you for your assistance and cooperation. Give my regards to your husband, and may you both rest well tonight."

CHAPTER SEVEN

etsy waited in the saddle for a laconic Stoddard to mount his
horse before nudging her mare north behind him. Her thoughts
tumbled, and her pulse fluttered like a caged songbird stalked by
a housecat. What a predicament she'd woven. The redcoats expected
her to surrender Arriaga's letter the next day, but she couldn't risk their
uncovering a cipher that might incriminate Clark. She saw no option
but to forge a copy of the letter for them while everyone slept. Why,
oh why, had she ignored David's warning to stay away from Alton?

Five lots north, they passed tanner Givens's shop and home,
where Clark had visited that afternoon. A crash from within prompted
Stoddard to halt their horses. "Did you hear that?"

A man on horseback galloped from behind the house out onto the
street and flew north past them, his expression shadow-gouged and
contorted with malice. Enough light existed for Betsy to recognize the
sensual lips and dark eyes and hair of a Spaniard — not one of the
men who'd visited Clark in the middle of the night, but a Spaniard
nonetheless.

"Bloody hell!" Stoddard groped for a pistol at his saddle.

No other soldiers were within hail, and Alton's civilians were snoring abed, imbibing at the Red Rock, or losing money over the cockfight. Betsy steadied her spooked mare. "Lieutenant, you mustn't give chase! The Givenses! I fear for the family!"

He stared from the gloom of night, where the Spaniard had vanished, to the house, to Betsy before he expelled a breath with decision, recognizing his priorities. "Wait here. I shall check on the family." He dismounted and handed her the reins and one pistol. "I presume you know how to fire this." He removed the other pistol and cocked it halfway. "If the Spaniard returns, shoot him."

Night at the rear of the Givens's house swallowed him, and anxiety slicked Betsy's palms. She darted a jittery glance about the deserted street, startled at the distant hoot of an owl, leaves clattering on the humid breeze, and raucous laughter erupting from the nearby tavern. Her relief at seeing Stoddard emerge a minute later dwindled at his expression.

"Madam, your concern is well-placed. Mr. Givens and his wife lay murdered most foully in their shop."

***

Two soldiers combed the yard for clues by lantern light, footprints mingling with those of Stoddard, the Spaniard, and his horse. The lieutenant, who'd been conversing with a stout sergeant, noticed Betsy's yawn, paused, and faced her. "My apologies. I should have escorted you back after you completed your statement. You've been most cooperative."

She favored him with a weary smile. "My mother's house isn't but a couple minutes away. I can ride by myself —"

"With that murderous Spaniard on the loose? I wouldn't dream of letting you do that. I shan't be but a moment longer completing my instructions to Sykes here."

The lieutenant turned back to Sykes, missing her subsequent yawn of resignation. Her gaze caught on a lone man on horseback trotting toward them from the direction of the Red Rock. He absorbed night, shadow his ally, stealthy in the dark like a creature of primal myth born to prey in the folds of a foggy, ferny forest. Although the air was warm, she shuddered and moved closer to Lady May, hoping he'd ride on past, the ground would cave in, or she'd become invisible. No such luck.

Metal clinked against leather as Fairfax dismounted. "Why wasn't I contacted earlier?" He drew up almost nose-to-nose with Stoddard. Sergeant Sykes's attempt at a salute went ignored. He slipped away to join the investigation in the yard, obviously used to such treatment by Fairfax.

Stoddard glanced at the time on a watch from his waistcoat pocket, replaced the watch, and swelled out his chest. "You weren't contacted because you're due to leave Alton in eight hours, fifty-two minutes. Sir." His smirk was audible.

"Indeed, but I still have eight hours, fifty-two minutes in Alton. Sir." The same height as Stoddard, Fairfax outweighed him by at least twenty-five pounds, all of it muscle, making Stoddard look spindly in comparison. Betsy shuddered again. Stoddard would be most fortunate if the two men never traded more than verbal blows.

Fairfax's attention snagged on the men in the yard, and dismay bit at the chill in his voice. "What the devil are they doing?"

"Searching for evidence."

"They're *destroying* evidence, fool. Footprints, hoof —"

"I remind you that you're speaking to a fellow officer."

Betsy squirmed. This rivalry went beyond epaulet crowding. "Cause of death?"

"As you'll soon be gone, it's immaterial to you." Stoddard hummed a few seconds. "Oh, very well, blood loss."

"They were stabbed?"

"Their throats were slit from ear to ear."

"By a Spaniard." Fairfax sounded certain. "Any witnesses?"

"Beside myself? Yes. You now have eight hours, fifty-one minutes."

"All who visited the tanner recently are potentially accomplices to murder. You will question them."

Clark had visited the tanner that afternoon. He had friends who were Spaniards. Betsy sucked in a breath of shock. Had he really gone to the Red Rock Tavern that night?

"Perhaps you've misunderstood. His Majesty doesn't require your investigative skills here. He requires that you pursue your next assignment on the morrow: escorting Mrs. Sheridan and her husband to Augusta."

Just when Betsy had begun to hope she'd escape Fairfax's scrutiny, his frozen stare rotated to her. "*You* are a witness?" She fought the urge to shrink when he advanced on her, his expression mobile and victorious as he no doubt considered angles through which she might be involved in rebel schemes. He lowered his voice. "Stoddard, if by some chance your *investigation* reveals that Givens was a member of the Ambrose ring, this woman is an unsuitable witness."

Ambrose ring? What the blazes was that?

Stoddard snorted. "We've examined what you call 'evidence.' A parasol and veil. Bah. No secret rebel messages hidden in those. The lady is willing to surrender the letter to Colonel Brown on the morrow in Augusta."

He caught her eye above Fairfax's shoulder. "I shall escort you back now, madam." He strolled around to face Fairfax and granted the Givens property a magnanimous wave. "Have at it if you like, sir. You've still eight hours, fifty minutes. And were I you, I wouldn't harass Mrs. Sheridan. She's performed admirably as the king's witness, and Captain Sheffield thinks well of her."

***

Not a ghost of a breeze cooled the stuffy bedroom, even though it was near eleven o'clock. The servant, Mary, was asleep in the tiny room across from Betsy's room, and Susana had gone home to her family, but Clark hadn't yet returned. Annoyed and fretting, Betsy shoved the window open further, undressed to her shift, and hung her clothing on pegs. Then she set her pockets and the lantern on her mother's desk and withdrew Arriaga's letter and Clark's cipher. Blue letters and numbers reappeared on the message from the boot when she passed it near the heat of the lantern. While its cipher faded to invisibility, she pushed the boot message aside and opened Arriaga's letter.

Almost afraid to confirm her suspicions, she waved the letter above the heat. A shiver scurried down her backbone, and she whispered, "Gods." The familiar, bluish cipher-scribble appeared between the lines of Arriaga's script, too.

What she knew of Clark little more than scratched the surface of the life he led. Even worse than her confirmation that he concealed so much was her certainty that he was in the thick of a multinational plot. She clamped down on her fear. Without a level head, she wouldn't be able to help her husband.

The Portuguese were supposedly neutral in the war. Sheffield had suggested the Portuguese captain's letter might have been intercepted before it left Havana. After exhaling a deep breath, she passed the letter over the heat again. The cipher portion was, indeed, written by a hand other than Arriaga's.

Without knowing the key to the cipher, trying to decode it was almost impossible. She studied the cipher on the letter, set it aside, and reheated for the message from the boot, searching for something in common between the two. 402. Say, hadn't that been a number from the letter, too? After she'd refreshed the letter's cipher, she saw the number 402 written there twice. What was the significance of 402?

Clark must have kept everything from her thus far to protect her, but she was through carrying the burden of what she'd discovered alone. She doubted he'd confess if she confronted him directly. No, she'd have to trick him or convince him he could trust her. 402. She'd wait up for her husband, and perhaps she could find out what it meant.

To pass the time, she copied Arriaga's letter with the stationery, quill, and ink on her mother's desk. By the time she sprinkled fine sand over the finished forgery to help dry the ink, she'd grown so sleepy she had difficulty holding her head up. She nodded several times, folded the cipher and both letters, slid them into her pockets, and extinguished the lantern. She'd stretch out on the bed for a few minutes and wake up when Clark came in.

She never remembered falling asleep, but early Thursday, a thunderstorm trundled over Alton and awakened her. Oblivious to the tempest, Clark snored beside her. When had he returned?

Rain spattered the floor beneath the window. Fuzzy-headed, she rolled from bed and shoved the window shut, and after using the chamberpot, lay abed listening to the assault of rain on roof and pane. Alton needed the rain. So did Augusta to the north.

Clark's snores deepened. Intermittent lightning flashes cast his skin blue, almost the same hue as the cipher message. When the storm abated, she reopened the window and crouched in the cool moisture, her pregnant nose reveling in raw scents of predawn, her hand stroking her belly. Several roosters crowed, and she peered out at the sky. In the east, it had blanched.

Clark coughed, and his murmur sounded groggy. "Betsy?"

Glad for the cover of darkness, she slid back in bed and began stroking his chest. Sweat dampened the sheet beneath him. "Hush. Go back to sleep."

He yawned. "Too much on my mind."

No doubt. She whispered, "Then let's play our game. Tree."

He sighed in deep contentment, eyes closed. "Sunshine."

"Wine."

"Purple." He yawned again.

"Bucket."

He nodded at the edge of sleep. "Mmm. Water."

"Four hundred two."

"Cornwallis."

She didn't miss a stroke, despite the fear that rammed her gut. Charles Lord Cornwallis was running the show in South Carolina. What business did a shoemaker from Augusta and residents of Spanish Havana have with a British general?

Clark stiffened, and she saw him stare at the ceiling, trying to decide whether he'd dreamed spilling the information. Then he pushed away and stood. "Bloody damn." He stumped to the desk, lit the lantern, and turned on her, his glare demanding an explanation.

She sat up. "Monday I received that box from a sea captain named Arriaga. His letter said he gave the enclosed parasol and veil to my mother while she was on his ship, and she lost them when the redcoats captured her in Havana, so he sent them to me. You and I didn't have time to discuss it Monday.

"Tuesday morning in the shop, I saw a piece of paper in the heel of a cowhide boot. When I held it close to the lamp, blue letters and numbers appeared all over it —"

"Christ Jesus —"

" — and again I didn't have time to ask you about it because we had to clean 'Tory Scum' off our house. I woke in the middle of the night and overheard you talking with two Spaniards who were taking away the cowhide boots. Basilio, you named one of them. The dogs never barked at them. They knew them from previous visits, same way they know Sooty Johns."

"Ah." Clark rubbed his eyelids.

Betsy wrung her hands. "Yesterday afternoon, Lieutenant Fairfax came here to the shop to post a letter. He recognized the parasol and veil from when he was in Havana and concluded that my aunt and I

were spies. I denied involvement, but I'd swear he *knew* I had
Arriaga's letter and your message."

Clark paced the length of the room in his shirt. Panic thrashed
his expression.

"Husband, rebels write between the lines of letters with invisible
ink that turns blue when heated, the way letters and numbers appeared
on your message from the boot heel —" She kept her voice low,
conscious of the servant in the bedroom across the stairway. " — the
same way letters and numbers appeared on Arriaga's letter last night
when I exposed it to heat. Between the two, I noticed the number 402
several times, so I knew it had to be significant.

"How many times have Basilio and his partner visited you in the
middle of the night? Did they get you the Cordovan leather? What's a
Loyalist doing in secret meetings with men from a country at war with
Britain? To whom are you sending secret messages? Did Sooty paint
the slur on our house, and if so, why? What has all this to do with
Cornwallis?" She drew a deep, shaky breath. "Are you spying on the
redcoats for the rebels?"

He kept pacing. "I cannot tell you."

"Or you *will* not?" At his silence, she intercepted him, planted
her feet, and braced her fists on her hips, her body quivering with
betrayal. "How dare you conceal all this from me? Does this baby
mean nothing to you? *Think*, man! Do you want me widowed, or —"
She cringed, recalling Fairfax's threat to loosen her tongue. "Do you
want all this half-knowledge tortured out of me? Tell me enough to
protect myself and not betray you. Let me be your comrade and help
you out of this." She hugged him. "I cannot raise this child alone.
Stop what you're doing!"

"I tried to leave," he muttered, "when I found out you were
carrying the baby. They won't let me go until it's over." He wrapped
his arms around her. "It's gigantic, Betsy. It reaches the entire length
of the Colonies, across the water, into Cuba, the Caribbean, France,
Spain, Holland —"

"Rebels." Her voice emerged choked the way hope felt in her
chest. "A spy ring. Dear gods, you're spying for the rebels."

"If I walk away, I'll be executed within days. After my attempt at
backing out two months ago, I was marked as suspect."

She clung to him, her head spinning with horror and indignation.
"What is your mission?"

"I swore on my sacred honor not to tell you or anyone else."

What did fanatics who raided farms and ravished women and girls know of sacred honor? "When will it be over?"

"Another six weeks. And then I'm out, I promise."

"Six weeks is a long time. The redcoats aren't stupid."

"Yes, I know." He disentangled himself and headed for the desk. "And we've a seven-hour ride today in the company of one with a fiend's love of interrogation." He laughed without mirth. "I'd the good fortune to meet Mr. Fairfax last night in the Red Rock, and — ahh, gods —" He ran his hand over his face, as if to banish memory of the encounter. "Where are the letter and note? I must destroy both."

Relieved that she'd had the prudence to forge Arriaga's letter, she withdrew the original and the boot message from her pocket and handed them to him. While she crawled back into bed, the quilt of despondency settling over her, Clark ignited the note and dropped it into a metal dish on the desk. Arriaga's missive he first warmed to expose the cipher and silently translate. Then it, too, was fed to the flames.

The bitter stink of evidence permeated the room and shivered premonition through Betsy. Fire, the beginning and the end. Clark blew out the lantern, crawled into bed, and took her in his arms. "I'll be out by September, I promise. Trust me."

Did she have a choice? Her soul writhed with foreboding over the chasm her husband straddled between two battling Olympians: punitive parent and recalcitrant child. To them, the life of one mortal named John Clark Sheridan was of no consequence.

CHAPTER EIGHT

Neither Betsy nor Clark slept while dawn brightened the sky. She withheld knowledge of the Givens murders from her husband, uncertain how to tell him. Perhaps he'd heard the news in the Red Rock before coming home and hadn't mentioned it to her because he didn't want to alarm her further. The possibility that he already knew of it from plans made with Spaniards made her want to shrink from his touch. Was Clark capable of plotting murder? On Monday, she'd have scorned the suggestion. But with each passing day, she'd gained greater discernment that she didn't know the man in bed beside her at all.

Mary rose at five-thirty and thumped downstairs to revive the cooking fire. When Susana arrived half an hour later, Betsy pulled from Clark's embrace without a word and dressed. He did the same. Then they descended the stairs together to the aroma of coffee and cornbread and met Susana's grim visage in the shop.

The older woman thrust mugs of coffee at them. "I hate bearing ill news first thing, but the Givenses have been murdered."

Clark coughed coffee, so Betsy surmised it was news to him. "How dreadful, Aunt. When? How?"

"Last night about nine-thirty or ten. Lieutenant Stoddard saw a Spaniard on horseback gallop away from the house, and so he investigated."

Clark coughed again. "A *Spaniard*?"

From the magnitude of his gape, he was either an excellent liar, or knowledge of the murderer's nationality had unsettled him as much as news of the crime. Susana sighed. "Yes, a Spaniard. Another Spaniard. Unfortunately this rascal wasn't caught, either. After the horrific murder of that Spaniard here last month, I hoped we'd seen the last of Spaniards. It's just as well that you're headed back to Augusta today. I fear Alton is no longer a safe place to live. Now, let me see whether that lazy servant has finished preparing your breakfast."

Betsy studied Clark's peculiar fenced-in, wary expression over the rim of her coffee mug after Susana walked away. "You visited the tanner yesterday, did you not?" she said low, keeping her face neutral.

"Yes, but — but you don't think I had anything to do with his murder, do you?"

"Did you?"

"Good god, he was my friend!"

"And the Spaniard who murdered him?"

Clark looked away. "I don't know who he might have been."

The coffee soured in Betsy's mouth. From the horror and suspicion in her husband's eyes, she surmised he did know something about the murderer. That he was unwilling to confide in her about it filled her with more anxiety. The least Clark could do would be to tell her how the tanner's murderer figured into his mission.

Upstairs after breakfast, while Betsy was cleaning her teeth, she heard the jingle of spur and harness outside in the front yard. She rinsed her mouth and looked beyond the porch overhang to see Lieutenant Fairfax dismounting his horse while five other soldiers remained in their saddles out on the road. Will's hounds rose from the front porch, their toenails scraping the planks, and trotted over to investigate the visitor. Halfway out, both dogs changed their minds and dove back beneath the porch — not a reassuring gesture.

The clock in the shop struck seven, followed by a rap on the front door. Betsy slung her tote sack over her shoulder and left the bedroom. Susana gave her a matronly hug downstairs in the shop, handed their wrapped dinner to Clark, and hugged him. "I may have the biggest mouth in Alton, but no one ever walked away from my table hungry."

As soon as Betsy opened the door, Fairfax glared in at the three of them. Without a word, she walked past him, Clark behind her, to where Clark had tied their saddled horses, noting the stiff expressions on the other five soldiers, none of whom had accompanied Lieutenant Stoddard to fetch them from Augusta. She and Clark sure weren't going to supplement any soldiers' rations with homemade goodies during dinner this trip.

The Sheridans waved goodbye to Susana. On the road, their escort of six spoke little. Attempts at chitchat between Betsy and Clark fizzled in the ambiance that they were a mere liability to the soldiers.

They stopped at nine and again at eleven, and Betsy, understanding the complaint of "pregnant bladder," trekked through foliage west of the road to relieve herself. Wandering out into the brush far enough for privacy made her feel like an escaped prisoner. And to think they had several more hours in Fairfax's company.

Her return was curtailed by pistol fire and the appearance of a dozen bandits descending on the escort.

At first she gaped in shock. Horses skittered and neighed through blackpowder smoke. Fairfax whipped out a pistol, blew a bandit's face away, and vaulted into his horse's saddle. Clark discharged his fowler into another bandit's midsection, sending the man screaming and thrashing in agony.

A volley erupted from the soldiers' muskets. The arc of sunlight on the lieutenant's hanger made Betsy flinch in horror, too late to avoid seeing the spurt of blood and the bounce of a bandit's severed head.

She crouched behind a tree, shaken, nauseated, Stoddard's words hammering her memory: *I was the target, sir. Had the men not performed commendably, I'd have been assassinated.* So this wasn't indiscriminate highway robbery and murder, then. Was she witnessing part of a conspiracy to assassinate British officers?

More pistol shots, more screams from dying men, the thud of someone running toward her — she gasped at a bandit fleeing into the woods and huddled lower in the brush. Best to stay concealed.

Her gaze followed the retreating man and widened when a Spaniard emerged from the brush thirty feet from her, the reins of his horse in one hand. He studied the bandit's noisy flight before looking toward the road, his expression as full of purpose as it was devoid of warmth. Betsy's stomach lurched, and she almost lost her breakfast. He was the Spaniard who had murdered the Givenses.

When he spotted her, menace and recognition condensed in his piercing, black eyes. He tossed the horse's reins over a branch and lunged. Betsy bolted for the road and blundered straight into the arms of a second retreating bandit.

He hauled her around and, with one arm pinning her to him, faced the soldiers, a knife pressed to her throat. Out of the frying pan into the fire — dark specks rotated through Betsy's vision of stunned soldiers and a horrified Clark. Clark faltered forward a few steps. "For the love of god, please let her go!"

"Stay there, you hear me? All of you — or I'll cut her!"

In the background, moribund bandits moaned. One began a death rattle. Clark spread his hands, beseeching. "I haven't much money with me, but it's yours if you let her go."

"I'll take your money, all of you, and I want every horse. After all, it's what's due us for our efforts. Drop your weapons and keep your hands where I can see them. Lieutenant, drop that pistol, I say!"

Betsy's gaze riveted to Fairfax, who'd dismounted. He finished reloading one of his pistols and replaced the ramrod with the calm and ease of a preacher reviewing a frequent sermon for a familiar flock. Then he lifted the pistol and took aim with a steady hand. "Drop the knife and let her go unharmed by my count of five, and I shall grant you a thirty-second lead before I hunt you down."

"Does your lordship think me a fool?"

Agony bloomed on Clark's face. "Lieutenant, didn't you hear him? Put that pistol away, or he'll murder her!"

"Stand your ground, Mr. Sheridan."

"You've lost your wits! Pistols aren't accurate enough —"

"*Stand your ground.*"

Betsy's gaze wrenched back to Fairfax. Angelic radiance suffused his face, and a half-smile teased his lips, as if he agreed with Clark's assessment of his pistol's accuracy. Again, she almost vomited. The pistol was aimed right for her. Did he have no regard for her life at all?

"Ensign, if Mr. Sheridan interferes, restrain him."

"Yes, sir."

She darted a glance around — from edginess on the four privates' faces, to discipline on the ensign's face, to terror on Clark's face, to the radiance that transfigured Fairfax in such a breathtaking, preternatural way. Gods. The only time she'd seen such virility imbue Clark's expression was during lovemaking.

She felt close to fainting. Sweat streamed between her thighs. If the bandit didn't kill her, Fairfax or the Spaniard would. She was on her own. Tensing, she spotted a small branch nearby: a good weapon to wield after she raked her heel down the bandit's shin and into his instep.

He firmed his grip on her, and desperation snarled his voice. "I'm tired of dancing with you buggering bloodybacks. Give me what I want, or I'll cut her throat."

"As I said, let her go unharmed," said Fairfax, "or I shall put a ball between your eyes on my count of five. One."

"All your money and horses! And drop that pistol!"

Humming filled Betsy's ears at the look of torment in Clark's expression.

Fairfax cocked the pistol. "Two."

"Meet my demands, or I'll kill her!" The bandit pricked her neck with the point of the blade. Fire burned down the side of her neck and into her tucker: blood. Her knees knocked. Terror wrenched her breath away and fed it back to her in puny gasps. Rage fueled the bandit's shriek: "The devil damn you black for a liar —"

"Three."

The tiny movement of Fairfax's forefinger pulling the trigger preceded the *kerr-poww* of the pistol a millisecond before the searing breath of the ball skimmed the mobcap at Betsy's right temple and plowed through cartilage, bone, and brains of the bandit with a wet thump. Blood sprayed the back of her neck, and he collapsed. Her hand groped for her neck. The world tinted yellow, sounds about her muffled, and her knees buckled.

Clark caught her before she hit the ground. Seconds later, the feeling of him dabbing off her neck with his handkerchief and water from his canteen anchored her, steadied her pulse. "Thank heavens it isn't deep. It's already stopped bleeding. I've cleaned blood off your clothing." He hugged her from behind, his chest warm against her back. "How do you feel, Betsy?"

The dead bandit's booted feet haunted her peripheral vision, and her tucker felt pasted to her shoulder. She moaned.

"Ah, sweetheart. We haven't much time. I hope you're well enough to ride."

On the road, soldiers cut purses and confiscated weapons from corpses before dragging the bodies into the brush east of the road. Betsy's gaze sought the cumulus-smudged sky, where turkey buzzards would be circling soon enough, and then shifted to the edge of the thicket, where Fairfax appeared and dusted off his hands. Somewhere behind her in the brush, the Spaniard lurked. Her voice emerged little more than a whisper. "I will ride." And the sooner the better. Something about the attack didn't seem valid.

Fairfax strode for them, his face expressionless. She focused her gaze on the horses. Dried weeds and coarse grass crunched beneath his boots. He bypassed them, scouted in the brush, and returned alone to the body of the bandit. Perhaps the Spaniard had witnessed his marksmanship and taken cover again. The bandit's booted feet jiggled as Fairfax relieved the corpse of purse and knife. "One of them escaped and may return with support. Let's be on our way." The lieutenant walked off.

Her life had been imperiled, but had Fairfax's satisfaction derived from heroism? No, his concept of honor was frightening and fluid, more like that of a cat playing with prey. She murmured to Clark, "Five. He'd shoot on his count of *five*, he said."

Clark pressed her arm with his hand. "Hush. Up you go." He rose and helped her to her feet.

Over his shoulder, Fairfax dosed her with his gray-green stare. "Did I say five, madam? Of course, I meant three." He continued to the horses.

Clark made sure he was out of earshot before lowering his voice. "How did Captain Sheffield put it yesterday? 'I assure you he's quite capable of handling any problems that might arise on the road.' Thank you, Captain."

Her gaze shifted north, toward Augusta. In three hours, she'd be home, rid of the company of a brilliant, blighted British officer. There was no place like home.

***

They reached Augusta just after two Thursday afternoon, and Betsy's heart lightened at the approach of her foster-father, Lucas O'Neal, on horseback south on the main street. With him were Adam

Neville and the Sheridans' nearest neighbors, stocky Ephraim
Sweeney and wiry Caleb Cochrane. They held up their hands and
pulled their horses to a halt, waiting. Her buoyancy collapsed at their
expressions. No welcoming committee, they were conveyors of bad
news. Someone close must have died.

Clark and Betsy sent their horses ahead. Pain wreathed Adam's
genial face. "Good god, Clark, we hate to be the ones to tell you this.
Your house burned to the ground this morning."

Betsy stared. She hadn't heard right. "Our house burned?"

Clark whispered, "Is this your idea of a poor joke?"

Weariness rimmed Lucas's blue eyes, and he shook his head. The
shop and Clark's craft and livelihood, gone. Betsy's grandmother
Elizabeth's china and cabinet, gone. Their clothing, their heirlooms,
their — no, this wasn't real.

Caleb sputtered, "We ran for the buckets, but it was too late.
Thank heaven you weren't inside. It went up so fast."

Ephraim pressed his hat to his chest. "We're sorry, folks."

A snarl whipped Clark's face. He kicked his gelding in the sides,
sending it northward.

"Clark, wait!" Adam extended a hand, but Clark was beyond
hearing.

Lucas reached out to Betsy. "Dear, there's nothing left."

Anguished, she sent Lady May galloping up the street after Clark.
In their yard, the henhouse and gardens were intact and undamaged,
but nothing remained of the house except a foundation, charred
timbers, and stone fireplace and chimney.

"My god," Clark whispered, supplicating the wreck of their lives
to resurrection. "Please, not *this*!" Betsy found her way to him, and
he took her face in his hands, tears in his eyes. "How can I provide for
you and our child now?" They fell into each other's arms, too
devastated to do anything but stare at the charred, stinking wreckage
that had been their home not two days earlier.

CHAPTER NINE

Hush now," Betsy whispered. They released each other and assembled composure while their friends dismounted and walked over to join them. The soldiers arrived and began dismounting.

Caleb removed his hat. "Jane found some extra material and can make quilts for when winter comes. Folks in the neighborhood donated clothes, and Vicar Glenn started a collection."

Ephraim beamed. "Ellie's organizing a house raising."

"Thank you. You're all kind." Clark's voice sounded hollow.

Lucas patted his shoulder. "Stay with us while you rebuild. You can have the room Betsy shared with my daughter."

Betsy saw Clark's shoulders relax. The thought that they might get through the disaster and have a home by the time the baby arrived didn't penetrate far into her numbness.

"You're a good neighbor. Catastrophe happens, folks head to another town where kinfolk help them —" Ephraim snapped his fingers, felt inside his waistcoat, and withdrew a sealed letter. "Before I forget, this came for you in yesterday's post." Clark, his actions still wooden, transferred it to his waistcoat pocket. "We'd all hate to see you leave. None of us has much money, but we'll help the best we can."

Fairfax strode into their midst, curiosity slicing his stony composure. "An unfortunate occurrence, Mr. Sheridan. The men wish me to give you this."

Betsy met Clark's gaze after he took the purse of the bandits' coin from Fairfax. Well, money was money. Clark gave the lieutenant a curt nod and caught the eyes of the soldiers, who projected dismay and commiseration at his loss. Gratitude struggled to his face. "Thank you, fellows."

Fairfax clasped his hands behind him. "Do you mind if I have a look about your property?"

Hair stood up on the back of Betsy's neck. They needed him poking around the ruins of their home like they needed more fire. Clark licked his lips. "Uh — why? There's nothing left to see."

"I may be able to discern how the fire started. If it was accidental, such information might help in designing your replacement home."

The emphasis Fairfax placed on the word "if" announced his suspicions as to the nature of the blaze, and Betsy remembered something else Captain Sheffield had said about him. *I know he'll get to the bottom of it, if anyone can.* Brilliant, blighted Fairfax had a knack for investigation. Oh, joy.

Adam cleared his throat. "Pardon me, Lieutenant — er —"

Fairfax roved his gaze over Adam's attire and regarded him without expression. "Fairfax. Lieutenant Dunstan Fairfax."

"Pleased to make your acquaintance, sir. Lieutenant Adam Neville, Brown's Rangers. We investigated the fire this morning and believe a lightning strike caused it. You're welcome to read the report I made for Colonel Brown." He smiled. "I suggest we withdraw and allow these folks time to deal with their loss."

"Colonel Brown won't object to having another set of eyes on the incident." Fairfax turned back to Clark, and Betsy saw Adam pinch his lips together in annoyance: a royal provincial dismissed by a British regular. "As I was saying, Mr. Sheridan —"

"Pardon me, again, Lieutenant." Adam's posture stiffened. "You must clear further investigation with your superior officer in Augusta."

Fairfax glared at Adam, and Betsy felt wretched for the Ranger, who was only trying to help them. "Regarding protocol, on this site, I, being the regular, am *your* superior officer. As I commented earlier, another set of eyes never hurts —" He looked at Clark again. " — wouldn't you agree, Mr. Sheridan?"

Adam's gaze met Clark's, the Ranger's expression imparting apology, and misgiving swam through Clark's face. Under the circumstances, Fairfax's request couldn't be declined. Clark shrugged. "Be my guest, Lieutenant."

"Thank you." Fairfax bowed. "Lieutenant, accompany me. I have questions." He ambled toward the remains of the house, and after Adam echoed Clark's shrug, he trailed after Fairfax.

Lucas lowered his voice. "Who the hell's the lobsterback?"

"Someone we're well rid of today."

Betsy suddenly recalled that Tom Alexander had promised to help watch the house. "Has anyone seen Tom?"

Ephraim slapped his thigh. "Ellie will yell at me good for forgetting. The lad's at our house recovering from the bump on his head he got while trying to stop your house from burning."

Betsy's eyes bulged and she and Clark said in unison, "What?" But the story about Tom had to wait, for the onslaught of Augustans — the nosy, the curious, the sympathetic — began, and townsfolk quickly thronged the yard.

In between hearing accounts of the fire and accepting gifts and commiserations, Betsy noticed Adam had returned to speak with fellow Rangers while Fairfax picked his way through the blackened ruins that had been Clark's shop and studied footprints. At least she needn't worry about producing Arriaga's letter. Later, she spotted Fairfax squatting out near the road, examining wagon ruts and more footprints. What evidence could he hope to find?

Lucas, Ephraim, and Caleb, seeing how spent the Sheridans were, shooed away townsfolk after half an hour. "Come over to the house and get out of the sun," said Ephraim. "Ellie will get us some ale, and you can talk with that apprentice of yours."

"Drink one for me, Clark," said Caleb. "I'm headed back to work."

"Me, too." Lucas hugged Betsy. "See you at the house for supper." He shook Clark's hand.

Fairfax, striding to meet them again, called out, "Before you depart, gentlemen, may I have a word with all of you?"

"Doesn't that one ever smile?" muttered Caleb.

Ephraim snorted. "From the looks of it, he for sure doesn't shit. Oh, pardon my language, Betsy."

Fairfax drew up at attention before them. "Mr. Sheridan, be so good as to introduce me to your companions here."

Clark sighed. "As you fellows heard earlier, this is Lieutenant Dunstan Fairfax out of the garrison in Alton —"

"The Seventeenth Light out of South Carolina, Mr. Sheridan."

Betsy cocked her eyebrow. So Fairfax had been transferred to the Seventeenth Light Dragoons in South Carolina, cavalry. Perhaps poking about that colony for Mathias Hale wasn't such a good idea just yet.

"These are my neighbors Ephraim Sweeney and Caleb Cochrane, and my wife's cousin by marriage, Lucas O'Neal."

Fairfax nodded. "Mr. Sweeney, I understand you were first on the scene this morning."

Ephraim sniffed. "My son Jeb woke me saying their house was afire. I roused the family and sent him running to the Cochranes so they could help with the water buckets."

"Yah, it was too late by the time we got here." Caleb shook his head. "Flames were shooting fifty feet high."

Fairfax craned back his neck and looked at the ancient oak that had cooled the house with its summer foliage. "Fifty feet high, eh? I suppose so. The bottom branches of that tree look a bit scorched. Did either of you see anyone leave the premises when you arrived to put out the fire?"

"Leave? Nope."

"Me, either."

"And both of you are Whigs."

No one spoke. Betsy saw Caleb's jaw clench and Ephraim's fist tighten. Clark said, "They're my good neighbors."

"I certainly hope so. Your Ranger friends told me about an incident the day before yesterday. Someone painted 'Tory Scum' across the front of your house. Had your property been vandalized before?"

"No."

"Lieutenant Neville is unaware of similar incidents since his arrival here. Why might you be singled out for persecution?"

Clark opened his mouth and then studied the burned house. "You believe the vandalism and burning are related?"

"Answer my question."

He swallowed at Fairfax's dagger-sharp tone, and empathy welled through Betsy. Clark took a deep breath. "I've no idea."

Ephraim slapped Clark on the back. "He's a good Loyalist. He don't bother nobody, and he keeps his mouth shut."

Ugh. Where did Ephraim come by that gutter grammar all of a sudden? Betsy watched Fairfax wilt Ephraim's jollity with the frigidity of the North Sea. After more silence, he said, "Curious that a Loyalist lives between two Whigs in harmony."

Caleb picked his teeth and spat something to the left of Fairfax's boot by a couple of inches. "Oh, you think we Georgians go killing each other over politics like them South Carolinians. Nobody in Augusta argues politics with his neighbor no more." He laughed. "It don't get you nowhere. In two years, we've had so many peacocks claiming to be the local government that we got a joke about it. You don't like who's in charge, just wait a week, and it'll change."

Baffled, Betsy wiggled a finger in her ear. Caleb, like Ephraim, sounded like an uneducated wretch — peculiar for a man who was the chess champion of Augusta.

Caleb grinned. "And why shouldn't we live in peace with Clark? He don't have a splinter up his arse like some Britons we know. By the by, Lieutenant Fairfarts — did I get your name right? — I don't recollect who pleaded for your help."

Betsy fought the urge to hit the dirt. Clark's gaze shuffled between Fairfax and Caleb, and she could tell he was groping to divert the subject. On the street, five redcoats and three Rangers listened, alert to the beginnings of an altercation.

But rather than seeing rage climb in Fairfax's expression at Caleb's slurs, she saw amusement. "Mr. Cochrane, Georgia is a Crown colony. As representative of the legitimate government, it's my duty to administer justice. I find no evidence that the fire destroying Mr. Sheridan's house was accidental. Therefore, someone must be apprehended and punished for committing arson."

Clark stared at Fairfax in anguish and astonishment. "What evidence did you find for arson in a charred wreck like that?"

"It's what I didn't find. Furniture. You had a bed, cupboards, chests, chairs, workbenches for your shoemaking?"

"Yes, of course we had all that."

"There's no trace of such in the debris."

Lucas stirred. "The fire got awful hot, Lieutenant. Everything probably burned down to ashes."

"I've seen burned houses before. Invariably, there's a remnant of the larger pieces of furniture: the frame of a bed, the leg of a dining table. None of that is here. Furthermore, I found no metal — candlesticks, pots, spoons."

Hair stood up on the back of Betsy's neck again. "I don't understand."

Fairfax faced her with eyes glittering like arctic stars. "Your property was removed before your house was set ablaze." He gestured north. "It was loaded on a wagon prior to a rainstorm about four this morning and driven north on that road after the rain — and after your virtually empty house was set afire. Where did the culprit go? Will your possessions turn up?" He eyed Clark. "Did you participate in the execution of this plan?"

Clark glared at him. "What? You believe I stole my own furniture and set fire to my house?"

"Did you?"

"No! That's the most ridiculous — Are you crazy?"

"*Rebels* are crazy."

"Rebels? Surely Adam told you my loyalties."

"Indeed." He contemplated Clark and Betsy. "A peculiar entity, fire. Almost a god — creator, destroyer. You can obscure evidence with it. A letter from a sea captain, for example." He pinned his gaze on Betsy. "I know a man who dug up another man's corpse, dressed it like himself, and set fire to it to make everyone think he'd been burned at the stake. It allowed him at least two days lead time over his pursuit."

"I'll be damned," said Lucas. "You're one of the redcoats who chased my wife's cousins and their father down to Havana."

Caleb scraped his teeth again and spat something to the outside of Fairfax's other boot. "Havana, eh? Yeah, I figured he didn't get to be the color of a quadroon chasing Will's broadsides around Georgia."

Ephraim grinned and poked Caleb's shoulder with camaraderie. "Will's 'Tarleton's Quarter' broadsides. I wager there's enough of them floating around that Tarleton can clean his nockhole with them every day. Oh, pardon my language again, Betsy."

A faint smile curved Fairfax's lips. "I hear Colonel Tarleton is flattered by them and collects them for mementos. But let's return to the business at hand. You've each been far more helpful than you've imagined with this game you've played, pretending ignorance and stupidity. Cease with the peasant pageantry and tell me who, beside your families, witnessed the fire."

Tom Alexander. Betsy saw, as Fairfax could not help but see, momentary widening in the eyes of Ephraim, Caleb, Lucas, and Clark. "Other witnesses?" Ephraim looked away. "There weren't any others. Somebody would have come forward by now if they'd seen anything."

Fairfax allowed another discomforting silence to elapse. Then he motioned them all closer and pitched his voice low. "Obstruction of the king's justice is an offense of the same magnitude as treason. Each of you is lying to me about this crime. I'm certain none of you wants to end his life on a gibbet, so out with the name of this witness, or I shall have all of you arrested and interrogated."

"Oh." Ephraim grafted a pleasant smile to his face. "You'll be wanting to talk with Tom Alexander, then."

CHAPTER TEN

Exhaustion under Ellie's eyes sank deeper than usual. "Oh, Betsy, I'm so sorry, dear. Sit and have some hot chocolate."

Anxious about what would transpire between Fairfax and Tom, Betsy glanced at Clark, last in the procession upstairs. "Let me make sure Tom's all right first."

Ephraim introduced Tom to Fairfax as she slipped in the room upstairs. Propped with pillows, Tom lay on the bed Jeb shared with his brothers. His cheeks colored at the sight of Betsy.

"Relax, son." Tom's widowed mother, Rose, shoved faded sandy-colored hair back beneath her mobcap, dampened a cloth in a basin, and dabbed his forehead with it. "Doctor says he can come home tonight. I never thought I'd be thankful for Tom's hard head. He doesn't ever give up, bless his heart."

Across the room, Fairfax inspected the occupants: Rose, Ephraim, Adam, Clark. When his gaze found Betsy, it swept back and forth between her and Tom like a beacon, flustering her, so she shifted close to Clark. Fairfax nodded to Rose. "Indeed, he's fortunate to have survived. I'm curious about the incident and have a few questions about Mr. Alexander's head injury."

"Oh, now, that can wait until the morrow, after he's had a good night's sleep." Rose fanned a fly off Tom's brow.

"No, I leave for South Carolina on the morrow —"

"You're probably going to ask the same questions the soldiers asked him at noon today — "

"Madam, if you would be so kind as to step outside —"

"I will not." Rose bristled. "You won't tire my boy —"

"Mama." Tom grasped her wrist. "Let him speak."

After Tom released her, Rose dropped the cloth in the basin and stood, glowering at Fairfax. "Thank heaven *most* soldiers aren't obnoxious." She swept out on a whiff of poultice.

Tom sighed, eyes closed. "I'm not feeling well this moment, Lieutenant, so I will appreciate your being quick about it."

Fairfax stationed himself beside the basin, and Tom blinked his eyes open. Betsy watched Fairfax's icy gaze reach out and clutch Tom by the throat, and anxiety wrenched her again. "Mr. Alexander, what is your relationship with Mr. Sheridan?"

"I'm his apprentice."

"For how long?"

"Four years."

"And how old are you?"

"Seventeen."

"He says you're an early riser. What time do you usually arrive for work at the shop?"

"Around seven."

An awkward, sickening silence fell over the room, the silence that evolves when a yawning metal trap has been baited and left to do its business. Tom stared at the foot of the bed, tense against the pillow. "What time did you arrive at the Sheridans' house this past Tuesday morning?"

Tom wrinkled his brow, remembering. "That would have been about the usual time. Seven o'clock."

"Was something amiss that morning?"

"Why, yes, someone had —" Tom broke off and darted a look at Clark before returning his stare to the foot of the bed. "There was a slur painted red across the front of their house."

"What slur?"

"It said 'Tory Scum.'"

"And you were the first person to notice it, just as you were, supposedly, the first person to arrive on the scene of arson this morning."

Clark stirred. "Now see here, Lieutenant. Tom had nothing to do with either incident. I'd stake my life on it."

"What makes you so certain?"

"I know him. And besides, he's a political neutral."

Fairfax's gaze slithered over to Betsy, and she looked away from the smile that toyed with her again. "A neutral. *Another* neutral. Peculiar. Here in Augusta — but nowhere else in the colonies — we have happy Whigs living alongside happy Loyals with happy neutrals wending through their midst. I'd inform His Majesty that the Garden of Eden exists in the Georgia colony but for some disgruntled serpent with a love of red paint and, two days later, a love of arson."

He paced before the window, three steps across and three steps back. "Mr. Alexander, what time did you arrive at the Sheridans' house this morning?"

"A little after four."

"How little after four?"

"I — uh — maybe four-twenty. Four-thirty."

"And the occasion for such an early arrival?"

"I woke during a thunderstorm and couldn't get back to sleep, so I went to collect eggs from the Sheridans' hens."

"It was dark at four-thirty in the morning. You took a lantern? Good. What did you see when you arrived?"

Betsy, noting Tom's lips tighten, knew he'd seen *something*. She also knew Fairfax had marked the tightening of Tom's lips. She could almost hear hinges in the trap groaning and quivering, eager to be sprung.

Tom fingered the upper back of his head and winced, still studying the end of the bed. "This is where my memory goes fuzzy. I walked into the yard, and something heavy fell on me from overhead. A limb, I reckon. The next thing I knew, Mrs. Sweeney and Mrs. Cochrane were standing over me, and people were shouting and running about, and the Sheridans' house was afire."

Another uncomfortable, Fairfax-induced silence ensued while the lieutenant's gaze roamed Tom's clothing and profile. "Were you injured anywhere beside your head, Mr. Alexander?"

"No."

"Any bruises or scratches on your shoulders, neck, or arms?"

"No."

"And that's the clothing you were wearing this morning when you were knocked out. Allow me a look at that knot on your head. Here is where you were hit? Ah, yes." Fairfax fingered the back of his own head. "I know exactly how much that must pain you." He strode to the other side of the room, turned about, and faced Tom, triumphant. "Let's go over this again. What did you see when you arrived at the Sheridans' house this morning at approximately four-thirty?"

"I told you I didn't see anything."

"You also said you were struck by a falling object — a limb, you conjecture. Were you bending over to examine something on the ground when it hit you?"

"No."

"Then you weren't hit by a falling limb. Mr. Sweeney and Mr. Cochrane told me there was nothing on the ground around you such as branches or limb debris to substantiate your claim that you were struck by a falling limb. Furthermore, you received no injury to your upper body or damage to your clothing, common when a limb falls on a person. And there is a clearing in the overhead foliage above where you were found. No limbs or branches could have fallen on you at that spot.

"Your injury was caused from a blow to the back of your head with a blunt object — likely a piece of wood and not metal, since your skull doesn't appear to have been fractured. You *know* someone struck you from behind. So here we have arrived at the same question. What did you see just before you were struck from behind?"

"I — I don't remember."

"Let me assist your memory, then. You saw a wagon loaded with the Sheridans' property sitting in the mud of the yard, ready to be driven off, did you not?"

Wham! Betsy tensed, feeling the trap slam about Tom. Dear gods, why wasn't he divulging information to Fairfax? Why was he letting the lieutenant disembowel him with interrogation? She resisted looking at Clark, fear and suspicion swirling in her stomach. Had Tom witnessed something that might compromise Clark's integrity?

Tom turned from Fairfax and stared through Betsy to the door. Escape, she read on his face, escape. His voice emerged dull. "Yes, I think I remember the wagon now."

"Excellent. And how many men were with the wagon?"

"I don't know."

"There must have been at least two?"

"I'm not sure. But one man couldn't have loaded all that furniture alone." Tom's face muscles clenched.

"What were they saying to each other?"

"I was only there a few seconds before I was knocked out."

"But you heard them speaking — what words?"

"I — Another language, I think."

A chill prickled Betsy's spine. Fairfax drilled his attention on Tom. "Which language?"

Tom shook his head, his eyes filled with desperation. "I don't know. I only speak English."

Like many in the Georgia colony, he understood Spanish. Why was he lying again?

Fairfax's eyes glittered with that unholy, archangelic light. "*Parlez-vous Français? Sprechen Sie Deutsch?*"

"I don't understand what you're saying."

"*¿Habla usted Español?*"

Tom turned back to him. "If you want my help, ask me in English." He sighed, his color gray, and shut his eyes. "My head hurts, and I don't care to answer more questions now. Come to my house on the morrow if you must, but I'm too tired to continue today."

Betsy had seen tabby cats watch field mice with the same intensity that Fairfax regarded Tom. "Very well. I shall leave you to rest. Thank you for your time. You've been of tremendous help toward solving this crime. Don't leave town tonight — not, at least, until I can ascertain whether I've further questions for you." Tom made a vague motion of acquiescence, and the lieutenant redirected his attention. "Mr. and Mrs. Sheridan, rest assured that I shall get to the bottom of this incident, find out who stole your furniture and burned your house, and then bring them to justice. It's my duty to see the Crown's justice executed. You're loyal subjects of His Majesty. I'm at your service." He inclined his head.

Clark's response sounded mechanical. "Thank you, but I don't see how you can help us. You're due shortly to catch up with your cavalry unit in South Carolina."

"The world, sir, is not so large as you might imagine. I guarantee you it isn't large enough to hide a wagonload of furniture — perhaps sodden furniture." He gestured toward the door. "I've a few more questions of all of you. Shall we repair downstairs and allow Mr. Alexander his rest?"

They filed from the bedroom, Fairfax first, followed by Ephraim, Adam, and Clark. When Betsy moved to follow them, she heard Tom whisper her name. He motioned her to close the door. "Quickly — before Mama returns." She sat at his bedside, afraid of what she saw in his eyes. "Clark's in deep trouble."

She made a furtive glance over her shoulder. "Hush."

"The Cordovan leather. How did he get hold of it? He had to deal with Spaniards somehow, and he's a Loyalist."

"Forget you ever saw it."

"Done. What's his business with Spaniards?"

"I'm not exactly sure."

"Trust me, I shan't breathe a word of it." He lifted his jaw. "I wouldn't betray Clark. I've known him most of my life. You — both of you — have been so kind to me. Tell me what he's into so I can cover for him."

"Oh, Tom, I don't know what to tell you. I honestly don't know enough myself to say for sure, but it's growing deeper and deeper with each day, and it —" Her hands shook, and she clasped them to still the trembling. "It frightens me."

He brushed her wrist with his fingers. "I lied to Lieutenant Fairfax."

Her heart skipped a beat. She glanced at the closed bedroom door again. "You lied about the men you saw with the wagon?"

"Yes. There were at least four, and I did hear one speak just before I was hit on the head. He was a Spaniard. *¡Cuidado, Basilio, un hombre!* he said. 'Look out, Basilio, a man!'" Tom swallowed. "The dogs — Caleb is holding them for you — they weren't barking or nervous with any of those men. They'd seen them all before."

"Good gods," she whispered. Disillusionment crashed over her world and splintered what remained of it into glistening shards of betrayal. How could Clark have done such a thing? That night, she *must* confront him.

Tom's gray eyes searched her face. "Find me on the morrow and tell me about it."

Involve him further in what was almost certainly suicide? "I cannot." She squared her shoulders. "I will not."

"I don't care about this war — you know that. I want to help Clark. And you. You're going to need help."

The stairs creaked with Rose's ascending footsteps. Betsy grafted serenity into her expression and stood. Tom was a decent fellow, undeserving of being stomped underfoot by Britain and an international ring of spies. "I won't involve you." Before he could protest, she turned her back to him and opened the door for his mother. "You get well, you hear me, Tom Alexander? The shop may have burned, but Clark still needs his apprentices." Then she smiled at Rose and trotted downstairs.

CHAPTER ELEVEN

I n the wee hours of Friday morning, Betsy rolled onto her back in the bed she'd shared growing up with a cousin. Scents of pine and dewy earth and the music of frogs and crickets drifted in through the window. Against the tumult of her thoughts, it all proved useless at relaxing her for sleep. Her life threatened by bandits, her home burned to the ground, her husband's business snarled with that of international spies...

Men's murmurs rose from the ground floor. Imagining how Clark acquiesced to offers of community aid revolted her. For hours she'd pondered how to dissuade him from further endangering them and defrauding the community, but she had no answers.

Chair legs squawked on the floor below. She heard Clark thank elders and friends. After they mounted horses and rode away, the house quieted. Betsy detected the low, diplomatic tone of Lucas. His tread preceded Clark's upstairs. The bedroom door creaked open. Clark shut it and peeled off his coat. When she sat up, he cleared his throat. "Sorry to wake you, darling. I tried to be quiet."

"I was already awake." Her voice sounded steady. Good. She swung her feet over the side of the bed and groped for the tinderbox. "Let's talk."

He yawned and hung his coat on a peg. "On the morrow. I'm exhausted."

"No. This won't wait." After dropping a spark on charcloth, she ignited spunk and lit a candle with it.

His mouth tugged downward, Clark sat at the foot of the bed. "As I feared, it will take us at least a year to rebuild. I must buy all new tools and make furniture. Fortunately, my business has been robust, and Lucas says we can live here until the house raising." She said nothing, and he shifted on the bed, unable to read her. "Support me through this. Dear heart, I need you."

She kept her voice quiet. "Basilio and his friends stole our furniture and burned our house. I demand to know why."

Shock splintered his expression. "The devil — how — ?" He regained composure, and his gaze on her narrowed. "*Demand*? Neither of us can demand a thing at this point."

"You must not mind the taste of charity. Did they destroy our home to intimidate you into compliance?" She exhaled fury. "I'm your wife, yet never once did you consult me about pursuing this appalling scheme with the rebels. Do you realize how angry I am? I could spit fire right now, Clark. I wonder whether I can trust you, especially since we're getting sucked deeper in.

"I don't support your decision or activities. It's wrong to endanger the three of us and take advantage of our neighbors' and friends' goodwill. I insist that you pull out of this mission."

Bleakness crawled over his face. "I cannot."

Betsy clenched her jaw and then relaxed it. "I want to support you, but if the baby and I are going to be at risk, I *must* know the stakes. Otherwise —" She pursed her lips. "Otherwise, I'm leaving you. Lucas and Sarah will protect me."

"Betsy, no!"

"Tell me why Basilio stole our furniture and burnt our house. You seemed on such good terms with him two nights ago, when he was sneaking about the house with his partner."

Clark spread his hands. "*If* he did it, I honestly don't know why. I feel just as betrayed as you do. I thought they understood that I could be trusted to complete my assignment."

"What's Basilio's partner's name?"

"If I tell you more, and the redcoats learn what you know —"

"Ignorance isn't a risk I'm prepared to take. Out with Basilio's partner's name."

He hesitated. "Francisco."

"How many times did they come in the middle of the night?"

"Eight."

Her head reeled. "Eight? When did they start?"

"May twenty-sixth of this year."

Two weeks after Charles Town and the southern rebel army surrendered to the British. As long as Betsy had known Clark — almost two years — she'd been convinced of his devotion to the king, but he'd been in the employ of the rebels far longer than the two months since the capture of Charles Town. Had he *ever* been loyal to King George? "Explain the Cordovan leather."

"It arrived after I resumed my activities with them."

A carrot instead of a stick. "Where were the Spaniards taking those boots?"

"To an operative in the Carolinas. I don't know his name. The way we're organized, each of us only knows the names of two or three others, and we have aliases and false identities."

"Who is Ambrose?"

His gaze on her became shrewd. "The alias for our leader. Where did you hear the name?"

"From Lieutenant Fairfax."

"Damnation."

"What does all this have to do with Cornwallis?"

He shook his head again.

"What's your mission?"

His lips tightened. "Some things I just cannot tell you. Perhaps later, but not now."

He'd put her off by telling her the least important information. "Did Sooty Johns write 'Tory Scum' on our house?"

"Yes, to tighten my cover here, although if Basilio and Francisco did burn the house, the ring must have changed direction and be leading to additional responsibilities for me."

"Without a home for a base? Hah." Betsy threw up her hands. "Even I can see how thin your cover is. To involve you deeper would destroy it."

"At least Fairfax will be gone soon."

She thought of the Givens murders and the horrendous encounter with bandits on the road back to Augusta. "How many Spaniards are in your ring?"

Wariness returned to his face. "Basilio and Francisco are the only ones I've met."

"I witnessed a Spaniard leaving the Givens home right after their murder. He tracked us on the road today."

Clark gaped. "You said nothing of this earlier —"

"When have we had the chance to talk? I blundered from cover into that bandit because the Spaniard was skulking in the woods, recognized me from Alton, and came after me."

"Why didn't you tell Fairfax?"

"Fairfax." She snorted. "At the time, I was far too terrified and just thankful to be alive. Something about the attack of those bandits tells me we weren't random targets. Perhaps the Spaniard hired them and planned it. So who is he?"

"I don't know." He flicked his gaze away. "I've no word of another Spaniard in the ring."

Clark was lying to protect her. "What if he isn't in the ring?"

He shrugged, moroseness and stubbornness setting his jaw. She wouldn't get further with him that night.

"Very well, then. I shall turn in for the night." Her jaw also defiant, she scooted to the far side of the bed. "Blow out the candle when you've undressed."

He rose, unbuttoned his waistcoat, and then patted the inner pocket with a frown. "Almost forgot about this letter."

She lay on her side watching him. "The one Ephraim gave you this afternoon? Who's it from?"

"Isaac Sheridan, King Street, in Camden, South Carolina."

"Sheridan?" Her eyebrows rose. "A relation?"

Without answering, he broke the seal and brought the paper close to the light. Expression faded from his face when he skimmed the letter. Then he warmed the paper over the flame.

Betsy, seeing his face empty of emotion, realized the letter contained a ciphered message, and she sat up again, her chest tight with omen. He turned the paper to her, where pale blue numbers faded, sandwiched between a spidery scrawl of dark ink:

9 July 1780, Town of Camden

My dear nephew John Clark:

It has been half a Year since last I heard from you. I hope All is well with you and your new Wife. How much a Blessing it is to have the Wife for Helpmate in the Shop. I do so miss your Aunt Catherine.

There are Soldiers aplenty in Camden these Days since the Capture of Charles Town, and All of them needing Boots, it seems. My Business flourishes, as does all Business in Camden.

Alas but that I could say the same for the Health of my Hands and Heart. How my Hands pain me with Rheumatism! The Surgeon tells me he does not believe my old Heart can survive another Year. I must rest and give up operating my Business. The very Thought of letting an Outsider direct the Apprentices and manage the Books pains me almost as much, so I shall make you an Offer.

Move to Camden with your Wife and assume the Operation of my Business for the next Year. I shall give you sixty percent Profit off old Business and ninety percent Profit off new Business. I shall also establish you in a decent Dwelling near me. All I ask, beyond my small share of Profit, is the comfort of your nearness in my final Days.

Think on it, dear Nephew, but do not think too long. My Days grow short, and I would go to my Maker knowing my Friends and Family are with me and my Business is well-tended.

I am Sir

Your devoted Uncle
Isaac Sheridan

Her chest still tight, Betsy reread the letter before handing it back. "I take it you don't have an Uncle Isaac," she whispered, "but this fellow is posing as such. The spies want you in Camden. What's in Camden?" She thought of the number 402 again. "Surely not Cornwallis."

"He's in Charles Town. Lord Rawdon now holds Camden." Clark set the letter afire and watched it blacken to ash in a pewter dish at the bedside. "Camden's a central location for Crown patrols that report from the backcountry. Much by way of rumor and strategy flows through Camden these days."

"You're to be the eyes and ears of the rebels in Camden." Intuition brushed her but faded before she could grasp it.

He dragged his gaze off the cinders. "Yes. I realize you hate this, but I beg you to stay with me. I need your loyalty."

"What about the rebel cause has earned *your* loyalty?"

He regarded darkness in a corner. "Their passion, their fever, their love of life. They want all men to live out their dreams in this huge land of opportunity. No land restrictions. No taxes. No one telling you to worship a certain god or bow to a certain ruler. No limit to life except what your own two hands can produce." His eyes grew fervent. "If the Patriots win, all men will be free and equal."

She kept her voice low. "Even the Negroes?"

"Soon enough, yes."

He couldn't have thought that part through. The agricultural economy of the South was quite enmeshed with slavery, and she didn't see anyone freeing slaves anytime soon. "You said no taxes? The Congress taxes colonies even now."

"Only until the war is over."

"Do you really believe all that?"

"The Ambrose ring is like my family."

He might mouth rebel dogma, but his true motive for sticking with the spies was the camaraderie and bond he'd found with them. In dismay, she realized the depths to which his insecurity from being orphaned had dug. How important were she and the baby in his life? Unwilling to drag from him an answer she wasn't ready to hear, she decided to confront him with the obvious. "Fairfax will be in South Carolina. He'll consider it significant when we, already suspects in his mind as spies, turn up in Camden."

"South Carolina is a big colony. I trust the lads in Camden to take care of us, make our cover plausible. Should our paths cross with

Fairfax's again, he may fret and pace with suspicion all he wants, but he won't be able to pierce our cover."

She recognized the prod to her consciousness. "Our furniture. Will we find it in the 'decent dwelling' near your Uncle Isaac?"

"Ah, yes, now I see why they burned the house. They're relocating me to Camden."

Monstrous! "At the Sweeneys', Fairfax took inventory of what was stolen from our house. Suppose he gains access to our home in Camden and assesses what's there — the exact pieces of furniture that went missing, down to the clothing and quilts. Even I'd consider the coincidence to be too great."

Clark seized her hands in his, his determination intense. "Trust me. We know what we're doing. We shall make it work."

She shook her head. "I don't want to leave family and friends here, and I have a bad feeling about Camden. Stay, rebuild your business, continue spying if you must, but write 'Uncle Isaac' and tell him you aren't coming."

"That isn't an option." His grasp of her hands grew almost painful. "Trust me, dear heart."

Gazing into his eyes, she felt desperate. In the past ten minutes, he'd let her see a man she didn't know. She resisted the urge to pull away from his touch. After all, he was her husband, and she'd exchanged wedding vows to stay at his side. But the fiery determination she saw in his eyes reminded her too much of the angelic radiance in Fairfax's face just before he killed or interrogated. Surely, if she pondered it long enough, she could find the argument to dissuade her husband from his association with the rebels. "Heaven help us," she murmured.

CHAPTER TWELVE

The humid, pearly dawn of Friday, July 14, found Betsy walking to the home of the Alexanders, a loaf of Sarah's molasses bread in her basket. Lack of sleep muddied her thoughts. She'd lain awake most of the night listening to Clark's snores.

Two days earlier, she'd wished for a plausible reason to go to South Carolina so she could search for her parents. Now, her house was gone. Her husband perpetrated treason against the government — not that she could muster exuberant praise for that government, but still, it was *lawful*. And she must move to the most war-torn colony in British North America so Clark could continue spying. The world had turned upside down. She had to be more careful what she wished for.

Augustans opening shop for the day called out sympathy over the loss of her house. A lump formed in her throat at their goodwill, kind-hearted people she'd known most of her life. Leaving such a solid community disturbed her even more than the knowledge of Clark's role in her distress.

Scant community awaited her in Camden, home of a third cousin, Emma, who'd married the owner of the Leaping Stag, Camden's most prosperous tavern. Betsy hadn't seen Emma in almost eight years and wondered if she and her family would ever feel like community or Camden would ever feel like home.

She detoured to the stationer's shop, where the plump proprietress behind the counter offered coffee. "We're so sorry about your house. But I'm making a blanket for that baby of yours, and Matthew, you know how fancy he gets with carpentry, he's hard at work on a couple of stools for you."

"Thank you, Molly."

"How can I help you this morning?"

Betsy set down her coffee cup, withdrew from her basket the letters she'd written before leaving the house, and handed them to Molly. "Please see them posted today."

"Gladly." Molly squinted at one address. "Joshua Hale, Hale and Sons Smithy, Alton, Georgia. It should reach him later today. I'm expecting a southbound rider presently. And, hmm, Emma Branwell, the Leaping Stag Tavern, Camden, South Carolina. That letter may take a few days."

"I understand. Thank you." Betsy had debated breaking Clark's confidence because she so needed someone to talk with. She'd finally settled for brief, scant-detail letters to her uncle and cousin about their burned house and relocation. She hoped Joshua would accompany her to Camden.

Molly waved away Betsy's postage money. "It's on us, dear. It's the least we can do for you right now."

Stumping along beneath her cloud of preoccupation after she left Molly, Betsy passed through town center, where some of the wealthier Augustans resided. Realizing her name had been called several times, she turned about in the street to spot widow Abby Fuller approaching her with a bundle, a timorous smile on her sensuous lips. "Good morning, Mrs. Fuller." She bobbed a curtsy, wondering at Abby's business with her. Abby's business had been mostly with her Uncle David.

"Good morning, Mrs. Sheridan." Abby dropped a curtsy, dainty blonde curls peeking from beneath her lace mobcap, a wave of expensive floral scent greeting Betsy at the movement. "I — I brought you this." She extended the bundle. "It — It's a ham."

"Thank you, Mrs. Fuller." Betsy, transferring the ham to her basket, wondered at the socialite's stammer, trembling hands, and haunted, red-rimmed eyes. Maybe she was concerned after their well-being. "Mr. Sheridan and I are both all right, you know. We weren't at home during the fire."

"I know it, but — but —" Abby darted a furtive glance about the street before lowering her voice. "Take care of yourselves, please, dear?" Fresh tears crested her eyes. "I'm sorry — so sorry." Her voice withered to a whisper. "Tell your Uncle David that, and may he forgive me someday." She burst into tears, caught up her silk petticoat, and rushed off.

Baffled, Betsy regarded her retreating figure a moment while her mind replayed David's predawn visit Tuesday morning to her back yard. Obviously he'd sneaked into Augusta late Monday to spend the night with Abby before heading to Williamsburg. Risky business, but if anyone knew how to sneak around, it was David St. James. However, he wasn't Abby's only suitor. Maybe they'd argued over her other gentlemen. Being a wealthy widow in no way guaranteed liberty from possessive beaus.

She'd all but dismissed Abby's peculiar behavior by the time she reached the Alexanders' little house. From out back, she heard the rhythmic strike of an axe — one of the Alexander brothers chopping wood. Diana knelt in the scrawny garden out front, trying to coax weeds from around herbs. A year younger than Betsy and sandy-haired like her mother and brothers, she rose with delight at the sight of Betsy, wiped her hands on her threadbare apron, and rushed over for a hug. "It's so good to see you safe!" She grasped Betsy's hand. "Come inside. Mama will make you herbal tea."

Herbal tea grown from Rose's garden — Betsy resisted the urge to wince at Alexander hospitality when they had so little. Diana, in particular, was looking rather thin. "I don't have much time. I brought food for all of you." She extended the basket. They could use Abby's ham more than the Sheridans could.

"An entire ham." Diana swallowed, her mouth watering.

"And Sarah's bread." Betsy wondered when the girl had last eaten red meat. The potluck she'd given Tom hadn't been much.

"I love her bread. Thank you. Mama? Mama, Betsy's here, and look what she brought us!"

Betsy trailed Diana inside the tiny but tidy house, where Rose straightened from before the hearth and came forward to hug Betsy. Her eyes misted at the gift of food, and Betsy declined the offer of tea

again after glancing out the back window, where Tom chopped wood
in his shirtsleeves. "It's good to see him up and about. Looks like
he's feeling better."

Rose pursed her lips. "Doctor Norton says he should rest another
day. I don't know any young men with harder heads." She plucked at
Betsy's sleeve. "Go out and have a word with him. He listens to
you."

She laughed. "Me? Since when?"

"About once a week he comes home from the shop, and it's
'Betsy says this' or "Betsy says that.'"

Betsy saw Diana's shy smile and looked away to hide a flush of
astonishment and bewilderment. "Surely I don't talk all that much. I
just manage the books." She glanced away. "That is, I managed the
books when there were books to manage."

"Oh, my poor dear, here you are, helping us with food when
you've lost your home. I'm so sorry."

Rose tucked her into a sound, mama's embrace. It felt like
Sarah's embrace, like *Sophie's* embrace, and Betsy bit her tongue hard
to keep from bursting into tears. She ached for her mother — her
soothing touch, her sensible advice. How she needed a mother that
moment, someone to stroke her head, kiss her, and tell her everything
would be all right. Here she was, going to be a mother herself in a few
months, but she figured most folks never stop needing a mother.

She wobbled out a smile when they parted. Rose squeezed her
hand, echoed the smile, and gestured toward the window. "So would
you have a word with that hard-headed son of mine, tell him to come
in here and get some sustenance?"

"Very well."

Tom pivoted from the woodpile, spied Betsy strolling toward
him, and set down his axe to take up a towel. "Morning!" He
swabbed off his face, leaving a smile behind. "Don't tell me. Mama
sent you out here to get me to quit working."

"No, indeed. I brought a ham and some of Sarah's bread."

"Food!" Tom cupped his mouth with his hand and hollered, "I'll
be right in, Mama!" With a grin, he reached for the axe again. "I can
get a few more logs split before she has it on the table. You sticking
around to eat with us?"

"No, I — I have too much to do today."

Crack! A log split in two with a clean stroke from the axe.
"Such as — ?"

Her tired brain refused to concoct an answer. What did one do while waiting to move hundreds of miles with nothing to pack? She fingered corn silk on a four-foot stalk. The Alexander's vegetable garden looked healthy. "Such as talking with people."

"I'll be there to help at the house-raising. I know you and Clark are eager for your own home again." *Crack*!

She wasn't at all eager for that house in Camden. What a lie everything was. "Yes."

"Diana says the ladies scheduled a quilting next week. She and Mama have some of the most even stitching in town and cannot wait to help." *Crack*!

"Yes."

Not hearing the crack of more wood, Betsy glanced over to find him studying her, hands on hips, the axe resting against his thigh. "You know, I've seen more enthusiasm from men being marched to the gallows."

"I didn't sleep very well last night."

"I don't blame you." He rubbed the back of his head. "I didn't sleep very well, either." His voice lowered. "Shall we continue the chatter, or are you going to tell me all about it?"

She felt her lower lip quiver and bit it to no avail. Tears stung her eyes, and her nose started running. "It's far worse than I imagined," she whispered. "I don't want to get you in trouble."

He set down the axe and gestured over the corn patch. "Would you take a look at my beans? You have a magical touch with vegetables, and the beans aren't doing too well. Maybe not enough sunlight?"

She trudged around the corn to the bean plot, squatted, and inspected the beans. "Put a little more potash on them." She sniffed and dragged the back of her hand beneath her nose.

"Thanks. I'll do that." He sat down next to her, so they were hidden from the house by corn, and he grew quiet.

Birds twittered while Betsy tested out preambles in her head, thinking to ease Tom into the unreality of the situation. She finally realized he wasn't the sort of fellow who liked to be eased into anything. "Clark's a spy for a ring of rebels. I don't know how many of them are in the ring, and he only knows a few, but I get the impression there are at least a dozen. You saw several of them yesterday morning before they knocked you out. Two Spaniards are named Basilio and Francisco.

"The rebels want him in Camden. They packed our furniture up and then burned our house. We'll find the furniture waiting for us in Camden, along with Clark's next assignment. A rebel in Camden is posing as his aging uncle who needs him to assume his shoemaking business. 'Uncle Isaac' will have our furniture set up in a house for us by the time we arrive." She trailed off. The mission sounded even more insane spoken aloud.

Tom plucked a piece of straw off the ground and shredded it. "What are you going to do?"

"Keep quiet and go with him." She emitted a dry laugh. "I'm his wife."

"Will you help him spy?"

"Oh, gods no. I might find a way to talk him out of such madness, and perhaps my presence will give him solace."

"Who takes care of you?"

She shook her head, unable to speak.

"Have you no family in Camden you can call on for help?"

"A third cousin."

Tom muttered phrases that sounded like, "Preposterous," and "Endangering the baby," before he said, "When do you leave?"

"As soon as we find an escort." She coughed out a laugh. "One that doesn't include Lieutenant Fairfax, that is."

"I shall go with you."

"No."

"I'm his apprentice. He'll need help with business."

"I shall manage the books."

"See here, a rebel spy purports to operate the façade of a shoemaking business in a town full of soldiers who need boots. Even with Clark at the last eighteen hours a day, I doubt he'll be able to fill all his orders in a timely manner. I shall go along as his apprentice. I don't agree with what he's doing, but I owe a great deal to him, and so I shall help him maintain his deception. No one has to know that I know."

"You cannot do that, Tom. Your mother needs you."

"She needs monetary support, and what better way to do that than to follow my master and send her my wages?"

"South Carolina isn't Georgia. We just have an occasional skirmish or battle here. They fight daily there. We could all be killed. How much good will you do your mother dead?"

"I'm going with you. I shall find Clark this morning, tell him you've told me you're moving to Camden to care for an ailing uncle, and offer my continuing services as his apprentice. I shan't breathe a word that I know the truth of his business."

"He won't listen to you."

"Maybe not, but I got a horse. I'll follow him. And that settles it."

Misery swam through her soul. "You *are* hard-headed."

He stood and helped her up, enclosing her hand a moment longer in the callused warmth of his hand while gazing into her eyes. His gaze placed her troubled heart in the realm of acceptance and non-judgment — the way she felt around Sarah, Lucas, and Sophie. "I prefer to think of myself as devoted, rather than hard-headed."

Scarlet in Betsy's peripheral vision fragmented the peace, and she and Tom dropped each other's hands in surprise. Rising sunlight on Lieutenant Fairfax's face failed to thaw his gaze and emphasized the blood red of his coat. "Ah, if it isn't *both* happy neutrals."

CHAPTER THIRTEEN

Fairfax smirked and strode forward. "I'm not surprised to find you two together. At least it spares me an extra trip before I leave Augusta."

Rose flew from the house flapping her apron. "Shoo! I told you out front to question him after he eats his breakfast. How dare you set foot in my back yard without my permission? Now shoo, you vile critter, and take those men out front with you!"

Tom eyed Fairfax. "What do you want?"

"I've more questions for both of you."

"How long will this take?"

"Five minutes."

Exasperation flooded Tom's face. "Five minutes, Mama." With a loud sigh that echoed her son's irritation, Rose marched back inside, slamming the back door after her. Tom strode toward Fairfax. "Make haste. I'm not courteous on an empty belly."

Betsy followed him, reading Fairfax's expression: the infinite patience of a predator stalking prey. Her stomach flip-flopped. What further questions could he possibly have?

"Mr. Alexander, do you think the foreign language spoken by those men yesterday morning might have been Spanish?"

"I already told you I don't speak foreign languages."

"Colonel Brown has reports of Spanish agents involved in a rebel spy ring in Georgia and the Carolinas. The agents are known by multiple aliases, but their true names are Basilio San Gabriel and Francisco de Palmas." His gaze darted back and forth between Tom and Betsy, scouring her face for the smallest flinch that betrayed her recognition of the names.

"I don't recognize those names. As I told you, I didn't see or hear much before they hit me."

"Did Mr. Sheridan have business with Spaniards?"

Tom shook his head. "Not that I ever noticed."

"Madam, you kept the books. Any Spanish customers?"

She hoped Fairfax didn't plan to instigate a witch-hunt among the Spanish families in the area. "José Garcia ordered shoes from Clark in March. He's our only Spanish customer."

"Who supplied Mr. Sheridan's leather?"

"Mostly Dutton and Sons out of Charles Town or George Gaskins in Savannah. There were some traders who made the rounds several times a year, like Sooty Johns."

"Any Spanish suppliers?"

Betsy shook her head. "Not that I'm aware of."

Fairfax opened a portfolio and withdrew an incinerated piece of leather about twelve inches square. Just before he handed it to Tom, Betsy spotted the rich, red Cordovan finish on a corner spared the flame. It required all her discipline to keep acknowledgement from her expression, and she sensed Tom doing the same. Fairfax was baiting another trap. "Identify the type of leather for me, please, sir."

"It's too badly burned. Cowhide, I'd guess."

Fairfax pointed out the reddish corner. "Does that help?"

"No, I've never seen anything like it."

"Curious, Mr. Alexander. You're reportedly Mr. Sheridan's most skilled apprentice, and yet you cannot identify Spanish Cordovan leather while his next most experienced apprentice did so last night. He also said a new shipment of it waited in Mr. Sheridan's shop the morning everyone was outside cleaning 'Tory Scum' off the house. I found this piece of leather in the ruins of the Sheridan house. What a coincidence." He replaced the burned leather in his portfolio and closed it up.

"I never entered the shop Tuesday. I was outside all day cleaning the house."

"That's true. He stayed outside all that day." Too late, Betsy reminded herself not to volunteer information.

Fairfax homed in on her. "But *you* saw the Cordovan leather. When did the delivery arrive?"

She wouldn't be able to repair the slip. "The night before our house was defaced."

"Who delivered it?"

"I don't know. I was asleep."

"You were asleep when a delivery of expensive, exclusive Cordovan leather arrived? Is it standard procedure for your husband to receive deliveries in the middle of the night?"

She shrugged. "I don't know about standard procedure, but it isn't unknown. Those traders can keep late hours. Sometimes they'll close down the taverns before paying Clark a visit."

"When was the last time you saw Sooty Johns?"

With another shrug, she regarded a cumulus cloud. "A few weeks ago."

"How about Monday night, delivering the Cordovan leather?"

How in hell did Fairfax find that out? "No." Betsy heard the extra firmness in her voice and regretted it.

A smile slithered across Fairfax's mouth before vanishing into the granite of his expression. "When was the last time you saw the Spaniard who killed the Givenses?" Mind-reading creature of the netherworld, he leaned into her hesitation with victorious eyes. "Last night, here in Augusta?"

"Actually I — I saw him in the brush yesterday. That's why I blundered out into the bandit. The Spaniard recognized me and was trying to kill me as a witness."

Mock sorrow pinched Fairfax's face. "A pity you didn't inform me so I could hunt him down and rid us of the menace. Alas, poor Mr. Johns has paid for your hesitation with his life."

Betsy scowled. "What are you talking about?"

With his forefinger, Fairfax drew a line across his neck. "Just like the Givenses. His throat slit from ear to ear some time last night. We found his body stuffed in a rubbish barrel behind the Bronze Boar tavern this morning." He jutted his chin north. "Just a few streets in that direction, you know."

Betsy felt her face drain of color. Poor Mr. Johns indeed. "He wasn't worth a Spaniard's knife. A local wretch followed him when he left the tavern drunk and then robbed and murdered him."

"He hadn't been robbed." Fairfax's gaze hopped between Tom and Betsy. "And assassins from *Casa de la Sangre Legítima* slit their victims' throats from ear to ear."

Casa de la — what? Tom stirred. "You've lost me. What language are you speaking, Lieutenant?"

"It's Spanish." Betsy swallowed, liking the sound of it less with each passing second. "It means House of the Righteous — no, Rightful — Blood."

"Ah, so you speak Spanish, Mrs. Sheridan?"

"A little. But I don't know anyone who goes about calling himself by such a preposterous title, and I don't know why an assassin would kill tanners in Alton or waste his time on a slimy little peddler."

Fairfax fondled the silk on the nearest corn stalk and cocked his head to study both of them, his eyes green mockery. "Does Mr. Sheridan know you two are cuckolding him?"

In the stunned silence that followed, a crow cawed. A flush climbed Betsy's neck. Tom whispered, "I — I beg your pardon?"

"His business is robust. He needs you, the most talented apprentice in Augusta, so he cannot afford to let you go, no matter the indiscretions you commit beneath his nose." His fingers continued stroking the corn silk. "I imagine the tension is incredible for all three of you. How much easier if he was out of the picture. So you paint a slur on his house and then burn it the following night after some Spaniards conveniently cart off all the furniture —"

"How dare you accuse me of such atrocious deeds?" Tom snarled. "You're a scoundrel. You haven't the decency to take your miserable carcass from this town where your company is sought by no one —"

"Tom, no!" Betsy gripped his upper arm, halting his advance toward Fairfax.

A great cat toying with prey, Fairfax was still caressing the silk. "Ah, so even though I saw you and Mrs. Sheridan holding hands behind the corn a few minutes ago, you aren't —"

"No, we aren't!"

He released the silk and snapped his fingers. "The deuce. How conveniently that would explain several motivations. And how you, madam, maintain neutrality amidst your family's rebel infamy astounds me. The pressure to yield to them and convert to the rebel cause must be tremendous. I wager it was overwhelming this past Tuesday morning."

She squinted. "Tuesday morning? I don't understand."

"You know, when your Uncle David popped in on you for a quick visit before he left town."

She felt lightheaded and worked her mouth in shock and futility. Fairfax most certainly saw the truth blaze across her expression in those seconds, but she had to save face anyway. "My — my uncle is free of the Indians? Is my mother free also?"

"Come now, I knew you were lying in Alton when you told me you hadn't communicated with them. Thanks to my — er — persuasive abilities with a certain widow here in town, I've discovered he paid her a visit Monday night."

The reason behind Abby Fuller's haunted, red-rimmed eyes became clear to Betsy then, and her stomach knotted when she imagined how Fairfax might have "persuaded" information out of the widow. She lifted her chin. "Did this widow say my uncle had planned to visit me on his way out?"

"I find it hard to believe he'd leave town the next morning without saying hello to blood kin, without telling you where he, your grandfather, your mother, and that half-breed Creek Indian who was helping them were headed."

"I never saw him."

Fairfax sighed. "Let's be reasonable. You come from a family of traitors. I believe you know where most of them are hiding. If you refuse to cooperate, you aren't a neutral. You're as much a traitor as they are. Tell me everything you and your uncle discussed Tuesday morning, and I shan't arrest you."

Tom rolled his eyes. "You cannot arrest her. Did someone see her with her uncle? You've naught but circumstantial evidence."

"A mountain of circumstantial evidence creates warrant for arrest." His tone lashed Betsy. "Out with it, or I shall see you lodged in Augusta jail this morning!"

"I never saw my uncle." Her chin trembled, and she pressed both lips together.

"Mr. Rainey!"

A redcoat stepped from the shadows of the house. "Sir."

"Place Mrs. Sheridan under arrest."

"Yes, sir." The soldier headed for them unwinding rope.

Tom clenched both fists. "You cannot do this, Lieutenant!"

Betsy glared at Fairfax. "Tom, find Clark and tell him everything that happened. See if he can find Colonel Brown."

Fairfax shook his head. "Colonel Brown won't bother with such a trivial matter as the imprisonment of yet another rebel."

"We shall see about that. I may come from a family of rebels, as you label them, but I'm married to one of Augusta's leading Loyalists." The soldier Rainey had reached them by then. "Oh, put that rope away. I shan't give you a fight."

Fairfax nodded. "A wise decision."

Tom growled at Fairfax. "You dung-eating pig, if you hurt her in any way —"

"Mrs. Sheridan knows her place, Mr. Alexander." Fairfax presented him with a smile that his lip muscles stumbled over, so unaccustomed were they to the motion. "You do well to review yours."

CHAPTER FOURTEEN

L et me out of here, you bleeding sod! I ain't buggered nobody's
ten-year-old son."
        Her fingers plugging her ears, Betsy could still hear the drunk
in the cell across from her. The jailer pounded on his door. "Shut up
in there, or I'll gag you and put you in irons." The drunk subsided,
and the jailer muttered, "Sorry about that one, madam," through
Betsy's grate.

En route to jail, she'd held her head high, proud to follow the
footsteps of another neutral, her mother, who'd been arrested and
imprisoned. But the glamour wore off as soon as she smelled the piss,
puke, and mold inside jail and heard the drunk's tirade. Sophie Barton
must be made of tougher stuff than her daughter was. At least Betsy
had a cell to herself.

The jailer had done her a favor and let Clark visit earlier. Seeing
his expression of outrage through the grate had brought her close to
tears. "What brutality! I'll find Colonel Brown, Betsy, I promise, and
we'll have you out of there this morning!" In the interim, though, she
had plenty of time to think.

Even had she confessed David's visit to Fairfax, she doubted he'd have believed her. As Joshua Hale had cautioned, Fairfax had something broken inside his head. He was correct about most of the circumstantial evidence he'd amassed against her. Unless he got sidetracked, he'd eventually substantiate his claims.

She pondered what he might have done to extract information from Sophie and Abby. Then she rubbed her temple and abandoned the thought line. Not only was it a waste of her energy, but she doubted, chilled, whether her imagination was capable of envisioning Fairfax's boundaries with forms of interrogation.

Women's voices drifted back. Through the grate, she heard Jane Cochrane: "For goodness sakes, you know she isn't a traitor, and this isn't about Betsy Sheridan being a spy, either."

"No, indeed!" That was Ellie Sweeney's voice. "This is about some odious *man* harassing a helpless *woman* — and her with child, too. For shame! Times are hard enough without decent women being thrown in jail for no good reason!"

"That's right!" chorused other women whose voices blended. "Let her go. Let her go. Let her go." The chant gathered momentum, and Betsy wondered how many women had assembled in the office. At least a dozen, she guessed, and a smile touched her lips as she imagined them in their straw hats and cotton aprons, holding baskets and wagging fingers at the jailer.

"Ladies, please!"

"We won't stand for this!"

"Men shan't take advantage of *us* any longer!"

"We've washed your laundry, mended your breeches, and cooked your meals, and this is how you thank us?"

"Let her go. Let her go. Let her go."

In the other cell, the drunk no longer sounded surly. "Jesus Christ, I'm going to die at the hands of a mob of women."

"Ladies, calm down!" Nervousness spiked the jailer's command. Betsy wondered whether he'd ever been harassed by a group of indignant goodwives. "Surely you understand my position! I can only release her with the approval of an officer of the Crown."

"There's a dreadful stink coming from those cells. You let us back there to make sure she's all right."

"I cannot, but trust me, she's quite well, and —"

At least half a dozen women booed him, and Betsy identified the voice of Ruth Glenn, Loyalist wife of the Anglican vicar: "You'd even deny her the civility of morning coffee? How barbaric!"

"Ladies, be realistic about this. I cannot allow you serve coffee to an inmate. I shall lose my job over it!"

"Better your job than something else." Betsy didn't recognize the woman's voice, but the corrosiveness in her tone gave her a chuckle.

"And we have the means of slicing bread in our baskets."

The drunk's voice rose in lamentation. "Ohhhhh, sweet Jesus, spare me. I won't ever do it again, I promise."

Panic charged the jailer's tone. "Shall I interpret that as a threat to a government official?"

"And put all of us in jail, too? Excellent idea. I've no qualms about keeping Betsy company."

Betsy heard spurs and harnesses outside. Adam Neville's voice pierced the clamor. "Whoa, there. Why, Mr. Moore, what's this at jail this morning? A quilting?"

"Er, no, Lieutenant. It's a misunderstanding."

Rose piped up. "That it is. Betsy Sheridan's imprisoned on false charges." Several women voiced agreement.

Adam murmured something to quiet them and then spoke up. "I have orders to escort her to a meeting to clear that up with Colonel Brown this very moment over at the ferry."

Ellie said, "We'd best follow to keep an eye on them."

While other women agreed to join the procession, Betsy heard the jailer confer with the lieutenant. "Your paperwork's in order, sir. Very well, have your men wait here while I fetch her. Er, you, too, Mr. Sheridan." Betsy took heart at the thought of Clark waiting outside for her. "All right, ladies, step aside. That's it, step aside, and don't go crowding her after she's out."

The clink of key in lock sounded at the door of Betsy's cell, and she clasped her hands. After the door swung open, the jailer motioned her out. "Colonel Brown wants to chat, and here's Lieutenant Neville to escort you."

A smiling Adam motioned her to the exit. "Right this way."

The ladies of Augusta phalanxed her, fussed over her, and clucked sympathy and outrage over the arrest, all the while conveying her out to her horse, where Clark waited with opened arms. After an embrace, he helped her mount Lady May. In the saddle, she inhaled a deep breath of morning, amazed at how marvelous Augusta's summer humidity smelled and felt compared to the interior of jail. Standing near the ladies, Tom saluted her with a grin, and she grinned back. Thank you, Tom Alexander!

Adam mounted his horse and led the way, Betsy and Clark falling in behind him, two Rangers bringing up the rear on horseback, while Tom, Sarah, Rose, Diana, Ellie, Jane, and a number of women followed on foot. In a minute they arrived at the ferry crossing, where the Savannah River sparkled in the morning sunlight. They dismounted to meet those awaiting them on foot: Colonel Brown and several Rangers, and Lieutenant Fairfax and the five soldiers who had accompanied him out of Alton.

Betsy's gaze swept over Thomas Brown, called "Burntfoot" after drunken Whigs had assaulted him in 1775 at his plantation, tied him semi-conscious to a tree, and burned off two of his toes. Brown returned her appraisal, gaze steady. Had she not known, she'd never have guessed that he, dressed in an ordinary hunting shirt and wearing a battered hat to cover where he'd been partially scalped in the Whig attack, was a lieutenant colonel. He bowed and touched the brim of his hat. "Mrs. Sheridan."

She curtsied. "Thank you for the audience, sir."

He flashed her a smile before directing the smile at Clark, standing behind her. "You're fortunate to have caught me in Augusta. I'm spread thin these days. But I can usually find time for the King's Friends."

Betsy marveled over his poise. His ropy, slight frame and his face, weather-beaten beyond his thirty years, clued her that those tales she'd heard about him roughing it in the Florida swamps with his Rangers, helping Governor Tonyn repulse rebels from East Florida, were accurate.

His smile faded into all-business. With a motion of his head to indicate the stone-faced Fairfax, at attention fifteen feet behind him, he returned his focus to her. "Lieutenant Fairfax has related some evidence against you. Even though it's circumstantial, it casts suspicion on you as a conspirator with rebels. That your house was recently defaced and then burned is also quite peculiar. Counterbalancing all that are the character witnesses of citizens who assure me you've never displayed an inclination toward the rebel cause. And I know your husband to be a leading supporter of His Majesty here in Augusta.

"So, we've naught but circumstantial evidence and character witnesses for a case, and I ask myself whether we even have a case against you." Hands on hips, he leaned a few inches closer, his gaze on her sharpening. "Are you a rebel?"

"No, sir."

"Are you helping the rebels?"

"No, sir."

He rubbed his chin. "There's a rebel spy ring operating across Georgia and the Carolinas, affiliated with spies in the Northern colonies. We know the Southern branch to contain at least a dozen members including two Spaniards, one Frenchman, and two women. Have you communicated with anyone in that ring?"

Such as her husband? Betsy's stomach clenched, but she didn't bat an eyelash. "No, sir."

"Did you communicate with your Uncle David this past Monday or Tuesday?"

Heaven help her and David St. James. "No, sir."

Fairfax stirred. "She's lying, sir."

Irritation seasoned Brown's tone. "Lieutenant, as you were. Madam, are you willing to swear allegiance to His Majesty that I might be assured of your intentions?"

She swallowed. "Sir, I claim neutrality. You know there are a good number of neutrals out there. If I must swear an oath as a Loyalist to avoid being returned to jail, then I shall do so. But would I not be a more effective witness to other neutrals of the king's intentions if I swore such an oath of my own volition, having come to my decision after being treated justly by representatives such as yourself?"

In the background, she saw Fairfax clench his jaw and then relax it. Thomas Brown leaned back from her, evaluating her sincerity. Clark cleared his throat. "Colonel, sir, I believe her to be telling the truth about not having seen her uncle. She knows I've been worried about him also. If she'd heard from him, she'd have told me. I don't believe they made contact."

Betsy watched the colonel discern the honesty in Clark's face, and she thanked the heavens she'd never confided in her husband about David's visit. Fairfax also perceived Clark's honesty, and his jaw clenched again. Brown nodded, a brief motion, and raised his voice a bit. "Very well, Mrs. Sheridan, I'm satisfied for now that you're clear of involvement with the rebels. You're free to go."

Approval and applause rose from the clustered spectators. Relief swamped Betsy, and she wobbled a curtsy. "Thank you, sir. I shan't forget your fair dealing."

Clark shook Brown's hand. "Indeed, thank you, sir."

Sarah and Rose bustled over and hugged her. Over Sarah's shoulder, Betsy saw Fairfax step forward, his nostrils expanded. "Sir, I remind you her blood relations are rebel spies —"

"Thank you, Lieutenant." Brown faced him, irritation tightening his lips. "Again, I appreciate the brilliant investigative work you've performed since yesterday, particularly when it comes to Mrs. Fuller's involvement, and I've commended you to your superiors. As you've a critical assignment awaiting you in South Carolina, I shan't detain you. The ferry is ready to convey you. Good day. God speed." The undercurrent in his voice was as clear as if he'd spoken aloud: *Good riddance.* Stoddard and Sheffield had said the same.

"Yes, sir." Fairfax made a stiff salute.

Brown returned the salute, swiveled to Betsy and Clark, and bowed. "Good day, madam, sir." He headed for his horse, held ready by one of the Rangers.

Sarah stroked Betsy's cheek, her gray eyes kind. "My sweet lamb, I'm so glad that's over. Coffee back home ought to settle your nerves."

From the corner of her eye, Betsy noticed the approach of Fairfax. She faced the horses and tittered out a nervous laugh. "That sounds delightful."

Clark crooked his arm for her. "Shall we, then, darling?"

"One moment, Mr. and Mrs. Sheridan."

Rose coughed out disapproval, her tone curdled. "Good Lord, what else do *you* want?"

Betsy turned back around with reluctance, her apprehension escalating at how soft Fairfax's voice had become. Clark stiffened. "Yes, Lieutenant, what *do* you want?"

Fairfax looked them over, and a midwinter chill scraped her at the soothing tone he invoked. "How fortunate that Colonel Brown grants the benefit of doubt where integrity is concerned, and your friends and neighbors in Augusta are so supportive. I presume I shan't encounter either of you in South Carolina. You see, that which is circumstantial often lacks little additional effort before being rendered substantial." After a curt inclination of his head, he pivoted and strode for the ferry and the soldiers under his command.

Clark pulled her against him and pitched his voice low. "That tick-bitten rat."

Her skin crawling, her muscles twitching with the instinct for flight, Betsy clung to him and stared after Fairfax. Now her husband *must* see the folly of his assignment in South Carolina and agree to abandon the mission. Surely he must.

CHAPTER FIFTEEN

Visitors plagued the O'Neals until past dinner, tongues wagging in curiosity and concern, preventing Betsy from discussing the move to Camden with Clark. He slipped away with Lucas after dinner to the White Swan, returned at three to the bed where Betsy napped, and awakened her with kisses on her brow.

Alerted by perturbation on his face, she sat, pulled on her shoes, and grabbed her straw hat. Then they rode their horses north to the burned foundation of their house, where, in the open, both could see passersby on the road: free at last to speak without the fear of eavesdropping.

Clark propped his fowler against the back of the hen house. Upwind of the bitter stench of burned timber, they strolled through the garden plot. He snapped a twig and flung away the pieces. "Why did you tell Tom we were moving?"

She kept her voice low. "I needed to confide in someone."

"I didn't give you permission to talk with anyone about it."

She squared her shoulders. "I didn't give *you* permission to spy for the rebels. See here, we're in this together." She placed a hand over her belly. "All *three* of us. Let's not make decisions independently of each other from here on."

His gaze measured her a few seconds, and then his shoulders dropped an inch. "All right. Exactly what did you tell Tom?"

"That your uncle needed help with his business in Camden, and with our house destroyed, moving seemed like a good option."

He nodded. "That's the story he told me. I'm glad you were sensible enough to keep the rest of it from him."

Sensible. Betsy wanted to scream with irritation. She wasn't the party lacking sense — unless one considered the way she'd lied to Colonel Brown.

"Have you told anyone else?"

"I posted letters to Joshua and my cousin Emma this morning. They got the same story Tom heard. We could use Joshua's company on the road, and Emma can help us get settled in Camden."

"Who else have you told?"

"No one."

"Good. Perhaps we can trust those three to keep quiet about it because frankly, I'm not sure we should go to Camden now."

She gasped. "Oh, can you mean it?"

He nodded again. "Lieutenant Fairfax is too close to figuring out everything. With a broken cover, I'm a threat to the mission. The Seventeenth Light must surely pass through Camden. I cannot place our lives or the mission at risk by going, so I shall post a letter tomorrow advising my contacts of my position and alerting them of Fairfax."

"Oh, thank heaven." Relief plowed through Betsy, and she hopped across the plot to embrace him.

He removed her straw hat and kissed the top of her mobcap. "And after what happened Wednesday, I imagine the British in South Carolina will be on their toes for awhile anyway."

"Wednesday?" She frowned up at him.

"British under the command of Captain Christian Huck were in the Catawba Valley, burning houses and plundering plantations. Some of Thomas Sumter's men caught up with them early Wednesday. Huck was killed, and his men surrendered." He smirked and dropped the hat back on her head. "They're damned lucky we *allowed* them to surrender, what with the cries of 'Tarleton's Quarter' resounding through the land."

Betsy shivered in the July heat. Tarleton's Quarter. Back in May, rebels had labeled the bloody victory of Tarleton's British Legion over Continental forces "Tarleton's Quarter." Her grandfather Will St. James had printed broadsides about the incident — crude pictures of a British soldier bayoneting a kneeling militiaman — before he slipped through British hands and fled Alton, bound for that ill-fated meeting with Spaniards in Havana.

Clark stroked her cheek. "I see how this has stressed you. I can still do the Patriots good by continuing my observations and reports from Augusta. Let's stay and rebuild our home."

Joy flooded her heart, and she flung her arms about his neck and hugged him, not caring that it knocked her hat into the parsley. "Oh, thank you!"

"It's good to see you smile again, sweetheart."

"I'd smile more if we had our furniture back."

He sighed. "I'm not sure it's prudent for all of it to turn up in Augusta straight away. For now, let's assume we won't see it again for awhile. I'm truly sorry."

After catching her hand in his, he scooped up her hat, led her from the herb plot, and replaced the hat. He grabbed the horses' reins and picketed them out of sight behind the hen house. During his embrace, she didn't allow her disappointments and misgivings to spill into the response she gave him. But projecting the appropriate warmth cost her. Since Wednesday, her trust in him had decayed. Although he'd come to his senses about Camden, she wasn't certain what priority he placed on family safety. Ah, but surely trust could be regained?

He nibbled her fingertips and whispered, "When we rebuild the house, I shall make certain we have at least six bedrooms to accommodate our multitude of children, my Betsy, my love. Mmm, your wrist, so soft, so delicious. Plead fatigue after supper tonight so we can retire early, and I can massage your naked shoulders abed."

She snickered. "Safety agrees with you, my husband."

"Mmm." He kissed her hand. Then he released her, pivoted for the edge of the shed, took a half-step from concealment, and jumped back behind again. "The devil!"

She registered the stiffness in his posture. When he snatched up his fowler, she frowned. "What is it?"

"Shh." He peered around the edge of the shed a second or two. "Stay out of sight. Don't make noise," he whispered.

"Why not?" she whispered back.

"It's that Spaniard I saw watching me in the tavern today. He's snooping in the ruins of the house."

"*What* Spaniard?" Dear gods, not the same man tracking them the day before, the one who'd murdered the Givenses?

Clark cocked his fowler and peeked back around. Wind sighed in pine needles, and the hens in the shed gave occasional, soft clucks. Betsy peered around the other side of the shed.

He faced the road in what had two days earlier been Clark's shop, his dark hair queued up beneath a broad-brimmed hat. When he swung back around, dark eyes scouring the charred remains, Betsy slunk for cover, chilled with recognition. Amid the ruins of their home, his face was just as cold with determination as it had been at the Givenses' shop and out in the brush.

In half a minute, she saw Clark's shoulders sag with relief, and she heard the whicker of a horse on the road. "Good," Clark muttered. "He's leaving."

"He's the one. He killed the Givenses and tracked us yesterday."

"You're certain?"

"Yes. Who is he?"

"I don't know." Clark rolled his shoulders back.

Betsy took a deep breath. "*Casa de la Sangre Legítima.*"

He sucked in a breath and gripped her shoulders, his expression belying the fact that he was all too familiar with the Rightful Blood. "Where did you —?"

"Lieutenant Fairfax again. You heard about Sooty's murder? That Spaniard killed him. Who are these assassins? Why did they kill the Givenses and Sooty? Why are they stalking us?"

Betrayal crawled through his expression. "Good god, they didn't tell me there were more than five of them — I — I cannot believe they'd do this to me —"

"Clark!" Her stomach roiling with dread, Betsy shook his arm. "Are your rebel 'friends' hoping you'll get killed by this assassin because they don't trust you?"

"They didn't mistrust Givens and Sooty, yet now they've been assassinated. Perhaps Ambrose doesn't know about this assassin."

Or perhaps Ambrose was allowing unproductive branches of the tree to be pruned. Clark was running out of people to trust. Fear and disgust galloped through Betsy. "We're no longer safe."

Remembering the Spaniard's face so empty of warmth, she wondered where they would be safe. She reached for the reins and mounted Lady May without Clark's assistance.

"Where are you going?"

"To report the Spaniard's latest movements to Colonel Brown." A nudge in the sides sent the mare into a trot.

"No! I'm your husband, and I forbid it!"

The assassin who'd murdered the Givenses and Sooty was stalking them. Time to seek His Majesty's protection for loyal subjects. She reached the road without acknowledging Clark and encouraged her horse into a canter toward the center of town.

**

Brown traced his forefinger along the handle of a teapot on the O'Neals' mantle. No tea had steeped within it for several years, the rebels who controlled imports having turned their noses up at anything British. The Ranger moved on to regard the clock, poised on eight that evening. "Where had you seen the Spaniard before?" Face devoid of cordiality, he swiveled and scrutinized Betsy.

He kept returning to the question, as if convinced she knew Clark's attacker. She squirmed, her lower back aching from having sat on the stool too long. The questioning wasn't going well. Brown seemed to have changed his mind about her innocence. "Two nights ago, when he left the Givens shop in Alton, and yesterday on the road back to Augusta."

"What were you doing when you saw him in Alton?"

"Riding with Lieutenant Stoddard back toward the print shop."

"And on the road to Augusta?"

"I was in the brush back from the road — of necessity."

"What did Lieutenant Fairfax do yesterday when you told him about the Spaniard?"

"I — I didn't tell him then about the Spaniard."

Brown's scrutiny sharpened. "The Spaniard menaced you twice, and you failed to inform Lieutenant Fairfax?"

She bounced a glance off the two Rangers in the doorway, and her stomach gurgled. Interrogation didn't sit well with her digestion. "I ran from the Spaniard straight into the capture of a bandit. It was horrifying. After Lieutenant Fairfax shot the bandit, I was too shaken to do more than mount my horse."

Brown slammed down a stool before her and sat. His ever-present hat shaded the upper portion of his head, and his eyes trapped flecks of lamplight, making him resemble a night creature with a gleaming stare. Imagining scalped spots beneath the hat filled her with a blend of pity, revulsion, and dread.

"You told your husband about your encounters, yet he hasn't filed a complaint about this scoundrel's activities. Why not?"

"We arrived home to a burned house. We've been in shock."

Brown braced his hands on his knees, his gaze searing her the way summer sun beat upon pine barrens. "This morning I all but dismissed evidence brought against you by a fellow officer. Now it appears you lied to me, and he was correct in his assertions that you're a spy."

She shook her head. "I'm not a spy, and I don't understand why our being attacked by a Spaniard makes me so. Spaniards support the rebel cause and would attack *Loyalists*."

He watched her expression. *"Casa de la Sangre Legítima."*

"Lieutenant Fairfax told me of this House of the Rightful Blood. What is it?"

"It's an extreme faction dedicated to purging Spanish culture of contamination from the Bourbon French."

She pulled back to focus on him. "An impossible endeavor, considering how long the Bourbons have influenced Spain."

"Nevertheless, the faction has infiltrated this colonial uprising with assassins directed to murder those who side with the French or stand in the way. Your husband is part of the Ambrose ring, allied with the French, is he not? What is his mission? How long has he been a traitor? Who burned your house and stole your furniture?"

Casa de la Sangre Legítima. The Ambrose spy ring. Betsy spread her hands, baffled. "I — I know nothing of these matters, Colonel. Perhaps the assassin mistook him for someone else."

Brown smirked. "Some of these assassins followed your grandfather, mother, and uncle all the way to Havana." That was news to her. She stared. His mouth tightened over frayed patience, and he straightened on the stool. While the clock struck eight, he waited for the vibrations from the final bong to fade from the air. "Where are *your* loyalties?"

"I'm not a rebel spy, sir —"

"The devil you aren't!" The stool toppled when he stalked away before turning on her with a growl. "Last night, a spy from the Ambrose ring named Ralph Johnston, alias Sooty Johns, bungled an attempt on my life. Although he managed to escape my bodyguards, he'd fumbled his cover. *Casa de la Sangre Legítima* tracked him down and executed him.

"In the past five years, I've had my fill of rebels and interrogating them. I've no time for your lies. Were it possible, I'd recall Lieutenant Fairfax and invite him to finish this conversation, since he seems to have a knack for it." He stabbed a finger at her. "You lied to me this morning."

She wrung her hands. "No, I'm not a rebel spy!"

"At this point, your credibility is in the vault, madam. Upon further interrogation, Mrs. Fuller confessed that your uncle planned to drop in on you Tuesday morning. I ask you again, did you make contact with David St. James earlier this week?"

Well, damn. Betsy lifted her chin. "No."

"Very well. Since you claim you aren't a rebel spy and didn't make contact this week with a suspected spy, you shouldn't object to taking that oath of allegiance to His Majesty." He pounced on her hesitation. "Either you swear allegiance, or I shall escort you to jail tonight."

She hated being backed into a corner almost as much as she hated that jail cell. "The king has my allegiance. I swear it."

"Excellent. Your husband renewed his vows when I questioned him earlier. If you commit treason, your lives are forfeit. Endeavor to prove yourselves blameless subjects." His expression darkened with ancient pain, no doubt that of his torture at the hands of rebels in 1775. "I cannot express how much satisfaction it gives me to see a traitor dangle from a gibbet."

"What of the assassin?" Betsy whispered, appalled at the pit she was mired it. "Has he been caught?"

"No."

"He may continue to try to kill my husband."

"I cannot spare soldiers to guard you day and night, but I can increase the patrol frequency in this neighborhood. Given those limitations, you and Mr. Sheridan must remain on this property until we ascertain that the danger to you is past."

"Wha — ? Does that mean we're under house arrest?"

Brown crossed his arms over his chest, a smile twisting his lips. "Madam, I've no grounds to arrest a *faithful* subject who has committed no crime. It's in your best interests to remain where we can find you at all times. That way you insure your own safety, and you assure us of your loyalty."

CHAPTER SIXTEEN

Hair disheveled, Clark paced back across the bedroom. "Why in bloody hell did you report it? I thought surely you had the sense to realize it would incriminate me!"

"*Sense*?" Exhaustion stripped away Betsy's diplomacy. "That assassin might have killed us all. You didn't even have the decency to warn me."

"I didn't know. I was told that two assassins were killed last summer, one was killed in Alton last month, and the others followed your mother to Havana, where they perished."

"How is it the British knew of this extra assassin but your fellow Patriots didn't? Oh, face it, Clark. Brown knows all about the ring and is ninety-five percent certain you're a spy. For all the help the Ambrose ring gives you, they must either want you dead or locked up."

She stretched out on the bed in her shift and closed her eyes. "I'm too tired to beat my brain more with it." The chair legs at the desk squawked, and she heard the scratch of quill on paper. "What are you doing?"

"Writing a letter." The scratch of the quill continued for another quarter minute. Then she smelled melted sealing wax. "Find a way to post this letter for me on the morrow — but only if it looks as though Brown isn't intercepting our mail."

Betsy yawned. "Post it yourself."

"I won't be here."

She chuckled. "As if you'd ride to Camden in the middle of the night."

"That's precisely what I must do."

"Oh, stop being foolish and come to bed." After opening her eyes, she rolled on her side and watched him stuff his shirt back inside his breeches. "What are you doing?"

"Getting dressed." He hopped into a shoe.

She sat up. "You cannot be serious."

"If I don't draw off the assassin, he'll keep trying for me, and he may kill you or someone we love in the process."

"We're both under house arrest, and Colonel Brown increased the patrols. The assassin won't make it through. Come to bed."

Clark slid on his other shoe. "If Brown knows much about these assassins and he's certain of my involvement with the Patriots, he intends for the assassin to take my life. Let the Spaniard be my executioner as he was Sooty's. To all appearances, Brown will have done everything he could to protect a loyal subject." He buttoned his waistcoat. "Don't think I shall wait here to be butchered like a fox in a hole."

Betsy rolled out of bed and seized his elbow, mortified by the fervent gleam in her husband's eyes. "This is madness. I cannot let you go. I will not let you go. I shall wake Lucas and have you thrown in Augusta jail to keep you safe."

"Please, you're making this more difficult for both of us."

"You're my husband, the father of our child. I need you alive, here by my side. I cannot raise this baby without you. It makes no sense for you to leave in the middle of the night."

He nodded. "War often makes no sense."

Tears of desperation and disbelief heated her eyes. She flung her arms around him. "For the love of heaven, my husband, don't do this."

He disentangled himself. "I must."

"Then take me with you."

"No. You're safe here with Lucas and Sarah." He reached for his coat.

Her throat constricted. "I cannot believe you're leaving me." The first tears squeezed out. "Don't go. Not this moment. Please stay with me the rest of tonight."

He hesitated and then dropped the coat back over a chair before stroking her cheek. "Now, now, dry your tears, sweetheart. I'm here."

He removed his shoes and waistcoat and followed her down onto the bed — unresisting when she removed his breeches, responsive when her mouth and fingers built his arousal, attentive when she needed her own arousal addressed, compliant when she mounted him. A stellar performance to the very end, when a sleepy Betsy heard the clock downstairs strike one. Yet as she drifted off to sleep, her legs wrapped around Clark and imprisoning his sweaty body against hers, she sensed he'd never been there making love with her. He'd sent a life-sized poppet in his place, and John Clark Sheridan was long gone to Camden, South Carolina, in the service of the Continental Congress.

***

The clock striking five in the morning jolted her awake, and she reached beside her to feel the sheets still warm. A horse whickered outside. She scrambled to the window to glimpse Clark in the yard walking his gelding to the street, fowler in one hand. In the next instant, he swung up into the saddle and kicked the horse into a trot south on the road. She raced from the bedroom down the stairs.

She'd almost gained the front door when a blob of masculine darkness rose from before the window, lunged for her, and propelled her backwards into the wall. Having clapped his hand over her mouth to muffle her scream, he prodded something cold and sharp to her neck — a knife meant for slitting a throat from ear to ear. Terror squeezed Betsy's throat.

"Scream, *señora*, and I kill you, *comprende*? Where did he go?" He peeled his hand off her mouth while retaining the point of the knife at her throat.

Her chest aching, Betsy gasped for breath. The knifepoint pressed inward, burning. "He wouldn't tell me. Said he wanted to p — protect me. Please. D — don't kill me. I don't know."

The wine-drenched warmth of the Spaniard's breath washed over her face. "He went to Camden, did he not?"

"D — don't know."

He chuckled. "To Camden, *sí*, with all those French-loving dogs who dream *ensueños francés de bobalicones*. Stripping mighty Britain of her military command — bah! How the Rightful Blood loves ridding the world of such imbeciles, *idiotas francés*." The knife pressure at her throat released. "*Gracias, señora*."

He shoved her away, and while she stumbled against a chair, flung open the front door and bolted outside. His running footsteps faded into predawn, and somewhere farther away, a horse was startled into activity. Straightening, she drew a deep breath and screamed for Lucas and Sarah, even though she suspected it was too late to catch the assassin, even though she knew in her soul that it was also too late for Clark.

***

"Madam, my irritation grows with each meeting." Brown's glower clouded the Saturday morning sunshine. "You're withholding information. He told you where he went."

A broom propped against the fireplace seemed the safest place for Betsy to look. "He only said he had to leave, and then he sneaked from bed while I slept."

"With an assassin from the Rightful Blood chasing him. Your husband is a rebel spy."

"The assassin didn't kill me. Surely that proves *I'm* not a rebel spy."

"It proves you're damned lucky." *Whack*! He swatted his booted calf with a riding crop. "Beneath my very nose — how long has he been an operative for the Congress?" She remained silent, her soul resounding with grief, her brain numb with fatigue and doubt. "Answer me!" After stalking forward, he kicked the leg of her stool.

She flinched and hung her head. "I don't know."

"Where did he go?"

Into the depths of sprawling, bustling Camden-hell: fallen angel. "I don't know."

"What's his mission?"

Depriving the British military of its command, if she believed the assassin. Cornwallis: 402. Was Clark supposed to assassinate him? The rebels *were* idiots if they'd given a shoemaker such an assignment. "I don't know."

He hovered like a panther on a tree limb, lord of the swamp, flicking his tail, waiting to spring and eviscerate. After half a minute, he lowered his voice. "Are you a rebel spy?"

"No."

Whack! "Look at me when you answer. Are you a rebel spy?"

She lifted her head and met stone for an expression. Someday, Brown was going to find the rebels who'd tortured him, and the sight of their corpses dangling from gibbets would purge his soul of torment. "I'm not a rebel spy."

He forced her to ride the steel of his gaze for what seemed an eon. "You're either telling the truth, or you're made of stronger fiber than many men I've known." At the window again, he scrutinized the day outside. "You will remain on this property while our investigation continues. Should you venture away without permission, I shall consider you a traitor and mark you for execution. However, should you recall significant details that might advance our investigation and inform me of them, I shall release you from confinement. Do you understand?"

"Yes."

Whack! "Good day." He strode to the front door and yanked it open. The two Rangers posted at the door followed him out.

Their footsteps were almost soundless — each trained by Indians in furtiveness. Provincials — individualists, sometimes radicals. Yes, Thomas Brown was an individualist — a clever and deadly individualist. She couldn't see him wasting time finishing up the investigation to uncover her lies. When he returned to haul her back to jail, she'd have had no choice but to wait for him in Lucas's house, trapped.

Her foster-parents entered through the front door. Sarah drew her into her arms. Lucas's face looked old, drawn with worry, and his hunched shoulders projected that he knew they'd be back. "Did you tell him what the assassin said?"

"No." She was surprised at how firm her voice sounded.

"You've everything to gain by telling him what you know."

"I'm neutral, regardless of what oath I had to swear."

He shook his head. "He'll figure it all out, and then you'll be sharing that jail cell with Widow Fuller."

She repressed a shudder. What had Abby done but try to convey the best escape odds possible on a man she loved? Surely Abby's silence for three days had bought David the time he needed to get to

Williamsburg. Surely her own silence would increase Clark's chances of getting to Camden. However the worst part was believing that silence was the only way she could help her husband. Passivity. How she hated passivity.

CHAPTER SEVENTEEN

R uth Glenn sniffed over her coffee cup. "A rebel spy."
Betsy looked up from her own cup. "No one has proven him
to be a spy."

"Bah. He lived a double life. You never knew him. None of us
did." She handed Sarah her empty cup. "Fugitives don't often escape.
I doubt he'll come back."

Betsy felt her face pale. What a brutal thing to say. She'd never
have believed it of Ruth, a model Christian woman, always so busy
tending the poor.

Jane handed her empty cup to Sarah. "Men do foolish things. He
shouldn't have run off. He's not worthy of your devotion."

"At least he isn't a double agent." Ellie looked hopeful.

Ruth waved off the suggestion. "We've all had far too much
excitement lately, especially you, Betsy. We're your friends.
Sometimes friends have to deliver honesty that hurts. In all honesty,
it's time for you to move on."

"Move on?" Betsy cocked an eyebrow at the vicar's wife.

"You must put this behind you and focus on keeping yourself well for the sake of the baby. And that means smiling."

"Smiling?" Betsy could hardly believe her ears.

"Yes, try smiling. It will make you feel better."

Dull anger churned Betsy's soul, bruised by women she'd trusted. She fantasized giving Ruth a gesture other than a smile.

Ellie frowned. "I hope you don't run off after him."

"She won't do that," said Jane. "She's too sensible. But Betsy dear, your primary concern right now should be your baby. Thank goodness you have a home with Lucas and Sarah."

"That's right." Ruth stood. "It isn't like Mr. Sheridan left you homeless. What time is it getting to be? Goodness, Sarah, I've drunk far too much of your coffee. Thank you ever so much. I must be off, ladies."

Ellie and Jane stood, taking Ruth's cue, each seeming relieved to be leaving. Betsy bit her lip, speechless with hurt and indignation. How did the women expect her to put Clark behind her? He was still her husband.

The warmth of Sarah's hand rested on her shoulder, but her voice held an early frost. "Thank you for coming."

Ruth situated her straw hat on her head. "Thank you for taking care of her, Sarah. You're a sensible, good woman." And what did that make Betsy — a lunatic for loving Clark? "Call on my husband anytime. We shall pray for Mr. Sheridan to come to his senses and surrender peacefully." Ruth grasped her basket. "Poor, foolish man."

"Take care, Betsy," said Jane.

Tears blurring her vision, Betsy stared at her cup while the women exited. When they were gone, Sarah removed the cup from her lap and sat next to her. Pain strangled Betsy's voice to a whisper. "Yesterday they supported me. Today they shun me."

Sarah took her hand. "They're frightened, confused. Most folks cannot handle a big misfortune. They resent you for disrupting their lives with it." She sighed. "Folks do the best they can to give comfort. That's where their platitudes come from."

"Their *best*?" Betsy blinked back tears. "Did you hear them? They expect me to make them feel better when *I'm* the one who hurts. And they want it all fixed overnight! My problems won't be fixed overnight."

"Lucas and I understand. You can count on us."

***

In the shade of an oak that afternoon, the two women snapped beans in the back yard. Sarah might have prattled about social events and the weather, but she remained quiet, receptive to Betsy in a way empty talk would have prevented. The tranquility she invoked enabled Betsy's thinking to clear. Sure, remaining silent and passive was an option, but it wasn't a good one because she might as well be in jail. Lucas had returned from the stationer's shop with Clark's letter unposted and Molly's warning that Brown was inspecting all mail for the Sheridans. If Betsy wanted to help her husband, she'd have to take some risks.

Sarah brushed her forearm. "Lieutenant Neville is here."

Adam strolled around from the front yard, jangling suspicion and ambivalence through Betsy. She didn't want to talk with anyone, especially another Ranger. However, his face expressed condolence, so she set the bowl of beans down and folded her hands in her lap to await him.

He bowed. "Good afternoon, ladies. Mrs. Sheridan, may I speak with you?" Seeing the forbearance in her eyes, he added, "This is personal, not business." Sarah rose, curtsied, and left, taking both bowls of beans with her. At Betsy's gesture, Adam took Sarah's seat. "I cannot believe Clark's a rebel spy."

She wished she could unburden herself on Adam, but had she been in Brown's position, sending Clark's friend to dig information from her would be a logical first move. She smoothed a wrinkle in her apron. "I'm as shocked as you are."

"Poor lad. He's probably run scared, hiding and hoping it'll all blow over. Where did he go?"

"I already told Colonel Brown that I don't know."

"Do you suppose he went to Camden?"

Why would Adam mention Camden specifically unless Brown suspected Clark had gone there? "This is a business visit, not a personal one."

"I apologize." He shook his head. "I want to help. Clark sees the best in people and doesn't have much bad to say about anyone. Most men at the tavern deride their wives. Not Clark. He praises you for your help with the books or what delicious biscuits you make, and it shuts up the men. Few men love their wives the way he loves you. He has a good soul in him."

She bit her lip and turned away. "Good day, Lieutenant."

"I didn't mean to upset you more. I'm worried about him. If I found him, I might be able to mediate, straighten things out."

Betsy felt a tear roll down her right cheek. Exasperated for not containing her distress, she fumbled for the handkerchief in her pocket. Adam extended his, and she dabbed her eyes with it and returned it. "Thank you."

"Please help Clark, even if you won't involve me."

In the depths of his eyes, fire clutched for her. Loyalists could be just as fanatic as rebels. She pulled away, afraid to look further. "How can I help him? I don't know where he is."

He withdrew a paper from his tote bag and unfolded it, his voice silk in the sultry air. "We got a copy of this last week from Camden." He turned it to her. "Does it mean anything?"

On the paper, three-digit numbers were paired with words or names in columns. Betsy's gaze swept the page, where it lodged on the number four hundred two, the name *Cornwallis* scripted beside it. Good god. Listed above it was four hundred one: Sir Henry Clinton, Commander in Chief. Horror blossomed through her. Four hundred three: Lord Rawdon. Four hundred seven: Cruger, British commander at Ninety Six, South Carolina. Four hundred eight: Tarleton, commander of the British Legion. The names went on and on. Thomas Brown's name was there, too.

Her heart hammering, she batted the paper away. "You think to trap me with privy military information. Away with it."

Adam seized her hand. "Colonel Brown doesn't know I'm showing it to you. It's the key to the cipher used by the Ambrose spy ring. You've seen something like it before?"

"No, never!"

"Something on this page looked familiar to you just now. I saw it in your eyes. Perhaps a letter Clark received or sent, coded in such a fashion?"

She snatched away her hand and stood, her nostrils flared, her body trembling. "Good day, Lieutenant!"

His expression closed. After returning the paper to his tote, he rose. "Forgive me for deepening your distress, but I don't believe I'm wrong about your knowledge of this cipher. I want to help Clark. I don't want to see him executed. If Brown finds him before I do, he'll hang." His face glowed with the fervor of holy cause. "If you recollect where he went, send for me. I shall come in an instant." He bowed. "Good day."

In disbelief, she watched him saunter for the front yard. So the redcoats had decoded the Ambrose cipher. How long had they been intercepting Clark's letters and learning rebel schemes? Perhaps they'd even authored that letter from "Uncle Isaac" to lure Clark to Camden and capture him, along with other spies.

She massaged her temple. How the British toyed with her, waiting for her to break. She'd no idea how much longer they'd wait, but it was obvious she couldn't afford to remain passive and under house arrest much longer.

The back door opened. Astonishment shot through her when she spotted Joshua Hale exiting, and she barreled forward to greet him. He grinned and caught his niece up in a solid embrace. "My dear, you look exceptional for someone caught in a hornet's nest."

Sarah smiled and waved out the back door. "I told your uncle he's welcome to stay with us tonight." She ducked back in.

"But you'll want to head home on the morrow. I shan't be going to South Carolina after all. I cannot leave the O'Neals' property right now."

"Not that anyone in his right mind would want to go to South Carolina right now." He linked arms with her and guided her back into the shade. "House arrest is no fun, so I shall stay a day at least to cheer you up before I return."

"And I shall be delighted for your company."

"Tell me, have you heard the latest news out of South Carolina Spartan District?"

Spartan District was some seventy-five miles northeast of Camden, but the way Whigs and Loyalists bashed each other around, hostilities could shift any day to another district. "I heard of a battle in which Captain Huck was killed."

He shook his head. "That was Wednesday. This started Thursday in Cedar Springs. Rebel militia under Elijah Clarke lured a couple hundred Loyalists and British cavalry to their camp. About thirty-five were killed."

She winced. Colonel Clarke liked creating a stir.

"And Thursday night, Loyalists who'd escaped Cedar Springs returned to Gowen's Old Fort near North Carolina with some Whigs who were passing themselves off as Loyalists."

"Trojan Horse."

"Exactly. Middle of the night, Whigs took the fort. Fighting and retribution are a way of life in the Carolina backcountry." Her uncle glanced around to ensure their privacy, withdrew a letter from his waistcoat pocket, and passed it to her. "I trust you'll know how to deal with *this*."

She stared at the name on the return address: Isaac Sheridan, Camden. "How did you come by it? I thought Colonel Brown was intercepting all of Clark's mail."

"My timing was extraordinary. While the lady who runs the stationer's shop and I were chatting about you, the afternoon post arrived. That letter to Clark was in it. No sooner did she give it to me than a Ranger walked in and inquired whether there was mail for the Sheridans. She waved me on my way and told him no. So there you have it."

Betsy hoped Molly wouldn't be keeping Abby Fuller company in jail — although from Joshua's news, it sounded as though Thomas Brown had his hands full keeping up with the actions of rebel militia leaders. She broke the letter's seal. "Uncle Isaac's" spidery scrawl greeted her from within:

11 July 1780, Town of Camden

My dear nephew John Clark:

I regret to inform you that I took a Fall yesterday Afternoon and sprained my Ankle and Wrist. The Surgeon tells me Nothing is broken. However, I am at a Loss to run the Business adequately now, as my Accident necessitated my sharing the Home of an old Friend, Samuel Taylor, until I mend and can get about properly again. Please come in all Haste and assist me, at least for Awhile, with my Business.

I remain Sir

Your devoted Uncle

Isaac Sheridan

Not doubting another message resided, invisible, between the lines, she reread the overt message and pondered its urgency. Someone wanted Clark in Camden right away.

Who was Samuel Taylor? The letter Lucas had been unable to post was addressed to Taylor, also on King Street in Camden. "Leaving 15 July," Clark had written. "Expect me 18 July. Blood follows." Blood follows. Yes, the Rightful Blood.

"It sure is taking you a long time to read one little letter." Joshua smiled at her over the top of the page. "Unless you got more than one letter there, that is."

"Actually —" Betsy eyed the house. " — there may be a second letter hidden here. If we had a source of heat, like a candle, I'd be able to show you."

Joshua studied her face. "You aren't joking." After groping his waistcoat pockets, he extracted pipe, tobacco, and tinderbox. "Time for a smoke." He began stuffing tobacco in the bowl of the pipe.

Betsy knelt and cleared a patch in the grass. In a moment, the two of them had a small blaze going with the kindling they found beneath the oak. Joshua lit his pipe and enjoyed a few puffs on it, mingling the sweet smell of tobacco with the tang of wood smoke. With him crouched beside her, Betsy hovered the letter as close as she dared to the flames. The Ambrose spy ring's characteristic three-digit cipher blued between the lines of brown ink. "Look there. You see?"

He removed his cocked hat and frowned at the letter. "Amazing. Now, I've heard spies use invisible ink, but I never thought I'd see it demonstrated. What does it say?"

With a cough, she fanned away smoke and squinted at the numbers. "I only know a little of the code." In fact, the names of each British commander she'd seen on Adam's key were represented in the cipher, and Cornwallis and Rawdon were mentioned twice. Despite sweat running down her back, she felt cold. She passed the paper close to the flame again to refresh the hidden writing. "Clinton, Cornwallis, Rawdon, Cruger, Tarleton, Ferguson —"

"Whoa, there." Joshua sat back on his haunches. "What the deuce has your husband fallen into?"

She regarded him. "Didn't town gossip spell it out? He's part of a rebel spy ring."

"I heard it, but I didn't believe it." Joshua scowled. "I thought he'd more brains. You're going to have a baby. And what are these spies up to?"

"I think they're trying to kill these British officers."

He sat back on the turf cross-legged like an Indian and laughed a few seconds, his pipe in his right hand. "Why, that's outright crazy. Suicide. Each of those men has a small army of bodyguards around him." He sobered and patted her shoulder again. "Gods, Betsy. You must be worried sick. Doesn't sound like you've been helping the redcoats with your knowledge. You helping the rebels, then?"

"No."

"Whom have you told?"

She studied Joshua, as comfortable in his presence as she felt with Sarah and Lucas. "A strategic few other neutrals."

"Smart woman. I reckon you got me figured out."

She settled beside her uncle and wondered what to do next. Disgust trickled into her voice. "I was forced to swear allegiance to King George to stay out of jail."

Her uncle shrugged. "Plenty of folks do that to stay alive. If a man put a pistol to my head, I'd tell him whatever he wanted to hear." He indicated the return address on the new letter. "Did Clark go to Camden?"

"Yes." She exhaled exasperation and anguish. "He's so obsessed he cannot see that his cohorts have grown mistrustful of him and are setting him up for failure. I tried to make him see what's happening, but it was all for naught." She snorted. "I suppose that if a man makes up his mind to do something, he'll keep after it."

"Men do think like that, yes."

"I hate giving up. I've seldom given up at anything."

He chuckled. "It doesn't sound as though you're ready to give up. It sounds as though you're going after him."

"Colonel Brown will have my head if I leave without helping him find these spies." She stared into the distance. "But that hasn't stopped me from fancying that I sneak away in the middle of the night, like Clark did. Somehow, I must leave. Otherwise I'll land in jail anyway."

Joshua puffed on his pipe and smothered the fire. "Write Brown a letter and tell him something he doesn't already know — just enough to convince him you're doing your duty to the Crown."

She pursed her lips. "He'd still have me followed."

"And your idea of night travel is a good one. Makes it more difficult for pursuit."

"I need an escort."

"I'm yours, and two fellows waiting on Mrs. O'Neal's front porch are prepared to ride to South Carolina with us."

Dismay screwed up Betsy's face at the thought of his being indiscreet. "Whom else have you involved?"

"Sehoyee Yahuh and Assayceeta Corackall."

"Creek." Her dismay faded. "The same warriors who rode to St. Augustine last month with my parents?"

Joshua patted her knee and leaned closer, in conspiracy. "Write your letter to Brown and then find yourself one or two other neutral fellows to accompany us. We shall be in excellent shape to start the journey to Camden before dawn on the morrow."

"Joshua, I realize you're hoping to find your brother. Camden is on the other side of South Carolina from Keowee."

"Uncle Jacques used to say, 'Sometimes a man travels to the very end of a road just to see what is there.'" Especially if he wanted to get away from a shrewish wife for awhile? Joshua had reasons aplenty for embarking upon such a journey. He craned his neck around toward the house. "Say, who's the handsome fellow?"

She followed his gaze to where Tom Alexander trotted down the steps with a chair hooked beneath his arm. In the open doorway, Sarah waved again. "Betsy, look who stopped by for a visit!" She withdrew inside the house.

One chair. Hmm. Sarah was leaving them to their conference. Betsy looked from Tom's approach to the letter in her hand. "I believe we've found another man for the escort."

CHAPTER EIGHTEEN

With a yawn, Betsy considered the blank page, reached for the quill, and wrote.

Colonel Brown:

I have thought back to the Moments early Saturday Morning when the Assassin held me at Knifepoint. My Terror from those Moments was so great as to make the Event a Blur in my Memories, and I've scarce wanted to reconsider such Peril. However, it is my Duty to impart upon you such Information as I can recall in Effort to speed your Investigation.

As I told you, while he held me Prisoner, the Assassin did demand of me the Destination of my Husband, and I informed him that I did not know. I now recall that he referenced the Ambrose spy Ring, labeling them "French-loving Fools." He also said that their Mission was "Stripping mighty Britain of her military Command." He said Nothing else to me. I trust this Information is of value to you. As my Part in the Affair has been blessedly small, I have Nothing else to contribute.

The Events of the past several Days have generated unwelcome and unwholesome Publicity for me. I find myself ostracized and ridiculed by Residents of Augusta and have grown fearful of losing my Child from the Strain. Therefore, it is my Decision to venture to the Home of a Relation and remain there in Seclusion for several Months. Of necessity, I have kept my Destination secret, even from the O'Neals. If you must pursue me and execute me en route, so be it. But I shall not endanger my Unborn by remaining here in a condition of such Disfavor.

I am Sir

Your humble servant

Elizabeth Sheridan nee Neely

She reread the letter before sealing and addressing it. Then she placed it in full view on the desk, blew out the candle, and reclined in her chemise to take what rest she could. In five hours' time, she, Joshua, Tom, and the two Creek warriors would set off for Camden, some 110 miles distant and four days travel through a portion of South Carolina populated largely by Loyalists. The O'Neals' official story would be that they'd risen Sunday to find their foster-daughter gone.

Lucas had given her his extra musket and cartridge box. Sarah had packed trail rations. And Betsy had tucked both letters in her pockets in case she needed to verify her identity with the Ambrose ring. Then all of them, even the Creek, had sat in the O'Neals' front room after supper and discussed the route and its perils.

Not the least of those perils would be the pursuit of the Rangers. Rebel leader Elijah Clarke stomping around nearby wouldn't make Brown forget that the Ambrose spy ring had operated within his jurisdiction. Plus she wasn't asking his permission to leave. She was just leaving. Unless he searched for her first in Alton, she'd have no more than eight hours lead.

Even if she made it to Camden, she might not be able to find Clark. Since the fall of Charles Town, the military population in Camden had increased to several thousand troops, and she doubted Clark would publicize his arrival and whereabouts under those circumstances. But remaining passive in Augusta — never venturing forth to find him — was no longer an option for her.

Had Sophie wrestled with similar thoughts before she violated house arrest to chase after Will, her father? Father. Betsy tried to assemble a picture of Mathias Hale from memory, but it had been too long since she'd seen him. Before she lost herself to sleep, she hoped that somewhere in the chaos of South Carolina, she'd find not only her husband but her father, too.

***

Afternoon sun emerged from behind cumulus and bathed the road in blistering waves. Cicadas surged and subsided with the passage of horses, and the scent of pine loaded the humid air. "More sand and turkey oaks." Tom removed his hat and swabbed a kerchief over his face.

"And South Carolinians are butchering each other over this?" Betsy's tailbone ached from twelve hours' astride and so little sleep. At least the road had taken a turn east, placing the sun at their backs. She halted Lady May beside Tom's horse on the road.

"Not over sand, no. They've transplanted clan feuds across the Atlantic."

"And the army has no idea how to keep the peace." Joshua reached the top of the rise and pulled back on his horse's reins.

Betsy studied Tom. "How do you know so much about these people?"

He shrugged. "I listen to what men say in the taverns. I read every paper I can find."

"If I'd been half that wise when I was your age, lad, I'd be twice as smart now." Joshua grinned. "Take a break, shall we?"

Tom replaced hat and kerchief. "How far have we come?"

"Thirty-five miles. The Ninety Six road isn't far ahead."

Thirty-five miles: small wonder Betsy's arse hurt. Such a distance was a challenge for cavalry soldiers. She squinted at her uncle. "Where do you suppose the Rangers are?"

He smirked. "Since the Creek haven't seen them today, I wager they followed our false trail and went to Alton first."

He hadn't witnessed the fanaticism in Adam Neville's eyes. "I wager they followed us straight away, soon as it was light," she said.

With a yawn, her uncle dismounted and led his horse off the road. "Come out of the sun for awhile. Let Assayceeta Corackall catch up and give us the latest report from the road south."

Remembering how the assassin from *Casa de la Sangre Legítima* had tracked them through cover of trees alongside the road, she nudged Lady May over to Joshua, and Tom helped her dismount. "Suppose the Rangers followed us without using the road?"

"They'd be hard-pressed to keep up in those pines without one of my cousins noticing them."

"But the Rangers were trained by the Creek."

"Betsy, relax. We're far enough ahead for a respite." Joshua groped in his haversack for his pipe.

Tom seized his musket. "I hear a horse."

Runs With Horses trotted his steed over the rise, and Joshua signaled him over. "What news, Cousin?"

"No sign of Rangers —" A little smile curved the warrior's lips. " — but three White peddlers ride our way."

Joshua cradled his rifle. "We'll stay out of sight and allow them to pass. No telling what caliber of men they are."

Runs With Horses' smile broadened. "I know them. They are harmless except for loving the sound of their own voices."

Tom turned to Joshua. "If they've been through Augusta, perhaps they've word of the Rangers."

"All right, then, we'll travel together aways and hear what they have to say." Joshua motioned the Creek down. "Join us in the shade, will you?"

"No. I ride ahead to find my brother." The Creek's smile became toothy, and he steered his horse back toward the road. "We follow, stay out of sight."

"You don't want them to recognize you, eh?" Joshua snorted.
"Most settlers cannot tell you two from Catawba or Cherokee."

"Take no risk." A grinning Runs With Horses kicked his gelding
in the ribs and sent him eastward on the road after Standing Wolf.

Squatting, Joshua lit his pipe. "Don't mind him. He's just
weaseling out of a boring conversation with old friends."

***

Paunchy Harry the peddler leaned forward in his saddle and gave
Betsy a wink of conspiracy. "Got a roll of yellow silk in Charles Town
for a good price because some fool spilled coffee on it. I hung onto it
all through Georgia. I knew them soldiers' wives in Ninety Six didn't
have nothing so fine, so pretty.

"So I says to myself, 'Harry, today is your lucky day. Work the
ladies up to the silk. Show them cotton, wool, and linen first. When
they see that silk, they'll fall in love and pay your price, see?' Well,
do you think I got my price, eh?"

While maintaining the expression she reserved for tea parties,
Betsy wondered whether Harry ever shut up. Over his shoulder, she
saw Joshua roll his eyes. "I don't know, sir."

Harry slapped the pommel of his saddle. "Them soldiers' wives
argued over the silk like it was gold. I got quadruple my price. That
was double what I paid for it. Was I clever?"

A bark of laughter escaped spindly Rob, peddler of deer hides.
"Sure, Harry, you was clever, and it was the last time you was clever."

A surly look enveloped Harry's face. "You ain't sold too much
lately, so you got nothing to brag on." He flung a look behind him at
the carrot-headed herb peddler. "You, either."

"You hear me say anything, Harry?" The third peddler scowled.
"Get off my back. Rob's too. Folks ain't buying much these days, and
here in the Carolinas a man cuts his neighbor's throat, just because the
neighbor looks at him wrong."

Rob gestured eastward. "Aye, and you cannot even blame it on
them redcoats in Camden and Charles Town."

The herb peddler continued: "They're just plain crazy here. I
ain't making another trip to the backcountry until this war is over."

Sullenness settled over the peddlers, and Tom, who'd been riding
in the rear, sent his gelding forward. "I take it you fellows were

unable to sell your wares at the homes we passed earlier on the Augusta road."

Rob sneered. "Last trip those folks was happily trading. This trip they told us to go away like we was banditti. Some of the houses looked abandoned."

"Come to think of it," said Joshua, "we haven't seen anybody else on the road today."

"Us, either." Harry sniffed with clear disdain for settlers who would forgo backcountry traveling, just because a war was on.

So no one had seen the Rangers. Betsy's intuition prodded her to remain vigilant. Adam Neville was coming after her; she felt it in her bones. "Not even out of Augusta?"

"Nope. Haven't seen a soul except you folks since we started out at dawn."

"Harry, look yonder at the road to Ninety Six."

They all gazed a quarter mile ahead to the crossroad, where eight men waited on horseback, a battered wagon hitched to a riderless horse with them. Joshua frowned. "Recognize them?" The peddlers said no, and Joshua tightened his lips. "I know you lads were headed for Ninety Six today, but let's stick together getting through that group."

Betsy cast about wondering, as she was sure Joshua and Tom were wondering, why the two Creek warriors hadn't emerged from hiding to tell them about the men on the road. Were the men bandits? Unease prickled her scalp, the bandit attack south of Augusta vivid in her memory. If her party turned about and bolted back westward, she wasn't sure Lady May could outdistance the eight men's horses after a full day's travel.

The distance closed. She saw that the men wore the hunting shirts and trousers of backcountry folks and ranged from Tom's age to men in their forties. A day's beard growth and bloody bandages on several, plus grime on their rumpled clothing implied they'd just come from a skirmish. Her unease deepened. Each man carried a firearm.

Joshua trotted his horse to the front of the party and squared his shoulders. "Afternoon, gentlemen." He tipped his hat and rode through the intersection, making sure his rifle was visible. The men scrutinized them and said nothing. Betsy, Tom, and the peddlers rode by unchallenged, their firearms in the open. She let out a deep breath.

Matching the speed of their horses, the men encircled them, the last bringing the horse and wagon in tow with a clatter. A man paced Joshua, his expression steely. "Are you a Duffy?"

"Indeed not, sir."

"Where you headed?"

"East."

"I can see that. You trying to be a crafty fellow?"

"No, sir. I answered your question. We don't mind the company if you and your men are headed east also."

The spokesman and several others blocked the road, bringing everyone to a stop. "Holy gods," muttered one of the peddlers. Betsy stroked Lady May's neck with trembling fingers.

"I reckon I was too subtle." The spokesman pulled out a pistol. "You folks tell us whose side you're on, and don't be claiming neutrality. There ain't no neutrals here."

Memory furnished Betsy with details of a proclamation issued by General Clinton in the aftermath of the Crown's victory at Charles Town. Any man in South Carolina not swearing allegiance to the Crown was deemed a rebel, allowing Loyalists to identify and persecute potential traitors from among their own neighbors.

A nervous laugh tumbled from Rob. "I'm on whatever side you lads are on!" The other two peddlers chimed in with gusto.

"Shut up, all three of you!"

A man to the right of the spokesman gestured to Rob. "I know him. He buys and trades deer hides."

"Yes, sir, I do, and they're the finest hides you ever —"

"Shut up. Recognize anybody else, Zechariah?"

"That one over there sells cloth. My wife got a decent bolt of linen off him this spring."

Harry wobbled out a smile. "I'm delighted to hear my customers are —"

"You shut up, too. Anybody else?"

"We bought horehound from that red-haired fellow."

Pistol still in hand, the leader leaned toward the peddlers. "You three — begone!"

Harry tipped his hat. "Yes, sir. Good day!" He kicked his horse in the ribs and sent it and his packhorse in tow back to the crossroad, where he broke into a gallop headed north on the road to Ninety Six. The other two peddlers and their packhorses allowed him little lead space.

Dust settled while the leader pinned his gaze on Betsy, Tom, and Joshua. His eyes were bloodshot, and blackpowder spattered his right jaw. "Now, we ain't never seen you folks before. What side are you on?"

Tom said in a quiet, firm voice, "A pox on King George."

One of the men tittered. "To be sure, that old fart is as poxed as a body can get."

"Quiet, Cain. They were guessing. They ain't Patriots. I wager they came from *Georgia*." He layered such loathing on the word "Georgia" that it seemed to hang in the air like swamp gas.

"Colonel Clarke works Georgia," one man volunteered. "Dan and Fred are from Georgia. There's good folks there."

Betsy lifted her chin. "We're from Augusta. What of it?"

"Thomas Brown." The leader spat on the ground, and several men followed suit.

Betsy felt her heart flip-flop. "We suspect a group of Rangers to be following us some four to twelve hours behind."

"Why?"

She took a deep breath and considered how much she dared tell. "The Ambrose ring."

Cain scanned her fingers for some sort of jewelry. A blank look transcended the leader's face. "The Amberly — What the deuce are you talking about, woman?"

"Since you've yet to produce the appropriate countersigns, I'm not permitted to release more information to you."

"Countersigns? What countersigns?" The leader cocked his pistol and aimed it at her, a scowl on his face. "You think I'm stupid, don't you, woman? No woman ever called me stupid."

Betsy gripped her reins to still the shaking in her hands. "Perhaps not, but your commander *will* label you stupid and then some if you shoot us and mire this portion of the mission."

"Jesus," said Zechariah, "she's a spy for the Continentals!"

"She's a lying harlot."

Zechariah prodded the leader. "Joe, the Continentals use women to deliver messages across lines. The bloodybacks don't think 'em capable of spying."

Joe waved his pistol at Joshua and Tom. "I'm not getting a word of sense out of her. Which one of you doesn't want his brains blown out?"

Joshua said, "You'll find us equally unhelpful, sir. Madam over there is the leader of our triad."

Tom nodded. "We're organized in triads with the senior member — Madam, in our case — given most of the information. Our business is merely to see her safely to the end of her mission."

Even though he lowered his pistol, a snarl etched Joe's mouth. "Well, then, *Patriots*, we got Patriot business in these parts. You come with us, and then we'll take you to the captain and let him decide what's to be done with you."

"Sir." Betsy flared her nostrils with what she hoped looked like indignation. "Our mission is of the gravest import."

"So is ours. You'll just have to wait."

"We dare not spare the time to accompany you."

Joe pointed a finger at her. "Shut up and stay quiet the way a woman should, or I'll gag you. You understand me, Madam Triad Leader?"

CHAPTER NINETEEN

Panels of late afternoon sun pierced the pine copse and bathed the cabin in the clearing with pastel yellow. Joe hollered from behind a pine tree, "Liam Duffy, are you home?"

A woman's voice rang from inside: "He ain't home, MacCrae."

"He ain't home because he's out killing Whigs."

"Too bad he missed your vile hide. Go away, or I'll use this here musket to fix it so as you never sire another beast."

Joe snarled. "Liam's found himself a whore!"

Musket fire from the cabin peppered the woods. Men scrambled for better cover and returned fire. One ball smacked the tree shielding Betsy, and Tom shoved her flat. "Stay down!"

"How did you know the MacCraes were rebels?" she whispered.

"This is Loyalist territory. The MacCraes look out of place and were in a recent skirmish."

Joshua scuttled over to make sure they were uninjured. "These men are taking a risk coming out here. I'm surprised the neighbors haven't ridden over to investigate the noise."

Betsy shivered when the obvious answer occurred to her. Joe

MacCrae had killed Liam Duffy and his neighbors in the skirmish and planned to exterminate the rest of the family. "Joshua, we have to get out of here."

"Suggest a plan. They're guarding our horses and weapons."

A ball ricocheted and hit a man in the thigh. Joe ordered his men to stop firing and collect kindling. Cursing low, Joshua brushed his hand over pine straw beneath him. "Dry as a bone. No rain here in a couple of weeks. He's going to burn their house down."

"But — but there's a woman inside and perhaps children with her!" Visions of her own house in Augusta burning rammed a knot of horror into Betsy's gut. "That's cold-blooded murder!"

More shots erupted from within the house. One showered them with pine bark and green needles, but Joshua's attention was elsewhere. "Listen. Crow caws — do you hear them?" He lifted his head and cawed: three, one, two.

"Indians!" Tom lifted up on elbows. "Where are they?"

"In the Duffy's corn near the road." Frustration puckered Joshua's brow. "They aren't able to help until dark — too late for the Duffys." The MacCraes had started a fire near the house. Joshua cawed several more times, and determination tensed his lips. "I told them to stay put for now."

A lobbed firebrand rolled five feet from the house and extinguished. The pitcher had better luck with the following two brands. With the left front corner of the house asmolder, Joe announced, "Your house is afire! Come out here without your weapons, and I promise I won't shoot you in your front yard."

An infant wailed, and people coughed inside. Flames crawled up the left side of the house, and an older child joined the baby in lamentation. Tears of helplessness and horror blurred Betsy's vision. Had the Duffys chosen to burn to death?

The front door whammed open, and they staggered out filthy and gagging: an elderly man, four women (one with a babe in arms), and five youths. The grandfather shook his fist. "You'll pay for this, MacCrae, I promise!"

***

The pain in Betsy's backside clawed up into her shoulders, distracting her from mulling over their fate. Although the MacCraes had smothered the fire, they'd bound the Duffys and loaded them into the wagon. Through early evening the party plodded westward. She couldn't stop thinking the MacCraes meant to murder the family and then loot the home.

The presence of three witnesses hobbled such a scheme. Joe had allowed them to ride their horses but had bound their hands. She suspected their lives had been spared because he half-believed her charade about being a spy.

Close to sundown, at the deserted intersection with the Ninety Six Road, he halted and ordered two men to escort Betsy, Joshua, and Tom into the woods. Then he and the rest of his men continued on the road with the Duffys.

Lady May plunged after the lead horse into the murk of pine barren on what appeared to be an old Indian track. Betsy's eyes grew accustomed to gloom, enabling her to maintain pace and avoid getting snagged on vines and low branches. Behind her she heard the horses of Joshua, Tom, and the second escort.

A putrid metallic odor intensified with each second, and they emerged in a small clearing. She gaped. Joshua whispered, "Ah, no." And Tom gulped.

Torchlight threw garish shadows over the carcasses of dead horses and bodies and severed limbs of men laid out by half a dozen filthy men in hunting shirts. Three other men, their heads just visible, heaved shovelfuls of sand out of a mass grave, and one cupped a hand to his mouth. "It's about got ready, Captain."

Betsy was unable to block out the stink of death, blood, and feces. Her bound wrists thwarted her attempt to reach her handkerchief. She panted, and her stomach churned.

"What now, Malachi? This is no place for a lady."

The MacCraes dismounted and saluted a sun-weathered man in his thirties. "Joe picked these three up on the road, Captain. They was headed out of Augusta. Wait 'til you hear their story."

"Cut their bonds. Get them down off their horses and bring them to me." The captain walked away, shoulders sagging.

The MacCraes marched them, unbound, to the north end of the clearing, where the stench wasn't intense. By torchlight, Betsy saw the captain's horse picketed in the brush and could hear a brook meander. He studied them. "I'm Captain Ned Murray. Who are you?" A musket shot sounded from about a mile distant, and the captain glared at Malachi. "What the devil — ?"

"It's my brother, sir. Cherokee stalked us while we was scouting." Another musket shot echoed through the dusk. "One shot Hosea. Joe spotted them again and gave chase ten minutes ago. Sounds like he finally found them. We got enough to deal with here without worrying about savages trying to loot us."

Betsy's initial fear was for Standing Wolf and Runs With Horses, and she flung a look of despair and grief at Joshua and Tom. Then the shots continued, eleven of them in all, and she read in the faces of her companions the realization of who had been on the receiving end of those shots. She hung her head. Every one of the MacCraes deserved to be hanged for murder.

Captain Murray's face was granite. "Good work." He braced his fists on his hips. "You three, I require your names."

Betsy firmed her jaw. "Our names aren't as important as our mission and the Ambrose ring."

His eyes widened, and his lips parted in surprise. "Well, I'll be — Knight to Queen."

Damn, he'd given her a password, and she'd no idea of the counter. Better keep bluffing. "Knight to *Bishop*."

Expression emptied from his face. "Give the two men food and drink if they require it, and see to their horses. I must have private conversation with this lady."

Joshua and Tom were marched away. Murray's shrewd look fixed on Betsy. "Hungry? I've small beer and dried venison."

She tried to consider the needs of the baby growing inside her, rather than murder and carnage. "Yes, sir, thank you."

After handing her a flask and satchel, he began a thoughtful pace back and forth. "The skirmish occurred about one-thirty this afternoon. We were sent on reconnaissance by Colonel Clarke and ambushed by Tories. They're all Tories around here. We prevailed." Well, that confirmed why no neighbors rode over to help the Duffys; they were dead. "I lost half my men and several horses." He glanced toward the mass grave. "Had it just been Tories dead out there, I'd have left them for scavengers, but the men and I felt it best to bury all of them. I hope the delay doesn't set us up for retaliation." He stopped pacing to eye her. "I must decide what to do with you and your companions."

She swallowed venison. "Let us go so we may continue our mission. Mr. MacCrae has already delayed us."

"You gave me the wrong counter awhile ago."

She tossed her head to cover her nervousness. "It was what I was given in my last correspondence."

"Blathering, incompetent fools," he muttered, "who never let the right hand know what the left hand is doing."

"I appreciate your caution, sir, however I have but three days to complete my mission. You must let us go."

"With all due respect, I must escort you to Colonel Clarke."

The last person she wanted to see was Elijah Clarke. Despairing that she wouldn't reach Camden in time to help her husband, she flung down the food and drink and frosted Murray with a glare. "Brown's Rangers are pursuing us." Murray's eyes bulged. "They won't pause to chat when they find you."

"How far behind are they?"

"When we were detained by MacCrae, no more than four hours."

Urgency tensed his face. "Thank you. I shall expedite our departure. There's Joe this moment, returned from dealing with those savages." He grasped his musket and ammunition box.

She snagged his arm. "It wasn't Indians that he executed. It was a family of Loyalists for whom he had personal enmity."

"Madam, do you know what you're saying?"

"I do, sir. MacCrae and his men weren't scouting. They were burning the Duffys' house. My companions and I saw it with our own eyes. Just a few minutes ago I counted eleven shots — one for each Duffy. They were murdered. As MacCrae's commanding officer, I charge you with dispensing appropriate justice."

Wrath chilled his face, and from the complexity of emotion that followed, she wondered whether he were more outraged at MacCrae for his barbarism or her for exposing it. He snatched his arm away from her. "Attend me."

At the mass grave, men were shoving in horse carcasses and militiamen's bodies. The battered wagon used to haul the Duffys sat off to the side, and Betsy shuddered at bloodstains blotching the wood. "Captain, he used that wagon to transport the family."

"And that looks like fresh blood on it." Murray raised his voice. "Joe, over here. George, Fergus — cease work for now. Pete, Raymond, Jeremy — get out there and help the sentries. Step lively. Brown's Rangers are in the neighborhood."

Betsy motioned Joshua and Tom to join her. Captain Murray drew up tall and imposing before Joe MacCrae, whose lower lip took a sullen downturn during his salute. "Mr. MacCrae, this woman says you murdered civilians with whom you had personal grievance and disguised it as military action."

Joe feigned being flabbergasted and gaped at Betsy. "She said that?" He laughed. "Captain, she's lying. Did she also tell you some crazy story about being a spy for the Continentals? And you believed that, too?"

"She isn't lying, sir." Tom stepped forward with Joshua. "All three of us watched the MacCraes burn the Duffy family's house this afternoon and load them into that wagon."

"Notice the blood stains on the wagon, sir," said Joshua.

"MacCrae, you'll hang for it."

"I don't think so."

Betsy heard the sound of muskets being cocked and realized that MacCrae kinfolk had taken aim on them and the non-MacCraes in the clearing. Her palms grew sweaty. Murray scowled. "This is treachery!"

"I ain't ending my life on a rope."

A musket discharged from the road. Everyone heard the warning of a sentry — "Rangers!" — before the sentry howled in agony.

"To arms, men!"

The issue of civilian murder tabled for the moment, the MacCraes trained their muskets on the incoming trail while the other men snatched their weapons. Betsy, Tom, and Joshua rushed for their horses, but sneering MacCraes blocked their escape.

Everyone waited while seconds spilled past. The militiamen in the clearing sweated and listened to sounds of the forest night and the sputtering of torches. "Rebels!" Adam Neville's voice ended minutes of taut nerves. "You're surrounded. Lay down your weapons, and we promise you quarter!"

"Quarter, hell!" A MacCrae spat. "Tarleton's Quarter!"

"No, men! Listen to me, and do as he says! I recognize his voice. You'll be treated well. Lay down your weapons." The captain threw down his musket and knife. Other Whigs followed his example, even the MacCraes, until the shush of muskets, fowlers, knives, and tomahawks landing on pine straw had ceased. Remembering that fanatic look in Adam Neville's eyes, Betsy couldn't envision him granting quarter to Murray's party. What made Murray think otherwise?

"The lady and her two companions remain where they are, off to the side. The rest of you walk to the center of the clearing. Keep your hands where we can see them."

Murray's men shuffled like skittish sheep past the firearms. Rangers emerged from cover, soundless wraiths, weapons ready. They passed Betsy, Tom, and Joshua and hemmed in the Whigs. "Be still, men." Murray radiated calm and trust.

Joe sneered. "Look at them sons of bitches. Damn them."

"Keep your mouth shut, MacCrae." Murray smiled at Adam.

"I won't! Damn you, Captain, you've sold us out!"

MacCrae dove for a discarded musket, rolled to a crouch, and fired. Four more Whigs dove through the rotten-egg stench of blackpowder smoke for firearms, and one even managed to discharge his before the Rangers opened fire and transformed the clearing into a fusion of sulfur and scarlet slaughter.

CHAPTER TWENTY

Cloaked by the chaos, Joshua and Tom hoisted Betsy astride into Lady May's saddle and thrust Lucas's musket into one hand. "Hold on! Yee-aww!" Tom slapped the mare's flank. Joshua whizzed past on his gelding, and Betsy, clinging to musket and reins, guided Lady May after him toward the road. Branches swiped at her face, and she bent low behind the mare's neck to dodge them.

Betsy emerged on the road with Tom bringing up the rear. Joshua's horse gave a nervous snort, and he stroked the beast's neck. "Fly for Ninety Six!" He sent his gelding galloping northward.

"Ninety Six?" Betsy kicked the mare after him.

"That way they won't look for us in Camden!"

Admiration for her uncle's ingenuity overcame the fatigue locking her muscles. For the next few minutes, she focused on encouraging and maintaining Lady May's gallop. The orb of the moon, near full, painted their escape route silver and lent excellent visibility ahead and behind. However as Betsy had feared that afternoon, the mare was too worn for flight. Joshua and his mount pulled ahead, and Tom's gelding inched past, and their lead over her increased.

Joshua threw a look over his shoulder. "Faster!"

"She's too tired!" As Betsy spoke, she felt the mare's first shudder. She might have used the riding crop to exact another quarter mile gallop from the poor beast, but after a glance behind, she realized it wouldn't have helped.

Riders pursued them, and from the way they were bearing down, only a rested Lady May might have outrun them. Joshua and Tom continued to pull ahead of her, and tears of frustration mingling with sweat stung her eyes. Was the musket clenched in her hand loaded? She flung another look behind to spot a rider out in front closing on her, and she gritted her teeth. By all the gods, she wasn't going down without a fight.

Lady May continued to lose speed, and foam rose to her lips. "Steady, girl. This is going to be terribly loud." Betsy cocked the musket and snatched another look behind. The Ranger out front had eaten up the distance between them and was only about thirty feet behind her. "Good, my Lady. Good girl." The road ahead lay flat and even. "Now's our chance. Steady, there!"

Betsy twisted about, dragged up the musket, and squeezed the trigger. Holding it one-handed, she'd no strength to aim, and when the musket belched saffron fire, the kick nearly flung her from the saddle. Lady May neighed in fright and stumbled, and Betsy regained control, her right shoulder knotted from wrenching backward. A grim smile stretched her lips. She'd heard the pursuing horse's scream of agony, and she'd seen it collapse and fling the rider off. One down. How many were still back there?

Lather spewed off Lady May's mouth, and her breathing grew labored. Another shudder wracked her. Tom and Joshua had reduced speed, realizing she was in trouble after hearing the musket. Betsy flung another look over her shoulder. "Give me whatever you can, girl! Here comes another of those Rangers."

Her musket grasped by the still-warm barrel, she waited until she heard the breathing of both Ranger and horse. Peripheral vision furnished her with correct timing. The butt caught the man on the jaw and knocked him clean off the saddle. Even though the musket was yanked from her hands in the process, she let out a whoop of primeval victory that would have done her Creek grandfather proud.

Adam Neville was upon her seconds later and received a taste of riding crop before falling back to reassess his strategy. When he bore down on her again, he deftly hooked the crop from her hands with the butt of his musket. Her efforts at fighting him off with her bare hands would have yielded doubtful results, but Lady May had given her all and dropped from gallop into canter, thus putting an end to Betsy's flight.

Rangers flew past to apprehend Joshua and Tom, but Betsy's companions brought their own flight to an end upon her capture and waited in the road to surrender. Adam gripped her hands, and, controlling his own horse with his knees, pried the reins from between her fingers and slowed their horses to a walk. "Madam." He took a couple of deep breaths. "I hereby arrest you and your accomplices in the name of His Majesty King George the Third."

***

Exhaustion avalanched upon Betsy. The Rangers hauled her up on Adam's horse, on pillion, took Lady May in tow, and headed back south, where they met more Rangers and a caravan of riderless horses. All Whigs who'd survived the original battle now lay with their compatriots and enemies in the mass grave they'd spent the afternoon digging. No muss, no fuss. How convenient for Neville and the Rangers.

They established camp with pines and oaks shielding them from the road and lit no fire, picketing horses beneath an oak. Betsy sat on a blanket spread by her uncle and stared at pairs of boots and moccasins traipsing back and forth before her in the moonlight. Tom brought water and trail rations and fussed over her because she showed no interest in either. She'd been awake for almost twenty-four hours. Food wasn't what her body craved. Wild flight on horseback couldn't be good for the baby.

Adam walked over, fists on hips. She glanced at him and resisted the urge to smirk at the damage her riding crop had inflicted on his lower lip. The swelling was evident even by moonlight. "Why were you headed for Ninety Six?" His injured lip fuzzed his speech.

"We were trying to escape you."

"Don't waste my time."

"You're wasting your own time. You're within the law to hang me. There's room for my body in that mass grave."

"Are you such a shrew with Clark?" She bit her lip and squeezed her eyes shut. Had Clark escaped the assassin's knife? "You headed to Ninety Six to join your husband, didn't you?" She opened her eyes and remained mute. "Such devotion. Misplaced, I assure you. Haven't you wondered why he married you?"

"He loves me."

"Perhaps, but he appreciates your intelligence more. He abhors working with numbers, you see, and no other young lady in Augusta had quite the bright mind or knack for the ledger as you do. Having you around means he isn't bothered by the less appealing aspects of business." Adam leaned closer. "And what a clever way to circumvent paying your most valuable employee. Marry her." Betsy's exhaustion didn't quite deflect his dart of doubt. "If I were you, I'd think twice about blind devotion."

Could Clark be that callous? The trust between them was just rickety enough to start teetering. Her head drooped, concealing her disillusionment. "I don't know where my husband is. Did you not read the letter I left for Sarah and Lucas?"

"Letter? A good-bye letter for the O'Neals?"

Her heart sank. He hadn't seen the letter. "Yes."

"We left Augusta at four o'clock in the morning, having received a tip that you were headed to Alton. I admit admiration for the trail your Creek friends left. We almost followed them back to Alton, thinking there were five of you headed south, rather than the two Creek." Interesting. Adam didn't realize Runs With Horses and Standing Wolf had come with them to South Carolina, and he didn't suspect the brothers were out there in the woods somewhere. "When I left Augusta, the O'Neals hadn't yet awakened to find you missing and read your letter. Apprise me of the content of this letter."

"I intended it for Thomas Brown."

"Of course you did. Cease stalling."

"I told him I remembered that the Spaniard who held me at knifepoint referenced the Ambrose spy ring as French-loving fools and implied that their mission was to strip Britain of her military command." Adam stared at her. "I also related to him that I'd become a subject of ridicule to the inhabitants of Augusta. I found this distressing, body and spirit, and deemed it best to spend the duration of my pregnancy with a relation elsewhere. That's why I was headed to Ninety Six."

"And Clark shall meet you there — when?"

"I've already told you I don't know where he is or what his plans are." She studied the blanket again, her head nodding. It was becoming as difficult to stay awake as it had become obvious that Adam meant to capture Clark and administer the King's Justice, despite his profession of friendship and concern.

"Who is this relation in Ninety Six?"

"I've not told anyone, not even my foster parents."

Adam knelt, grasped her upper arms, and forced eye contact. "If you don't tell me who you're visiting in Ninety Six, I shall consider that portion of your story to be a lie."

"Martha Neely, my father's aunt." Perhaps the old woman was still alive.

He released her and stood. "Bah. Women run after their husbands and forget about their kin when they're distressed."

"The sampling of women on which you base your conclusion appears to be —" She searched for the right word. " — rather *small*. Sir."

He digested the insult without retort in a moment of icy silence. "I doubt you'll provide me with more useful information tonight. However, on the morrow we shall resume this conversation. Geoffrey."

One of the Rangers trotted over and saluted. "Sir?"

"Bind these three."

"Yes, sir."

Joshua, who'd been sitting nearby, struggled to a standing position and faced Adam. "Bind us? Why, Lieutenant?"

"We've been on the road almost as long as you have. I don't plan to post a sentry tonight and won't let you run off after going through such lengths to capture you."

"We're too tired to run far."

"You'd be surprised how far rebels can run when they're tired. Good night, madam. And good night, gentlemen."

* * *

Betsy fell asleep with her eyes full of Altair, Deneb, and Vega, brilliant blue-white stars forming the Summer Triangle. Too exhausted for her bonds to impact sleep, she also ignored her grimy clothing and the sultry, stifling night. She jerked awake, exhausted, to the stench of rancid bear grease. Starlight glinted on a knife in the hands of an Indian kneeling beside her. The first second, terror tore through her. Then she recognized Standing Wolf, who signed for her silence and cut her bonds.

After he helped her up, she trudged with Joshua, Tom, and the warrior to the horses, where Runs With Horses held their mounts and firearms ready. Lady May dragged along, as unrefreshed as Betsy. Runs With Horses brought the mare into the moonlight, caressed her flanks, withers, and neck, and whispered to her, whereupon the mare revived a bit. He turned the reins over to Betsy.

The five walked their horses well around the camp of snoring Rangers in the pre-dawn humidity, and only when they reached the road half a mile south did they risk speech. Joshua clasped arms with both Creek. "Thank you."

"Thank Creator, who opened a way at last." Runs With Horses gestured west, where the Rangers lay asleep. "Why you don't let us slit their throats?"

"Trust me, they'll head to Ninety Six at dawn, not Camden."

The warrior grunted. "We must ride for Camden until dawn, then, two hours at most. Horses are tired. We are tired. But we know a place safe for rest."

CHAPTER TWENTY-ONE

W hen the Creek guided them back to the Duffys' cabin, Joshua concurred with his cousins on their choice of haven. Neither the Duffys nor their neighbors were returning. Betsy was too tired to object out of principle.

The horses picketed out back, the travelers took turns at watch. Mid-afternoon Betsy awakened with her right shoulder knotted from one-handed musket firing. While the men waited outside, she washed and changed her shift to the spare she'd taken with her to Alton. Then all of them polished off a pot of rabbit stew full of vegetables from the garden and mopped out their bowls with slabs of day-old bread from the beehive oven. To replace the knives Runs With Horses hadn't been able to recover from the Rangers, they confiscated three pristine hunting knives from the family's stash.

They left the cabin in the evening about six, bypassing the road south to Orangeburg within minutes. By sunset their road had taken an east-northeast bearing. Beneath moonlight, the swelter eased from the air. They put twenty miles between themselves and the cabin before camping off the road near a creek in the pine forest at the west edge of the Saxagotha Territory.

One homesteader they'd passed just after the Orangeburg Road
had given them a cheery wave and mentioned they were the first
travelers he'd seen all day. Still, they ate trail rations for supper and lit
no fire. The odds were great that the Rangers had galloped to Ninety
Six in search of their escapees, and the homesteader's greeting seemed
to confirm it, but no one wanted to risk being caught.

Tuesday morning dawned clear, and the party took to the rolling
road again before full daylight. The excellent time they made placed
them near Fort Granby and the junction of the Broad and Saluda
Rivers before noon. The swampy terrain hosted the first mosquitoes
Betsy had encountered on the trip; alas, she and her companions
waited several hours amidst the mosquitoes for the ferry that crossed
the Congaree River.

After debarking the ferry, they pressed on northeast. Nightfall
found them camped north of the road leading to King's Mountain: an
easy day's travel to Camden on the morrow.

They built a campfire and partook of roasted rabbits, dried fruit,
trail bread, and coffee. Betsy studied the Creek, and for the first time
she wondered how far her father had adopted Indian ways. Did he
look like Runs With Horses and Standing Wolf, an oiled, muscular
mass of tattoos with a shaven head and teeth glinting white in the
firelight? She visualized her mother in the arms of a Creek warrior,
and the picture her imagination yielded was alien, queer, disquieting.
How much did she and Mathias Hale have to share with each other
beyond blood? Supine on her bedroll, she fell asleep contemplating
the familiar territory of her dilemma with Clark. But later she dreamed
that Laughing Eyes, wise and unsmiling, whispered Creek in her ear.

***

Camden, South Carolina entered history as the Fredericksburg
township on the east side of the Wateree River circa 1733. However,
not until the late 1750s did trade in the area assume cohesion and an
actual town emerge. Fredericksburg metamorphosed into Pine Tree
Hill, a quaint name that yielded to the politics of prominent citizens,
predominantly one Joseph Kershaw, who wished to honor Charles
Pratt, Lord Camden, for his intercessory measures in Parliament on
their behalf. In 1780, Camden was one of but a handful of South
Carolina towns to possess a genuine courthouse — no small

accomplishment for a backcountry hamlet that had, one generation earlier, been just a few plantations.

Five major roads fed the town like anchoring strands that draw insects into the heart of a spider's web. Betsy and her companions entered Camden on the afternoon of Wednesday, July 19, after passing Fort Cary and taking the ferry across the Wateree.

Camden's non-wartime population probably equaled that of Augusta, but the presence of Francis Rawdon's portion of the British army and its camp followers doubled that population and quadrupled the business opportunities and headaches of residents. The five walked their horses on the main east-west road, taking in the throbbing, laughing, stinking, sweating colorful life cluttering the streets. Betsy had never seen so many redcoats in one place; and the excursion provided her first exposure to Jägers and Hessians. Many soldiers weren't "coated" at all and had, in deference to the relentless, un-British heat, doffed their wool coats to become "white shirts."

Sutlers spilled over from Market Square into the town square: entrepreneurs taking advantage of soldiers ready to part with their coin. Tom ogled a bosomy chicken vendor, and when the young woman pulled a feather off the mound of one breast where sweat had pasted it and blew it after him, a grinning Joshua brushed Betsy's sleeve. "I wager he doesn't remember later that she sells chickens." Betsy chuckled. Tom's bright hair would, no doubt, attract the attention of many ladies.

They turned north, away from the portion of city enclosed in a palisade by the British, onto Broad Street, once a Catawba trail. Betsy and Joshua rode side by side, the Creek followed, and Tom brought up the rear. Joshua leaned over to her. "You think you'll be all right here with your cousin?"

"Oh, yes. You're headed west on the morrow, then?" His nod of confirmation brought a wave of ambivalence to her. She couldn't be two places at once, and she'd convinced herself that tracking down her husband was more important than locating her parents. "Does he resemble you — my father?"

"We both look like Mother, but I'm half a head taller and have more meat on my bones." A rakish grin ate his expression. "And I'm more handsome."

"With half a head more room to absorb flattery." Still unsure of herself in the realm of the Creek, she smiled back. "When you find them — both of them — tell them where I am. Tell my mother I love her. And when you go back through Augusta, give my love to Sarah and Lucas."

"I shall do that."

Tom trotted his gelding ahead to them. "You cannot miss the Leaping Stag in this town. Look yonder."

In retrospect, Betsy realized she'd expected to see a homey little bed-and-breakfast tavern. What greeted them instead was a two-story brick hybrid inn and tavern the size of several townhouses. From the look of it, the place could sleep two-dozen guests. At least as many horses stood hitched out front, and it wasn't yet four o'clock.

Joshua craned back his neck. "Jove's arse, Betsy. All of Alton would fit inside that place. I wonder what one week's worth of rum costs."

"More than any of us make in a year." Tom seemed just as impressed as Joshua did.

"Excellent location. Well-to-do district, and there's the courthouse yonder —"

"Out of the way, you rabble, out of the way!"

The five coaxed their horses to the side of the street as a gaudy carriage rolled up to the Leaping Stag, accompanied by ten redcoats on horseback. After it squeaked to a stop, the doorman leaped down to yank open the door for a stout colonel who waddled to the entrance of the tavern with bodyguards marching behind. The remainder of the entourage made no effort to remove themselves from the road.

After Colonel and company disappeared indoors, Betsy caught the whiff of a fragrance even Widow Abby Fuller couldn't have afforded — though whether it came from the colonel or the tavern she couldn't tell. "Cousin Emma's done quite well."

Joshua gestured for the door. "Well, don't just stand there catching flies on your tongue. Go on inside and find her. We'll secure the horses and join you in a moment."

Tom assisted her in dismounting, and she did what she could to straighten her homespun petticoat and short jacket, even though four days of travel had creased in the dust and grime. Just inside the warm, cavernous common room smelling of tobacco, yeast, and human musk, a tall, ropy man in linen and silk blocked her way. "May I help you?"

Betsy looked up his nose. "I'm here to see Emma Branwell."

"I don't think so."

"I *do* think so."

"She doesn't have an appointment scheduled with you for this afternoon. There's the door. Good day."

What an obnoxious cur. "I'm her cousin Betsy, just arrived from Augusta."

"Hrumph!" He eyed her from head to foot. "I shall convey word of your arrival." He turned to leave. "And don't move from that spot while I'm gone."

Afraid she'd pickpocket the clientele, eh? Betsy blew out a sigh of exasperation and propped her fists on her hips.

An ensign from a nearby table swaggered up and strolled his gaze over her in a way she didn't find comfortable. "I heard you ask old Todd for Mrs. Branwell. You new in town?"

"I just arrived from Augusta."

"Ooh, an exotic lady from faraway Georgia colony." He made a bow straight out of King George's court. "Terrance Halsey, Ensign, at your service, madam. I'm off duty until the morrow at eight and would consider myself the most fortunate man alive to be able to show you a bit of Camden." He extended his hand in expectation that she'd give him hers.

What a rude bore, and how dared he fancy her a slattern in so fine an establishment? She turned back in the direction the other obnoxious fellow had taken. "No, thank you."

"I was just paid this noon," the ensign whispered.

She scowled and faced him. "I said no. Which are you: deaf or half-witted?"

One of the leering soldiers from Halsey's table imitated to perfection the sound of chair legs collapsing to deposit someone's arse on the floor. Halsey flashed Betsy a mirthless smile. "Perhaps another time, madam." He bowed and slipped back to the jeers of his tablemates.

"Betsy? Oh, it *is* you, dear!"

Betsy beheld a pretty, plump brunette in her early twenties bustling through the common room for her. "Hello, Emma." She smiled and hugged her cousin. "You're looking quite well." Not just well, but wealthy. The material for Emma's polonaise gown cost more than all of Betsy's petticoats together.

"And you're looking — er — happy to be at the end of your travels. Oh, you poor dear. Everything gone in the fire, and now you and your husband have come here to start anew."

A gust of wind signaled the entrance of Joshua and Tom. The doorman rushed over to throw them out, and Betsy waved at him. "Yoo hoo, excuse me, but those two gentlemen are with me." His sneer shoved subsurface, the doorman allowed them to pass. "Emma, this is my Uncle Joshua Hale, from Alton."

"Pleased to meet you, madam." Joshua kissed Emma's hand.

"Likewise, Mr. Hale. Oh, and you must be Betsy's husband." Emma rushed past in a cloud of lilac perfume, caught Tom by the elbow, and dragged him into their little circle. "My, such a handsome fellow. You two make the perfect couple." She turned on Betsy. "Forgive me if I seem a bit distracted, dear. I wasn't expecting all of you so soon, and I was hoping you might arrive a few days later, after the criminal for that horrific murder had been caught."

"Murder?" said Betsy, Tom, and Joshua at the same time.

"Oh, it was ghastly. They found a Spaniard flayed alive in town square last night after first being shot in the knee."

Joshua coughed. "Excuse me, did you say a Spaniard was flayed alive?"

"Horrid, isn't it?" Emma lifted white fingertips to her pearl choker.

Hair polarized on the back of Betsy's neck. Something about the murder sounded familiar.

Joshua licked his lips. "Mrs. Branwell, might I inquire whether the Seventeenth Light has been through Camden recently?"

"Why, now, Mr. Hale, I do attempt to keep abreast of the units in town because as you can see —" She indicated the common room, inhabited by nearly thirty redcoats, including the Colonel, who drummed his fingers on a tabletop with impatience. " — soldiers are important clientele. I shall inquire of Margaret to be certain, but I believe she entertained an officer from the Seventeenth late last night."

Shock emptied Joshua's face of color, and Betsy and Tom rushed to his side. "Are you all right, Uncle? You look ill."

His gaze passed between them, and he lowered his voice to a whisper. "The coincidence is too great. Watch yourselves. Lieutenant Fairfax has been in town, I'm certain of it."

CHAPTER TWENTY-TWO

E mma peered over Betsy's shoulder. "Shall I fetch you some spirits, Mr. Hale? Of a sudden, you look rather pallid."

He shook his head. "I'm fine now, madam."

She clasped her hands. "Well, then, I still haven't been introduced to Betsy's husband."

Tom opened his mouth to clear up the misunderstanding, and Joshua slapped him on the back. "Where are your manners, lad? Mister Thomas Alexander Sheridan. Mrs. Emma Branwell."

Tom covered up astonishment by kissing Emma's hand. In the next second, Betsy understood her uncle's logic. Searching for a rebel spy in a town of British soldiers was risky enough, but if Fairfax knew they were in Camden, he'd make good on his threats to her at the Savannah River ferry crossing.

"Such a majestic name." Emma fluttered her eyelashes at Tom. "No doubt you were named for Alexander the Great, master cordwainer that you are. Betsy was stingy with details in her letter, but at least she told me your trade, if not your name. I've a client list for you if that uncle of yours can spare you."

"Thank you, madam."

Jitters in her stomach, Betsy eyed Tom. With each passing
second, the lie deepened. Tom, her friend and an apprentice, had
become her husband and a master. For the moment, he seemed to be
rolling with the deception — a good sign since Emma had offered
built-in business for a cordwainer. However, Tom would have to
acquire a set of tools. Betsy cleared her throat. "Ah, speaking of
Tom's uncle, his name is Isaac Sheridan. Do you know where we
might find his shop?"

"Isaac Sheridan?" Emma frowned. "And he's a cordwainer?
I'm not familiar with the name."

"How about Samuel Taylor?"

"I'm afraid his name isn't familiar to me, either."

Both names must be code names. Without "Uncle" Isaac or
Samuel Taylor, she wasn't sure how to find Clark, and there was also
the matter of tools for Tom. "Perhaps both gentlemen are members of
a multi-partner business."

"Perhaps. There are several here. I shall write the names and
directions for you under the condition that the three of you return and
dine with Abel and me tonight for supper."

Betsy cast a skeptical look at Tom. "If we find your uncle, he'll
want us to dine with him tonight, too."

"Don't worry. I'll manage Uncle Isaac. Dining with your cousin
will provide far better company." Tom kissed Emma's hand again, and
she flushed with appraisal and flattery.

***

In the street with their horses and the Creek, Tom shucked the
confidence he'd mustered indoors. "Joshua, why did you mislead Mrs.
Branwell into thinking I'm Betsy's husband?"

"You two don't need the name of John Clark Sheridan following
you around. I suspect Fairfax murdered the Spaniard last night. You
want that species of varmint tracking you? Even if *he* never returns,
Neville has figured out by now that we've duped him. He won't waste
time riding here to search for Clark."

Tom sighed. "I see your point. But it isn't ethical. And I'm not
even a journeyman yet."

Irritation gripped Joshua's face. "Lad, look around you. Do you think you'll find a rebel spy in this town using ethical means? You aren't in Augusta anymore. Play the part."

"But —" The two Creek were giving Tom knowing grins, and a blush crawled up his neck. "But Betsy's your niece —"

"See here." Joshua clapped a hand to Tom's shoulder, and Betsy heard sarcasm in her uncle's tone. "This is rough business, but you have to do it. Betsy won't find a better friend anywhere than you. Settle up with Clark down the road if you feel you have to —" He gave the street a baleful glance. "If you can find him, that is."

Betsy peered at Joshua. "You don't think we'll find him? If the murdered Spaniard was the assassin who chased Clark, perhaps Clark is somewhere nearby."

"I wager the Spaniard *was* the assassin tracking Clark. Very few Spaniards in these parts. Suppose Fairfax captured him and tortured him to death, obtaining what information he could about the Ambrose ring. Suppose Fairfax also found out Clark is in town. Can Clark afford to surface right now? No. He's gone deep underground."

Betsy scowled. "But I'm his wife."

"And if Fairfax gets hold of you, he won't waste time adding what you know to what he knows. The Ambrose ring isn't going to let you and Clark within a mile of each other until some of this blows over. Sure, we'll see if we can find Isaac Sheridan this afternoon, but I'm doubtful he'll show. My advice is to sit tight with your heads down, ears open, and mouths shut."

Tom nodded, looking none too happy. "I'll need a complete set of tools. I brought what I have, but it isn't enough."

"Well, then, we'll shop around for tools."

"I haven't much money."

"Show the shoemakers on this list Mrs. Branwell gave us how talented you are. I cannot imagine any of them hurting for business in a town hosting the British army."

Betsy sensed Tom was still weighing his worth. Clark really should have given him journeyman status months earlier. "Tom, forget being an apprentice anymore. You're a journeyman now."

She watched him grow an inch taller. "Right."

"That's it. Play the part, both of you, and after awhile, perhaps you'll be able to extricate Clark from this web he's woven for himself." Joshua unfolded Emma's list. "Now, let's see whose name is first."

***

Shadows lengthened on Camden's dusty streets. A block over from the courthouse, Tom received yet another invitation to return on the morrow for employment at a handsome rate of pay. Alas, he informed his traveling companions, shoemakers Gamble and Wade hadn't heard of Isaac Sheridan or Samuel Taylor, either.

Joshua glanced at his watch. "Six o'clock. We're due at the Leaping Stag soon." He assisted Betsy into the saddle.

"I wish we'd had just one clue. I feel so useless."

"Clark cannot hide forever. But since we didn't find Uncle Isaac, we need to consider where to spend the night. I've little money for the return journey and must be frugal with it."

"Emma might house us tonight and suggest a place to live."

"Her tastes are more expensive than what you and Tom can afford. By the by, he's a fine fellow. Part of me's hoping you won't find Clark." He grinned. "Whoa, there, do I detect a blush?"

"He's my friend."

"I'm mighty glad to hear it. The two of you put your heads together. You'll do some fancy thinking." He mounted his gelding and then craned his neck. "Where's the lad got off to? Ho, there he is down King Street with his horse." Joshua nudged his gelding in Tom's direction, Betsy coaxed Lady May into a walk, and the Creek followed. "What have you got into, Tom?"

Afoot, one hand holding the reins to his horse, Tom examined the sideboard of a large wagon parked before a two-story wood house. As Betsy caught up, he ran his fingers along a wheel. Then he pivoted to them, discovery lighting his expression. "This is it! The wagon!" Seeing blank gazes, he hopped from one foot to the other. "Remember? The wagon your furniture was hauled away in!"

Betsy clicked her tongue and sent the mare up ahead. "How can you be sure? You said you only saw it for a second or two."

"I lied." Tom helped her down. "I was actually standing there watching the men load the wagon with your belongings for about three minutes before somebody hit me."

"Tom, wagons all look alike."

"Not really. See how the left rear wheel is newer than the others? I remember that. And look at that big knot in the wood just above the axle. It rather looks like — er — um —"

"Like a woman's bum." Joshua joined them beside the wagon. "I wouldn't have forgotten such a detail, either."

Men. Betsy grinned and then gazed the length of the street. "This *is* King Street, where Sheridan and Taylor supposedly reside. Perhaps my furniture is in one of these houses."

Tom passed his reins to Joshua and rubbed his hands together. "Let's peek in windows, starting here."

Leaving Joshua and the Creek with the horses, Betsy and Tom headed for a first-floor window of the house. He stared inside. "Clark's workbench!"

Her breath fogging the glass, she peered in, too. "Zounds, it *is* his workbench — at least a part of it. And there's the wardrobe from the bedroom. I wager my extra clothing is still in the top drawer. I see two of our dining chairs, too. Nothing's in order. Looks like they just unloaded the wagon and didn't sort furniture." She backed away, unsure of whether to feel jubilant or angry. Had Clark planned to set up house there?

Joshua waved them on. "Don't just stand there. See if anyone's in. We shall watch the horses."

They climbed the steps, and Betsy knocked at the door. No one answered, so Tom knocked loudly, still with no response from within. They found the door unlocked and entered.

A lack of dust inside implied the house hadn't gone long unoccupied. She plunged forward around furniture. "Clark? Clark, are you in here? It's Betsy and Tom!"

Tom slid open a drawer in the workbench. "His tools. They must plan for him to occupy the house."

"Looks that way. Hello? Hello, is anyone home?" She opened a drawer from the wardrobe and heaved a sigh of relief. "My shifts, petticoats, jackets, stockings." After a pause, she began lifting out each piece. "I don't know when Clark's coming back, but I need clean clothing now."

"Take it." He shook out a canvas sack and handed it to her. As soon as she'd stuffed in all her clothing and her extra pair of shoes, he walked the sack out to Joshua.

The bottom drawer still held Clark's shirts, breeches, and waistcoats. She ran her fingers over them and fancied she smelled the faint citrus of his soap.

"May I help you, madam?"

With a jump, she turned to the foot of the stairs, where a heavyset, blond man in his thirties stood, a huge gold ring emblazoned with a family crest gleaming upon his right forefinger. Lace at his throat and wrists failed to soften the chill in his pale blue eyes. She swallowed, shut the drawer, and straightened her shoulders. "Where did you get this furniture?"

"Perhaps I should be the one asking the questions. You have, after all, entered my house unbidden." Somewhere in that perfect English of his lurked the trace of an accent.

"We knocked. Several times. No one came to the door."

"Common courtesy dictates that you return at another time when the occupant is receiving guests." He twirled a silver-handled ebony walking stick and pointed it toward the door.

She lifted her chin, aware that Tom had returned and hovered in the doorway. "I hardly need the courtesy. This furniture is mine, stolen from my home in Augusta, Georgia a week ago."

An aristocratic gust of laughter escaped him. "I purchased it from an estate sale in Charles Town back in June."

She frowned, as much perturbed by his arrogance as her own inability to place his origins. "You may have spent your coin on it, but I assure you a crime was committed, and it's my stolen furniture. I found my clothing in this drawer and that of my husband in the drawer below it. His tools lie in that drawer over there. And I'm certain my grandmother's china is somewhere in this house, along with our bed, dining room table —"

"To whom would madam report this crime?" He dabbed a perfumed handkerchief across sweaty eyebrows. "Madam wishes to see my receipt for this furniture, perhaps?"

He had her there. If she told the British, the entire story would unravel, and she'd land in jail. "Where is my husband, John Clark Sheridan?"

"I do not know such a person."

"Play dumb, then. He told me the Ambrose spy ring was multinational, and you most certainly are not a colonist. Nor are you British, French, or Spanish — but from your sunburn and obvious discomfort with Carolina heat, I wager the summers are quite cool where you call home." His eyes widened just a bit and glittered with menace on her. "Perhaps you know Clark by some code name, not unlike the code names Isaac Sheridan and Samuel Taylor. Is the entire ring in hiding now? Camden's a dangerous town for you these days.

After all, if assassins from the powerful Rightful Blood can be flayed alive, you never know when one of your own allies might be murdered."

"Camden is also a dangerous town for those who pry where they have no business. Leave this house and do not return."

Betsy pursed her lips. "You look like someone accustomed to delivering messages. Deliver a message to my husband. Inform him I'm here and have grown annoyed at chasing him around the colonies. He knows where to find me." She stomped from the house. Tom exited after her and shut the door.

Shadows of evening engulfed the house where her belongings resided, beyond her ability to recover for the time. Damn the Ambrose spy ring. Damn the British, too. Camden wasn't half as colorful as it had seemed that afternoon.

CHAPTER TWENTY-THREE

J oshua dismounted and helped Betsy off Lady May. "I fancy you flung the gauntlet back there."

"You fancy correctly. He claimed he bought my furniture in Charles Town and denied knowing Clark."

Seven blond-haired, big-boned Jägers rode up before the Leaping Stag in a cloud of dust and bombast: "Out aff zhe vay!"

Betsy led her horse down the crowded hitching post with Tom and Joshua and then stared at the rosy-cheeked Jägers, swaggering to the door of the tavern. "Tom! He's German!"

"Of course. Jägers are German."

"No, that obnoxious macaroni at the house. Did you hear his accent? He looked and sounded like those Jägers. He's German."

"German?" Joshua frowned. "That makes no sense. Germans are allied with the British. Spaniards stole your furniture."

"If a faction of Spaniards ignores Spain's alliance with France and sends out assassins, a faction of Germans could be working with the Continentals and the Spanish."

"Uhhhh, Betsy." Tom grabbed his head as if it hurt. "My head is spinning with too many plots and intrigues."

Joshua clasped her shoulder. "You're grasping at straws. Slow down."

"I want my furniture back!" She bit at a quiver of impotence and loss in her lower lip. "I want my husband back, and I want my *life* back."

"I doubt you'll ever get back the life you had in Augusta."

She gaped at him, her doubts escalating, and squashed down panic. She'd given chase because she loved Clark, but at every juncture, he receded from her.

"The answers aren't going to come easy, I fear. The Ambrose ring is crafty. Each member has at least two identities. Perhaps that fellow at the house pretended a German accent, just to keep you pondering why Germans would steal your furniture." He released her.

Tom took her hand and pulled her around to face him. "On the morrow, I shall accept the situation with Gamble and Wade. They're right off King Street. It will give me the opportunity to keep an eye on your furniture and that fellow at the house." When she hung her head, he squeezed her hand. "Let's not draw attention to ourselves. It may chase the Ambrose ring away."

"I know it's frustrating, but listen to Tom." Joshua kissed her forehead. "And listen to your stomach, because if it sounds like mine, it's empty of trail rations and ready for a meal."

Suspend the chase. Wait passively. Betsy grimaced. How she hated passivity.

***

The slave placed a second two-inch-thick filet mignon on Tom's empty plate, and he swigged red wine. "I'm not a prolific writer. I should have written Uncle Isaac three months ago, when he first proposed the partnership. We were so busy in Augusta, and there was that fuss over the capture of Charles Town. I didn't think he'd move on to Cousin Edwin's in New York, just as I never dreamed my house would burn. But here we are in Camden, and no Uncle Isaac, and no home, and Betsy's with child —"

"You're with child?" Emma, her face flushed from wine, smiled at Betsy and fanned herself. "How wonderful, dear. I'm envious. You aren't showing yet. When will the baby arrive?"

Betsy ignored the soft grunting sounds from her right, where Emma's middle-aged husband, Abel, packed away a third filet. Where did the scrawny fellow find room for it? "By Yule."

"Will you follow your Uncle Isaac to New York, then?"

Tom shook his head and swallowed a chunk of steak that would choke a mountain lion. "With this war, further travel is out of the question. I start work with Gamble and Wade on the morrow."

"A prestigious firm. How fortuitous." From the way Tom squirmed in his chair, Betsy realized her cousin was toying her foot with his beneath the table. Emma folded her fan and leaned toward her husband, offering him a view of her cleavage. "Don't you think so, Abel dear?"

His mouth full of buttered rice and string beans, dark-haired Abel grunted a noncommittal response. Then he returned to the steak without so much as a glance at Emma's bosom.

Because Tom had just plugged his mouth with more steak, Betsy picked up the conversation. "Naturally we cannot afford a house yet. Might you recommend a rental arrangement?"

Emma crossed her arms on the table and leaned forward, offering a view that neither Tom nor Joshua declined. "Housing is scarce these days, even with the bulk of the army camped a mile north in Log Town. Of course —" She grew thoughtful and sipped her wine. "We could let you rent the room you three are sharing tonight." Her expression enlivened, and she put down her goblet to wiggle forward again, breasts bulging her bodice. "I've a fabulous idea. You and Tom may live in the room rent- and board-free if Betsy will help with the business."

Hope sprang to Betsy's heart. She longed to be useful. "Why, of course. I'm excellent with accounting, and —"

"I perform the accounting." Except for mumbled greetings during pre-supper introductions, the words were Abel's first.

"All by yourself, sir? It must be an ordeal with so robust a business. I managed all the books for our business in Augusta, and I assure you that —"

"Perhaps you didn't understand me, madam. No one touches the books except me." His voice rose on the "me," and he glared at her, bloody beef skewered on his knife.

The stares of Tom and Joshua echoed Betsy's astonishment. Emma fluttered out a laugh and stroked her husband's forearm, and he resumed his aggression toward his steak. "There, there, dear. Of course she understood. She was merely trying to be helpful." Emma smiled at her guests. "Abel always has been very protective of the finances. I'm ever so much better suited to managing the 'people' portion of the business." She twitched her nostrils at Tom. "We've the perfect arrangement, you see."

From the flush advancing up Tom's neck, Betsy knew he'd comprehended the Branwells' "arrangement." Jealousy prickled her, and she dashed it away with a gulp of wine. She'd no right to censor his behavior.

"So since helping with the books is out, we could use your assistance with housekeeping. Lotty, our chambermaid, didn't show up for work Monday morning, and when she finally arrived Tuesday noon, she was so drunk she couldn't stand up. I fired her. The slaves Hattie and Sally have temporarily assumed her duties." Perceiving the downcast look on Betsy's face, she reached across the table as if to take her hand and then rested her fingertips near Betsy's wine goblet. "I know a woman of your station is hardly suited for a chambermaid's work, especially after you've helped your husband in such a cerebral capacity. But Fate has brought us together when we need each other's help, and in truth, you need work here only long enough for you and Tom to get back on your feet financially. What do you say?"

The deal sounded repulsive, and Betsy had never felt more like saying no. But Tom prodded her ankle with his toe, and Joshua watched her with an expectant smile, so of course the men must be right, as the deal *did* sound like the perfect cover under which to sniff around for Clark. "Very well, but you mustn't expect me to lift anything too heavy."

"In your delicate condition? Of course not, dear."

"And to help us recover faster financially, please don't tell anyone who comes asking that we're here."

Abel stopped chewing and narrowed his beady eyes on them. "You in trouble with the law?"

Tom breezed out a smile. "No sooner did our house in Augusta burn then three fellows who'd loaned me small amounts of money came asking for their funds. And don't you know that the five fellows who owe *me* money are nowhere to be found."

With a grunt, Abel returned his gaze to his plate and continued chewing. At Tom's quizzical look, Emma giggled. "Abel knows about those kinds of men. He won't say a word."

***

A wave of masculine laughter and tobacco smoke surged in from the first floor when Tom opened the door to admit Joshua. Candlelight gleamed in Joshua's eyes. "I wonder what time they quit serving the rum. We've over two hundred drunken redcoats downstairs." He shut the door and muffled some of the noise.

Betsy wondered whether she'd be able to sleep through it. She combed a final tangle from her hair and began braiding. "Are you sure your cousins don't mind spending the night in the stables?"

"It's quieter, and they want to keep an eye on the horses."

Tom smiled. "Don't they trust a weasely accountant to not be thieving horses in the middle of the night?"

"No, they don't trust the weasely accountant's drunken patrons." Joshua yawned. "What time has it gotten to be?"

"After ten." With a yawn, Betsy tied the end of her braid.

Joshua unrolled his blanket on the side of the bed nearest the door and positioned his loaded rifle on the floor next to it. While Tom unrolled his blanket on the opposite side of the room, Betsy shoved her shoes and stockings out of the way and reclined on the bed near the nightstand. The bed creaked and sagged, begging to have the ropes tightened, but she was just too tired. "Lights out, gentlemen?" They both answered her with a yawn, and she extinguished the candle, plunging the room into a darkness made incomplete by light filtering in through a small window. Noise from the floor below seemed amplified.

Joshua's breathing deepened into sleep within a minute. Shortly after, she heard Tom's soft snores. But she lay awake buffeted by unfamiliar sounds and smells from a tavern in revelry. She told herself she was lucky to have made it to Camden unharmed, to have a generous cousin like Emma, and to have uncovered clues of Clark's whereabouts on her first day. Yet she didn't feel lucky.

Instead, she felt overwhelmed and despairing, surely feelings her mother must have experienced when her second husband died and she was left to raise a child alone. Betsy remembered circles of fatigue beneath Sophie's eyes each morning after she'd worked a print run and the way her mother dragged around, almost too tired to care for either of them. By the time Betsy had been ten years old, she'd resolved to never land herself in the same situation. No, she'd marry a fellow who didn't travel, a man who worked a safe trade, because she didn't want to raise a child alone. In fact, the very idea of raising a child alone terrified her because she was sure she couldn't do it. Maybe some women could do it, but she didn't have the gumption and iron backbone of Sophie. Now here she was, alone, and Clark was nowhere on the horizon, and —

...what a clever way to circumvent paying your most valuable employee. Marry her. If she thought about it hard enough, she could envision her husband smirking out just such a comment to the men in the White Swan, but she didn't want to think about it. Not yet, at least.

Instead she experimented with her anger toward him for getting involved with the rebels and putting the baby and her in jeopardy. She blamed Loyalists and Whigs, too, who couldn't stop fighting long enough to hear each other's grievances, and who'd battled it out yet again four days earlier up in Spartan District, where Joshua was headed on the morrow. When all was said and done, she realized she had herself to blame, too.

It had been her choice to put herself, her baby, and four men in danger, all because she'd hated the thought of waiting in Augusta for Clark to return — or not to return. In the wee hours of the morning, the reality of her folly tossed and turned sleep from her. If she'd had even an inkling of the dangers she'd encounter on the road or the drudgery she'd be required to perform, just to be in Camden, she'd have remained in Augusta, for waiting and passivity were her lot in Camden, too.

CHAPTER TWENTY-FOUR

After seeing Tom off to work the next morning, Betsy and Emma waved farewell to Joshua and the Creek. Then they strolled from the stables through the birdsong and humidity of a garden redolent of bread baking in the beehive oven. Sally straightened from weeding beans when they passed, her smile broad. "Mornin', Miz Emma. Mornin', Miz Betsy." She extended her basket. "Just look here at all the beans that come ripe since yesterday. Musta been that rain we had five days ago."

"We need another hard rain just like it soon, or the corn will dry up."

"Yes, ma'am, fixin' to be another hot one today."

In a dining room fragrant with bread dough, Hattie, her fingers floury, poured coffee for Emma and Betsy, set out biscuits and strawberry jam, and returned to kneading. Betsy sipped her coffee, relaxed, and listened while Emma apprised her of how they needed help each day. Sweep, air, and dust the four guestrooms. Empty the chamberpots. Make sure each room had candles and stocked tinderboxes. Bundle heavily soiled towels and sheets for the washerwoman, and see that every bed had sheets on it that didn't look too dirty. Patrons paid extra for fresh sheets. And make sure each guestroom had at least five clean towels in it. Hattie opened a cupboard and showed her a ring of keys that held the upstairs linen storage key.

All in all, Betsy heard nothing unusual in Emma's requirements until her cousin specified that the rooms had to be cleaned by one o'clock, since a few patrons began arriving that early. Betsy gave the ceiling a glance and considered how late the revelry had extended into the night. "Aren't some of them still asleep up there this moment?"

"Oh, no." Emma spread jam on her biscuit. "Standard patrons are all out by four o'clock in the morning. Todd and his men see to that, thank goodness." With a lovely smile, she bit into the biscuit.

Such a policy hardly made sense to Betsy's sleep-fogged brain, but she had plenty of other questions. "Will you need my help in the afternoon or evening?"

"Only if we've a frightfully messy patron."

Betsy wrinkled her nose after catching a whiff from the common room — alcohol, tobacco, sweat. "Who cleans out there?"

"Henry and Philip, who'll be arriving any moment."

"Shall I tidy Abel's office?"

"Absolutely not. He's peculiar about who sets foot in there. Just sweep the hallway outside if it's dirty."

Betsy shrugged, glad to have one less room to clean. "You said four guestrooms. What about those four other rooms on the floor? Shall I clean those, too?"

Emma waved away the suggestion and washed down her biscuit with coffee. "The ladies clean their own rooms."

"You've residents besides us?"

Hattie chuckled, not missing a stroke with the bread. "Lawd, child, but Augusta must be a small town."

The nature of the Branwells' auxiliary business dawned on Betsy. Recalling Ensign Halsey's attention in the common room the previous afternoon, she felt herself blush to her toes. "This is a *bordello*?"

Emma smiled. "Not exclusively, no, but we do such a brisk business pouring cheer that it seems only natural to offer it in other forms, too."

"This *is* a bordello."

Emma's smile became practical. "Betsy, if I need a sermon, I'll

walk down to Church Street. Let us have an understanding, shall we?"
She leaned forward and steepled her fingers. "Georgia hasn't been in
the forefront of this war. In the last six months, more atrocities have
crossed Camden's doorstep than most people witness in a lifetime.

"Unfortunately, the victims aren't brutal men. If they were the
victims, wars wouldn't last but a day. No, the victims are women like
us, and their children.

"What happens to them when their men go to war? Many follow,
and it's a hard life for them — washing, mending clothes, tending the
injured and sick, never enough to eat, never a moment to rest, never
safe. When their men die, the army has no use for camp followers.
Consider what happens to women and children who've no kin to take
them in."

Every day for more than a week, Betsy *had* considered it. The
stark terror of it ached like a lump of ice in her soul.

"Janet's nose had been broken and two back teeth had been
knocked out when she came to me in February. She'd run away from
her husband, who got drunk so he could beat and ravish her. The other
three ladies followed Janet in the spring. Dolly's husband abandoned
her, their son, and her grandmother, and she's no other way to care for
the boy and old woman. Maria and her daughters were beaten by both
Whigs and Loyalists on their farm when Maria's husband and brothers
vanished into the war. One of the daughters died from the brutality.
Margaret's husband was killed at Charles Town, leaving her to care for
two sick children by herself. After her children died, she followed
Cornwallis's army here last month to shelter with her only relative, a
brother, and then he died, too."

Emma sat back and folded her hands in her lap. "Each woman
receives room and board here and may keep forty percent of her
earnings. Two women donate to charity. What war does to women
and children is heinous, and I shall do my part to ease that wherever I
can.

"If my business were more robust, I'd offer this arrangement to
other women, for they come to me every day, begging for help."
Emma shook her head. "Most of them have been cast away from a
church, where they sought protection and charity. Imagine that,
having a congregation that preaches love and giving turn its nose up at
you because you suddenly have no money and no husband.

"You and I are the lucky ones, Betsy. We've husbands to provide for us. Let us not judge what other women must do to survive and help innocent loved ones survive in a war not of their making, a war that drags on and on, simply because men won't listen to each other."

***

Betsy spent most of the morning sweeping, airing, and dusting guestrooms that reeked of various forms of gentlemen's diversions — mostly British officers' diversions, if Emma was accurate about her clientele. Though Clark had been her only lover, she concluded that it didn't matter whether a man was a colonel or carpenter, rebel or redcoat. They all smelled the same when they wallowed in carnal bliss. In the moment they gave themselves to *le petit mort*, they were each vulnerable, each very human — despite the rebels' insistence on demonizing the redcoats.

Each room was furnished with a sturdy bed, handsome chair, and wardrobe with drawers. To verify that no patron had left personal articles behind, Betsy opened a drawer in the first room and discovered an education in silk, leather, wood, and lubricant devices. As she found out, the other rooms were similarly equipped.

Mid-morning, she paused to glance out the window toward the kitchen, where Sally stirred stew for the patrons that night in a cauldron. She remembered a night Sophie had fallen asleep telling her a bedtime story while stretched out next to her in bed. Betsy, eight years old, leaned over, stroked her mother's cheek, and pulled the blanket over her shoulder. "Always so tired, Mama. You sleep now." In retrospect, she wondered whether those circles of fatigue beneath Sophie's eyes were less from weariness than from worry.

Her lip curled when she recollected the imperious attitude of Ruth Glenn. "It's time for you to move on," Ruth had said. She envisioned pastors from churches in Camden saying the same thing to widows knocking on their doors: *Begone. Beg elsewhere. Stop bothering us.* There, but for good fortune, might any widowed mother with hungry children walk. Had circumstances been otherwise, Sophie might have walked that route, too.

Betsy finished the rooms just before eleven and carried a basket of soiled linens, mostly towels, downstairs in time to accept a delivery of wine. Neither Emma nor Abel was to be found to remit payment to the vendor, so she shoved the invoice in her pocket and promised the vendor she'd give it to Abel. Henry and Philip, the lads cleaning the common room, carried the crates of bottles down to the Leaping Stag's wine cellar and left Betsy with a lantern to sort things out in the cool dampness of the cellar.

With the lantern held high and her eyes wide in awe, Betsy wandered aisles of wine bottles, more wine than she'd ever seen in one spot, and took the time to decode the floor-to-ceiling storage plan. She found places for all the new bottles in the system and stood back to survey the cellar again, wondering how often Emma ordered wine. She'd cleaned at least five empty wine bottles from each guestroom.

Back upstairs in the dining room, she delivered the soiled linens to the washerwoman, who had just arrived. When Hattie informed her that Abel was in his office with a client, Betsy groped in her pocket for the invoice and headed for the closed office door. When she raised her hand to knock, the invoice in the other hand, she hesitated, hearing Abel's voice: "I cannot give you anything today. Next week I should be able to work it into the books."

"Next week will be too late." Betsy's eyes bugged at the heavy Spanish accent of Abel's visitor. Why, it sounded just like Basilio's voice! "*Señor* Carter wants storage fees up front."

"See here. I find it exceedingly poor planning on your part to move all that rubbish this morning, in such a rush. Poor planning on your part does not constitute an excuse to squeeze my pockets. You shall just have to make do in whatever other way you can."

She heard menace in the Spaniard's voice. "Ambrose will not like this."

Her jaw dangled open in shock. Ambrose.

"Ambrose may bugger himself for all I care. Tell him I said so. And next time, you'd bloody well better use the *back* door — and come after midnight."

Abel yanked the office door open and caught Betsy in a perfect pose of surprise: her mouth open, one hand raised to knock, the other hand clenching the invoice. For the second that she darted her gaze from Abel to Basilio — yes, it was indeed a tired looking Basilio — and then back again, she felt her heart stop beating and her ears buzz with faint. But Basilio showed no sign of recognition, and she realized with a tremendous surge of relief that he wouldn't have recognized her from his visits to Augusta anyway because she been upstairs in bed each time he'd come. She drew a deep breath. "Oh, Mr. Branwell —"

"What the devil do *you* want?"

She thrust the invoice at him. "Wine shipment this morning, sir. I told the vendor you'd send him your payment."

Abel snatched the invoice from her, and his expression relaxed but little, even if some of the harshness seeped from his voice. "Where's the wine?"

"In the cellar sorted and stored properly."

"Good." He squinted at the total on the invoice and pursed his lips. "That will be all."

With a curtsy, she turned and strode away, her legs somehow managing to not convey that her insides felt like jelly, for she recognized the symbolism of the bloody beef skewered on Abel's knife the night before at supper. Abel had an excellent reason for not wanting her help with the accounting for the Leaping Stag. He was siphoning money off his business with British soldiers into the ravenous maw of a rebel spy ring.

CHAPTER TWENTY-FIVE

Beneath the shade of an oak in the garden, Tom made short work of bread, yellow cheese, and fried squash and then applied himself to a mug of beer. Betsy smiled. Much had changed in the past two weeks, but not his appetite. "When are you due back?"

"One o'clock." He lowered his voice. "I reckon Clark won't be needing his tools anytime soon, so I took them."

She stared. "But — but how? Surely you didn't go into the house after that man's threats? He'd arrest you for burglary."

He shook his head. "I'd planned to sneak in before work, so I took a sack. But when I got there, your furniture was loaded on the wagon. Clark's workbench was easy to reach." He drained off his beer. "The German was talking with two Spaniards who'd stolen your furniture from Augusta. I couldn't get near the wagon without them seeing me.

"The Spaniards left with the wagon, and the German went back inside the house, and I ran behind and jumped up on the rear. I unloaded Clark's tools into the sack and jumped back down with the Spaniards none the wiser."

Betsy regarded him with admiration. "You amaze me, Tom Alexander. Did you see where they took my furniture?"

"It's in a barn about a mile east of town."

"Hmm. Clark's plans to set up business in Camden with Uncle Isaac went quite awry, and now we've made the Ambrose ring nervous." She cocked an eyebrow. "Weren't you late for work?"

"Yes. I ran all the way back. But Mr. Gamble had overslept and wasn't angry about me being tardy because I helped the apprentices and him open the shop in no time."

"Let's visit that barn tonight after supper and inquire after my property." She yawned. "But then return at a reasonable hour. I need sleep."

He studied her. "If it's all there, you won't confront anyone about it, will you?"

"I will, indeed. It was stolen from me, and I want it back."

"Betsy, I realize all that furniture is difficult to replace, but the spies have already threatened you once over it. Now, if you believed there was a way to find Clark from the furniture —"

"Of course! Of course there's a — a connection." She heard herself sputter and then took a deep breath. "I'm not ruling any clues out at this point."

"Very well, but you realize the spies will be even more nervous after tonight. Their primary business isn't moving furniture. We're costing them valuable time. Were I them, I'd hide it in several locations. It's less difficult to conceal on short notice."

"Less costly, too — which explains why Abel Branwell doesn't want me helping him with the books." Curiosity sparked in Tom's eyes, and she plunged on. "From a portion of conversation I overheard between Basilio san Gabriel and him late this morning in his office, it would seem my cousin's husband is supporting the Ambrose spy ring with funds embezzled from his business."

"Zounds!" Tom rubbed his jaw. "What irony — the British army supporting rebel spies. Assuming you could access his books without endangering yourself, how would you recognize such a falsification to confirm it?"

"Well, he might break up a large sum and lodge it under loans or charitable donations to false entities." Her lip curled. "More likely he's creating donations. They're a charitable lot here — especially the four talented ladies lodged on the upper floor."

Tom studied her the duration of several heartbeats before his eyes widened with understanding. "This is a bawdy house?"

"Officially it's a tavern, but the Branwells discovered earlier this year how lucrative such a side business could be."

"I should think so." He leered at the house. "And you've met the ladies? Are they very lovely?"

"No, I haven't met them. They were all asleep in their quarters when I cleaned the guestrooms earlier." She crossed her arms in a huff at the look on his face, feeling her own expression sour. *Men.* "But you may as well save your coin. Their clientele is almost exclusively officers."

He turned back to her, his leer diffused into a smile of friendship. "Are you jealous?"

"Why should I be? Your business is your own."

He pried one of her hands from its defensive position and held it in his. "I've no urgent desire to get myself poxed."

"Yes, I suppose every profession has its hazards. Consider, though, how the employment of four such ladies might place Abel in a situation of learning sensitive military information."

"Indeed. But the redcoats aren't stupid. If they discover what he's about, they won't waste any time widowing Emma and closing down the tavern."

And Emma had considered herself lucky that morning. Betsy wondered how much her cousin knew of Abel's activities with the spy ring. But that wasn't the most pressing of her concerns. "Tom, if Abel's involved, the spies know where to find us."

He sighed. "I shan't sleep easier for that."

"But Abel may know where to find Clark."

He firmed his grip on her hand and captured her gaze in his. "Walk carefully around him. We don't know what he'll tell Clark about Betsy and Tom *Sheridan*, lodged together beneath his roof."

***

She sent him back to work and carried his dishes from the garden, trailing despondency. Not even the aroma of stew perked her spirits. Clark — wherever he was hiding — was her husband, and Tom was their friend. So she and Tom hadn't acted on the growing attraction they felt for each other. But what reward would virtue deliver if Abel told Clark his wife was sharing a bed with his friend? She doubted things could get much worse.

Sally waylaid her from the side yard, her hands soapy from a washtub. In exchange for dirty dishes, Betsy carried a tray of clean tankards inside. As she entered the dining room, Emma flagged her down from the common room. "In here with those tankards."

Betsy spotted a brunette seated at the dining room table, a coffee cup before her. She smiled. "Good afternoon."

Her rosy lips perfect and full, her dark eyes sultry, the woman returned the smile. "Good afternoon." Whoever she was — Janet, Dolly, Maria, or Margaret — she was quite fetching. She looked to be in her mid-twenties, and her silk bedgown advertised luscious curves.

In a common room swept and tidied by Henry and Philip, Betsy helped Hattie and Emma stack tankards in preparation for the night. Through a thin haze of pipe and cheroot smoke, Emma's early-shift tavern maid ambled between three tables of soldiers playing cards and dice and filled their tankards.

Betsy followed Emma and Hattie back to the dining room, where two women had joined the brunette at the table. Emma ushered her forward. "Ladies, this is my cousin Betsy from Augusta. Betsy and her husband, Tom, are living with us until he's established in business." She introduced a thin blonde with a crooked nose as Janet, a chunky brunette with bouncy curls as Dolly, and the sultry, gorgeous brunette as Margaret. Janet and Dolly, also adorned in bedgowns, were about Margaret's age.

"How do you do." Betsy bobbed a stiff curtsy and wondered what flavor of small talk one pursued with high-class harlots.

"Pleased to meet you, Betsy," murmured each of the women, just as skeptical.

Sally brought in a tray of damp, clean tankards, and Hattie whisked it away to the common room. Emma beamed at the three ladies, not indifferent to the awkwardness. "Betsy's helping me with the cleaning. Have you seen the rooms upstairs yet?"

The apathy on Janet's face transformed into pleasant surprise. "You did that, Betsy? Why, you did a wonderful job. Thank you." Despite her crooked nose, Janet was pretty when she smiled.

Margaret smiled, too. "Emma's needed reliable help."

"That girl Lotty just couldn't keep herself out of the bottle." Dolly's curls bounced. "Welcome, Betsy."

When Emma mentioned that Betsy and Tom were expecting, the ladies murmured congratulations, and Betsy followed their thinking. What a wretched time to be bringing a child into the world. She said to Dolly, "Emma tells me you've a son. Where is he?"

"With Mr. Fitzgerald two streets over, learning his letters and arithmetic. Emma has such a big heart." Dolly's dark eyes sparkled. "She's arranged for Maria's daughter to receive schooling, and she's found someone to look after my grandmama."

For a fleeting second, Betsy fancied changing professions because Emma had made the benefits so attractive. Then Hattie returned to the dining room, her expression stoic. "Captain Robert Harding's arrived."

Emma drew a watch from her pocket. "One-fifteen." She snapped the watch shut.

Surliness puckered Dolly's lips. "He's early again."

"Well, then, keep him waiting again. I must check on the stew, ladies." Emma tucked the watch back in her pocket and reached for the back door. "But don't keep the captain waiting *too* long, Dolly."

Margaret and Janet snickered. Hattie filled two cups and set them before Janet and Dolly. "Have yo'self a cup of coffee before you rush off, Miz Dolly."

"Fetch her some ham, too, Hattie. She shall need the sustenance after Bouncing Bob takes command." Janet grinned, and Betsy spotted the gap where her husband had knocked out her back teeth. Pity shot through her before she could get a grip on it and dismantle it. The women didn't want her pity, and she sure didn't want their life — regardless of Emma's generosity.

Hattie set to work unwrapping and slicing a ham on the sideboard, and Margaret addressed Betsy. "You're from Augusta? How far is Alton from Augusta?"

Betsy regarded Margaret with surprise. "Alton's about thirteen miles south, but I'm amazed you've heard of it. It's such a small town."

Janet waved away Betsy's words. "Oh, we've heard of Alton, to be sure. Alton, Alton, Alton for the past two days."

Dolly smirked. "Indeed, you'd think it was Jesus Christ himself who came from Alton."

That sultry look captured Margaret's face. "You're all jealous because he took his time with me."

Janet laughed. "Bouncing Bob takes his time with Dolly, but no one's jealous of her for it."

Dolly's lips pinched again. "He'd take his time with any woman. That man's forge is so cold that even the bellows seldom revives it." For emphasis, she thrust her cupped hand several times toward her open, rounded lips, a familiar gesture that earned a flush from Betsy and merry peals of laughter from the other two ladies. When they'd subsided, Dolly winked at Betsy. "Take our advice. Give your Tom a little of it every now and then. It's one way to keep him from straying. All men are the same, even husbands."

Betsy flushed again. As for what Tom wanted, she'd best not consider it.

"Not *all* men are the same."

"That fellow from Alton again? Pshaw, Margaret, let it go."

"He called me his priestess."

Dolly shrugged. "One fellow last week called me Queen Charlotte."

"And a few have called me Venus." Janet frowned. "But a man never called me a *priestess* before. That's right peculiar."

"You weren't pretending to be a virgin led to a sacrifice, were you?" Dolly sipped coffee.

"Not with him, no."

"Maybe Margaret's fellow wasn't a man. With that red hair of his, he might have been Mars in disguise." Dolly slapped her thigh and laughed.

"You saw him?" Janet picked at ham Hattie set before her.

"Mmmm. Tight bum on that handsome young lieutenant. I sure wouldn't have minded spending four hours with him." Dolly shoveled ham into her mouth.

The pieces condensed in Betsy's reasoning, and she felt her skin crawl. Alton. Red hair. Lieutenant. Oh, no, surely it wasn't so. But hadn't Emma said something the day before about Margaret entertaining an officer from the Seventeenth Light?

Janet shook a piece of ham at Margaret. "You'd best take hold of yourself. The delectable ones don't often come back."

Mystical conviction curved the corners of Margaret's mouth. "He'll be back. He said so."

Emma entered through the back door, a bottle of wine in one hand, a lit lantern in the other. "Dolly, is this the red Captain Harding so admires?"

Dolly squinted at the bottle. "Yes, it is."

"What luck. More bottles arrived with this morning's delivery." She motioned Betsy over and handed her the lantern. "Dear, please run down to the cellar, fetch another bottle of this vintage, and set the two bottles up in room number four with a couple of glasses —" She grinned at Dolly. " — while we ensure the good captain is made merry."

Betsy grasped the lantern and headed for the cellar, not knowing whether to scream or puke. The second or third step down, she tripped and just managed to catch herself from falling. The lantern banging the wall, she clung to the railing, steadied her breathing, and announced to her audience of wine bottles, "I'm a fool, an utter and complete fool."

The worst she might have expected in Augusta for sticking to her principles was sharing a smelly jail cell with Abby Fuller. Now, in Camden, she had to live under the roof of odious Abel Branwell, who might, at any moment, dispute her marital fidelity with the husband she loved. And if that weren't enough misery, she'd need to stay on guard day after day, her nerves wracked all to hell. For if Margaret's confidence were any indicator, Lieutenant Fairfax would return. He'd been a satisfied customer.

CHAPTER TWENTY-SIX

What a mucking mess." Tom glanced behind, as much to gauge the angle of the setting sun as to make sure no one sharing the dusty road could hear. "Did you tell Margaret you knew Fairfax?"

"No." Betsy mopped her forehead with her kerchief and scurried to keep up with his stride eastbound on a road rippling with heat.

He noticed and slowed. "I keep forgetting my legs are longer."

"We cannot stay hidden to avoid him."

Tom shifted his musket from one hand to the other and flexed the muscles in his empty hand. "What do you propose?"

"Approach Margaret with a story about why we don't want him knowing we're here, and ask her to alert us when he returns."

"What story are you considering?"

"I don't know. I've contemplated it all afternoon. Whatever we say, she'll relate it to the others and Emma, so we must use their gossip to our advantage."

A smile crinkled the corners of his eyes after he considered a few seconds. "Let's build on the story we told the Branwells about our creditors. Fairfax is a creditor. I lost money to him at piquet back in June, when we visited your family in Alton. We agreed I'd make him a pair of boots to cancel the debt."

"Keep talking. The story sounds plausible."

"When he came to Augusta to collect, the house and shop had burned the night before."

"Good. Margaret will spread it around, and you'll become the honorable fellow who intends to pay his debts as soon as he emerges from adversity."

"Do you think she'll swallow it?"

She grimaced. "Who knows? She was quite taken with him."

Tom's expression soured. "Of course she was. He didn't interrogate *her*. Were she exposed to his tender ministrations, she'd avoid him like malaria." They crested a rise, and he pointed with the musket. "Yonder."

The pine barren thinned southward to reveal land cultivated in gentle slopes. Presiding over miles of cornfield and pasture, several barns caught the setting sun. Smaller buildings phalanxed them, and oaks shaded a two-story manor on a hill.

In Abel's office, Basilio had mentioned someone named Carter wanting storage fees, presumably for the furniture. She suspected they'd discover "Carter" owned the property surrounding the barn. From the appearance of the land, he didn't look like the sort who lacked for money, but Southern gentry weren't given to publicizing hard times, preferring to maintain the facade of aristocracy by selling off a slave here or a few acres of land there. "A fellow named Carter was asking for storage fees."

"Then that's probably his land."

They walked downhill and left behind the scent of pine resin to head south on a path. Cornfields swallowed them, stalks and leaves dull green from lack of rain. After another few minutes, the first building — slave quarters — came into sight, along with a couple of Negro women up to their elbows in laundry. When the women straightened to eye them and Tom's musket, Betsy said, "Where might we find Mr. Carter?" Her face shiny with sweat, one woman pointed toward the house, and soapsuds dripped off her forearm.

They passed more cabins. Tom cleared his throat. "The corn is ready for harvest, but where are the slaves? Even assuming that most hands are working another field, I don't see enough slaves here to occupy these cabins, and I certainly don't see enough to have planted all these fields in the spring."

"I didn't see but a half dozen cattle in the pasture. Perhaps the fall of Charles Town wasn't kind to Mr. Carter."

"That would explain why he couldn't pass up an offer to store your furniture. The barn we want is to the left."

Startled doves winged away, and a sonata of cicadas encircled Betsy and Tom. Corn cleared to reveal the north end of the barn and three other buildings. From one, the ping and clank of a blacksmith's hammer pierced the cicada-buzz, but otherwise, the area seemed deserted.

Around the front of the barn, Tom lifted the latch to the door, and he and Betsy stepped inside, leaving the door ajar. During the seconds it took for their eyes to adjust to the gloom, Betsy noted that the barn retained the musty smell of livestock, even though desiccated droppings told them no animals had been there for several weeks. They bypassed farm equipment and found her furniture, draped with canvas, in the northeast corner.

She fondled everything she could get her hands on with a mounting sense of loss until Tom flung canvas back over the cabinet holding her grandmother's china. "It won't do you any good moping over it. We cannot carry it back with us. We need to find this Carter fellow and get to the bottom of the theft."

The barn door whammed open, and they pivoted in surprise. Four men backlit by waning daylight darted in and took cover behind farm equipment. One called out. "We finally caught you rabble stealing our supplies. Lay down your weapons, put your hands up, and get out of that corner where we can see you!"

Taking care to make no sudden movements, Tom dropped his musket and knife in the straw underfoot. Then he and Betsy walked forward with hands visible. A musket held ready, one man rose from concealment and slunk forward to kick Tom's weapons from reach. Bewilderment creased his expression at the sight of them. "Come outside where we can see you better."

Outside, daylight made Betsy aware from the fine linen and wool on her captors that they weren't farm hands. After examining Tom's musket and knife, a man in his early forties swiveled his dark-eyed gaze back and forth between them. "You aren't the thieves we were expecting in my barn. Who the devil are you, and why were you in there?"

"Are you Mr. Carter?"

"Yes, Josiah Carter. And who might you be?"

"Betsy Sheridan." Seeing that the name "Sheridan" went unrecognized by them, she pondered how to continue. "I was verifying that the furniture stored in the barn is mine."

Carter shrugged. "It was delivered this morning."

"Yes, and stolen from my home in Augusta last week."

From the blank stares on their faces, she could tell the men knew little, if anything, of the spy ring. Carter said, "Here, now, I saw a receipt for the sale of the furniture."

"An estate sale in Charles Town? We've heard that story. I assure you the receipt's false."

Tom shifted his feet. "I was in Augusta last Thursday morning at her home and witnessed the furniture being loaded onto a wagon by Spaniards. One of the thieves knocked me senseless and set the house afire."

"Spaniards! Did you see who delivered the — ?"

"Quiet, Jeremiah." Josiah Carter assumed an expression of diplomacy. "Perhaps there's a misunderstanding about the furniture. I certainly don't want any trouble. Why don't you query the gentleman who purchased it and paid me to store it? He's at the house right now."

Betsy crossed her arms. "The obnoxious German."

"German?" Carter stared at her. "He's Dutch, not German."

Dutch. Of course. That puzzle piece dropped into place, and Betsy and Tom exchanged a look of comprehension. Holland had sided with the Continentals against Britain. But Holland didn't have the resources of France or even Spain. The Stadtholder was putting himself out on a financial limb to ally with a ring of rebel assassins and spies — unless the assassination of British military figures furthered an agenda for the Dutch.

"No matter what country he hails from, he's a thief."

Carter's lips twitched with nervousness. "In principle, perhaps, but professionally Jan van Duser is a surveyor whose grandfather was one of Camden's first settlers."

"I will appreciate the opportunity to speak with him."

"Then I shall escort you to him this moment."

***

The mysterious Jan van Duser made them wait in Carter's drawing room for an hour. By the time he deigned to meet them, a slave had made the rounds of the drawing room and lit candles to banish the twilight descending on the countryside. Carter led Betsy and Tom to gardens behind his manor, where torchlight in no way warmed frostbite in van Duser's eyes. Two strapping fellows Betsy hadn't seen before flanked the Dutchman. "Mr. Carter, I require a private audience with these *persons*." He motioned toward the house with his ebony walking stick.

Watching the flicker of Carter's gaze over van Duser's henchmen slid fear up Betsy's spine. Did van Duser presume to harm them on Carter's property and still maintain his storage arrangement with a man who now suspected him of burglary? But perhaps Carter was under van Duser's thumb.

After Carter hurried for the house, the Dutchman signaled everyone to follow and strode into the gardens while his ruffians assumed position behind Betsy and Tom. Betsy sensed the tension in Tom but kept her eyes on van Duser.

"Mrs. Sheridan, it surprises me to see you here."

"Why? You stole my furniture. I want it back."

He turned on them, much of his sunburned face in shadow, and in one fluid movement, the henchmen pressed knives to her throat and Tom's. When she swallowed, the steel ached against her throat. Fear zinged through her veins like rivers of fire. "I received the distinct impression from your husband that you were intelligent. Yet you and Mr. Alexander are about to have your throats slit. Hardly the move of an intelligent woman. Did you not understand my warning yesterday?"

She licked her lips. "D — Do you plan to tell Clark we were both murdered by banditti?"

He smiled, and even by twilight it wasn't a lovely sight. "A horror of war, I'm afraid — outlaws prey upon the innocent."

"How do you think Mr. Carter will feel having contributed to two murders in his garden, especially since he already suspects that you did indeed steal my furniture?"

"A few more guineas will ease his conscience."

Horrified, Betsy realized she had nothing to lose by blasting van Duser with everything she knew. "With so much coin to throw around, you must be Ambrose. Do you plan for Clark to assassinate the Earl Cornwallis, or is Lord Rawdon his target? Who will Basilio and Francisco assassinate? The British won't be duped much longer by Abel Branwell's operation. What more do the Dutch get out of this besides assassinated British officers?"

"Madam, I fail to understand why you never took such conclusions to the British. They might have completely unraveled our operation by now had you done so. True, they'd have thrown you in jail for complicity, but at least you'd still be alive on the morrow. Apparently you've as little love for them as you have for Continentals. I wonder that any mortal can straddle such a fence for so long. Surely you cannot stay on that fence much longer, and when you fall off, I cannot afford for you cast your lot with the British."

Bitterness clawed through her fear. "I don't expect you to understand. Issues superior to asinine causes inspire my loyalty. My husband's welfare, for example."

The Dutchman frosted her with his scowl for almost a quarter of a minute. Then, after the barest movement of his head, the pressure from the knife on her throat released. In her peripheral vision, the henchmen backed off and Tom massaged his throat, but in no way did she feel invincible. The ring on his forefinger glinting golden by torchlight, Jan van Duser stroked a fern before addressing her again. "Your husband is not of your concern these days. However I assure you he's well."

She drew a shaky breath. "I want to see him."

"He's unavailable to meet you. He's performing admirable service for King George by helping escort a convoy of supplies to the British base in Hanging Rock north of here." The smile slithered across his face. "They'll never reach Hanging Rock, thanks to intelligence from Mr. Sheridan."

"Ambushed by Whigs," muttered Tom.

"Yes. The supplies are badly needed by Major Davie and his North Carolinians. I expect the arrival of a messenger at any moment to confirm his good fortune. Never fear, I shan't allow Mr. Sheridan to languish a prisoner of war very long."

Something in his admission about Clark being a prisoner of war activated Betsy's instincts that a double-cross was in the works. "I want to see Clark, and I want my furniture back."

"Madam, you apparently haven't understood your place in all

this. Because 'asinine causes,' as you label them, don't motivate you, I'm convinced you don't intend to spill all this to the British, so I'm letting you go. During the course of our mission, Mr. Sheridan may initiate contact with you." Van Duser shrugged. "His choice, but you see, he's a very busy man.

"Be assured, however, that we shan't permit *you* to initiate contact with *him*, nor shall you have your furniture back, until our mission is completed. Whether you die by our hands or ever see him or the furniture again depends entirely on whether you can keep your mouths shut and cease meddling in our affairs. I advise both of you to not forget the feeling of steel against your throats. The next time we put it there, you *will* die.

"Now get out. At the front door to the manor, you'll find your weapons. Take them and return to Camden. And do not give us cause to suspect you of interfering again."

CHAPTER TWENTY-SEVEN

Two blocks from the Leaping Stag, Tom yanked Betsy around to him. Torchlight gouged concern into his face. "God's teeth, calm down!"

Her voice hissed out, even though she realized passersby could eavesdrop. "Those rebels have ruined my life —"

"And lower your voice." He released her arm.

With her next breath, she complied. " — swayed my husband, burned my house, stolen my furniture — and I'm *neutral*!"

"If they swayed Clark, it was because he decided months ago to follow this course. Nothing you do will stop him. His fellows remind him of his priorities and prevent his straying.

"If they burned your house and stole your furniture, you've the company of thousands who've been ground underfoot by the injustices of this war, also for no reason, and you cannot stop that, either. Van Duser can buy attorneys and judges who manipulate the law and perform perjury. You've naught but truth to fight with, and it's meaningless against legal perfidies."

She glared at him and choked back the vile taste of her own helplessness and impotence, hating all devotees to asinine causes who had the financial backing to create victims of war from decent, honest folks. "God damn them all to hell!"

Tom nodded in agreement, outrage flooding his expression. They both strove for self-control. His voice emerged low but firm. "We shan't find Clark until he desires it. We shan't recover your furniture until the Ambrose ring is ready to release it."

"I want my life back!"

"Forget about Clark and your furniture! They aren't worth your life."

Joshua had said the same. She bit her lip and averted her face from him. Men didn't understand.

"Our priority now is assuring your safety. Have you relatives elsewhere who might give you sanctuary?"

Seeking her parents among the Cherokee might open the gates of hell on them all. Tom couldn't know. Still looking elsewhere, she gnawed on her knuckle.

"Who is it?" he whispered. "I'll see you get to them safely, I swear it, or I'll die in trying —"

"Tom, please, don't make an oath like that —"

"Why not? You know how I feel about you. I've never been good at hiding it. Nor have you minded my showing it."

She turned back and held his gaze. Abandoned by her husband and threatened by his partners, only a conservative minority would blame her for seeking solace, protection, and affection with another man. In war, folks did what they had to do to stay alive. But Tom was being dragged to the doom of her husband. If anyone deserved an out, it was he. "I have a duty to Clark," she whispered.

"*Clark*? He hasn't enough brains to come in out of the rain." The corrosion in his voice stung her. "He's like all the rest of those damned fools out there, men without honor, men who leave families and pregnant wives to fend for themselves while they indulge in bloodlust and call it duty."

Shadows covered his face. "Duty to *what*? To some hopeless cause? Whatever happened to duty to loved ones?" He grasped her shoulders. "You've lost too much. Where must we go to find your relations? I would at least see you regain your safety."

She shook her head. "If we're caught, we shall all hang."

His lips tightened. "Ah. Your mother and uncle aren't really prisoners of the Lower Creek. And your uncle *did* visit you on his way out of Augusta."

She hoped that somewhere down the road she wouldn't have to justify confiding in Tom to Laughing Eyes. "Surely Colonel Brown has extracted all the details from Abby Fuller by now and even knows where Uncle David went. I cannot return to Augusta, or I shall be arrested."

"Well, you cannot stay here. Adam Neville is *en route* spitting nails because you've slipped through his grasp twice. Fairfax will be passing through to partake of Margaret again. And if I were van Duser, I'd have second thoughts about letting us go. Abel Branwell just might ease the Dutchman's conscience by murdering us both in our sleep. Your cousin's whorehouse is no sanctuary. So where are your mother and uncle?"

She looked up at him. "Uncle David was headed to Williamsburg, but he's very good at laying low to avoid a rival in cards or love. My mother is hiding with Cherokee Indians in the wilderness near Keowee." And Betsy, recalling the oiled, tattooed Creek, wasn't so sure she could live among Indians. "Perhaps the British will move on soon and take the focus of hostilities with them."

"The British have held northern cities for years at a time. General de Kalb is in North Carolina with the Southern Continental Army, eyeing Lord Rawdon's portion of the British army here. Rawdon's pacing nervously with almost a thousand troops sick of yellow fever and malaria. Cornwallis is scrutinizing them both from Charles Town. They're all bound to do something enormous and messy soon — and on our doorstep.

"You're with child, and you need protection. Clark isn't protecting you. With his head full of Patriot garbage, I doubt he even knows how to save his own hide. You're only going to get protection from another neutral. Your mother's neutral."

"I won't endanger her."

"Cease being noble about this. If she knew the danger you're in, she'd put herself at risk to assure the safety of her only child and unborn grandchild."

Betsy's throat tightened. Tom had met Sophie twice, and yet he knew her well.

"My mother would do the same for me. Mothers are a special breed. I reckon you'll be that kind of mother someday, too."

She swallowed. Perhaps she could manage living among the Indians for a short while, as long as Sophie was with her. "All right, I shall try to find her, but I haven't money to travel right now, and neither do you. We'll need to save money so we can get out."

He nodded. "On the morrow I shall ask Mr. Wade about overtime. Sniff around, find odd jobs that pay decent coin."

Betsy detested the obvious solution, yet it was a superb source of income. "I've time off in the afternoons. Little as I like the work, I shall present myself to the town printer on the morrow and inquire whether he needs an assistant with layout." She grimaced. "If need be, I can even pull the press."

"Excellent." Tom's teeth flashed in a smile, and he took her hand. "Between the two of us, perhaps we can escape this hellhole in a month and get you to safety."

***

After another night in a tavern throbbing with rowdy redcoats, a bleary-eyed Betsy waved Tom off to work on Friday. Then she forced down coffee and a biscuit and trudged back upstairs — first to tidy their room, and by eight o'clock to clean the aftermath of bliss in four guestrooms. The night had intensified her feelings of loss and anger. Every time she ran fingers over the fine finish of Emma's furniture, it reminded her that she had no furniture or home. The furniture and home from Augusta were gone. So was the Betsy Sheridan of Augusta, she realized with a tremor of fear. She began to wonder who she was.

She envisioned Ruth Glenn sipping coffee in Augusta and saying in a sweet voice, "Furniture and a home are only things of this world. Lust for them but sets your feet upon the path to hell." Betsy scrubbed the very hell out of the guestroom floors, effacing good Mrs. Glenn, upstanding Mr. Branwell, and eminent Mr. van Duser. Furniture and a home were only things of this world until she was deprived of them, and then she recognized them for what they were — not just shields against starvation and disease, but keys to her own identity.

Finished cleaning by ten-thirty, she proceeded downstairs with dirty linen. A delivery of rum arrived, and when she knocked on Abel's door, invoice in hand, she found the door unlocked and no one within. Tom's comment about caution with Abel came to mind, and

she flushed it out with a scowl, daring the weasely accountant to make
an attempt on her life.

After shoving the invoice in her pocket, she marched in.
Monitoring the hallway and the window, which faced the street, she
looked over Abel's desk before finding the business ledger in the top
drawer of a cabinet. Savoring her catch, she snooped in other drawers.

The expected invoices were there — liquor, food, glassware,
furniture, repair of the roof after a tornado, labor of employees — but
she hadn't a clue what the invoices she found to and from "Messrs.
van Duser and der Waal, Surveyors" and other men and business
entities were about. A pity she couldn't put those in the hands of the
British to make sense of them, but she didn't want to implicate Emma.

While poking about the third drawer, she discovered the key for
the Ambrose ring's cipher. Hidden beneath the mattress in her room
was the final ciphered letter sent to Clark in Augusta. She committed
to memory the first ten number-word combinations from the list that
followed those for the military figures. Then she replaced the key as
she'd found it, closed the cabinet, and left, resolved to snatch future
peeks at the cipher key.

Emma was in the dining room talking with Margaret and Maria, a
slim brunette. Betsy smiled good morning to the ladies, and her
cousin beamed and hugged her with affection. "I just inspected the
rooms. My word, but you've done a marvelous job this morning.
Thank you ever so much."

"You're welcome. Some rum arrived a few minutes ago. I had
the men unload the kegs in the common room." Betsy retrieved the
invoice from her pocket. "Abel wasn't in his office."

"I shall give him the invoice when he returns. He takes morning
coffee on weekdays with two surveyor friends of his." Coffee wasn't
the only thing Abel was taking with van Duser and der Waal. If the
accountant kept a regular schedule, she'd have the cipher upstairs
decoded in no time. "You look tired, dear. Are we working you too
hard?"

"Not at all. Tom and I aren't used to sleeping in a tavern." She
flashed Emma a smile. "Taverns are noisy, and we're just not getting
enough sleep, so he's going to work overtime to see if we can save
enough money to at least rent our own place in a few weeks."

"I do understand, dear."

"And since you don't often need my help in the afternoons, I
shall assist him by finding jobs around town."

"I admire you for working with your husband that way. A month will give me plenty of time to find a reliable chambermaid — although I doubt any could measure up to your efficiency."

Betsy refreshed her smile and eased out a sigh of relief. One hurdle down. Emma wasn't going to fight her. She shifted her smile across the dining room to where Maria sipped coffee and Margaret studied them with those endless dark eyes of hers. "Er — Margaret, yesterday afternoon, you mentioned a client from Alton." Maria set down her cup, all ears. "He sounded like a soldier I know. Perchance is he Lieutenant Dunstan Fairfax?"

Margaret's expression didn't change, but Maria leaned over to her with a grin. "Watch out, Peggy. She's sweet on him."

Betsy felt her ears heat. Margaret's smile grew seductive. "I wondered if you were the same Sheridan he was looking for."

Fairfax expected her in town. Gods, he'd a demon's sense for investigation. Betsy tried to stay calm. "He — he asked about *me*?"

"No. He asked if I'd keep my ears open for someone named John Clark Sheridan."

"Oh. I see." Betsy swallowed, not at all relieved. "John Clark Sheridan, you say? I've not heard of him. I shall ask my husband if the name is familiar. Perhaps he's a relation."

"But you do know Dunstan."

Maria purred, and Betsy felt indignant at her implication. "Well, I'm acquainted with him. When Tom and I visited my family in Alton, he played piquet with the lieutenant." Betsy twisted her lips with what she hoped was remorse. "I'm ashamed to admit that my Tom lost more money than he should have. He and the lieutenant agreed that a new pair of boots would cancel the debt, and since the lieutenant was coming to South Carolina by way of Augusta, he escorted us back.

"Unfortunately, we didn't have a home to return to, or a shop for that matter, because our house had burned in our absence. Tom's creditors descended on him like turkey vultures. While his intentions to pay off Lieutenant Fairfax are honorable, it's going to take us awhile to get back on our feet."

"You don't want me to let him know you're here."

"I will be grateful if you don't mention it. When he returns to visit you, let us know, and we'll stay out of sight. Tom will get the debt repaid before the end of the year."

Maria snickered. "You'd best find a way to keep your man away from piquet."

Betsy rolled her eyes and heaved a sigh meant to sound forbearing. "You have the right of it there."

"Ladies." Emma came forward. "If *anyone* asks for the Sheridans, don't let on that they're here. This war deals bad knocks to good folks. Betsy and Tom need time to recover."

Margaret and Maria sealed the pact with silent nods that communicated they'd pass the word along to the others. Betsy wiped sweaty palms on her apron. She felt like she'd danced on a rope above a pit of lions.

Sally entered and bobbed a curtsy. "Miz Emma, they's sent word from th' hospital in Log Town. They needs more linen. Rebels ambushed a supply train yesterday, and they's lots o' King's Friends injured right now needing bandages."

Betsy stared. Clark had been in that supply train.

"I suspect they'll need more than bandages. They'll need some of Hattie's salve to fight infections, and willow bark for tea, and —" Emma turned and grasped Betsy's elbow. "Dear, can you spare a few hours today to help me in Log Town?"

And place herself in a superb position to discover what had happened to Clark? Betsy threw back her shoulders with dedication. "You can count on me."

CHAPTER TWENTY-EIGHT

Above the smells of dirt, horse, and scorched pork, the stenches of putrefaction, human waste, and vomit brewed beneath the blazing sun and bore down on Betsy when she and Emma dismounted at the perimeter of Log Town. They waited, sweating, in the scant shade of a pine tree. Guards secured their horses and inspected the contents of their baskets. Two privates then escorted them through camp to the hospital.

While walking avenues of canvas tents draped with scarlet wool coats too warm to wear, Betsy smelled rum and unwashed humans. She heard pennywhistles and fiddles and the laughter of young men on a one-way passage to obliteration before their lives had even begun. Conversation paused in their wake, and from the silent stares she and Emma received, she could almost hear the thoughts of the soldiers. *Not camp followers. Pretty. Young.* It made the hair on the back of her neck stand up, even in broad daylight, even with an escort.

Sutlers hawked fabric, ink, and tobacco. Wainwrights installed a new wheel on a wagon, and a blacksmith repaired a coffeepot. Her gaze pierced woodsmoke to haggard women toting water, cooking, and mending, and ragged children darting out of the way of oxen hauling supply wagons. She wondered how many camp followers had homes to return to and shuddered to imagine herself among them, raising her child in squalor.

The stench of death increased, and she saw canopies shielding hundreds of supine bodies. So many soldiers packed together, most still and quiet, some muttering or twitching in deliriums. Women in grimy aprons offered rum or water to those who were lucid. Flies swarmed over everything. How vulnerable the army was in Camden. There wasn't enough willow bark in all of South Carolina to accommodate such human suffering.

Their escort waved them beneath a canopy where the groaning of men was louder and pointed out several men clustered around a bloody table. Betsy and Emma set down their baskets, removed their straw hats beneath the shade, and fanned away flies. "Emma?" A tow-headed lad of fifteen rose on an elbow and plucked at her petticoat. Betsy sucked in alarm at bloody bandages swathing his lower right leg, and Emma knelt beside him. "Peter Griffin, oh, dear heavens, what are you doing here?"

He flopped back on a filthy blanket, his face twisted with agony, his voice a croak. "I left with the militia yesterday morning. Whigs ambushed us, tied us back to back, headed us out to meet Davie. Middle of the night, we fell into an ambush of our own men. They killed more than half of us. Couldn't see who we were in the dark. Got the fellow tied with me right through the heart. G - Got my leg, too."

Emma patted his hand. "Lie still and let the surgeon figure out how to fix your leg."

He rose again in terror. "He says the bone's too badly broke, and he'll have to take my leg! Don't let him take it!"

"Mr. Griffin!" Emma rose, and she and Betsy turned to the approach of the surgeon, a blood-spattered apron tied across his ample torso, his two muscular assistants following him.

"Noooooo!" Peter tried to roll up to a standing position, but the assistants were upon him. "No, I won't let you take my leg! I won't!" Betsy covered her mouth with her hand in horror, and a pallid-faced Emma lifted a handkerchief to her own mouth.

"I'm afraid the leg has to come off, sir. Lucky you are that I have something to ease the pain. You shan't feel a thing, I promise." The surgeon motioned the assistants toward the gore-spattered table.

"Noooooo!" Peter clutched for Emma before being borne away.

The surgeon lingered. "Mrs. Branwell?" Emma lowered her handkerchief and nodded. "I'm Dr. Daniels." He indicated the baskets. "I appreciate the donation. If you can help here for a few hours, I'd appreciate that, too, and see you get an escort out. My staff gets one fever after another." In the background, Peter's lamentations grew gurgled, as if one of the assistants had poured something down his throat. "You know the lad?"

"He's the youngest brother of one of my friends. I shall notify his mother."

"Thank you. Bloody shame when I have to take a boy's leg. Damn this war."

Daniels ambled for the surgery table flexing his biceps, and Emma turned away blinking back tears. Betsy took her hand. "Let's do what we can for an hour and leave. This is horrid."

Emma nodded. "If Peter's here, there are likely others from Camden also. Perhaps they even brought back the bodies of those killed in the ambush."

"The surgeon looks dreadfully busy. I wager he hasn't had the time yet to catalogue the casualties." Betsy's gaze ranged across the shaded area, taking in men who were reclining or sitting. "No doubt you'd be helping him further if you recognized —" Her voice trailed off as she watched an unshaven dark-haired man with a clean bandage on his left upper arm stand and look at her full on. "Oh, my god."

Clark's eyes widened with recognition, and then a blend of emotions traversed his expression: fear, flight, frustration, furtiveness. She gaped at him, the realization that he displayed no longing for her or regret for the situation pinioning her like a bayonet in her stomach and halting her instinct to bound forward and cast herself into his arms. Her reflection in his eyes was, in fact, that of a source of betrayal. The bayonet of anguish twisted upward and punctured her heart.

"Do you know that militiaman, Betsy?"

She unclamped her jaw and felt the ache in her head bleed through her soul. Her voice sounded dead. "He's from Augusta."

"Men travel quite aways to serve our king, don't they?" Emma gave her a nudge. "He looks none the worse. Go on over and chat. Maybe you can help him get word to loved ones in Georgia. I sure hope he didn't leave a wife and children behind."

"So do I." Betsy ambled over to Clark, who gestured to the east edge of the canopy: privacy if they kept their voices down. They regarded each other a few seconds until Betsy pursed her lips. "How's the arm?"

"A mere flesh wound."

"You're fortunate." She turned her gaze away from the bone saw at the table and tried to shut out Peter's babbling. "How ironic. Young Peter over there loses his leg for his sincere devotion to the king, and you walk away almost unscathed. You look surprised to see me."

Clark's lips tightened. "I am."

"Or perhaps you're simply surprised to see me *alive* after your friend van Duser nearly killed me last night."

He shook his head. "Jan wouldn't have killed you."

"Of course not. He'd planned to tell you it was bandits who slit my throat." Doubt flickered in Clark's eyes before he doused it. "Just as he'd planned for you to be accidentally shot in the ambush last night, tied back to back with a *true* Loyalist in a defenseless position. Fortunately for me, van Duser believed my assertion that your safety was what motivated me. Fortunately for you, the ambushing men couldn't see very well in the dark, and their aim on you was off by — oh —" She eyed his injured arm. " — one foot."

"I won't stand here and be insulted by you."

"Answer my questions. Our furniture is in Josiah Carter's barn. What are you going to do about it?"

"Nothing. It's safe there. I suggest you leave it alone."

"Clark, you may enjoy running around in the forest picking up ticks and stinking like a goat, but I want and need a home. In case you've forgotten, I'm carrying your child. I don't enjoy living off the charity of my cousin."

"Then you should have listened to me and stayed in Augusta."

She stared at him, open-mouthed, unable to believe how indurate he sounded. This was her husband? *...what a clever way to circumvent paying your most valuable employee. Marry her.* Adam's taunt didn't seem far-fetched at all. "You've taken off on this damned fool cause and abandoned me. All my worldly possessions are in a barn a mile and a half east of Camden. You've ruined my life —"

"If your life has been ruined, it's you who've done it by disobeying me and following me here after I told you to stay in the protection of Lucas and Sarah in Augusta."

"*Protection*? Can it be then that you don't know I left town to avoid being thrown in jail by Colonel Brown?"

"You're overreacting. It was house arrest. If you return, of course he'll throw you in jail for breaking house arrest —"

"Listen to me." She took a deep breath. "My Uncle David apparently spent Monday night the tenth with Widow Fuller and told her he might drop in on me on his way out Tuesday morning. Naturally the British interrogated that out of her, so you see, it really doesn't matter whether Uncle David saw me on his way out. In Brown's eyes, I'm an active link to my uncle, whom they're certain is a rebel. Even a lamebrain would realize there was no protection for me in Augusta, and after all my 'friends' began blaming me for your actions, I no longer even desired to remain there. So I'm in the protection of my cousin Emma, the only relation I knew how to reach quickly. And here in Camden, I find my only worldly possessions confiscated, and I receive confirmation that my husband has, indeed, abandoned me."

He leaned against a canopy post, scratched stubble on his jaw, and sighed. "I didn't know about your uncle. I presumed you were here to harass me into returning to Augusta."

"It's a bit late for that, wouldn't you agree?"

"It's been too dangerous for me to contact you."

"You don't realize the half of how dangerous it is. Was the Spaniard from *Casa de la Sangre Legítima* who chased you from Augusta the same who was found flayed alive several days ago?"

"Yes."

"Then you've Lieutenant Fairfax on your tail. He's suspected of flaying alive another Spaniard last month in Alton."

"Ye gods." Clark swallowed.

"You may also expect Lieutenant Neville to arrive in town hunting you sometime over the next few days."

"Thank you. I shall keep alert for his arrival." An awkward silence opened between them. "I still hope to make this up to you someday. Will you let me?"

She studied him and felt nothing inside, even though she suspected she'd feel a monstrous something later. "I doubt you can make this up to me. You've voluntarily placed yourself in a position where you're unable to protect me or the baby. Since I'm forced to take measures to do so myself, I shall leave Camden in a few weeks for a sanctuary in another colony. At this point, I'm not making plans beyond that day."

"But you'll tell me where you're going?" Incredulity exploded across his face at her silence, and he drew himself up to his full height. "You *will* tell me, dammit! You're my wife!"

"Am I?"

His expression returned to the guardedness it had held at the beginning of their conversation. "You know, I didn't want to believe Abel when he told me, but now I see it's true. My wife and my apprentice, sharing a bed."

"How dare you question my fidelity when you won't be a husband to me? And how dare you trust the word of Abel Branwell over me?"

He braced his fists on his hips. "Well? Is it true?"

She mirrored his posture. "I've not been unfaithful to you, though at this point, few would blame me if I were. And frankly, Clark, I'm weary of standing here defending my character. It suggests that you and I never trusted each other. I shan't waste more of my time with you when I'm needed over there among the wounded. You know where to find me. If you want to talk with me over the next few weeks, send word, and I shall attempt to meet you. But I'm through with chasing you."

CHAPTER TWENTY-NINE

From the clutter in the print shop on Littleton Street that afternoon, Betsy wondered whether her Aunt Susana had lent a hand at its management, too. She stepped around a bucket of lampblack, over a pile of ragpaper, and marched to the front counter.

The skinny, balding man behind the counter stood. "May I help you, madam?"

"I'm here to talk with the owner."

"His name is Frank Harker, but he's behind schedule arranging next week's paper."

"I thought so. I'm here to help him."

The man chuckled and wagged his forefinger at her. "Now, what does a young lady like you know about printing newspapers?"

"Column arrangement, for one thing." She spread Wednesday's paper on the counter. "This is all wasted space. Drop the point size on the columns, and you could get four columns to the front of the page with no wasted space." She flipped over the paper. "You could block in woodcuts and advertisements better."

The skinny man's jaw dangled open.

"You also could stand another pair of eyes editing the articles. This sentence fragment belongs at the beginning of the paragraph up here, while over on this article, you've double occurrences of the word 'the.' And you need to overhaul your type trays. A capital E looks like an F, and what is this letter over here — an r?"

The man cleared his throat. "Frank, come here a moment."

The owner, a big, stocky fellow in his late thirties, shuffled out wiping hands stained with lampblack and varnish and squinted at her. "What's the problem?"

"No problem. This lady knows how to arrange columns."

"You do?" Harker squinted again at her, this time with humor. "I suppose you've helped pull a printing press before?"

"Not since I was nine or ten, sir, but I haven't forgotten how it was done."

Harker's humor vanished. "And where might you have learned the printing business?"

"From my family's business in Alton, Georgia."

"Bust my buttons. You must be a St. James."

She frowned. "How do you know the St. Jameses?"

Harker belly-laughed. "Every printer knows Will St. James." He unrolled one of her grandfather's captioned "Tarleton's Quarter" broadsides with relish. "This here's a work of art."

Art? Alarm shot through Betsy. "I'd nothing to do with the printing of that broadside. I wasn't even in the same town when it happened."

Harker sniggered. "You needn't offer me any excuses."

"It's not you I'm worried about."

"Oh. Pshaw." Harker rolled up the broadside and stashed it beneath the counter. "Colonel Tarleton was in here several weeks ago laughing over it, asking if we'd seen new ones circulating. He's flattered by what it's done for his reputation." The printer emerged from behind the counter with his hand extended. "Frank Harker, madam."

She shook his hand. "Betsy Sheridan."

He grimaced at the copy of Wednesday's paper. "My — er — talent skipped town two weeks ago with the contents of the till. So you're interested in helping me?"

"Yes, but I require compensation."

"He didn't take *all* my money." Harker's jollity wilted. "See here, I'm in a pinch arranging next week's paper. If you've the talent and help me get the paper out on time, I'll pay you — uh — well, what exactly do you want to be paid?"

From the desperation in his posture, he wasn't in a position to bargain on wages. Betsy never believed she'd be able to name her price. Perhaps she could grow to appreciate the filthy, grueling business of printing after all.

***

In the sticky twilight of Friday night, she trudged back to the Leaping Stag embracing the exhaustion brought on by hours of work. She hoped to collapse in bed and be spared dreams of linen bandage strips, feverish soldiers, amputated limbs, and husbands abandoning wives. When she entered the dining room at the rear of the tavern, Hattie guided her to the table. "Child, just look at them hands of yours."

Betsy sat and regarded ink on her fingers. "Yes, I'm back in the printing business." Her stomach growled over the homey scents in the dining room, and she yawned.

"No food and no sleep ain't doing that baby of yours no good. I got the remedy for your belly, but then you got to get on upstairs and rest." A plate piled with string beans, turnip greens, ham, and buttered cornbread appeared on the table, and Betsy's mouth watered. She picked up her fork and dug in. "Lord, you and yo' man eat like you got hold of the last food on earth."

Betsy glanced around the dining room. "Did Tom come back yet?"

"'Bout half an hour ago. He eat three plates like yours 'fore heading up. Bless me if I know where he puts it all."

Three plates. "That's Tom for you."

Twenty minutes later, the cheer in the common room ramping up, Betsy climbed the stairs in time to encounter Dolly fumbling with the latch for the fourth guestroom while a portly captain slobbered on her neck. Betsy hurried past them: he smelling of brandy and tobacco, she of roses. The prostitute winked at her and kissed the captain's ear. "Oh, darling, has it been so long?"

"Grrrughmpugh." His meaty hand groped Dolly's breast.

Her cheeks aflame, Betsy opened the door to her own room, slipped inside, and exhaled. Just a little over a week since she'd made love, but the ladies made it feel like years.

A candle on the nightstand illuminated Tom's open bedroll spread between the bed and the door. Sprawled snoring on one side of the bed, Tom still wore his shirt, breeches, and one stocking. Betsy managed a tired smile. "I don't blame you after three plates of Hattie's cooking."

A huge yawn ran its course. She stripped to her shift and cleaned her teeth. By the time she completed a sponge bath and combed out her hair, she felt as though she was falling asleep standing up. Moving Tom from bed to bedroll would be sure to sprain her back or jolt him awake. She pulled off his garter, stocking, and breeches. Then she snuffed the candle and crawled into bed beside him.

He never showed any inclination to wake up, for which she wasn't sure whether she felt relieved or annoyed. She stared at the ceiling, tears salting her eyes, movement from the child in her belly by then definite. *...now I see it's true. My wife and my apprentice, sharing a bed.* Tears rolled down the side of her face into her ears, and she blotted them away. "Play hero, Clark. Enjoy yourself," she whispered to the night, and the night responded from the hallway with Dolly's laughter.

***

A cock crowed predawn, awakening her from a sound sleep. The bed sagged in the middle, plastering Tom's sweaty frontside to her sweaty backside. However, the bed wasn't to blame for Tom's right arm and leg draped over her body. "Good morning," he murmured. "I meant to sleep on the floor last night." His tone lacked guilt.

She matched the tone. "After Hattie told me how much food you'd eaten, I figured you weighed enough to break my back, so I just left you in bed."

His hand reached for hers, and his thumb caressed her palm. She felt his face in her hair and his breath on her neck. "You didn't braid your hair."

Her nipples tightened. "You weren't the only one who was exhausted."

"We both needed sleep." His fingertips trailed up her wrist to her forearm, brushed her sleeve, and stroked her neck. "Your skin is so soft."

Pressed between her buttocks, his erection burned and pulsed, summoning a slippery echo from her cleft. How little she'd have to do to tumble both of them over the edge of the precipice. Tilt her pelvis backward to provide the perfect angle. Roll onto her back and offer her lips to his. Guide his fingers to her aching nipple. In a town reeking of death and deception, why shouldn't she choose the affirmation of life and trust encoded in the essence of humanity? "Tom," she whispered.

"Sweet Betsy."

While she shifted onto her back, he pushed up on one elbow, took her face in his other hand, and leaned over to kiss her — stopped at the last moment by her fingers against his lips. Gods, how she wanted that kiss, how she longed to cast off her shift and his shirt and feel skin sliding together on a lusty film. She swallowed the fountain of saliva in her mouth. "I spoke with Clark yesterday."

After several heartbeats, she removed her fingers and heard him swallow, too. "Where?"

"Log Town. He'd received minor injury in the skirmish near Hanging Rock."

The cock crowed again. "I presume your talk went poorly."

"It's as you said two nights ago. His head is so filled with rubbish that he cannot save himself."

"Are you through with him, then?"

"I told him I'd leave Camden in a few weeks to protect myself and the baby. He expects me to wait for him, tell him where I'm going. We quarreled without resolution. I told him to send word if he wished to discuss it further before I left town."

"You still love him?"

When a woman was done with a man, she was done with him. "No. I'd fancied reconciliation before meeting him yesterday, but love for him is destructive, and I won't wait around to be destroyed."

The bed creaked with the transfer of his weight. He lay back, and she could just discern him staring at the ceiling. "So the plans we made the other night stand. Make money as quickly as possible and then leave Camden to find your mother."

"Yes. I've afternoon work helping the town printer. I'm paid well. He was desperate."

"Splendid. Mr. Wade will grant me as much overtime as I desire." He paused. "It does sound like you don't love Clark anymore. But if I were him, I'd want to know it."

"I need to tell him and be done with it before we leave."

"Yet you mentioned being open to discussion with him. Isn't it better for both of you to sever contact?"

Disquiet and frustration pricked her soul. The fluid nature of the immediate future might mean she was gone from Camden if Clark tried to meet her. She could lose track of him after that — never know whether he cared to be a part of his child's life. On the other hand, his actions weren't her responsibility. While she'd make a reasonable attempt to meet him before she left Camden, she'd forgo such a meeting if it meant being held accountable for him. "Although I'll have no part in being his wife anymore, I'm carrying his baby. He may want some say in the child's upbringing. If I can I'll ask him." Tom stayed silent, and she gulped. "I'm groping through a dark room without a candle, Tom. I know none of this is fair to you."

He remained quiet so long that she wondered whether he'd fallen asleep again, but then he groaned. "Emma was waiting for me last night. Hattie excused herself from the dining room while I was on my second helping of everything, and then Emma sat next to me, smelling of lilac, her hands soft, her breasts two damp, luscious mounds begging to be freed from her bodice."

Betsy could almost feel his hands aching and, in an arc of jealousy, understood why her cousin hadn't protested her plan to work afternoons. Few warm-blooded fellows Tom's age would refuse release offered in such a blithe and relentless fashion.

Irony stung his voice. "I was tired and hungry. Alas for Emma, *too* tired and hungry." Somberness replaced the irony. "I don't want her, Betsy."

Was Emma's desire for Tom Alexander's intelligence and courage, or was it for the physical delights of a strapping young fellow? Indignation smoldered within her, for she suspected Emma's motivation was the latter, and she reconsidered all those incriminatory invoices in Abel's study. "Do what you must." Indeed, they were all at war, and people did what they must in war — but her cousin had best not wound Tom.

"There you are being noble again. I've never wanted anyone but you. I shall wait for you."

She pushed up on her elbow. "Tom Alexander, that's the first stupid thing I've ever heard you say. What if I'm never available? Are you being fair to yourself?"

He stroked her cheek with the backs of his fingers. "I reckon it's as fair as it gets. The universe isn't accountable to dealing justly with any of us."

CHAPTER THIRTY

R evelry called no day of the week special, so Betsy readied the guestrooms for business on Sunday, the twenty-third of July. After dinner, she and Tom set off to explore Camden and walked the perimeter of the large palisade erected by the British. The British had also fortified redoubts and powder magazines.

So much done in so little time. Cornwallis realized it didn't build morale to let several thousand troops sit idle while 125 miles northeast, General de Kalb awaited the arrival of General Horatio Gates, granted independent command of the Southern Continental Army. Hence the flurry of palisade building.

Overheard conversations bespoke the concern of Camden's citizens. "Rawdon cannot stand up to Gates with half his men sick in Log Town." "Cornwallis sits in Charles Town and isn't lifting a finger to help." "Redcoats — always making promises they don't keep." Not a good *esprit de corps* for a major backcountry base.

She and Tom strolled north on Market Street. It would be three weeks before they could afford a packhorse, and they both realized General Gates wouldn't dally around after he met up with de Kalb.

She said, "How long do you suppose we have until the Continental Army rides into town?"

"Three weeks, maybe less."

"We're shaving it quite close."

"I don't want to run out of supplies while we're searching for your mother." He gave her hand a squeeze of reassurance. "I'm worried, too. But we'll get out, and we'll find her."

With the afternoon shadows grown long, they headed north on Campbell Street. Halfway to King Street, Tom gaped ahead among pedestrians, riders, and carriages and then ducked into an alley between two shops with Betsy in tow. He motioned for her silence, peeked around the edge of a baker's shop, and withdrew again. "That's Adam Neville up there with six Rangers!"

They peered back around to spy a road-grimed Neville and grungy Rangers dismounted before a shop. No one at the shop answered their knocks. The seven Rangers remounted, rode north on Campbell, and turned east onto King.

Betsy tugged Tom out of cover. "Let's see who they were calling upon."

Keeping a sharp lookout, they proceeded over and studied the storefront, expressions souring. "Messers. van Duser and der Waal, Surveyors." She cocked an eyebrow. "No surprise."

"I've the feeling the rebels' spy ring days are numbered in Camden. Let's go."

She gnawed her lower lip. "I don't like this."

"If Neville intends to haul you back to Augusta and throw you in jail, he'll track you down no matter where you are. But if he must go through the trouble of hauling someone back to Augusta jail, his priority will be Clark, not you. And we cannot stay here and debate it. I'm hungry."

"One thing we absolutely cannot hide from is your appetite." He smirked. "Just so."

***

"What you lookin' at in the common room, Mistuh Tom?"

He faced Hattie from the doorway, amazement flooding his expression. "For a Sunday evening, the Leaping Stag sure does a brisk business."

"Well, now, what you expect wit' all them dry British soldiers camped a mile north o' here? Hrumph." She turned her back on them to butter fresh cornbread.

Tom winked at Betsy and mouthed, "No Neville."

She exhaled relief and accepted the chair he pulled out. He sank into the chair beside hers, and when Hattie set plates before them, they had nothing to say for several minutes. They capped off the meal with blackberry cobbler, and in a drowse brought on by the afternoon of walking and the supper of good food, Betsy felt Hattie pat her shoulder. "That's right, child, you go ahead and eat fo' dat baby of yours. Bless me if you wasn't just skin and bones when you arrive here last Wednesday."

"Mrs. Sheridan." Betsy blinked at Abel, who stood in the doorway, and Tom turned his head to regard the dour-faced accountant. "I would speak with you in my office." Tom rose, and Abel sniffed. "*Alone*." He vanished down the hallway.

Too sleepy to conjure resistance, she shrugged at Tom and followed Abel. Only when she rapped on his office door did she suspect he might have figured out she'd snooped in his office Friday morning — but by the time her reasoning caught up with her groggy senses, the accountant was already beckoning her inside. She came fully awake when he shut the door behind her and Adam Neville rose from a chair in the corner shadows. "Mrs. Sheridan, what a pleasure to see you again."

She glanced from a stone-faced Abel, who had assumed position near the room's only lamp, to the floor, where she bit her tongue to stop herself from screeching, "Branwell, you stinking, miserable excuse for a double agent!" Then she looked back at Neville, whose lip was still swollen from the encounter with her riding crop a week earlier, and grafted on her tea-party smile. "Lieutenant, what brings you to Camden?"

He laughed and crossed the rug between her and Abel. "You're quite good at this, you know, sending my men and me on to Ninety Six. I even fancy you gnawed your way out of your bonds last Monday morning while we were all sleeping."

"You hardly seemed open to reasoning, and I didn't desire to birth my child in Augusta jail. As I told you, I was seeking the shelter of a relation to have my baby in peace. Here I am in the home of my cousin Emma. Have I satisfied your curiosity?"

"And where is Clark?"

She held his gaze. "I've no idea."

"You may as well dispense with the lies. One of our agents saw you talking with him in Log Town Friday. Where is he?"

"Random chance made that encounter possible. I accompanied Emma to donate medical supplies for Loyalists injured in the Hanging Rock incident. Clark was one of the injured men there."

"And you'll see him again — when?"

She shook her head. "Your guess is as good as mine. To protect himself, he never told me where he was staying, nor did he set up a time to meet me again."

Neville crossed the room and returned to the shadows. It was downright eerie the way he blended with darkness, just the way an Indian would do. "You're under arrest, madam."

"Yes, I do remember." She lifted her chin, feeling her game options run out, and extended her wrists. "Go ahead, then, take me to jail. There isn't a thing I can do to stop you."

His eyes glittered from the shadows, much as Brown's had done from beneath his hat. "You swore allegiance to the king, and I admire the grace with which you handle this. I shall give you the opportunity to prove your loyalty."

She lowered her wrists, liking the sound of his prelude even less than the threat of jail. "I've already proven it in the letter I wrote Colonel Brown before my departure."

"Then you shouldn't mind proving it again. Clark is working for rebels while posing as a Loyalist. The Ambrose spy ring, of which he's a part, aims to assassinate British military figures in high command positions. A great deal of funding for the ring's activities comes from the Dutch, although we aren't certain yet what the Stadtholder's motive is in all this.

"Last month, counterespionage activities enabled the Earl Cornwallis to learn of an ambush along his return route to Charles Town, so he took another route. But an operative from the Ambrose ring made an attempt on the commander at Ninety Six Friday. He killed an adjunct accompanying the commander and then swallowed poison to avoid interrogation. And, of course, there was the attempt on Colonel Brown's life by Sooty Johns. So you see, we really must put a stop to the activity.

"Clark will attempt to meet you again. Find out as much as

possible about the ring's mission — the names of the agents, where they're located, the Stadtholder's stakes. Ultimately we expect you to lead us to Clark, at which point you'll be exonerated from suspicion."

Betsy swallowed, horrified. "How can you expect me to just hand him over to you?"

The smile spread across Neville's swollen lips again. "You're sharing the bed of his apprentice, and when a woman takes up such an arrangement, she often dispenses with the man who is obsolete. Do we understand each other?" She nodded, flabbergasted. "Excellent. When you've information of import, send word to me through Mr. Branwell. I shan't stray far." He bowed to Abel. "Sir." He bowed to Betsy. "Again, madam, it's been a pleasure."

As soon as he exited, she pivoted to follow. "Mrs. Sheridan, I'm not finished with you yet." Abel laid his hand on the door latch. Here it came, a confrontation over the snooping. "I've a message to you from Ambrose." Black humor laced his tone. "Under no circumstances are you to follow Neville's orders. If you contact your husband, it shall be my pleasure to evict you and Mr. Alexander from my house on your adulterous arses. May heaven help you after Ambrose catches up with you."

God damn the bastard to hell. She returned his glare. "The conservative approach is a curious one for you, considering the four whores you've lodged upstairs."

His lips pulled back in a snarl. "Don't be clever with me, woman, or you shall deeply regret it. Now begone."

She trudged back up the hallway and through the dining room, dazed that she was expected to serve both rebels and British. All the way upstairs, she pinched herself, hoping she'd awaken from the nightmare, but when she reached the second floor, she realized the nightmare wasn't yet ready to release her. Beside the door to their room, her cousin had Tom pressed against the wall in a kiss so juicy Betsy could hear the moisture. In ruthless rhythm, Emma rotated her pelvis into his groin and rubbed his chest with her silk-covered, unfettered breasts. Betsy backed around the entrance of the stairway and down three steps, rage spreading within her.

She heard the kiss break off. "Mrs. Branwell, this is most unseemly of you."

Emma sounded breathless. "Darling, you must help me. My marriage is unconsummated. Abel has desires only for his accounting books, while I'm a warm-blooded woman with such diverse *needs* —"

"I'm not the one to gratify those needs. I'm very much enamored of my wife —"

"Oh, the mockery of it, that my drab little cousin could arouse a handsome young man like you more than I, and she stinking of chamberpots." Betsy balled her fists. Small wonder Emma felt such affinity for her prostitutes. "Smell my wrist. Lilac. Here on my throat, too. Feel how soft. Yes? I'm oh so ready for you to take me, even if for only two minutes —" Silk slithered, and Emma squeaked with surprise. "Oh! What did you do that for?"

"I already told you I'm not interested, madam. Good night!"

The bedroom door squawked open and slammed shut. Emma emitted a ragged sigh, muttered, "Damn," and shuffled for the stairs. Betsy straightened her shoulders, held the banister, and waited, her expression neutral. No surprise registered on Emma's face when she turned the corner and spied Betsy. "Oh, excuse me, dear, I'm having such trouble sleeping tonight and must have left my laudanum in the dining room." She glided downstairs in a cloud of lilac so cloying that Betsy almost gagged.

In the bedroom, Tom bent over the washbasin dousing his face and neck with cool water, his coat and vest cast onto the chair. He straightened and blotted his face on a towel, and they eyed each other in mutual misery too deep for words. "Betsy, I'm thinking if we work really hard, we can get out in two weeks."

"Even the morrow won't be soon enough."

He nodded, flung aside the towel, and cleaned his teeth. She waited on the bed for him to finish, and while he opened his blanket, undressed to his shirt, and lay down on the bedroll, she rushed through her own toilette. The candle extinguished, they lay in darkness, and Tom dropped off into sleep.

But she lay awake a long while, trussed up in the schemes of the Branwells, Jan van Duser, and Adam Neville. A fly blundered into a spider's web, she struggled without escape, awaiting the spider's pleasure, and she detested all of them with virulence that shocked her.

While she lay awake, she realized Abel wasn't omniscient. He didn't know she'd snooped in his office. If she did nothing else, she was determined to decipher the message in Clark's last letter. The intelligence locked there might give her leverage. Should she find Abel's office locked, that ring of keys in the cupboard downstairs included a spare key for his office.

It occurred to her then that she wasn't as trussed up as they all presumed. The revelation made her skin crawl. At her disposal was a weapon her antagonists weren't aware of, an elemental she might loosen upon them if she figured out how to contain him without destroying anyone she loved in the process.

Words and the printing press: her family legacy.

What a masterful piece of propaganda her grandfather had produced with that broadside. History was full of warriors whose only weapon was words. Words, yes, her means of directing the beast. With a smile of satisfaction, she rolled onto her side and slipped into sleep.

CHAPTER THIRTY-ONE

Monday morning, Betsy tidied the guestrooms in time to allow a visit to Abel's office — this time locked. Under pretense of fetching towels, she trotted the ring of keys upstairs to replace the spare office key with her room key — just in case Hattie or Emma counted keys — and then returned the ring to the cupboard. She'd leave early for the print shop, find an artisan to copy the key, and replace the original before anyone was the wiser.

In the accountant's office, she memorized ten more number-word combinations. Comparing invoices to entries in the ledger, she realized the expenses of the Ambrose spy ring were being subsidized by so many different "charitable donations" that it boggled her mind. Tempting as it was to pass invoices on to the redcoats, she resisted the easy gratification. Abel would figure out she'd undone him and get word to the spies, and then she and Tom might not escape Camden. No, she had something far more appropriate planned for Mr. Abel Branwell.

Emma was her usual ingratiating self, praising Betsy's cleaning before wheedling a pre-dinner trip from her to the butcher. On Market

Square, Betsy joined a gaggle of goodwives in straw hats, all haggling over haunches in the hot sun while the butcher's boy fanned flies off the cuts.

A brisk breeze seized Betsy's hat and sailed it over the butcher's stall. Annoyed to lose her place in line, she gave chase. Before a fabric stall on the next row, she found her hat in the hands of Josiah Carter.

He passed it to her as if afraid she might take his arm off at the elbow. She curtsied. "Thank you, Mr. Carter."

From his furtive posture, she wondered whether he was being followed. "Good day, madam." He plunged into the most densely populated portion of the market.

After tying the ribbons of her hat, she scurried after him. Carter, like her, was caught in the middle. "I've no hard feelings for you, sir."

He walked quickly without looking at her. "I'm glad to hear it. I wondered whether I'd see you alive again. Had I known the vipers with whom I'd be sharing a pit, I'd never have agreed to store your property. I haven't the slightest idea how to extricate myself from this intrigue."

"You must think me petty for wanting my property back."

"Not at all. I commiserate. I've lost eighty percent of my family fortune in the past four years. It's bad enough that I shall be forced to sell all but three hundred acres of my land to pay off my debts. Now Mr. van Duser and his attorneys dangle blackmail before my nose. I've not the finances to defend myself, so they push me around. I wish I'd never set eyes on that Dutch demon."

Betsy's heart wrenched. Three hundred acres was a pittance for one accustomed to the life of a gentleman. His life, like hers, had been ruined by manipulations of rebels and British. A pity neither had taken sides. They might have fared better.

Ambivalence tugged on her soul. If she executed the scheme she'd crafted overnight, Carter might get backlashed, and she could lose her furniture forever if she didn't protect him. She caught his forearm and turned him to face her, the bustle of Market Square around them. "Mr. Carter, I'm setting a plan in motion that will make van Duser rue the day he started pushing decent folks like us around. The problem with my plan is that you may fall under suspicion unless —"

"Ah, no, I want no part in what you're scheming. I'd rather stay out of jail, thank you."

She released him. "You needn't know the details. All you need do is move my property from your barn to a safe location on your land and play ignorant when people come asking for it."

"Van Duser will slit my throat if I touch your property."

Recalling the tale of Will's adventure in Havana, she smiled. "Tell him a — er — Spaniard appropriated it to a secure and secret location and paid you handsomely for your trouble. He'll hop like a rabbit after he hears that news."

"A Spaniard?" Carter frowned at her. "Why should that make him jump? And to be sure, he'll want the name of this Spaniard to verify my story."

"Give him the name Jaime de Gálvez."

"Gálvez. Ye gods, I've heard of them. Way up there in the Spanish court, aren't they?" Carter's lips paled as he began to ponder the extent of the intrigue he'd been plunged into. "But — but why would such a connection be significant to van Duser?"

"I've no time to explain, but I suspect the name is tangled enough with his intrigue to confer immediate credibility upon your story. What do you say — will you do it?"

"I shall give it thought."

"Don't drag your feet. I may have to execute my plan any moment. *Whoever* comes asking for that furniture, give them the exact same story, and make certain you leave my name out of it."

His gaze made another pass around the marketplace, and he bowed. "I must be off. Good day, madam." With a tip of his cocked hat, he vanished into the crowd.

She watched him go, a smile touching her lips. How she wished she could witness the obnoxious self-assurance wiped from van Duser's face when Carter explained the missing furniture, but she'd just have to settle for imagining the event and knowing it would soon be the Dutchman's turn, like Abel, to run scared.

***

Harker and assistant Saunders had started the print run for Wednesday's paper when Betsy arrived. She came prepared in her oldest clothing. Lampblack and varnish spattered everywhere, even if she didn't pull the press. Harker greeted her with a grin. "The first side's looking mighty good!"

On all the pages hanging to dry in the yard behind the shop, columns lined up without reading too cramped and with little wasted space. Type was crisp and clean, owing to her speedy sort job late Friday afternoon. Harker had trashed the cracked letters, so they wouldn't have sloppy type again.

At two-thirty, while she hung out front pages, the men ambled outside with lit pipes. "We're running ahead of schedule, thanks to you, Mrs. Sheridan." Harker wiped his sweaty neck with a kerchief. "The master calls for a fifteen-minute break. Sit down for a spell and rest your feet."

Just the opportunity for which she'd been waiting. "I shall pick up where you gentlemen left off, if you don't mind."

"You sure you want to get your hands dirty?"

She wiggled blackened fingers at him. "Like this?"

Harker laughed. "You're an angel, Mrs. Sheridan."

That wouldn't be the attribute others ascribed to her when she was finished with them. She curtsied. "It's my pleasure to be of assistance."

In the pressroom, she grabbed two empty composing sticks and opened type drawers. Five minutes later, she inspected her message: *The furniture you seek is in the keeping of Jan van Duser, surveyor, Camden.* She set the sticks aside, inked the galley of the front page of the paper, and pulled off five copies — requiring more physical effort than she'd remembered from her childhood. Upon completion, she headed outside with the pages. Neither printer nor assistant moved from the shade.

Back inside, she hauled out an extra galley and fit her two composing sticks into it. Then she inked it down, pulled off a copy, and inspected it. No letters inverted. Everything was lined up well and easy to read. Perfect. Setting the page aside, she fit the front page galley of the paper back onto the press and pulled off five more copies, at which point she could feel herself working up a sweat, and Harker and Saunders were stomping in through the back door anyway. She hastened to break down her galley and stash the composing sticks out of sight on a low shelf for disassembly later.

Saunders clicked his tongue as she bustled past with the six pages. "Look at her go, Frank."

"Best thing that ever happened to my business."

She camouflaged her page among dozens of front pages drying in the merciless sunlight, pausing to regard it before she returned inside. It would have been far easier to write a note, but she couldn't chance anyone from the Ambrose ring intercepting the message and comparing a sample of her handwriting.

As for Lieutenant Fairfax, she doubted he'd backtrack during the heat of the hunt just to query printers about the page. No, if he'd tracked down that Spanish assassin in Camden with such alacrity, she could be certain that while any scent was fresh, he'd stay with his quarry. And after he scratched the van Duser surface of the Ambrose spy ring, he'd be reaping far too much success to care who'd tipped him off. By then, she and Tom would be long gone from Camden.

She studied the page, her mood sobering, for there was no getting around the fact that after Fairfax got to digging, Clark's name would come up. Not that such a revelation would surprise the lieutenant. She was sure he'd known standing near the scorched foundation of their house in Augusta that Clark was a spy. He'd tried to snare him then, even though he didn't have quite enough proof.

Clark, however, was a groundnut in comparison to the giants of the ring, evidenced by the way he'd been sent on that suicide mission to Hanging Rock. If Fairfax could get hold of one of the top men in the spy ring and squeeze information from him, why would he waste time on drones like Clark or even Basilio or Francisco? Betsy chewed her lip. She hoped as much was true, because she didn't want to be the instrument of her husband's death, even if there was nothing left of the marriage. At least she'd alerted Clark in Log Town to Fairfax's proximity.

"Mrs. Sheridan!" Saunders jiggled papers from the doorway. "Where'd you run off to?"

"Right here, sir, making sure everything's drying properly."

Just after eight, she left the print shop exhausted but elated. Yes, she'd broken down the composing stick without Harker or Saunders knowing, and she had her prize trimmed, folded, and tucked inside her bodice, but the game of one-upmanship with the Ambrose spy ring wasn't the sole source of the spring in her step.

Of all the crazy notions — she'd derived satisfaction from her work in the pressroom. The men had praised her insights and helpfulness, but it felt *good* to pull the filthy, grueling press again. Perhaps printing was in her blood. The entire process filled her with such a sense of power and accomplishment that she couldn't wait to help print the back page of the paper the following afternoon.

Not until she'd returned to the Leaping Stag and caught sight of Janet and Maria in the common room laughing and flirting with soldiers did she put the pieces together, and it astounded her. Dependent on husbands and fathers for protection, Janet, Maria, Dolly, Margaret, and hundreds of women across the thirteen colonies were forced to whore their way through the war when their menfolk disappeared. They'd never learned skills to land them other work in demand.

But Betsy had been in a position to receive the legacy of printing as she was growing up. Will St. James and Sophie Barton had thrust the business down her throat at times, but she at last realized what they'd been about. She needn't be dependent on a man for protection. With her skills, so long as she settled in a town with a printing press, she needn't worry about being reduced to prostitution or raising her child in poverty.

Her stomach rumbled with hunger, and she smelled the supper Hattie had ready for her in the dining room. After sweeping her gaze across the common room once more, she whispered, "Thank you Grandpapa. And thank you, Mother."

CHAPTER THIRTY-TWO

O n July twenty-fifth, Horatio Gates arrived at de Kalb's camp on Deep River, their combined forces numbering anywhere between 2,500 and 7,000 troops, depending on the source's sobriety. On the twenty-seventh, Gates ordered a march on Camden straight through countryside with little resources to scavenge.

While Betsy and Tom doubted his wisdom over the march, they couldn't deny that starving Continentals would find Log Town and its invalid soldiers easy pickings. Lord Rawdon realized the same, mustering what able-bodied men he could to detain Gates. If ever Cornwallis's support in manpower and martial prowess was needed, it was then. But the British general remained aloof in Charles Town, and anxiety swelled among Camden's residents.

Many shop owners — Harker included — professed loyalty while trafficking with rebels, hoping their businesses wouldn't be confiscated whatever the outcome. Some threw diplomacy to the wind, enticed redcoats to desert, and then transferred deserters among safe houses to prevent their capture. The British remained baffled over desertions, missing the point that loyalty and proper conduct didn't possess a man's soul the way of a cause. But Betsy had witnessed fervor in Clark's eyes as he explained why he cast his lot with the rebels. Even if she didn't swallow rebel propaganda, she heeded the power of the irrational.

Monday night, the thirty-first of July, she pulled out the last letter to Clark and, thanks to Abel's regular meetings with the Dutchmen, ninety percent of the cipher key. She and Tom set out to decode the hidden message. "Ambrose, Cornwallis," it read. "Black, Rawdon. White, Clinton. Gray, Tarleton. Yellow, Hamilton. Red, Webster. Green, Ferguson. Blue, Brown ... Morton will also advance agenda of Stadtholder."

Tom paced while she thought aloud. "The colors: codes for agents in the ring? And each is paired with the officer he's supposed to assassinate." She wrinkled her nose. "If van Duser is Ambrose, I cannot imagine him assassinating Cornwallis. But *why* are the Dutch planning assassinations?" Tom continued to pace, and she wondered whether he was listening. "If all these men are killed, the British won't surrender and go home. Officers will fill their positions, and the war will go on."

Tom stopped pacing. "*Morton.* Do you suppose the reference in the message is to Major Morton, Thomas Brown's adjutant?"

"'Morton will also advance agenda of Stadtholder.'" Her eyes widened in amazement. "What if the Stadtholder bought replacement officers in advance of assassinations?"

"And after his men are in place within the army, he turns the tide of war to his favor. For example, the new commander of the Legion doesn't drive his dragoons quickly enough to prevent redcoats from being ambushed and slaughtered by Davie, and the rebels escape with captured ammunition and supplies."

"But Tom, ammunition and supplies aren't as great an issue as men. It takes time and expense to replace seasoned soldiers."

"Exactly, and His Majesty is already feeling the attrition. While Britain stretches herself to make an empire of the world, her trained soldiers are dying by the hundreds in the colonies. If Holland can accelerate those losses —"

"Here's another thought. The Stadtholder's officers will return to honors in Britain. They'll receive titles and land, perhaps posts in Parliament."

"Zounds, Betsy, the Stadtholder could be running Britain in another fifteen to twenty years!"

She gave him a wry grin. "Huzzah!"

"Whom do we tell?" he whispered.

"No one," she whispered back and echoed his smirk. "I cannot imagine Holland being worse at governing these colonies."

A tap on their door caused them to jump in alarm. Tom raised his voice. "Uh, a moment, please." They hid the letter, translation, and key, and he opened the door.

Margaret beamed at them from the doorway. "Our lieutenant will see me again at eight in the evening on the morrow."

Betsy felt color drain from her face. She hadn't told Tom about her plan to tip Fairfax off. He'd just try to talk her out of it along the lines of "Don't tempt the Fates." But she really wanted Abel Branwell and Jan van Duser running scared. The more preoccupied they were with saving their own skins, the more easily they'd let two neutrals go.

Tom draped an arm around Betsy's shoulder. "Thank you, Margaret. I shall work in a pair of slippers, just for you." Margaret curtsied and walked away. He closed the door and guided Betsy back. "Let's meet in here on the morrow before eight."

She'd have to find a way to get the note to Fairfax without arousing suspicion. "We print the other side of the newspaper on the morrow. I'll likely run late."

"Ah, that's right. Very well, if you aren't back by eight-thirty, I shall come looking for you."

***

The next morning, the household was abuzz with news of military action from the thirtieth of July. Rebel leader Isaac Shelby had besieged Thicketty Fort in northwest South Carolina, but because the fort commander surrendered before any shots were fired, the men inside were paroled without injury. Three companies of Loyalists from North Carolina weren't so fortunate near Hanging Rock — cut to pieces by William Davie's rebels before the garrison in Hanging Rock could help them. Cocky and irascible Thomas Sumter had besieged the garrison at Rocky Mount and set the main building afire. But an afternoon thunderstorm extinguished the blaze, and Sumter had withdrawn, thwarted.

A sealed letter awaited Betsy at breakfast, and she glanced over the contents: "B. — Minor injuries at Rocky Mount. In Log Town through Tuesday night. Must talk. Please come. C." Hattie exited the dining room, and Betsy showed it to Tom. "It's an opportunity to settle with Clark, but I cannot take advantage of it with Fairfax in Camden today. I don't want to run into him in Log Town, and I hope *Clark* doesn't run into him."

Tom nodded, expression grim. "With Clark's phenomenal luck at escaping serious injury, perhaps you'll have another chance to talk with him."

Espionage, Betsy decided, wasn't for heroes. It was the realm of fools. The sooner she cleared the field and could be mistaken for neither, the better she'd feel.

***

At seven-thirty, she left a completed print run and hurried back to the tavern. She approached with wariness and upon her arrival paused to scrutinize the traffic out front.

From the noise level and crowd at the hitching post, the common room neared capacity. Scrawny pre-teen boys mingled with the activity and begged off the soldiers. One lad spied her and ran over, evading horses and carriages like an eel, brown eyes alert, dirty face eager. "A full house in there tonight."

"I can see that, Andy. How's your mama's cough?"

"Much better. Bless you and Hattie for them biscuits."

"Sure." Betsy grasped his bony shoulder. "How'd you like to earn two pence tonight?" His jaw dropped open. "It could be dangerous, and you'd have to follow my instructions carefully."

"Oh, yes, madam!"

"And I must have your word that you'll tell no one."

The lad's eyes gleamed. "It's spy work, ain't it?"

"No questions."

The sparkle in his eyes remained unfazed. "Yes, madam, 'pon my word, I shall keep quiet."

"Good. I expect an officer from the Seventeenth Light to arrive soon. I've a message for him, but he mustn't know it came from me. I shall give you a penny to deliver it and another when you report to me afterwards." He nodded. "After he reads the message, he'll want to question you. He isn't a good man. He'll hurt you, and he may even kill you, so you must disappear."

"Don't worry. I know how to disappear."

"I'm sure you do. Watch your back for a few days, too." She patted his shoulder. "I shall monitor the common room from inside. When I see the officer, I shall come out the back door and give you the message and a penny. Complete your mission and meet me at the back door for the other penny."

"Yes, madam."

She described Fairfax to him before they parted company. Hattie had supper waiting for her, but she peeked out and scanned the common room first. "Child, come on over here an' set down. Yo' man eat only one helping and then go straight up to bed. You reckon he's taken a fever?"

Tom was upstairs, out of the way. Excellent. "He's just tired from all that overtime."

Betsy gobbled supper. As she finished her ale, she heard a soft knock on the dining room door. Hattie scowled, hands floury, and reached for a towel. "Who's that this time of night?"

"Not to worry. I shall get it."

A gleam-eyed Andy danced on the back step. "The rare bird flew in to roost."

"Wait right there." She strode over and peeked out into the common room in time to see Emma flattering Fairfax near the clients' stairway. He waved away her offer of wine and pointed upstairs. Considering that the ladies played games with clients, he might be made to wait awhile. Betsy smirked and slipped out the back door. "He's early for his appointment with Margaret, so here's your first penny, and here's the message."

The penny vanished from Andy's quick fingers, and he sprinted around for the front. With a sigh of anxiety, Betsy returned inside and assumed position to peek out again. Hattie chuckled. "I don't know what you's up to."

"Sometimes I just like to watch the activity in the common room." Her eyes bulged. Margaret glided downstairs fifteen minutes early, Fairfax strode over to meet her, and pompous Todd was interrogating Andy at the door to the tavern while a muscle-bound assistant gripped the lad's shoulders. Damn. Andy was going to miss his window of opportunity. After Fairfax got started on Margaret, who knew how long he'd be occupied?

Stymied at her scheme, Betsy watched delight flood Margaret's face when Fairfax kissed her hand and the inside of her wrist. They headed upstairs, and Betsy sagged against the doorjamb in frustration. But at the front door, Todd had finally allowed Andy to pass. The lad homed in on Fairfax and Margaret and then threaded for the stairs among partying soldiers.

Betsy sneaked up the service stairway and peered around the corner to find Fairfax and Margaret, hand in hand, entering the first guestroom. The door latched closed behind them, and two seconds later, Andy emerged at the top of the stairs. His gaze darted to Betsy. She held up one finger and pointed to room one.

With a curt nod, he walked forward and rapped on the door. "Lieutenant, I've a message for you."

"Leave it with Mrs. Branwell downstairs."

"It's urgent, sir — a matter of intelligence."

Fairfax yanked open the door and glared at Andy, who extended the letter to him. "This better be good, you filthy little urchin."

As soon as he snatched the letter, Andy bolted for the stairs. Fairfax's expression transformed from annoyance to rapture when he read the message. The paper clenched, he looked in Andy's direction, that appalling angelic radiance suffusing his face. Never mind sex. The game was afoot. "Boy, wait!"

After ducking in the room, Fairfax re-emerged with a perplexed Margaret trailing after. "But Dunstan, why cannot it wait half an hour?" If he responded, Betsy didn't hear. He thumped down the stairs, Camden's premier lady of the night forgotten.

Back on the first floor, Betsy surveyed the common room. Andy had navigated it by the time the lieutenant reached the foot of the stairs. Realizing he couldn't bowl through dozens of rowdy men to apprehend his quarry, Fairfax shouted, but the din of the room swallowed his words.

With Andy free and clear out the front door, Betsy ignored Hattie's cocked eyebrow and exited again. They met at the corner of the building, and she hugged him despite his grime. "You were brilliant!"

"Thank you. Let me know if you have any other errands."

"To be sure. Here's the other penny. And remember, this is our little secret."

"Yes, madam!" Something around the corner snagged his attention, and then he stared back at her, elation drained from his expression. "Uh oh. It's *him*, the lieutenant!"

She snagged his arm and hissed, "Inside that shed!" They raced for the shed where Sally stored gardening tools, closed themselves into humid darkness redolent of corn and earth, and looked out through cracks in the plank door. Enough light remained for them to see Fairfax skulk around the corner. He stood still a moment like a swamp cat casting for scent before walking to the back door and rapping on it.

Hattie shook her head at his low-voiced query. "Ain't no younguns fittin' that description come through this dining room, Lieutenant. No, sir. Good night to you, too." She shut the door on him, and he turned around on the step, again surveying the back yard and gardens. Then he idled toward the shed.

Betsy heard Andy suck in a breath of fear. With her left hand, she gripped his arm to prevent his flight. With her right hand, she grabbed the handle of a hoe.

Halfway to the shed, Fairfax paused, and his voice softened. "Lad, I apologize for being short with you." He reached inside his vest and jingled his purse. "A shilling if you'll talk."

A shilling was far more than two pennies. Andy tensed, and Betsy, fearing that he was ready to take the bait, clamped her hold on him tighter. In the next second, Fairfax moved his hand from purse to dagger. Andy gulped, understanding his true reward if he were discovered. Betsy thrust him behind her, took hold of the hoe with both hands, and bared her teeth.

"Surely a clever lad like you could use a shilling, eh?"

She held her breath, as did Andy, while Fairfax listened to the garden around him. Then he sheathed his dagger and strode back the way he'd come.

"Bloody hell!" whispered Andy. "He *was* going to kill me!"

Sweat chilled Betsy's brow. She propped the hoe against the wall of the shed and took a deep breath, remembering the way Fairfax had shot the bandit while toying with her. "I told you he wasn't a good man. He should be gone from Camden in a day or two. Stay clear of the Leaping Stag so he doesn't catch you."

"You ain't going to see me around here for awhile, madam."

Hattie wasn't in the dining room to question Betsy when she returned. Headed upstairs to her room, she wrestled with a scream of instinct. In myths of old, the gods used respect and deference when they released elementals. Now that the beast was loosened on the game, it was too late to wonder whether she, a mere mortal, had been cautious enough.

CHAPTER THIRTY-THREE

The next morning Betsy snooped in Abel's study for the last time. She hadn't slept well, unnerved by the brush with Fairfax and news from Tom that they couldn't afford a packhorse until early September. Fairfax was hard at work mining the lead she'd handed him, and Gates was hard at work driving the Continental Army south. Neither man would grant them a month to escape Camden. But since something about all those charitable gifts in the ledger nagged her, she pushed aside dread and grogginess to study ledger entries.

Charitable contributions for 1780 included multiple payments of at least two hundred pounds each from three men staggered over a period of months. Abel had collected — she tallied it in her head — 2,800 pounds in gifts during the first half of the year, a sum to lodge nobility in comfort. Astounded, she recalculated, but there was no mistake.

He'd skimmed money off for his household use. Hence the scrumptious furniture upstairs, Emma's wardrobe, the extensive wine cellar, and the well-stocked pantry. But 2,800 pounds? Who were these three men? What made them want to donate such sums to a rebel spy ring? How long had all this been going on?

For 1779, she found donations from other men. Entries appeared for charitable gifts in 1778 and 1777, too. Abel had been living in style for quite awhile. She stared at Josiah Carter's name, his gifts for 1777 tallying 1,500 pounds.

Odd. She had Carter pegged for a neutral, not a rebel, and certainly not a man zealous enough to hand over 1,500 pounds to a spy ring. Such a sum might bankrupt any plantation owner. Sure enough, his property was almost deserted of livestock and slaves, and he'd mentioned having to sell off all his land except three hundred acres. She closed the ledger, replaced it in the top drawer, and stared out the window at passersby. If Carter's motivation had been helping the rebels, none of it made sense.

At the time of his first contribution in March of 1777, the rebels didn't have a chance at victory. Washington was still holding his ragtag army together with the magic of his personality. France didn't display interest in helping him until late 1777, after Horatio Gates was victorious at the Battle of Saratoga. Soon after, other countries such as Spain and Holland announced their interest in the outcome by declaring war on Britain. But in early 1777, the American rebels' cause was too laughable in the courts of Europe for the Stadtholder to fund a spy ring.

The suspicion grew within Betsy that the men listed in the ledger hadn't donated massive amounts of their money to fund the Ambrose ring. Carter had said, "Mr. van Duser and his attorneys dangle blackmail before my nose." Were Abel Branwell and Jan van Duser in league all the way back in 1777, and did they blackmail Josiah Carter out of 1,500 pounds? Were the "gifts" of the other men the result of blackmail? What could so many men be blackmailed over?

Out the window, she glimpsed Abel stalking toward the tavern followed by a slender blond fellow about van Duser's age. What the devil? Abel was returning at least twenty minutes early from coffee with the surveyors. Betsy made a sweep of the office to ensure nothing looked out of place, slipped out, and closed the door. When Abel and his companion brushed past her, she was dusting paneling near the dining room.

She guessed the blond to be der Waal, Jan van Duser's partner, and had her guess confirmed when she heard the Dutch accent in his voice: "I do not know where he is, nor do I know why he should not have joined us this morning!"

Abel unlocked his office and snarled. "He's left town to double-cross me, and you're covering for him."

"Really, sir!" The blond drew himself up with hauteur. "Your insults carry you over the line of a gentleman's behavior. I do not know what business you and he engage in, nor do I care to learn, but I have endured enough of your conduct for the last year and will have no further dealings with you."

Abel stabbed a finger at him. "The next time you see Mr. Jan van Duser, you tell him I want to talk with him."

"Do you fancy me your servant? Seek him yourself." The Dutchman stomped out past Betsy and slammed the front door to the tavern at the same time Abel slammed his office door.

"Mercy! What was dat all about?" Sally stepped from the common room into the hallway and spotted Betsy. "Dere you is, Miz Betsy. Dis here letter come for you in dis morning's post." She handed her a letter.

"Thank you." Betsy glanced at the return address and, certain she'd misread it, blinked to clear her vision. Martha Neely, Ninety Six, South Carolina?

Sally grinned. "Looks like a good surprise."

"Oh, yes." She hadn't had communication with her stepfather's aunt in almost ten years. The letter meant the old woman was still alive — or did it mean that? Betsy tucked her dust rag in the waistband of her apron, sensing that someone was attempting to communicate with her using her aunt's name. "I shall run upstairs and read it in the privacy of my own room."

Run she did, as fast as her swelling midsection would allow her, and then, almost out of breath, she closed herself in the room and broke the seal on the letter.

22 July 1780, Town of Ninety Six

My dearest Niece:

I regret the Years that came between us and in my old Age am desirous of renewing your Acquaintance. Though the Times are troubled, and much Warfare tears the Colony, please find it in your Heart to pay your old Aunt a Visit before the Summer

*ends. I fear I shan't see many more Seasons
on this Earth.*

Your loving Aunt

Martha Neely

Betsy reread the letter, set it on the desk, and walked away. The tone was appropriate for an old woman wanting to settle her affairs, but the handwriting was that of a much younger person, and something about it looked familiar. She returned to the letter and examined the address: *Betsy Sheridan, the Leaping Stag Tavern, Camden, South Carolina.* That the writer hadn't addressed it "Mrs. John Clark Sheridan" was significant, as if her mysterious contact from Ninety Six had known that identifying her in connection with Clark would be a mistake.

Aunt Martha. Betsy closed her eyes and conjured a memory of the old woman, that of the two of them weeding a flowerbed. "Elizabeth, dear, if you don't use this spade, you won't get the roots of the weed out." Aunt Martha always called her "Elizabeth" and not "Betsy."

She stared at the letter again, addressed not to Elizabeth but to Betsy, and then she gaped at the curly "B." "Mother!" she whispered, astounded, and turned the letter upside down and flipped it over and over looking for more information before reading it a third time. Dared she believe Sophie would be waiting for her in Ninety Six?

On a hunch, she lit the candle and, with the letter warmed above the flame, watched a message appear between the lines: *We are in deep hiding and dare not risk journey to Camden. If you can make it as far as Mulberry Creek, twenty miles northwest of Ninety Six, we will find you and bring you to safety.*

Relief, anguish, and anxiety tearing through her heart, Betsy set the letter afire to destroy evidence and sat on the edge of the bed. She guessed *we* to encompass not only her mother and father, but Joshua Hale, who'd carried knowledge of her familiarity with invisible writing, and also Runs With Horses and Standing Wolf. With the armies converging on Camden, and military action all over the colony ramping up, her uncle and his Creek allies hadn't been able to escape back to Georgia. But at least they were all safe, and now she knew where to find them.

***

The door creaked, and she jerked awake to night near midnight. Her heart flip-flopped in her chest at the man-shaped blob in the doorway, and she dove off the side of the bed farthest from the door. Tom's voice sounded tired. "It's me. Sorry to give you a fright." He shut the door, closing out some of the jollification noise from below.

She rolled up to her knees, confused from having deep sleep interrupted, remembering she'd intended to wait up for him and relate the news about her mother. "Why are you so late?" Not the first time in the past two weeks that he'd come in late.

"Is there any water in the pitcher?"

"Yes, I filled it before I lay down." She waited, but he didn't answer her question, so she sat on the bed.

He strode across the room to the washbasin, stubbed his foot on the desk, and muttered, "Bloody damn."

"Let me light a candle."

"No. I'll manage."

She squinted at him, feeling a subtle change — distance, avoidance — and her heart sank. "Is there anything you want to talk about?"

Water trickled into the washbasin. "No." He stripped to his breeches and began scrubbing his torso.

Above the scent of soap, her pregnant nose detected lilac. More than the twangs of jealousy and betrayal, she felt a great sadness and loss. She lay back and wondered why she hadn't considered before that intimacy with Tom might have expanded their friendship, while Tom pursuing intimacy with Emma served only to rift the friendship.

Had she but realized it the morning she and Tom awakened in bed together, she'd never have given lovemaking with him a second thought. She'd lingered too long in an ideal that no longer fit with the revolution transforming her soul: fidelity to a man, just because a piece of paper claimed her as his wife. She was finished with Clark, but she'd yet to fully embrace revolution.

By meeting her mother northwest of Ninety Six, she'd disappear into the wilderness. Her mother — and perhaps the Indians — would help her stay disappeared. The legal piece of the marriage would remain, but it was meaningless. She considered herself free already — free to seek safety, free to seek a lover, free to *not* seek a lover.

However part of that freedom meant she had to accept that Tom might not want to leave Camden, now that he'd become intimate with Emma.

He sprawled onto his bedroll in a clean shirt and emitted a sigh laden with disgust, and she rolled on her side facing him. "I heard from my mother today and know where to find her, so I needn't worry about a lengthy search."

"Your mother?" He pushed up to a sitting position. "Excellent!

"Do you still want to leave?"

He sounded ornery. "Why shouldn't I want to leave?"

"I thought that perhaps since you'd taken up with Emma, you might want to stay with her."

"Shit." He reached for her hand and clasped it. "All right, yes, I said I'd wait for you, but I've recently had an amazing lesson in how youthful idealism and the carnal needs of young men collide. Alas, youthful idealism didn't survive the encounter, but in the learning process I discovered that Emma is nothing more than big breasts and buttocks, a hot, wet mouth, and a hot, wet crotch. That's all she'll ever be, despite her claims to be in love with me."

Betsy felt the inane urge to laugh at the image of her cousin falling in love with Tom. "I presume you intend to see her again."

Amusement shook his shoulders. "I may not be very idealistic anymore, but I'm still a young man with carnal needs."

She yielded to laughter. "But you'll break her heart."

"Pigs fly."

They guffawed, and the distance she'd imagined melted away. He sat beside her in bed and wrapped his arms around her, and they hugged each other until Betsy felt herself nodding off to sleep again. After he tucked her in, he caught her hand and kissed her palm. She yawned. "We'll get out of here and find my mother, you know that."

"I do know it. Now sleep, my sweet Betsy."

CHAPTER THIRTY-FOUR

On Thursday morning, Emma asked Betsy to run down to Market Square again and select steaks for them. "Your taste in beef is exquisite, dear." Despite the black humor, Betsy was envious of her cousin. Why should Emma have such fun with Tom? She fancied letting him find her naked in his bedroll and longed to be seduced — kisses tickling her neck, wet tongue lapping the tender skin of her throat, hot fingers kneading and stroking her flesh. Young men weren't the only ones with carnal needs.

Getting out of the tavern for awhile that morning was a good idea. Jan van Duser hadn't come running when Abel called, and the accountant prowled the common room heaping curses on the absent Dutchman. "...the double-crossing snake...may his soul rot in hell..." Altogether an unpleasant place to be that morning, the Leaping Stag.

In the sunshine before the butcher's counter, she stood shoulder to shoulder with goodwives and studied marbling in steaks. "I've a tip on a most excellent cut," Josiah Carter murmured in her ear. She turned, registered his good spirits, and smiled. He proffered his elbow and strolled her into the heart of the market.

"I admit trepidation after our last meeting, madam, but I decided to trust my instincts and follow your advice. Monday night, I had my slaves load your furniture onto a wagon and head east on the road with it. After a quarter mile, they took a small track that led to where your property is now stored."

"Ah. And what of Mr. Van Duser?"

"He called early yesterday morning with his own wagon, two bodyguards, and two Spaniards, desperate to retrieve the furniture. When I told him a Spaniard named Don Jaime de Gálvez had taken it all Monday, he called me a liar, had bodyguards restrain me, and put a dagger to my throat.

"The name Gálvez made him both paralyzed and terrified. He wanted to know everything that had transpired. I told him the Gálvez had laughed at my fears of receiving bodily harm from van Duser and said van Duser's days of causing bodily harm were over because he'd displeased too many of the wrong people.

"I said Gálvez showed me legal papers identifying him as the owner of the property, and I could do nothing to stop his taking it because he'd brought ten men with him. I thought at that moment van Duser would kill me, but he let me go and rode off like a rabbit running scared before a hound. I've the feeling he won't be bothering me again."

"I'm glad you've seen the end of it." Betsy smiled again.

Carter sobered. "Well, I'm not certain I have. Noon yesterday, the hound called — a lieutenant from the Seventeenth Light." He saw Betsy flinch. "You know him, eh? A mind reading devil. He asked me thorough questions about the furniture. When did I first receive it from van Duser, what did the legal paper from the estate sale say, what were the items I'd stored, had I heard the names Francisco de Palmas and Basilio san Gabriel —"

"Did he mention my name?" When Carter said no, Betsy let out a sigh of relief. "Good."

"I'd heard van Duser refer to his Spaniards as Francisco and Basilio, so I told the lieutenant that. The Gálvez name also conferred authenticity on my story with him, so I replicated exactly the details I'd told van Duser. He inspected the barn where I'd stored the furniture." Carter shook his head. "Would you believe he examined the tracks from the different wagons?"

She felt chilled remembering how Fairfax had knelt in the dirt and examined wagon ruts in Augusta. "Yes, but surely the traffic on the road obscured your wagon's passage."

"I presume so." Carter paused and glanced over his shoulder. "One more thing. When the lieutenant was in the barn where we'd first stored the furniture, he found the print of a woman's shoe. Yours, I presume. I told him my wife had been out once to have a look at the china."

Another chill crawled over Betsy. In Augusta, Fairfax had looked at footprints in the mud and compared shoe soles. "Did he believe you?"

"I'm not sure. He'd so little expression on his face. I'd hate to play piquet with him. His expression tells you nothing."

Except when he anticipated killing someone. She swallowed, wondering how much time she had. Days? Hours? Or perhaps she'd grown over-anxious. In truth, her furniture was a spent lead for Fairfax. Bound up back in July with the innermost schemes of the Ambrose spy ring, it was now cut adrift of the core mission in the rebels' frantic haste to divest themselves of evidence, avoid capture, and succeed — after several failures at assassination. Fairfax wanted the Ambrose spy ring, not her furniture. But Carter didn't know any of that, and she sensed his nervousness.

"Never fear, Mr. Carter, the lieutenant doesn't want my furniture half as bad as he wants something that was once connected with it. Finding it would be a dead lead for him."

"I hope you're correct. He treated me fairly, but I'd hate to be found on the wrong side of the law from him."

His mention of law revived her curiosity over the ledger entries. "Sir, I've a question of personal nature. Were van Duser and Branwell blackmailing you back in 1777?"

He stiffened and shot her a sharp glance. "Where the devil did you get that information? I know I mentioned the other day that van Duser was blackmailing me, but —"

"Is it how you lost your family wealth?" He nodded in disgust. "Are the names Richard Knox and Daniel Callahan familiar to you?"

"The first is a banker out of Charles Town. I don't recognize the other."

"Ah. Then I suspect van Duser and Branwell have blackmailed close to a dozen men in the past four years."

Carter stopped walking and frowned at her. "Who are you? Where did you get this information?"

She took a deep breath. "I'd tell you, except that I've no great wish to be found by Lieutenant Fairfax, and if he comes round again and questions you about Betsy Sheridan, any further information I give you this moment about myself would tell him exactly how to find me."

"Very well, if my ignorance protects you, you may have it."

"Thank you, sir."

They continued walking, and he said after a moment, "To my knowledge, I was their only local victim, and I was ordered to keep my mouth shut about the entire business."

"Well, if I'd plans to blackmail wealthy gentlemen, I wouldn't select many local victims, either. The word gets out sooner that way. If all of you are or were wealthy, how is it that no victim's attorneys were summoned to the rescue?"

"I assure you they were, but van Duser has his own attorneys, and they're quite fond of perverting the law."

"I've no need to spread details of your personal misfortune. Will you share with me their motive for blackmail? It may help me figure out why my furniture was stolen and my house burned."

He sighed and glanced again over his shoulder. "You don't strike me as a gossiping sort of woman. Perhaps I may indeed trust you with the story of my misfortune. I hope I can also trust Lieutenant Fairfax, because he didn't believe my story about making poor investments and prodded me until he got the truth about my financial adversity." Carter paused. "In October of '76, my wife caught a fever. Two of our four children succumbed and died by the end of the year." Grief spasmed his face. "Deborah lingered through the winter, and I scarcely left her side. They said she wouldn't last until spring.

"In February she rallied, but it became evident that she would remain an invalid in some ways. Understand that I'm overjoyed to have her with me still, and my love for her has become more profound and stronger since I almost lost her, but I'm a man, after all, and men have certain — ah —"

"Certain needs." Betsy stared out into the crowd, intuiting the rest of his story, almost unable to believe it.

"Mrs. Branwell was but nineteen, but she knew what to do to precipitate the situation, and Mr. Branwell knew how to take advantage of it. He found me in her bedroom after arriving home a day early from a trip to Charles Town, and there was no doubt as to the recreation I'd been pursuing with his wife. I feared for Deborah's frailty and what the news of my misconduct would do to her, and so I paid. And I paid and paid, and damnation, I'm still paying, although I've naught left to pay with."

Good gods, Abel and Emma had been working their scam for four years, a couple of fat spiders squatting in their Camden spider web, snagging the cream of the crop who passed through. Was Tom buzzing the same spider web? If so, the joke was on the Branwells, because he had no money. On second thought, the Branwells were shrewd enough to find ways to blackmail anyone, regardless of their income level, so neither she nor Tom was exempt from the Branwells' machinations. They'd best proceed with caution.

Sarcasm scored Carter's tone. "I've heard they landed their biggest catch this year — the cousin of a congressmen."

"You'd think folks would hear rumors and avoid Camden."

"Can't do that. It's on the main roads."

"This really must stop. It's time someone put the Branwells out of business."

He laughed. "Ah. Madam Mystery, I suppose you're in a position to do that, eh?"

She didn't answer his question, but possibilities started revolving in her head. "Such an unfortunate thing to have happen, Mr. Carter. You have my complete sympathy. And to think you've had to sell off most of what you own to satisfy those people."

"I'd rather not think about it too much, else I'd be tempted to acts most nefarious."

An idea occurred to her. "Have you a horse for sale? It doesn't have to be a well-bred animal, just one sturdy enough to serve as a packhorse."

Some of the gloom left his expression. "Why — why yes, I've a horse I could sell you."

And she'd get a good deal from him, too, because he needed the money. "I'm not prepared to purchase for another week or so, but surely by mid-August. Tom and I will appreciate the opportunity to come out and inspect the horse this weekend. Will that be convenient for you?"

"Yes." He captured her gaze, and they stopped walking. "Where are you and the horse going?"

Her mouth twisted. "Someplace where armies aren't stomping about."

He nodded. "Were it not for Deborah, I'd have left this area long ago. You haven't asked me yet about your furniture."

"That's because I'm not in a financial position to compensate you for storage fees."

"Do you intend to abandon your property when you leave Camden in a week or two?"

She tensed her lips almost in time to prevent the lower lip from quivering. All her grandmother's china — ah, gods — "Little as I care for the idea, I must do so. Someday, when this war is over, I shall have a home again, and furniture, and china, but right now, my immediate need is for my safety and that of my unborn child."

No, she wouldn't beg Josiah Carter to hang onto her furniture out of the goodness of his heart. He'd been scorched enough to have little use for goodness, but he sure could put to use the cold, hard cash he'd get from the sale of her property. So she must let it all go, for she wouldn't find safety unless she quit dragging the furniture around with her. But by god, nobody in the world could convince her not to grieve over it.

Carter studied her, his expression inscrutable. "Well, I must be on my way. I shall expect you this weekend to look over the horse." He lowered his voice. "And should you care to lose that dark-haired lieutenant back there who's been following you through the market, I recommend taking a left at the milliner's stall up ahead, a quick right onto the street, and then waiting out his passage in the apothecary's shop. Good day, madam."

She was being followed? Betsy resisted the immediate urge to look behind or run. After Carter blended with the crowd, she sashayed to the milliner's stall, pretended to examine hat pins, and tilted her hat to allow a peek at her pursuit: Michael Stoddard, all the way from Alton.

Panic jiggled her pulse a second or two before reasoning returned its rhythm. If he were in league with Thomas Brown and intended to arrest her, he wouldn't be dawdling over stationery at a stall in Market Square. Curiosity prodded her. Why was he in Camden? She drew a deep breath, mustered courage and a grin, and walked over.

"Why, Lieutenant Stoddard, what a pleasant surprise! I never expected to see you here."

When he swept off his hat and bowed, she saw the clench of fatigue and determination in his face. "Madam, the pleasure is mine."

He replaced his hat. "May I have the honor of your company for a stroll?"

Pleasure, bah. Stoddard hadn't cracked a smile: all business. Still, he didn't seem inclined to arrest her, so she took his elbow, and he escorted her among the pedestrians.

"I'm relieved to find you well —" He lowered his voice. "— what with your husband a member of the Ambrose spy ring."

Annoyance and alarm shoved a sigh from her. "Well, *I'm* not a member of the ring."

"Fortunately not."

"And I haven't the slightest idea where to find Clark. We're estranged. He hasn't confided in me, so if you're hoping I will lead you to him, I must disappoint you."

"Mrs. Sheridan, I already know that."

She studied him, puzzled. "Then why have you been following me?"

"I'm investigating the Ambrose ring."

"Good hunting, sir. Between you, Mr. Fairfax, and Mr. Neville, I expect the Ambrose ring to collapse within days."

"Ah, Mr. Neville. I've a need to consult with him, but he's quite a mobile fellow." Stoddard's dark-eyed gaze pinned hers. "When was the last time you saw him?"

She blinked at the vehemence in his expression. "Last Sunday, I believe."

"Where?"

"He and six Rangers were calling at the office of two surveyors in town."

"Van Duser and der Waal? Of course. Did you see Mr. Neville elsewhere last Sunday?" Betsy glanced away for a second and felt Stoddard lean into her hesitation. "Mrs. Sheridan, was he at the Leaping Stag? I know you're living there."

She sucked in a breath of fear and met his stare. "How did you discover that?"

His gaze upon her was level, direct. "The O'Neals told me."

And Betsy understood why, even though her reason tried to buck against it. From her first encounter with him in Augusta, Stoddard projected a quiet level-headedness and integrity that said *trust me.* "For god's sake, please don't tell Mr. Fairfax where I live."

Some of the fervor left his expression. "I assure you that isn't my intention."

She exhaled in relief. "Thank you. Yes, Mr. Neville was at the Leaping Stag."

"And with whom was his business?"

"Abel Branwell."

"The husband of your cousin." The lieutenant nodded as if he'd expected her response, and Betsy relaxed a little. They walked another quarter minute in silence. "Horrendous business, the murder of that Spaniard in Camden just before you arrived."

Betsy tensed again. "The murderer hasn't been caught yet, but — but another Spaniard was murdered the same way in June, in Alton, and I heard you'd solved that murder." Beside her, Stoddard stared ahead, jaw stiff. Through flutters in her stomach, she remembered Joshua's theory about the murder in Alton. She pitched her tone with care: even, calm. "Do you suspect the perpetrator is here?" Stoddard said nothing. Fear twisted Betsy's stomach again. "If so, why did you let him go in Alton? Someone who tortures people to death — ugh, he may kill again."

Stoddard's throat sounded clenched. "I assure you I'm as appalled by injustice as you are."

And powerless, Betsy realized with dismay and empathy, comprehending what had happened in Alton. Stoddard, the junior officer, had solved the murder but been duty-bound to swallow policy delivered by a superior. Her logic linked his line of questions then, transformed her dismay to horror. "Is — is Mr. Fairfax a spy, a member of the Ambrose ring?"

"Mr. Fairfax visited the Leaping Stag a few days ago. Did you see him there?"

She nodded, bit her lip, and turned away in terror. Stoddard hadn't answered her question — or perhaps he *had*, by not answering it — and he was tailing Fairfax. "I hid from him."

"A wise decision. Was his business also with Mr. Branwell?"

"No. He visited one of the prostitutes."

"And her name?"

"Margaret." Guilt flicked her. She hoped Margaret wasn't in trouble.

"Thank you, Mrs. Sheridan. If you see either Mr. Neville or Mr. Fairfax again, I will appreciate your sending word to me immediately through Charles Bledsoe, the tailor on Littleton Street. He's in the shop next to the printer where you're employed."

Where you're employed. Winter raked her backbone. She hadn't the slightest awareness that Stoddard had been tailing her and wondered whether Fairfax knew he was under surveillance. Stoddard also seemed interested in the Branwells. Did he know of their blackmail scheme?

He said, "Colonel Brown informed me that bandits ambushed your party during your return to Augusta from Alton and that the Spaniard who killed the Givenses was among them."

"The Spaniard wasn't exactly one of them, sir. He was following, watching the event."

"But he was the same Spaniard that you and I saw in Alton — and the same man who threatened you at the O'Neal's house?"

"Yes."

"Think back for me, if you will, to the attack of the bandits. Aside from the presence of the Spaniard, did anything strike you as curious about the attack?"

The vortex of memory flung her to those dreadful moments; immobilized, the bandit's knife to her throat, she gaped down the barrel of Fairfax's pistol. *The devil damn you black for a liar.* She shuddered. What a peculiar thing for one stranger to say to another — unless the bandit and Fairfax hadn't been strangers to each other. "It was almost as if Mr. Fairfax knew the bandits."

Stoddard released her arm. They stopped walking and faced each other. In the swelter of sunlight, ice scraped her. A thin smile of predatory resolve chiseled his face. Weeks before, on the road to Alton, he'd enjoyed watching a hawk stoop for a field rat. Michael Stoddard had become a hawk. "Curious, indeed."

The big picture assembled for Betsy and left her shaken. Fairfax, realizing that Stoddard had implicated him in the murder of the Spaniard in Alton, had commissioned ruffians to kill Stoddard during his trip to Augusta and disguise the deed as the work of highwaymen. That Stoddard and his men emerged the victors from the encounter didn't deter the ruffians from pouncing on Fairfax two days later in attempt to collect their commission. Stoddard's honor as an officer prevented his outright admission of the treachery, so he'd steered her to the conclusion, that she might comprehend the magnitude of her own precarious position in Camden.

He exhaled a deep breath and said in a mild tone, "You may be in danger at the Leaping Stag. Should you need help, send for me through Mr. Bledsoe. I shall see to your safety."

With all the surveillance he'd performed, he must know about Tom, but he hadn't mentioned helping him. Not for anything in the world would she abandon Tom. "Why should I trust you?"

"A shrewd question to ask, madam." A quirky smile snagged one side of his mouth before it sank back into the seriousness. "But one you must answer for yourself. You know how to reach me. Unless I'm occupied with an emergency, I shall come immediately." He touched his cocked hat. "I must be off. Thank you for the conversation. Good day." After a curt bow, he strode away, leaving Betsy to her doubts.

CHAPTER THIRTY-FIVE

Betsy! What a wonderful surprise!" Tom the journeyman navigated benches of apprentices hammering and sewing at Wade and Gamble's, gave her a hug, and eyed her basket. "Dinner?"

She nodded and rubbed her temple at all the pounding in the shop. "This isn't the place to be if you've a headache, is it? Might we find a spot in the shade of the porch and eat together?"

"Certainly. Give me a few minutes to finish a piece of cowhide, and I shall meet you there."

Outside, she removed her hat, sat in the shade, and fanned herself, trying to shove away anxiety over Stoddard, Fairfax, Neville, and the Branwells. Manage one problem at a time, she told herself. In about ten minutes, the hubbub within the shop dwindled, and four apprentices filed out and scampered home for a midday break, joyous to be soaking up sunlight. In another minute, planks creaked behind her, and Tom knelt to plant a kiss on the back of her neck.

They ogled each other until his smile slanted off into a grin of apology. "What's for dinner? I'm starved."

She laughed and poked his chest, and moments later they were making short work of bread, cheese, and ham Hattie had packed. "I shall spoil you if I bring dinner every day."

"Oh, I can never be spoiled enough by you." He swigged ale. "By the by, did you hear the news?"

"Oh, no, what is General Gates up to now?"

"Not Gates. One of van Duser's slaves found both his bodyguards' corpses in the pond on the property this morning."

She stopped chewing and reached for her ale, her mouth gone dry. "Abel's complained for two days that van Duser is avoiding him, not keeping appointments."

Tom's eyebrows rose. "Both bodyguards' throats had been slit sometime late yesterday afternoon or early evening. Do you suppose van Duser met the same fate?"

She suspected the Dutchman, deprived of the protection of his bodyguards since late Wednesday, may very well have met a different fate, and one neither as quick nor as tidy. "I'd rather not ponder it while I'm eating dinner."

"Ah — my pardon."

For the time, she'd decided to keep news of her encounter with Stoddard to herself. Upon hearing of it, Tom might seek the high ground — insist that she accept the lieutenant's protection and abandon him in Camden — and she wasn't in the mood to debate it with him. "Since we're trading news, I've some you'll find quite interesting. Abel and Emma haven't made their fortune solely from the tavern."

"I figured as much."

"They live like nobility and support rebel spies because they also operate a blackmail business."

Tom lifted his tankard. "Here's to Abel, the consummate businessman. Who are they blackmailing, and how?"

"Emma becomes irresistible for wealthy men passing through Camden, and when they're in her arms, Abel plays the outraged, cuckolded husband. The result being one of many charitable donations ranging from 1,200 to 2,800 pounds I found recorded in Abel's ledger dating back three years."

Tom's jaw dangled open. "Zounds!"

"I realize Emma's providing you with great sport these days, but I think it wise for you to discontinue your recreation."

He snickered. "Why? No money means no blackmail."

"Think again. Abel has a connection with Adam Neville. We could wind up in Camden jail and be hauled back to Augusta."

He sobered and looked away in annoyance. "It won't be easy stopping it, Betsy. I mean, you don't realize the sorts of persuasion Emma uses to lure me in."

"I can imagine. I fancy using some of it myself sometimes."

His expression was all eagerness. "Really?"

When it came to lust, it was true; all men were alike. "Is irresistible persuasion on Emma's part all that captivates you?"

"Yes."

"Well, then, let us think of a way to discourage her from using that irresistible persuasion on you."

He shook his head. "She doesn't take no for an answer."

"So she must want to stop persuading you."

He narrowed his gaze on her. "You look as if you're plotting something dastardly."

"When do you see her again?"

"Tonight, right after I finish supper."

"In her bedroom?"

"Yes."

Betsy felt a good purr coming on. "Let's arrange a surprise, then, and do be certain you leave her door unlocked."

***

Almost out of breath from running that evening, she flew in through the back door of the tavern and up the stairs, Hattie's voice following: "Child, where you goin'? I got yo' supper hot." Her stomach rumbled at the mention of food, but she was ten minutes late, and she couldn't let Tom down.

For a few seconds, she paused outside Emma's door to catch her breath. Then she stretched a fake smile across her face and let herself in. "Hello, everyone, sorry to be late, but we were having trouble with column alignment at the print shop!"

Emma, who was nude, gawked at her from a reclining position on the satin-draped bed. Tom, who was bare-chested, winked at Betsy and resumed kissing Emma's navel. Lilac-scented candles illuminated the room.

Betsy propped her hands on her hips and returned Emma's gape. "Didn't Tom tell you? He invited me tonight to watch. You two have been having such fun, and we've been trying some of it on our own, but there are a few techniques that I'd appreciate seeing demonstrated in action, so —" She opened her arms wide. " — here I am!" She beamed at her cousin.

Speechless, Emma sat up, fumbled for her sheets, and shoved Tom off her. With a growl, he buried his face between her breasts. Emma panted and pushed him away again, dangling her leg over the side of the bed in attempt to escape. "Stop it, you dolt, don't you see your wife is here? My cousin!"

Tom scooped her back into bed. "Join us, Betsy."

"I thought you'd never ask." She sashayed over pulling the tucker from her jacket and leered at Emma. "You don't mind, do you? Or is the thought of tender play with your own kin a little too bizarre, even for South Carolina?"

A choking noise issued from Emma's throat, and Tom kissed her nose. "Aw, Emma, honey, didn't Betsy's kin ever show you a real Georgia welcome? Maybe you'll come back with us next time we visit *my* kin. My little sister Diana is the prettiest thing."

"Aargghh!" Emma flung Tom off her. "Get out, both of you!"

Betsy glanced over her shoulder at the open door. "Isn't Abel going to join us? The more the merrier, you know."

"Didn't you hear me? I said out!" Emma backed into the corner, a silk dressing gown covering one pendulous breast, and burst into tears.

Tom dragged his shirt, waistcoat, and coat off the floor, his expression grumpy. "Well, all right, if you say so, but I didn't expect this of you, Emma." He bundled up his stockings and shoes and patted Betsy's shoulder in consolation.

As they were closing the bedroom door on a shocked Emma, Betsy leaned back in. "Let us know if you change your mind." A small object flew through the air and smacked the doorframe near her right ear. She shrugged and pulled the door shut.

Tom bounded down the hallway to the other end of the floor, and she bustled after him. Inside their room, they collapsed on the bed in laughter so merry it mingled with tears. After a few minutes, he caught his breath. "You're damned lucky she didn't take you up on your offer. God almighty, Betsy, you scare the saints out of me sometimes with how well you sham."

"How well *I* sham? I'm wondering now what sort of company you keep with your little sister."

"Are you now?" With a villain's leer, he rolled over and tickled her ribs. "Here's a sampling of the torture you'll incur should you ever breathe a word of that scene to Diana."

Betsy yowled and wiggled free a hand to jab his armpit. "And I possess retaliatory measures both excruciating and effective." They wrestled, legs tangling in her petticoat. She pinned him on his back, straddled him, and laughed. "Surrender!"

"Tell me your terms." Lips parted, expression relaxed, he gazed at her in the waning daylight, and his heat seeped through her shift to permeate her inner thighs. She loosened a hand and ran fingertips over his naked chest. When his groin stirred, he grasped her hips and nudged a pulse of hardness up against her. "Remind me who's the captive."

She slid down so her chest pressed to his and kissed the corner of his mouth. Her nostrils filled with his scent: clean, grassy. "You are."

He flipped them over so she lay beneath him, her head dangling off the bed: daring, different, decadent. A shudder rippled through her at the warmth of his lips on her shoulders and upper chest, so naked and vulnerable without the tucker. Far too often she'd wanted him when the timing wasn't quite right. But at that moment, she couldn't imagine why the whole night shouldn't be theirs. She seized his hair in her fingers and met his kiss with a mouth just as hard and wet as his.

Three hours later, he rolled to a sitting position on the edge of the bed and struck flint on steel. Light blossomed in the salty darkness, and he lifted the candleholder to illuminate the gleam of sweat on her naked skin and the mellowness in his own expression. "Lie there and let me look at you a moment."

She smiled, and since the looking went both ways, allowed her gaze to ramble the slender line of his pelvis into his nest of dampened pubic hair, where arousal already engorged him for the fourth time. The child within her kicked. She reached for Tom's free hand and drifted it over the spot on her belly, and amazement roved his face. He set down the candle and curled up with his cheek on her belly, his palm stroking her hip, while she ran her fingers through the sweat-darkened hair on his head.

How wondrous it felt to lie so at rest within a man and not fret over the sensation of incompleteness she'd experienced too often after making love to Clark — the knowledge of superficial lust satiated without either of them having penetrated the other. No matter how many times Clark brought her to *le petit mort*, she'd suspected she was connecting with but a fragment of life. His deep insecurity had deprived him of being the friend to her that Tom had become.

That morning, she'd fancied elaborate scenarios for capturing Tom's attention. Oh, how she'd wanted to be seduced by him. Yet he'd responded to simple tickle and play. As for seduction, well, she concluded it was a myth. Either a woman wanted a man or she didn't want him, and the response of her body would follow the predilections of her heart and soul.

Tom rose to his elbows. "You didn't eat tonight. Your stomach's growling."

"That's *your* stomach growling."

"In sympathy. Come on, up you go, and let's get you fed."

After dressing, they moseyed down to the dining room, where Hattie fussed over Betsy because it was well past nine and put a heaping plate in front of her at the table. When Tom sniffed at the plate like a starving dog, the slave set food before him, too.

Each time Hattie's errands took her from the dining room for a few seconds, Betsy and Tom sneaked kisses and gropes. For once, Betsy was able to tune out the revelry in the common room and soar above her worries. She didn't need rescue. All she needed was Tom's friendship.

While they were polishing off dessert, Sally entered from the common room, a wooden box about a foot cubed in her arms. "Hattie, you seen Mistuh Abel?"

Hattie eyed the box. "I seen him in his office 'bout half an hour ago. What's in dat box?"

Sally grimaced. "I dunno. Mistuh Todd say an old man bring it fo' Mistuh Abel just now. I sure don't like the smell of it, so I's ready to turn it over to th' master." She disappeared down the hallway, and about a minute later strolled through the dining room, headed for the back yard. "Yessum, he's in his office."

A howl of human terror rocketed down the hallway from Abel's office. Tom bolted to his feet, toppling over his chair. Abel howled again, and the hairs stood out on Betsy's neck and arms. Tom dashed out into the hallway, followed by Betsy, the slaves, and three redcoats who were standing near enough in the common room to hear. By the time Tom opened the office door, Abel had howled twice more. They found him babbling, cowered on the floor, expression contorted in horror. Tom bounded over, peered in the opened box on his desk, and recoiled. "Oh, my god!"

Abel howled a final time and fainted. While the slaves pulled the accountant out from underfoot, the soldiers surged forward to look in the box, recoiling much as Tom had done. One headed for the doorway. "I shall return with the captain straight away."

One of the others pulled on Betsy's arm when she inched forward. "Madam, you really don't want to see what's in there."

She really didn't want to smell what was in there, either — something in the early stages of putrefaction — but morbid curiosity and a thumping heart drew her onward until she glimpsed over the edge. The ebony walking stick of Jan van Duser lay inside, hacked into about eight pieces as if by an axe. Nestled atop the remains of the walking stick was the Dutchman's gold ring — except that it was still attached to his forefinger, and the forefinger was still attached to his hand, severed at the wrist, and turgid with decay.

CHAPTER THIRTY-SIX

Betsy studied her hands. They'd ceased shaking, but the dread that haunted her earlier had grown, and her attention kept straying from her discussion with Tom.

"So van Duser has met his demise." Candlelight imbued Tom with the appearance of a scholar. "I think Abel knows that whoever severed van Duser's hand will come for him next."

Betsy grimaced. What had she unleashed Tuesday night?

"Perhaps a blackmail victim has vindicated himself."

She remembered Carter's words: *tempted to acts most nefarious.* She could envision him murdering van Duser and Branwell but not chopping them up with an axe. No, he'd use a firearm — put a ball through those wicked hearts or heads.

His expression thoughtful, Tom paced their room. "I don't know. If Branwell and van Duser bilked me of my fortune, I'd shoot them. I'd shoot the bodyguards, too. But slitting someone's throat or hacking him up — Jesus, you have to touch the person you're killing." His face screwed up. "Maybe even enjoy your victim's agony. That's twisted."

I shall grant you a thirty-second lead before I hunt you down.
Betsy gulped, drawing Tom's attention. "Josiah Carter has a packhorse to sell us at a reduced rate."

"A packhorse?" His tension easing, Tom sat and wrapped an arm around her shoulders. "Wonderful news. We'll inspect it —"

"This weekend. I already made an appointment."

He seemed surprised but gratified. "Well, then, we may be able to get out of here in a couple of weeks."

Desperate to find sense in the madness, her brain tacked together a story. Fairfax's superior officers had granted him special dispensation to hunt the Ambrose ring, unaware that he was spying for the Continentals, and then the Ambrose ring had double-crossed Fairfax — no, that didn't feel right. She couldn't believe that Fairfax was spying for the Continentals, but she knew he was hunting the spies. And even if van Duser had lost consciousness before divulging details of her residence at the Leaping Stag, Fairfax would uncover all that when he went to work on Abel. She knew nothing to aid his hunt, but he might not be convinced until he'd mutilated her. Her shoulders sagged. "I want to be gone before an attempt is made on Abel," she whispered.

"I do, too. But if your mother's detained meeting you at Mulberry Creek, you mustn't go without food. You have that baby to think about."

"It's too dangerous for us to stay here."

He grasped her shoulders. "Sweet Betsy, I want to give us the best odds possible."

She met his gaze and felt her stomach knot with fear — not just for herself, but for Tom. For the first time since coming to Camden, she couldn't see the two of them as separate. They were a unit — exquisitely vulnerable for having become a much larger target than two individuals. Tom's emotions played into her decisions, and her emotions played into his, and she was no longer certain that two heads were thinking better than one.

The intimacy that evening had skewed their ability to think. In retrospect, she realized the timing couldn't have been worse for initiating the physical relationship. If she'd but known earlier — but how could she have known, never having experienced with her husband the tenderness and connection she'd found with Tom? For his safety and hers, she must disentangle her emotions and return to a state where she could reason again.

He frowned. "Why do I get the feeling you know more?"

She shook her head. "I'm just as stunned as you are."

"But you're acting as though van Duser's murderer is coming for you next, not Abel —" Shock slapped his face, and he leaped up. "It wasn't a blackmail victim who got van Duser. It was Lieutenant Fairfax! I don't know why I didn't see it before." He stared at her and lowered his voice in horror. "Betsy, tell me you didn't tip him off Tuesday night. Oh, no. Oh, heavens, no." Tom began pacing the room again.

Her lower lip quivered. "The Ambrose ring ruined my life!"

"You've made an avenging angel of a fiend. Oh, gods, I don't know why he didn't torture and kill you."

"He never saw me. I slipped him a note that informed him of the connection between van Duser and the stolen furniture."

"Lovely. Now he has a sample of your handwriting."

She stood and squared her shoulders. "No. He's no idea who sent the note, for I printed it on Mr. Harker's press."

Tom stomped back over to her, gripped her wrist, and waved her fingers in her face. "Ink on your hands! You're a St. James, for god's sake. Printing runs in your blood. All Fairfax has to do is ask Harker who helps him with the printing!"

"But do you think he'll care who tipped him off if he can destroy the Ambrose spy ring?"

"He won't leave loose ends untied. Sooner or later, he'll come for you."

She bit her lip. "We'll be gone by then."

"What's to stop him from tracking us? You've put your mother at risk, too." He released her. "What luck the Fates have handed Fairfax. The blackmail scam will yield easy motives and suspects for murder. Two armies are squaring off north of Camden, so it might be months before all suspects are cleared and the investigation probes elsewhere. Fairfax will have moved on — transferred elsewhere so he can seek new victims. That's what happened after he murdered the Spaniard in Alton back in June."

"The British will notice the trail of bodies after him." In attempt to console herself, Betsy envisioned Stoddard's raptor eyes, but the thought failed to comfort her.

"He's murdered enemies of the king. He's doing Britain a favor. They may pretend it isn't happening. But *we* don't know what threshold of suspicion confirms us as enemies in his mind. And we dare not let him know we suspect him of any murders."

She twisted her apron between her hands, wondering why she hadn't considered all that before Tuesday night. "I'm so sorry."

"Save your apologies for Clark if you ever see him again. If he's fortunate, he'll die on his next assignment, and Fairfax won't be able to torture out his confession of treason."

He flopped on the edge of the bed, propped elbows on knees, and put his head in his hands. She remained standing. "If letting Fairfax know about van Duser was a mistake, our making love this afternoon magnified the mistake tenfold."

His voice emerged dull. "How so?"

"We've forgotten how to reason together."

He looked up at her, his expression plaintive, and then reached for her hand. "I apologize for saying that about Clark just now. It's just that I'm so concerned for you — good god, I've never been so concerned for anyone before."

"Don't you see? Lovemaking clouded our judgment. We were thinking more clearly before."

His shoulders drooped. "You're right. We were."

Fresh in her memory, she tasted his kiss, felt his tongue encircle her breasts, and saw the glisten of sweat on his skin. The corners of her mouth tugged downward in mourning. "We must put it aside until we're safely away from here."

Irony speared his expression. "An excellent way of coercing me to leave sooner." He managed a lopsided grin. "I might have known I wouldn't be so lucky as to not sleep on the floor again."

***

Nothing else of van Duser was found. Investigators hunting for a motive questioned anyone with a connection to him or Branwell. Abel remained closed in his room babbling. His doctor convinced the redcoats that he'd been driven mad and might never relate to humans again.

From her cousin's haggard appearance, Betsy deduced she knew little of the Ambrose spy ring. Four days of interrogation persuaded Emma to spill the truth of her affair with Josiah Carter. The plantation owner's alibi was solid, and he named other victims. As Tom predicted, the investigation exploded with suspects and nary a whisper of Fairfax's name. The blackmail scam provided Lieutenant Fairfax with the perfect cover for his activities.

The redcoats pulled resources off the murder investigation after reports filtered in on the seventh of August that the Continental Army had entered South Carolina. Cornwallis remained in Charles Town, so a resigned and courageous Lord Rawdon headed out to intercept Gates's multitude with fewer than a thousand men. By Tuesday August eighth, the exodus of residents down Broad Street was commonplace. Even Frank Harker lost his ebullience. Although he insisted they'd print the paper, he wasn't eager to stand up to a mob invading the town.

That evening while eating supper, Betsy realized five days had passed since the severed hand. No move had been made on Abel. Another week more, and she and Tom could slip from Camden.

With no direct route to Ninety Six, they'd parallel the Wateree River on a northwest road through territory of the friendly Catawba Indians, thus giving pursuit the impression they were headed for Charlotte Town, North Carolina. The route entailed backtracking, hence Tom's adamancy that they build up provisions. Betsy appreciated his sense. Joshua had been right weeks ago about Tom: a good ally and friend, a man with a head for clear thinking.

For a moment, she recalled her final night with Clark in the O'Neals' house. Memory of it had haunted her weeks before, made her question if she'd contributed to his decisions. But the meeting in Log Town brought her a reckoning with her own insecurity. Deep inside, she'd never trusted him, never believed he'd come through for her. Insecurity had motivated her to follow him to Camden, as if by sheer proximity she could force him to assume responsibility.

But she understood that she couldn't change Clark and from the closed door in her heart knew she'd also passed beyond holding a grudge against him. Perhaps the Fates would extricate him from the mire they'd both created, but she wasn't sure she'd be able to settle with him before she left Camden.

Daughter, I sense a great restlessness in you, a fear. Beyond getting acquainted with your father, what is your reason for seeking him? Laughing Eyes had comprehended Betsy's desire to find a blood father. For unless Betsy did so, a crisis might prevent her from providing for her child through her skill with the printing press. With blood kin in her corner, she had a fighting chance of raising her child to respectable adulthood. Will St. James had helped Sophie in just such a way. Was half-Creek Mathias Hale such a father?

Boots scuffed in the doorway to the common room. "Where may a good sholdier phiss?"

Betsy started at the doorway, where a besotted soldier fumbled with the buttons on his breeches. Hattie marched over waving her apron and scowling. "You goes out th' door on the other side of th' tavern, sir, and the house o' easement is just outside." The soldier staggered back into the common room, and Hattie crossed her arms in annoyance. "Been like dat all night. Had t' chase one officer off these here stairs 'bout an hour ago. Turn my back for a second, an' in they wanders. Hrumph."

Emma burst into the dining room, her pampered and glamorous appearance spoiled by five days of investigators' questions and tavern maintenance. "Betsy, there's a wine spill across the bed in number two. We must have clean sheets."

Betsy swallowed ale and nodded. "As soon as I —"

"Are you deaf? Do it *now*!"

Betsy lounged back in her chair and took a deliberate swallow of ale. "As I was saying before you interrupted me, when I finish here, I shall take care of it."

Emma stalked over, yanked away the tankard, and handed it to Hattie. "How dare you ignore my orders, you ungrateful wretch?"

Betsy leveled a cold stare on her cousin. Five days ago, Emma had abandoned pretense of affection toward them, making them wonder how they could last another week in the company of such a termagant. Betsy had spotted Emma sneaking up to Abel's suite with the ledger and day's invoices. Abel, she suspected, wasn't as infirm as reported. The two were scheming something. "You're confusing your cousin with a servant."

"Room two. *Now*."

Betsy wiped her mouth on her napkin, obtained the keys, climbed the service stairs, and retrieved a clean sheet for the bed in number two. Back downstairs a few minutes later, she dumped the wine-covered sheet in a basket for the washerwoman and returned the keys to Hattie. Above the din in the common room, soldiers from several units were belting out a verse of "The British Grenadiers." Waving aside Hattie's offer of more food, she trudged back up the stairs. What she needed more than food was something she hadn't had since leaving Augusta: solid rest.

At the door to her room, she stretched. In response to the baby's movement, she rested her hand on her belly. Baby, sweet baby. Her expression softened, and she swept her thumb across the base of her ribcage. A tiny elbow or knee pressed her thumb before relaxing back into the protection of the womb. Dreaminess born of exhaustion and maternal glory brushed Betsy's lips, and she envisioned a newborn boy with dark hair, held high and proud in the arms of his Creek grandfather beneath winter sunshine. Regret misted her eyes. Would Clark ever see the child he'd fathered? Did he even care?

Hand still on her belly, she opened the door and took two steps into the room before halting. Like iron filings caught in a magnetic field, all the little hairs on the back of her neck stood straight out, but she wasn't sure why. Light from the opened door allowed her to see that no one lurked in the room, and all their belongings appeared safe and untouched, even the supplies for their journey. Still, her instincts vibrated. She seized Lucas's musket, swept it under the bed, and poked it along the other side of the bed in the shadows. She flung open the wardrobe, but no one was hiding.

After scratching her temple, she set the musket down, lit candles, and closed the door. She surveyed the room again before inspecting their supplies and assuring herself that nothing had been stolen. She peeked beneath the mattress where the key to the cipher and other papers lay just as she'd left them. She also rummaged through her clothes and Tom's, not sure what she was looking for, and not satisfied to find nothing amiss.

The entire time, intuition shot such peculiar, crossed signals through her, poising her on the edge of flight while causing her mouth to water. In exasperation, she pushed aside the puzzle and yielded to her exhaustion. Undressed in minutes, she crawled into bed and fell asleep.

A small portion of her brain allowed her to register the arrival of Tom half an hour later before plunging her back into sleep, but her dreams didn't offer her the rest she craved. Blood and lust they gave her, and peril scented dark, humid, savage. She jerked awake before the first cockcrow, Tom's soft snores on the floor beside her, her nose buried in her pillow, her mouth full of a dark, humid, savage taste. The taste was all over her pillow and the sheets, and when she bolted upright in bed, she smelled it, faint, throughout the room, as though whatever had deposited it there was still in the room with them. But she and Tom were alone.

"Go back to sleep, Betsy," she muttered. "It's just your imagination," yet after she lay down, sleep didn't come. Crazy as it seemed, she knew that what her instincts had picked up on when she first entered the room the night before had been that scent detected by her pregnant nose, a scent that had no business being in there and delivered dreams drenched in blood and lust.

CHAPTER THIRTY-SEVEN

On Sunday August thirteenth, churchgoing citizens united and bent their heads in prayers for deliverance, along with folks who hadn't considered themselves religious. General Gates had camped thirteen miles due north of Camden, while the multitude that had followed him from North Carolina filled in the surrounding terrain. Although Lord Rawdon ordered garrisons from Rocky Mount and Hanging Rock drawn in, along with four companies from Ninety Six, the redcoats were outnumbered. Even if Lord Cornwallis arrived with all his men, the Crown forces would *still* be outnumbered.

For lack of sustenance, the Continentals had razed the countryside on their southward march, concocting eldritch stews made of green corn, green peaches, and whatever else they could get their hands on, and thickening the entire mess with hair powder. Gates's army was a dysenteric, noisome, starving mob overendowed with militia as green as the produce they consumed. And according to reports, Gates was strutting about as if he had plumage worth displaying — forming his own strategies and not listening to his officers.

Granted bluster from rum and ale, British soldiers at the Leaping Stag that night boasted about plowing through the enfeebled Continental horde. But Betsy, in the doorway with Tom, saw it from another angle. Never mind conquest. The fevered, starving Continentals parked thirteen miles north of them could do plenty of damage in Camden just trying to lay their hands on decent food. Ever mindful of Hattie, she murmured in Tom's ear, "Can you not get Mr. Wade to give you last week's pay on the morrow instead of Tuesday so we can leave a day earlier?"

He shook his head. "Believe me, I've tried. He wants those dozen boot orders finished by Tuesday at five."

"How important are boots when armies are about to fight?"

"He's sticking it to all of us, not just me. If anyone leaves on the morrow, he loses all of last week's pay."

With a sniff, Betsy crossed her arms. "After I pick up the packhorse Tuesday at noon, I may as well help Harker pull the press." She and Tom could be ready to leave Tuesday evening. Their first choice of route had become doubtful with the Continentals sprawled across it, but much could change between Sunday and Tuesday evening, and they'd decide on their exact route when they were ready to set out.

A soldier burst in through the front doors, and above the din, Betsy distinguished his words: "Lord Cornwallis! The Earl Cornwallis!" The noise level plummeted, and everyone in the tavern fixed attention to the young man, who had outrun his breath and was waiting for it to catch up with him. "He rode out of Charles Town with his men four days ago. He's scarcely paused for need to reach us in time. He's here!"

The tavern exploded with "Huzzahs!" and hats and helmets rode the air. When the men settled down and called for bumpers of drink, Betsy heard a hubbub swelling outside, the parade of Cornwallis and his troops snaking through Camden. One private leaped for the door waving his fellows to follow. "He's headed right up Broad Street!" The common room resounded with the soldiers' stampede and the clank of tankards toppled off tables.

Betsy tugged at Tom's sleeve. "Come on." She motioned him across the hallway to the windowed pantry beside Abel's office.

Redcoats, Jägers, provincials, and militiamen packed the roadside, making the view out difficult. The military entourage flowed past on horseback. Lord Cornwallis rode near the front waving and smiling, his back straight and regal after four days in the saddle, his powdered wig impeccable. Not a speck of travel dust sullied the scarlet of his coat or its gold lace and epaulets. Every inch of him spoke assurance to the desperate faces around him that the king was superior and would triumph.

Betsy's smile was wry. "They've really needed Cornwallis."

"He knows it. He rode up Broad Street just for them."

"He should have come sooner. He'd have scared off Gates."

"Gates would have come whether he was here or not. He's spoiling for a fight, and I hope the redcoats give it to him."

She eyed Tom with an eyebrow cocked in amusement. "What, now, have you turned loyal without my knowing it?"

"Hah. I'm all too weary of this war. Perhaps a few more British victories like Savannah and Charles Town will make the rebels willing to talk more and squabble less."

***

She dreamed of a battlefield on a crisp autumn afternoon, with men in red and tartan and buckskin lined up on one side, and opposing them by a thousand yards, men in blue and buckskin standing in formation. Banners snapped in the breeze, and a drum beat: whump, whump, whump. Whump, whump, whump. No one moved. What were they all waiting for? Whump, whump, whump.

She dragged herself from sleep to find Tom crouched at her bedside, listening. Whump, whump, whump. With a gasp, she sat up, her heart drilling through her ribcage, and whispered, "What's that sound?"

"I don't know," he said, low, "but it's coming from across the hallway." Her gaze followed his outstretched arm. Abel's suite. Whump, whump, whump. "I'd better investigate. Stay here."

"Oh, sure, I'll stay here. Do you think I've lost my wits? I'm coming with you."

He sighed and fumbled for his breeches. Whump, whump, whump. "I should have known better than to try to reason with you. Better bring your musket."

Feet bare, throat dry, palms sweaty around the loaded musket, she listened with Tom at the shut door to Abel's suite. Whump, whump,

whump. With more courage than she could have summoned, Tom shoved the door open and pulled back outside next to her, his loaded musket ready.

Emma's muffled sobs greeted them, along with more whump, whump, whump. Tom hazarded a look into the room and straightened in astonishment. "Betsy, come here."

At the sound of his voice, the sobs became squealed entreaties spiked with hysteria. Her musket lowered, Betsy followed Tom inside the candlelit bedroom, where she stared, dumbfounded. Blindfolded and gagged, Emma, in a silky shift, sat bound in a plush chair. She'd managed to free her right foot, with which she'd been stomping the floorboards in attempt to draw attention.

Abel was nowhere to be found. Pillows fluffed into human form beneath the bedcovers attested to his absence from bed when his wife was restrained — and a good thing that was, too, for from the quantity of escaped feathers and shredded covers, the blade of a sharp knife or tomahawk had imbedded itself several times in the pillows where his body should have lain.

Betsy eyed Tom, and the sight of him gripping his musket made her tense her fingers about her own musket. "Fairfax," he mouthed. Her gaze darted to the darkness of the doorway and then back to Emma in sympathy and alarm. How long ago had this happened? Was Fairfax still prowling the house? Why hadn't he killed Emma and come looking for her after uncovering the Branwells' ruse?

Emma stomped again in misery and indignation, and Tom gestured in her direction. "Untie her. I shall guard the door."

After Betsy tinkered with the knot from behind, the blindfold — one of Emma's lacy tuckers — came off. Emma blinked at Tom, stared at the bed, and then moaned. Betsy stripped off the lacy handkerchief that had been used to gag her cousin, and Emma worked her mouth. "Abel! Oh, Abel!"

Her concern over her husband seemed shammed, another act in helping Abel maintain a façade of convalescence. But it didn't matter what Betsy and Tom believed. Emma's true trial would come when she fell under scrutiny of the investigators over the incident.

Betsy went to work on the ropes. "Don't worry, he wasn't in bed when the attack was made."

"Oh, but he was, I assure you, and he was fast asleep, and I just dozed a minute in this chair reading a book when I found myself blindfolded, and my hands being bound behind me, and then my legs. Oh, such horrors! I heard him strike the bed over and over, and I feared for Abel's life and my own. And oh, my poor, shocked heart, after he left the room, there wasn't a sound from the bed."

"Dawn isn't far off." Tom kept an eye on the doorway. "When did this happen?"

"I — I don't know." Emma rubbed her chafed wrists. "But I've sat here for at least half an hour struggling with my bonds and stomping the floor."

Betsy released Emma's left foot, and her cousin sprang up from the chair shivering, clasped her arms across her breasts, and reached for a shawl draped across the foot of the bed. Betsy pushed up from her kneeling position with Emma's book and glanced at the title. *Fanny Hill.* It figured. She dropped it in the chair. "Were you hurt by the intruder?"

Emma considered it a second before shrewdness filled her expression. "Why, yes, I was ravished!"

Incredulity permeated Tom's expression and voice. "While you were bound sitting in the chair? I should like to see such a feat demonstrated, madam. You don't look at all disheveled."

Emma glared at him. "He put his hands all over me after he'd bound me, touching me places I should never wish to be touched by a stranger, and — and he spent a goodly amount of time doing it —"

"He? So it was a man. You were blindfolded. He spoke?"

"No, but I — I assumed it was a man —"

"This presumed man had his way with you first, leisurely, before going to the bed and cutting it to pieces?"

Betsy caught Tom's eye and shook her head. Like Tom, she knew Emma lied about the intruder ravishing her. Her cousin's story had plenty of holes in it, but it wasn't their job to expose them. "Tom, let's get her downstairs and the household awakened, and then we must send for investigators."

The investigators didn't finish questioning the household until after six-thirty. Betsy and Tom took breakfast in the garden where they couldn't be overheard. "Too bad we won't be here in a few days when Emma breaks again." Tom gulped coffee. "It would be amusing to hear the real story."

"You don't think Fairfax was here, then?"

"No. I think the Branwells staged the incident. It was time for

Abel to lay low. He cut up the bed and tied and blindfolded Emma, ensuring that she'd be unable to identify her 'intruder' and be absolved of complicity."

"The investigators won't believe her story."

"Of course not. Abel was supposedly mad and infirm, requiring a nursemaid. So did this mystery attacker carry him out? Or did Abel walk out himself with the attacker? Very suspicious, you see. At the least, Abel will now be seen to collude with his attacker."

"I doubt he's been in that room for at least a day."

"I agree with you."

"So if he made good his escape yesterday, it still could have been Fairfax in there chopping up the bed."

Tom leaned forward with his napkin to brush a crumb from her chin. "Yes, it might have been, but don't you think realizing Abel had outwitted him would have enraged him, and he'd have said *something*? Cursed perhaps? And then trotted across the hall to vent his rage on Betsy Sheridan?"

She shuddered. "That's gruesome."

"I'm sorry." Tom touched her cheek with his fingers. "He must know where to find you by now. I don't see why he wouldn't have taken advantage of the proximity, made it worth his time."

She stared at a redheaded woodpecker on an oak limb. "What if he just wasn't ready to work me into his schedule yet?"

"Betsy, stop worrying. We'll be gone tomorrow night."

"Emma lied about being fondled. And given the circumstances, I don't think Fairfax would have fondled her."

"Oh, right." Tom snickered. "He's a scoundrel. We already know he fondled Margaret and then some. What red-blooded scoundrel who'd bound, blindfolded, and gagged Emma would resist fondling her a bit?"

"No. He wouldn't have wasted time with her. If given the choice, he'd rather kill than fondle."

Tom frowned and scratched the back of his neck. "You sound convinced of that. Why do I get the feeling there's something *else* you aren't telling me?"

She met his gaze. "I snooped on the delivery of my message to him. He'd already gotten started with Margaret, and yet he stopped everything when he read the message and went running off after the lead of van Duser, leaving Margaret behind."

Tom rubbed his jaw. "Are you serious? Margaret, eh? He's even more twisted than I imagined."

"Can you understand now why I doubt he fondled Emma? After he discovered the Branwells' ruse, he realized where he might find Abel hiding and rushed off to verify his hunch. It promised him more stimulating entertainment than Emma."

Tom let out a deep breath. "I see your point. All right, have Harker walk you home tonight and tomorrow. We'll barricade the door to the room tonight with all our supplies and sleep with our muskets loaded, and I promise, whether Wade and Gamble pay me or not, we'll leave tomorrow night. Feel better?"

Should you need help, send for me through Mr. Bledsoe. If she abandoned Tom, Fairfax would torture him to death.

"The precautions sound appropriate." But she didn't feel better because she suspected it was all futile. Assassins' training hadn't helped two Spaniards from *Casa de la Sangre Legítima*, and two experienced bodyguards hadn't helped Jan van Duser. If Fairfax wanted her, he'd figure out a way to get her.

CHAPTER THIRTY-EIGHT

By Monday evening, investigators had poked so many holes in Emma's story that she'd become a nervous mess. The Dutchman's partner der Waal volunteered information that the Branwell-van Duser relationship hadn't been healthy. Suspicion of complicity in van Duser's disappearance shifted to Abel, whom no one had seen for almost a week. Abel Branwell, wanted for questioning in the presumed murder of Jan van Duser — how ironic.

General Edward Stevens from Virginia arrived with his militia to reinforce Gates. Even though almost two-thirds of the Continentals' ranks consisted of militia, the Virginians bolstered the count by which the redcoats were outnumbered.

News of Stevens's arrival propelled soldiers in the Leaping Stag into a stomping, singing frenzy over the "rebel scum and whoresons" who dared camp within a day's march of them. Accustomed to the occupational activities of British soldiers in Augusta, Betsy found herself both appalled and fascinated by the bloodlust, sentiment she knew was echoed thirteen miles north around Continental campfires. They were all feral: rebel and redcoat. When battle descended, victory would go to those with the most cunning manipulation of feral rage. The men drawn to war as sport — predators that prowled the perimeter of humanity — would glut themselves, their atrocities ignored or condoned.

The tavern roared past three Tuesday morning, offering Betsy and Tom little rest. For all the intensity sweeping the first floor, no one attempted to break down their door in the middle of the night and hack them to pieces. Still, Betsy was never so glad to hear the cock's crow at the retreat of night, knowing it was the last night she'd spend in a tavern fashioned straight from hell.

Downstairs in the dining room, Hattie poured coffee and handed her a letter. "Just arrived, special courier."

After waiting for her to walk away, Betsy scanned the handwriting on the address and winced. Tom whispered, "Clark?" Intuiting the content, she broke the seal.

> *Darling, I should never have doubted your*
> *Fidelity. Please do not venture forth from*
> *Camden before speaking with me. I haven't*
> *much Time but can meet you inside the*
> *Tavern's Stables at 4:45 this Afternoon.*
> *Come, I beg of you.*

Her stomach knotting, she turned the letter to Tom and watched his lips pinch as he read it. "Gone a bit poetic in the eleventh hour, eh?" He clasped her hand and kept his voice to a whisper. "The meeting is fifteen minutes before I get off work."

"I don't want you there. I must go alone so he understands that my decision to leave him isn't influenced by you."

"And if he wants to be part of the child's upbringing?"

"Then we shall make arrangements. Periodic meetings at the home of a neutral party, perhaps."

"I've the feeling he won't let you go easily."

"He's bound to that militia unit he's been fighting with. They'd hunt him down as a deserter if he tried to follow me."

Tom nodded. "I'm glad he's arranged this meeting. If you'd left Camden without ever seeing him again —" He twined his fingers with hers. " — you'd always have wondered."

Tears prickled her eyes at his discernment. "You are my good and true friend, Tom. I must have done something right to be gifted with your friendship this day."

"And only a good and true friend would bruise his arse by sleeping on the floor night after night." He lifted the back of her hand to his lips. "Expect me a little after five o'clock. We'll load up the horses and head west by six. The Continental Army would capture us and steal our food and supplies if we take the road to North Carolina tonight."

So they were headed west, past Fort Cary and across the Wateree River. Perhaps it wasn't such a bad idea to make it appear that they were returning to Augusta.

After all the revelry in the common room the night before, Betsy was surprised to find the guestrooms needed little work. But the ladies were most occupied when soldiers were bored or celebrating. Monday night, masculine camaraderie and convivial spirits were their greatest needs. So while the ladies' duties had been light, the rum and ale was running short, and Henry and Philip swept up a good deal of broken crockery.

Mid-morning, word passed like a lightning bolt through town that rebel Thomas Sumter had surprised the garrison at Fort Cary, killing seven and capturing thirty. They'd also confiscated more than two-dozen supply wagons. Rumor spread among the shocked citizens that the redcoats couldn't protect Camden's residents.

Upon hearing the news, Betsy sat down, stunned to realize that the only other direct route to her mother was now in the hands of the rebels, the ferry blockaded. If she and Tom wanted to leave Camden that night, they'd have to head east or southeast, toward Charles Town, away from the help of kin. She wrestled with despair. Gods, she didn't want to spend another night at the Leaping Stag, and she yearned to be away from the aggression. If only they'd left town two days earlier.

Having completed her duties early, she saddled Lady May and rode out to Josiah Carter's plantation to pick up the packhorse and pay the balance due. The roads were thronged with wagons, refugees, and soldiers, and in the midst of the crowd, Betsy tasted rising panic. The monstrous storm that had born down on them for weeks was going to cut loose in the next day. In their desire to be prudent, she and Tom had waited too late to leave Camden. It now looked as though they'd have to depend on the redcoats for protection and weather it out with residents.

After stabling the sturdy old gelding with Lady May and Tom's horse, she walked to Wade and Gamble's. Tom guided her outside on the porch and lowered his voice. "Fort Cary, Jesus. We dare not ride west tonight."

"We cannot get out of Camden."

"We shall find a way out."

"Do we have the money and supplies to head east? I don't think so. We cannot leave, and we cannot stay."

"Betsy." He gripped her shoulders. "Let's have clear thinking, both of us."

"I am thinking clearly. I think Gates will march on Camden tonight. I can feel it out there. We have to leave now."

"No." He held her gaze with his. "I've heard he's still indecisive. It sounds like he doesn't have a plan for the morrow and will be sitting there when Cornwallis forms a battle line. And if Gates sends that jackal Sumter round again, I guarantee you the redcoats won't let him make off with more men and supplies." Tom enfolded her in his arms. "Listen, sweet Betsy. We're in this together. We'll get through it together, but we have to stay together in action. Are you with me?"

Her face pressed to his chest, she let the beat of his heart beneath her cheek ease tension from her. "Yes."

His shoulders relaxed, and his fingertips stroked her neck. "I shall be back right after five, and we can assess where to go from there. You've already fetched the packhorse. All you've left for today is printing work and that meeting with Clark."

She nodded as if to agree with him, but by then, she'd had enough of desperation, enough of watching worry carve hollows beneath Tom's eyes. It was time for a leap of faith — and hope that her persuasive skills were good enough.

***

Charles Bledsoe the tailor wasn't in, and his shop was closed up, but it was business as usual in the print shop, Harker and Saunders pulling off the back page. Betsy got right to work because it kept her from worrying about when Bledsoe would return. She found herself speculating ten minutes later whether she'd ever be part of a print run again, and realized she was going to miss the business of printing.

At four, just after they'd hung out the last papers, Bledsoe burst in through the front door. "Sumter's at it again! This time he got fifty wagons coming from Ninety Six with supplies and baggage, seventy recruits, and a couple hundred head of cattle!"

Harker roared, "What the hell are the redcoats doing about it? Sitting around on their lazy arses?"

The tailor danced back toward the door. "I heard they gave chase across the Wateree with a retaliatory force. If I were you, I'd close up. I've already sent my lads home."

"Mr. Bledsoe." Betsy stepped from behind the counter. "Please tell your friend Michael I must speak with him." She'd persuade Stoddard that bringing Tom along would be an asset.

The tailor stared at her, incredulous. "I shall do my best to get word to him, but with all this military activity —"

Dear gods. Stoddard was engaged with the army and unavailable to help her. She'd been a fool, indecisive too long.

"For god's sake, Harker, see her to safety. We'll have battle before dawn!" Bledsoe flung open the door and ran out.

Saunders was looking at Betsy. "He's right, Frank. Get Mrs. Sheridan to safety. You and I can finish up here."

Harker grabbed Betsy's hat. "Let's get you out of this."

Through streets boiling with chaos and summer heat, he escorted her back to the Leaping Stag. He didn't tell her good-bye. He didn't say his usual, "See you on the morrow." He just tipped his hat and vanished into the crowd. From his expression, he didn't expect her back.

"There you is, Miz Betsy." Her face grim, Hattie yanked her into the dining room from the back step as if she'd rescued her from quicksand. Betsy wandered into a common room empty of soldiers. "They ain't comin' tonight. They's all out there." The slave jutted her chin north. "Waitin' to get into it wi' th' rebels."

"Where's my cousin?"

"Upstairs in bed wi' a headache."

"Come to think of it, I feel a headache coming on, too."

Hattie's voice followed her up the stairs. "You want coffee?"

"No. I shall just lie down for awhile."

She reached the second floor. Maria and Dolly were chatting in Dolly's room. She slipped into the room she'd shared with Tom for a month, closed the door, and began packing clothing, followed by

toiletry articles and other personal effects. The hum of heightened
activity outside intruded. She tried not to think about the tailor's
warning of battle, focusing instead on Tom's promise that they'd get
out together.

Close to 4:45, when she'd finished packing, she lifted the
mattress and pulled out the papers they'd hidden. She no longer
needed the cipher key. The spies were in deep trouble, their operations
disrupted, their mission at risk. Best to destroy anything
incriminatory. After lighting a candle, she fed the translation and key
to the flame.

When she lit the letter Clark had received in Augusta, she
realized the page below it was blank. Frowning, she dropped the letter
in the plate to be consumed, flipped the blank paper over, and looked
about on the floor. Where was the letter Clark had written in Augusta
and Lucas had been unable to post? She pulled up the mattress again,
but the letter was nowhere to be found.

A more thorough search of the room proved fruitless, and she
tried to remember when she'd last seen that letter. The night she and
Tom had translated the cipher? Had she burned it with her mother's
letter or the note Clark sent from Log Town? She told herself to quit
worrying. Clark hadn't incorporated a secret message into the letter,
so there'd been nothing damaging in it for her. And she had far greater
concerns.

Oh, how she hoped he'd let her go when he heard her resolve to
leave, but she knew it wouldn't be an easy parting. A man could leave
his wife and go to war without a second thought, and other men would
support his decision. But let a woman leave her husband, and both he
and she earned a bad reputation. *Darling, I should never have doubted
your fidelity.* Bah. Why didn't he realize in Log Town that she was
through with him? Get it over with, she told herself, and squared her
shoulders.

She exited the house without encountering the slaves and crossed
the garden and yard to the stable. The smells of horse and leather
greeted her, as well as Lady May's welcome. Betsy smiled and
walked to the mare's stall. "Hello, girl. Ready to travel tonight?
There's my lady. I know I should have brought you a carrot, so
perhaps next time — say, what's this?"

She squinted overhead before plucking down a folded piece of
paper dangling from the beams on a string above the mare. Unfolded,

the paper revealed another note in Clark's scribbling: *I must use extreme Caution today. Meet me in the wine Cellar.*

"Leading me on a scavenger hunt." Annoyed, anxious to be done with it and free of Camden, Betsy crumpled the paper and lobbed it into a refuse bin beside the door. With a caress for the mare's nose, she strode from the stable.

Her first thought upon opening the cellar door was to fetch a lantern, but she spied a source of light below. Her next thought was far less concrete: a whisper from instinct that something unpleasant and unexpected waited in the cellar. She pursed her lips. The entire business of her broken marriage was unpleasant, but she saw no way around the meeting.

She proceeded down the stairs. "Hullo? It's Betsy." Following the light took her to the end of the second aisle and a lantern propped on the bench she'd used to reach bottles stored high. To the left of the lantern was a fresh red rose in an earthenware vase. Dejection prodded her. How like Clark to imagine a romantic rose would help him negotiate.

She noticed a straight-backed chair against the wall to the left of the bench and a musket propped between the wall and chair. A woolen blanket rested on the seat of the chair. She picked up the blanket by the corner, and as it unrolled she spotted rope beneath it, two pistols, a bayonet — Her gaze swept back over the musket and a saber near it. Saber. Cavalry. Dragoons.

Hairs on the back of her neck began a slow polarization, and she dropped the blanket. Scent released from it: dark, humid, savage. Every muscle tensing for flight, she spun around.

His laugh rich with joy, Lieutenant Fairfax stepped into her aisle from the shadows of the third aisle, one hand on his hip. "Darling, I should never have doubted your fidelity."

CHAPTER THIRTY-NINE

He allowed her to reach the steps before giving chase, as if holding off pursuit were the better part of sport for him. On the third step, he snagged her by the waist, and after she punched his shoulder, pinned her arms and reduced her to a portable, wiggling mass.

Hauled back down the second aisle, she shrieked. "Help! Hattie! Sally! Help me!" But no one could hear her in the bowels of the Branwells' wine cellar — just as no one had heard Jan van Duser's screams when his hand was severed.

Pressed to the brick wall, Betsy stared at the lantern and red rose, little black specks spiraling in and out of her vision and gray-tinting the whole scene. With each gasp, she tasted Fairfax's scent. With each second, she expected the burning thrust of his knife in her innards.

But no knife thrust came, and the specks in her vision faded. Still panting, she maintained her stare on the bench, even after he unpinned her and backed away a step. The pieces came together in her head. "You — You stole Clark's letter. You forged his handwriting."

"Would you have agreed to meet with Lieutenant Fairfax?"

The mockery she saw on his face sent her gaze darting for the lantern. "Oh — oh, g-god." But no gods she'd ever heard of inhabited the cellar. She tried to steady her breathing. "What do you want with me?"

"What does any man want from his greatest source of inspiration?"

"Huh?"

His gaze roved over her eyes, lips, and chin before sweeping across her forehead and capturing her gaze. Mockery vanished, supplanted by idolization. She felt him catch her hands up in his and stroke her fingers with his thumbs, and when she darted a glance back at the rose, incredulity and awareness slithered across her like a swamp fog. There were worse things than enmity to awaken in Fairfax.

"Weeks ago, Mr. Neville told me you'd declared your loyalty to the king. At the time I suspected it a pretense. I was certain you were covering for that rebel husband of yours and the Ambrose spy ring."

"Uh — uh, yes, I suppose it did look that way." Her heart ceased to stammer and assumed a more sedate pace. Perhaps she wasn't in for being murdered in a ghastly manner.

"I'd run out of leads on the spy ring the day I encountered Neville. Can you imagine how dejected that makes me when I'm unable to solve a puzzle because I've run out of leads?"

"Uh —"

"But then your note gifted me with a fresh lead." He brushed the backs of her fingers with his lips and for a moment seemed at a loss for words. "Men have attempted to match wits with me and lost. Never before has a woman done so and managed to stay so far ahead of me and for so long that I must retrace my steps, scouring where I have been for clues. Superior intelligence in a woman — madam, I am enchanted."

Disbelief punctured her numbness. Enchanted he did seem, but he still had her backed to the wall. Her attempt at a smile foundered. "I assure you, sir, enchantment wasn't my intent."

"Why didn't you simply write the message?"

"I didn't want it falling into the hands of the Ambrose ring and have them recognize my writing. I had a dagger pressed to my throat when I confronted van Duser about my furniture. He'd have killed me if he'd suspected my interference."

Fairfax nodded. "So you sneaked printing it. Excellent. Of course Harker and Saunders denied printing it, and I could tell they spoke the truth. It became a mystery to baffle me even in my dreams. I traced your furniture to the plantation of Josiah Carter and found the print of a woman's shoe where the furniture had been stored. At first, I didn't recognize that it was the print of *your* shoe." He kissed the palm of her other hand. "Mmmm, my mystery woman."

Betsy didn't like the way he kissed her hand. A monster that flayed two men alive, slit the throats of another two, and hacked a fifth man to death wasn't supposed to have soft, warm lips. "Mr. Carter may have stored my furniture, but I assure you he isn't involved in the Ambrose spy ring, and he isn't a rebel."

"Quite. Oh, I realized he'd used his own wagon to haul the furniture from the barn and hide it, but after I questioned him, I became certain he wasn't a rebel spy or sympathizer. How cleverly you worded your message to steer implication from him.

"I also appreciate your ingenuity at borrowing the Gálvez family name. I was so surprised to hear it that it threw me off for another half day. I might never have solved the puzzle of my mystery woman had it not occurred to me to return to the print shop and inquire whether anyone helped with the print run." He smiled down at the stains on her fingers. "Lampblack and varnish. Quite the chip off the old printing block, aren't you?"

He drew her right forefinger into his mouth and sucked on it, and for the first few seconds, Betsy stared at him in shock while his tongue twirled around her finger. No man had ever done that to her. A tide of gooseflesh, not unpleasant, crawled up her right side before she recovered the sense to yank her finger free. "Stop that." He smiled again and recaptured her hand. "I will appreciate your letting me go now since you're convinced of my loyalty to His Majesty."

While his thumbs continued stroking her palms, he bathed her with that look of idolization. "Such a heady combination, a woman who is both intelligent and loyal. Do you know, where I come from, County Wiltshire, the people thousands of years ago somehow hauled these massive stones about and formed circles and avenues and temples from them to appease the old gods. These weren't gods like that trio of gelded Christian gods. These were gods with power, and the supreme deity of them all was a woman. The great mother, the wise woman."

In one lithe movement, he reclaimed the step he'd taken away from her and encircled her waist with one arm, his abdomen and groin pressed to her mother belly. She tensed and pushed at his chest, all hard muscles and heat. When she attempted to back away from him, the brick wall left her no latitude. "You're too familiar. Take your hands off me."

"When warriors returned from battle, they spread trophies at the feet of her priestesses. From among the warriors, her priestesses selected champions and lay with them."

Eyes still wide, she remembered a black cat of her cousin's who'd hunted mice by night, leaving ears and tails on Lucas's back doorstep for the humans to find next morning. How proud and smug the cat had been, too. Trophies. Horror trickled through her soul. Van Duser's hand in the box hadn't been meant just for Abel Branwell. "I never asked for trophies," she whispered.

"Didn't you, though? Betsy, darling, why do I feel you're playing a game with me? I lay on your bed upstairs a week ago fancying I was your champion. But now I sense you've merely been using me to revenge yourself on people who stole your furniture and ruined your happy life in Augusta."

Horror climbed into her throat. "No, no, it isn't so. They're rebels, traitors to His Majesty."

"So I *am* your champion."

"I never asked for a champion, either."

He lowered his mouth to within an inch of hers. "Either I'm your champion, or you've used me. Let us be clear about this."

Damned if she did, damned if she didn't — but he didn't wait for her to sort out her preference of damnation. The lips that coaxed hers apart were soft and warm and sly, seeking the slippery assent of her tongue, inviting her descent. And descend she did into subterranean caverns carved from her own lust, stymied out of a month of sleepless nights and a physical relationship arrested in its genesis.

Across the roof of her mouth, between her lips and gums, and behind her teeth he painted promises, her introduction into the ecstasy of ancients with bronze weapons, stone temples, and gods of blood and human sacrifice. His hands slid beneath her buttocks, and her body rose in answer to the burrowing heat of his groin, flouting the predilections of her heart and soul and all she'd naively labeled as myth. While a sorcerer's lips explored the curve of her chin, the line of her jaw, the hollow of her throat — all softness no man had ever before sought — she recognized in the rattle of her own breath a woman who teetered on the fine line separating true fear and sexual fascination.

Her eyes rolled back, and a dreamy zephyr wove words through her memory. *He took his time with me.* Oh, yes, he was taking his own, inexorable time. He whispered against her throat, "Let me taste your shoulders. Take off your tucker." When she hesitated, he kissed the curve of her chin again. "Our greatest fancies are for that which we cannot, dare not do. So dare."

He took his time with me. Margaret had said that — Margaret who was infatuated with him because he'd taken his time with her, even as he was initiating his new priestess that very moment. A chill of strangeness wedged through the spell, granting Betsy the vision of boxes filled with severed hands following her wherever she went, trophies from her champion, a fiend's gratitude for his greatest source of inspiration. Her hands found his shoulders and pushed while she twisted her torso away and gained solid footing — even if her head felt far from solid. "I — I've an engagement elsewhere and will be missed, so I must go. I should think it obvious that I've not been using you and have told you all I know about the rebels." Hoping to be released, she pushed at his arms again.

He didn't budge and scrutinized her while his breathing evened. "You're leaving Camden. Where are you headed?"

"North Carolina."

"Why?"

"To get away from the war."

"With whom will you stay?"

"Relatives."

Seconds dragged past. "Where is Will St. James?"

Her stomach fluttered. "I don't know. The last time I saw him was last month. He'd made his way back from Havana and hid in my henhouse in Augusta. He had friends to stay with — somewhere in Virginia or the Carolinas, I gathered. He told me so few details."

Fairfax brushed her earlobe with his lips, just enough contact to scurry gooseflesh all over her body and tighten her nipples. "Where was your uncle headed the morning he met you in Augusta?"

She swallowed. No point in maintaining the lie. "Somewhere in the Carolinas or Virginia. He wouldn't say, either."

"And where is Soph — Where is your mother?"

Chill seeped from the cellar floor through the soles of her shoes and spiraled up her legs. Black lace in a box with a parasol — she tensed, and he felt it. "I — I don't know."

"I shall ask you again — where are you headed?"

She swallowed again. "I told you, to North Carolina."

"Not to Ninety Six? Neville told me you had an aunt who lives there. Martha Neely."

She sighed, still clinging to the hope that she could bluff. "Oh, very well, I may as well admit it. I'm going to stay with Aunt Martha in Ninety Six."

Fairfax showed his teeth in something that looked like a smile but wasn't. "Would it distress you to know that Mrs. Neely died back in May? Neville checked the town records."

A swell of despair rolled over her expression. "I — I guess I won't be staying with Aunt Martha."

He pulled her up against him again, one hand returning to her buttock and squeezing. "I have no compunction about taking the time necessary to extract the truth from you. In fact, I fancy you enjoying the process so much that two or three hours hence, all manner of truths will be tumbling from your lips. So unless you prefer to miss the engagement you alluded to earlier, stop playing me for a fool. You're going to Ninety Six. Your husband abandoned you, and you're with child. It's time to find the protection of your kin. It's time to find Mother."

Betsy gritted her teeth and squirmed. "I told you I don't know where she is. Take your hands off me!"

He tangled fingers in hair escaped from her mobcap at the back of her head, exposing her throat, filling her nostrils with his scent. "Betsy darling, Betsy sweet, I knew you were intrigued with me the afternoon we met in Alton. Shall I show you how it was with your mother in Havana?"

"You cur!" She freed a hand, grazed his jaw with her fist, and tried to stomp his foot.

While he scuffled with her for control, the door to the cellar opened. In the instant of her surprise, Fairfax blew out the lantern, plunging the aisle into shadow. She lunged away, and he reeled her back. She sucked in a breath to scream and felt the tip of his dagger prick through her petticoat to her belly above the womb. "Quiet," he whispered, "or you'll never birth this child." At her stiffening, the pressure of the dagger grew painful. "Do we understand each other?"

"Yes," she whispered, trembling, relaxing against his shoulder so he wouldn't injure her. Then she turned her attention to the wine rack separating them from the stairs, through which they watched a man with a lantern descend into the cellar.

CHAPTER FORTY

A second man followed him down and stood beside him at the end of the first aisle. Betsy sneaked a glance at Fairfax's face, but there wasn't enough light to see more than a glitter in his eyes, reflection of the two men's lantern.

The pressure from his dagger had vanished, but she doubted he'd sheathed the blade. As if reading her thoughts, he secured his left arm across her ribcage, her back snug against his left side. The alertness in his body permeated her, communicating that there'd be no quick dash for freedom. Fairfax wouldn't drop his guard.

Two more men descended with lanterns, and Betsy gaped in recognition at Basilio and Francisco. They were followed by a couple more, both strangers and young, before Betsy gasped at the seventh man: Clark.

Great heavens, was this a meeting of the Ambrose spy ring? If so, Fairfax was seeing one of his fondest wishes unfold: the opportunity to identify all the rebels.

Another three climbed down, all strangers, and then Betsy stared in confusion at the final man to descend. "You disgust me, all of you," said Adam Neville when he'd reached the bottom step and surveyed those arrayed before him. "You call yourselves 'Patriots?' You're dung-eating dogs, a continual source of amusement for the redcoats. 'Patriots' like you guarantee world domination for His Majesty."

"Ahhhhhh!" whispered Fairfax, the sound a cross between a sigh and orgasmic release. Betsy glanced at him again and shuddered with horror at the radiance in his eyes.

Lieutenant Neville planted his feet. "You're supposed to be an autonomous unit, but each of you has bumbled irreparably. I should never, *never* have had to compromise my position with the Rangers to ride here, just to realign this mission."

"Ahhhhhh!" whispered Betsy, echoing Fairfax's comprehension, niggling details about the adventure making sense at last. Jan van Duser hadn't been Ambrose, and Abel Branwell hadn't been the double agent, and Whig Captain Ned Murray had assumed he'd nothing to fear at the mass grave because one of his own would give quarter to him. But Adam Neville had his own code of honor.

"To tell you the truth, I don't know if it can be repaired at this point. Van Duser's gone, and the last time I saw Branwell was Saturday the twelfth of August, gentlemen, three days ago. Has anyone seen him since then?"

The men shook their heads in silence. Betsy's peripheral vision detected a gleam, and when she turned her head, she realized it was the reflection of the lantern on Fairfax's teeth. He was grinning. A wave of ice stormed up her spine.

"Assume he's dead, then." Neville scowled. "Where's Wilson? Posey, wasn't he with you?"

One of the men cleared his throat. "Yes, sir, but I haven't seen him since last night."

"Damnation." Neville pounded his fist into his palm. "That confirms it's not a blackmail victim. Assassins are working us, lads. How did they latch onto us, eh? Who gave 'em the tip?"

"My sweet," Fairfax whispered and brushed his lips on the back of Betsy's neck, above her tucker. She tensed, sickened.

"Oh, come now, surely some of you have thought about it. After all, we've had enough clues. Very well, let's waste no more time guessing. Sheridan, step forward." The other men allowed Clark room. His face inches from Clark's, Neville sneered. "Your wife tipped them off."

Clark shook his head. "She wouldn't have. She's neutral."

"Horse shit. There are no neutrals in this war. She swore allegiance to the king back in Augusta."

"She did it because she was cornered by Brown, you know that." Anger blazed through Clark's pallor. "If that's all you have on her, it's flimsy evidence. Look elsewhere. Betsy and I disagreed about politics, but she wouldn't have betrayed me."

Betsy blinked back tears and pushed at Fairfax's arm when he nuzzled her neck. "My darling." He tightened his hold on her.

Neville's sneer waxed to a vindictive smile. "Gálvez. Van Duser said the disappearance of your furniture was linked to the Gálvez family. Who gave Josiah Carter that name? It was someone who was familiar with how our efforts are connected with those of the Spaniards.

"You told me how angry your wife was over losing your furniture — reportedly so angry that she confronted van Duser twice and tracked it to Carter's barn. Coincidentally, her grandfather was involved in the attempt back in June to bring in the Gálvez family. She knows enough about the Gálvez to throw the name into our operations and confuse us.

"Sheridan, the shrew betrayed you. You fouled your own flight to Camden by picking up that assassin, so you couldn't set up shop posing as Kessler's nephew, and you couldn't set up house for Mrs. Sheridan. There's her motive for betrayal. Typical woman, she got angry with you. Typical woman, she consoled herself by bedding your apprentice. The two of them plotted vengeance. And now she's turned loose assassins on us."

A tear rolled down Betsy's cheek. "Clark," she whispered.

Fairfax licked behind her ear. "My lovely mystery woman."

"You're wrong! When she and I met in Log Town, she warned me that Lieutenant Fairfax was sniffing around. If she was plotting vengeance, why would she have done that?"

"Lamebrain, it makes her look guiltless, that's why she did it. Besides, I'm not convinced Fairfax is involved. No one's spotted him in the area since before Branwell disappeared."

"Don't underestimate him —"

"I shall deal personally with him if he shows up."

Betsy felt tremors course through Fairfax. When she looked up at his face, she saw his teeth shining again and realized he was laughing without sound. Horrified, she averted her gaze.

"Sheridan, describe your wife."

"She's seventeen. Pretty. Dark hair, dark eyes. About this tall." He indicated the bridge of his nose. "Slender."

"Since that describes a number of ladies in the area, men, note that she's also nearly six months pregnant. If you encounter her, capture and restrain her for my interrogation. If she attempts to escape or create a burden for you, kill her."

"Wha — ? You'd murder my wife? For god's sake, man, I'm telling you she didn't do it!"

Neville snarled at Clark. "Whose side are you on? Husbands and wives betray each other in this war. You're only safe with those whom you recognize as belonging to the cause. That's the men in this room." The snarl faded into granite. "If you aren't with us, we're all dead, because we've run out of margins in this operation. Now get back over there with your fellows so we can assess where the mission stands."

For the next ten minutes or so, Betsy was privy to schemes of the Ambrose spy ring. They reevaluated their chances of picking off British commanders, given distribution of their members among the Loyalist militia units. One man revealed intelligence that Cornwallis was debating marching the British north that night to take on the Continentals. Neville then reviewed strategies for completing the ring's mission beneath the cover of battle. Throughout it all, Fairfax held Betsy without making a sound. She felt his concentration and knew he was committing to memory every detail.

The men filed upstairs except Neville and the first fellow with the lantern. Neville waited for the door to shut. "What do you think?"

"He'll desert. He'll try to find his wife and warn her."

"Agreed. Stay with him. The first sign of it, kill him."

The other man chuckled. "We tried at Hanging Rock."

"May your aim improve."

They headed up the stairs. The door grated shut behind them, and in utter darkness Betsy was left in the embrace of Fairfax.

"Be still," he whispered. Men's voices faded from the entrance to the cellar. She felt her own pulse and heard the soft breathing of Fairfax and the ticking of the watch in his waistcoat. Minutes elapsed before he released her. "Forgive me if I take leave of you for awhile in service to His Majesty."

He moved away, and she backed in the opposite direction, hands groping for and finding shelves of wine bottles. Behind her flame sparked: the lantern lit. She raced around the end of the second aisle, and at the scuffing of his boots, seized a wine bottle by its neck and swung it at him when he bolted around the corner after her. He flung up his arm against her upraised forearm, jolting the wine bottle from her hand. It crashed to the floor and filled the cellar with bouquet.

"Bloody waste of an Italian red." He pinned her arms when she swung at him, hauled her back down the second aisle, and shoved her into the chair, emptied of blankets, rope, and pistols. "Where did you think you were going, eh?"

"You have all the information you need to destroy the Ambrose spy ring. You don't need me." She sprang up.

He pushed her back into the chair. "Remain seated. I don't need you? My dear, lovely lady, you underestimate your own charm and importance." He scooped up the rope and slid it between his fingers. "You and I aren't finished, and even if we were, I dare not release you to be apprehended, tortured, and possibly murdered by rebel scum."

He walked around, pulled her right arm behind the back of the chair, and began binding it with the rope. "How dare you! Let me go!" Betsy tried to yank loose her arm and gasped at the harsh fiber digging her wrist.

"I wouldn't do that if I were you." He kissed her ear. "As a representative of the legitimate government, I have the responsibility to protect loyal subjects from rebel atrocities — even if I'm forced to use restraint on a subject who has become so confused she doesn't know what's good for her."

"You're abusing your authority. You've taken me prisoner!"

"Prisoner? A delectable thought." He secured her left arm and proceeded to tie her legs to the chair. "If you were my prisoner, I wouldn't be ensuring that these ropes don't chafe your sweet skin. Only if you struggle will the ropes bite."

She'd been tied in a similar fashion to Emma. Over her shoulder, she watched him assemble his gear. "You're going to leave me here to starve, you loathsome creature."

"Now, now, you and I have too much to discuss for that."

"If you're killed out there, no one knows I'm down here. It could be days before anyone ventures into the cellar for wine!"

"Darling, I'm touched. You do care for me." Musket over his shoulder, saber strapped to his back, pistols at his waist, he grasped the stem of the rose and knelt on one knee before her — less a knight-errant before a princess than a Celtic warrior before a priestess. Light from the lantern captured the preternatural pulchritude and virility in his face. "Upon my honor, I shall return to cast trophies at your feet, and then perhaps you shall be more amenable to a discussion about your mother."

Trophies. Clark's head, perhaps? Betsy blanched. "I never asked for trophies or a champion. Untie me!"

Nestling the rose atop her apron in the hollow between her legs, he stood, caught her face between his hands to steady it, and trailed the tip of his tongue from her chin all the way up to her nose. Then he seized the lantern and sauntered away.

"Will you not even leave me a light? Lieutenant! At least leave me the lantern, I beg you!" He paused at the open door atop the stairs to extinguish the lantern. And after the door shut, Betsy was closed up alone in the night of her own making, her "champion's" kiss drying upon her face.

CHAPTER FORTY-ONE

I n darkness, her pregnant nose awakened to Italian wine spattered over the stone floor of the cellar: wine the hue of battlefield gore. She twisted about, fingers seeking loose ends of rope. Fibers stabbed her skin. She bit her lip and paused, her mind atumble with mounting disbelief, panic, and revulsion.

May your aim improve. The Ambrose spy ring had set Clark up to be murdered, just as she'd warned him at least twice. And as she'd dreaded, she'd become the instrument of his destruction. Staggered, unable to process the verdict she'd passed upon herself, she scampered her thoughts elsewhere.

Widow Abby Fuller's tear-swollen face haunted her memory. In Betsy's hair, on her skin, in her mouth, she tasted and smelled that dark, humid, savage scent. Sweat on her froze, and she struggled with her bonds again. Torture, ravishment, seduction: which had Fairfax applied to extract information from Widow Fuller about David St. James? Which did he have in mind for *her*?

She plucked at a knot and panted, wrists irritated, the knot still tight. Somewhere up there, Tom waited for her. He might have gone to the stables when he first returned from work. Not finding her, he'd have headed to the room, where he'd have seen their belongings packed, ready to be transferred to the horses. Perhaps Hattie would have informed him that "Miz Betsy" had gone upstairs with a headache. Puzzled, Tom would sit at the table and have a bite to eat, just to think things out. Perhaps he was on his second or third plate by now. Betsy's stomach rumbled.

At what point would his puzzlement yield to worry, and his worry transform to panic? No, Tom wouldn't panic. He'd search the grounds. He'd ask if anyone had seen her. Before dark, he'd conclude that she wasn't at the tavern, and something had happened to her. The thought would cross his mind that she'd run off with Clark, and he'd dismiss it, realizing she hadn't taken her clothing. He'd comprehend that she'd met with foul play. Tears filled her eyes at the thought of his anxiety. She yanked at the ropes and squeaked in pain. Would he suspect Fairfax had something to do with her disappearance?

A silky veil of black lace — *Shall I show you how it was with your mother in Havana?* Betsy strained legs and arms against her bonds, abrading her skin. Rage and terror burst from her at her immobility. *Two or three hours hence, all manner of truths will be tumbling from your lips.* She thrashed about, chafing her wrists more, releasing the scent of the rose from her lap, and collapsed against the back of the chair, fresh tears welling to her eyes.

In her memory, Laughing Eyes regarded her with a reproving look. *Use this forthcoming knowledge wisely, or you will invite suffering upon us all.* Wisely? What a fool she'd been. Her head drooped, and she wept. Unleash a fiend, and of course the whole thing must explode in her face, and she must end up betraying her own mother and the father she'd waited her entire life to meet. "Mother, oh, Mother, I'm sorry! You'll never forgive me, but I am so sorry!" The similarity between her despair and that of Widow Fuller — *Tell your Uncle David how sorry I am...I hope he forgives me someday* — throttled her in the darkness and ratcheted her weeping into sobs.

With what trophies from slain opponents did Celtic warriors return? What body parts did they cast at the feet of priestesses of the old gods, currying favor? "Clark, oh, Clark, I didn't know! I'm sorry!" Murder at the hands of his fellow Patriots would be a blessing for him, a swift ball of lead in the brain or heart, but she intuited he wouldn't be so lucky as that. Hard sobs wrenched her gut.

Twenty minutes or so spent in lamentation flushed the wild terror from her. Her face sticky and salty, she stared into night as complete as any tomb, the numbness of defeat settling over her brain and encouraging surrender. She'd invited death and destruction upon everyone she cared for and was powerless to stop the consummation of it. Might as well make it easy on herself — tell Fairfax everything. Maybe he'd be quick with her.

Flutters of life within her belly agitated her resignation, kept it from solidifying into capitulation. Baby, sweet baby, promise of life in the womb, black as any tomb — yet unlike the tomb, a covenant of continuation. Maybe she'd consigned everyone else to death, but didn't she owe at least birth to her baby? The child prodded her again, demanding of an answer and commitment. A tough, scrappy layer knit over Betsy's soul. She couldn't save the world, but perhaps she'd save her baby.

A grunt of pain passed her lips when she contorted her right hand to allow her fingers inspection of the knot. She did the same for the knot binding her left hand. Ignoring the fibers stabbing her wrist like needles, she pressed into the heart of the knot with her right forefinger and thumb and began wiggling — small movements that she hoped would loosen the knot and help her understand its composition.

After a few minutes, she rested, unsure whether she'd made progress. How much time did she have? How long did Fairfax need to lure prey into a trap and cut them to pieces? How many victims' deaths must he indulge in before his urge for blood was sated and he headed back to the cellar to sate other urges? Betsy shook the thoughts from her head, refusing to dwell upon them. She must extract what she could from the time given her.

Still she needed rest, for as minutes accumulated into an hour, two hours, her fingers cramped, and her shoulders ached. When her right hand fatigued, she attacked the left knot. When both hands fatigued, she slumped forward, trying to ignore her growling stomach, dry throat, and pressured bladder.

Once, about eight-thirty or nine, the faint voice of Tom calling her name roused her from drowse. "Tom!" Her voice emerged a croak, and she coughed to clear her throat. "Tom! In the cellar! Tom! Tom!" She listened but heard no response. He'd moved out of range. Despair sullied her determination, and with a snarl, she shoved it back, returning to the knots.

Exhausted an hour later, she realized the right knot was beginning to open. Muscle spasms coursed through her arm and up the side of her neck. Her wrist and palm were rubbed raw. She had to rest. She dozed, lost track of the time.

When she awakened, she returned to the right knot, probing its structure. What time was it — midnight? Over and over, she traced her fingers along the knot's mysteries, not understanding what fed one strand until she happened to move her left hand, and the whole mess on the right side moved with it. Just as with Emma, Fairfax had left a rope connection between her hands. That meant she'd have to untie both hands before getting either free.

Wearied again, she allowed herself to doze before returning to work, this time with the fingers of her left hand probing the other knot. Her left wrist and palm gained intimate knowledge of the spiky fibers imbedded in the rope. Shoulder cramps and the needling pain intensified and slowed her. She dozed and wakened, dozed and wakened. Whenever she could, she kept after the knot, long into the nightmarish night, long after the passage of time had ceased to flow in units she recognized.

The left knot loosened, and then, with both knots open, lacking just the unraveling of the rope between them, she heard the door to the cellar scrape open. Blinking into lantern light, she caught her breath, fear soaring into her throat. Oh, gods, no, it couldn't be so! With only five minutes longer, she'd have freed herself.

"Betsy? Are you down here?"

She gasped. "Tom!" She coughed. "Tom, yes, over here!"

He clambered down the stairs, a lantern held above him, and drew up, dumbfounded, at the sight of her bound to the chair. "Oh, my god. Oh, Betsy!" Knife drawn, he rushed forward and set down the lantern so he could cut her bonds, and then he dragged her up out of the chair and crushed her to him. From the confines of the chair, every joint in her body ached, and every muscle trembled with fatigue.

He bore her weight while she stretched limbs, restored circulation, found her footing. Then, after sheathing his knife, he took her face in his hands and kissed her eyelids, cheeks, mouth, and chin. "I thought I'd lost you, oh, my sweet Betsy. Who on earth did this to you?" He felt the tremor shoot through her and set her back at arms' length, stepping on the rose in the process. A snarl curdled his handsome face, and he snatched up the rose and flung it. "I swear to god, I'll kill the maggot."

"Please, let's just get out of here. I don't know when he'll be back."

He grabbed the lantern and caught her about the waist to help her ascent. Outside, frogs and crickets lauded night. She sucked in lungfuls of air that didn't smell of wine or conquest, and then, by the light of a moon one night past full, visited the vault and relieved her aching bladder.

A single candle burned in the dining room, where Hattie embraced her and set food before her. "Child, yo' man tried to get some help searching fo' you, but them soldiers was all too busy."

Tom read the blankness on Betsy's face. "The redcoats marched north last night to engage the Continentals."

"Last night? What time is it now?" Betsy crammed buttered cornbread in her mouth.

"Just on four in the morning."

"I've been down in the cellar almost twelve hours."

"Tied up all that time? You poor thing. An' poor Mistuh Tom, wishing he'd a thought to check the cellar earlier." Hattie's gaze took in Betsy's reddened wrists, and she scowled. "Who would do such a thing to a woman with child?"

Tom slammed his fist on the table. "A dung-eating pig."

Betsy covered his fist with hers, seeing the opportunity to explain their departure. "Hattie, a crazed British lieutenant is trying to kill me. Tom and I had intended to sneak out of Camden late yesterday, but I was captured and imprisoned in the cellar. He must have marched out with Cornwallis. Perhaps that's why my life was spared long enough for Tom to find me. We must leave before dawn. Will you wrap up some food for both of us?"

"Yes, but — but where are you goin'?"

She firmed her jaw. "To a safe place to have my baby."

With a curt nod of her head, the slave turned away to the beef roast on the counter and sliced pieces of it. "This here ain't no place to be havin' a baby, that's fo' sure. Hattie'll get a couple meals ready fo' you."

"Thank you. Where's my cousin?"

"Here." Wraithlike, Emma drifted from the darkened common room, her fingers plucking at the bodice of her bedgown. She flicked a haughty glance from Tom to Betsy. "I heard what you said." She paused. "At least remain until my husband returns."

Betsy held Emma's gaze. "He won't be returning. He kept the

wrong company."

Emma's lips trembled. "Then stay and help me. You wanted to manage the ledger. It's yours. I'll help you and Tom find a home in Camden, a lovely house. But please don't leave me."

Betsy wondered how many men Emma had smitten with that pathetic, helpless look. Not that she herself was beyond being moved by her cousin's plight, but running the tavern wasn't her problem anymore. She said in a quiet voice, "My first duty is to my unborn, making sure the baby is birthed in peace and quiet. There will be neither in Camden for awhile. I must move on."

Emma choked out a sob of despair. Then she swept past them, seized her bottle of laudanum from the windowsill, and ran upstairs. After her passage, Hattie averted her gaze to the meat she'd been carving. "Well, what you waitin' fo? You folks got to go. Finish up yo' meal, an' get yo'selves packed."

CHAPTER FORTY-TWO

B y the time they'd transferred everything downstairs and begun loading the horses, the eastern sky was paling on a muggy, warm day. Betsy handed one of the last bundles to Tom. "In the cellar, Fairfax and I witnessed a meeting of the Ambrose spy ring. Adam Neville is Ambrose — a double agent. He figured out that I led Fairfax to the spy ring, and he's ordered his men to kill me — and kill Clark, should he try to warn me."

Even in the darkness she saw the worry on Tom's face deepen. "Good god." He strapped the bundle on the packhorse.

"One of the Ambrose ring could be stationed at the ferry across the Wateree."

"Agreed. Shall we make for Charles Town, then?"

She considered. "If I remember the map correctly, the rebels are camped off the Waxhaws Road, almost due north. The first route we'd selected — the one that parallels the Wateree — doesn't it branch to the northwest well south of the rebel camp?"

"Yes, it does — south of Log Town, in fact."

"Let us ride northwest, then. With luck, we shall slip past all of them to the west."

"All right. I'm willing to give it a try."

They led the packhorse from the barn. Her gaze shifted north, and she blinked. "Did you see that just now? It looked like lightning, except that it — oh, look, there it is again."

Tom studied the northern sky. Intermittent flashes painted the horizon scarlet, and beneath their feet the earth vibrated. He walked several steps away for a view unblocked by trees, disbelief etching his face at the light display. "It isn't lightning. It's cannon fire."

She grimaced. Cornwallis and Gates had found each other.

Tom strode back to the stable, snagging her elbow on the way. "Regardless of who wins that battle, we'll be mired in heavy traffic on the road this morning if we don't get ahead of it now."

When they finished balancing the loads on the horses ten minutes later, the eastern sky smoldered with sunrise. The northern horizon had quieted. Tom helped her mount Lady May and handed up her loaded musket. Then he climbed into his horse's saddle and adjusted his musket and reins.

They headed north. She wished she could have felt enthusiastic about riding away from the month in hell, but her womb had begun to ache. Violence rippled the air ahead, expanding in all directions, dragging down her mood. Somewhere to the north, hundreds of men and horses surely lay dead or dying upon a battlefield, their spirits whispering for her to beware. She and Tom weren't safe yet. Before the morning was spent, disaster had plenty of time to seek them out.

***

The soldier at the blockade apologized. "We've troops patrolling all up and down the Wateree with orders to allow none but His Majesty's forces access to the road."

Betsy gazed with longing at the northwest road, her head fuzzy with exhaustion, and heard her frustration echoed in Tom's voice. "Trying to prevent rebels access to their men in Fort Cary, eh?" He indicated the Waxhaws road. "May we travel north?"

Another redcoat blocking the road shrugged. "I advise against it. We saw cannon fire that way not half an hour ago. Been a great battle six or seven miles north. We've no word yet on the outcome, but you might be taking yourselves into peril."

"That's right," said the third soldier. "Even if you miss getting your head torn off by a cannonball or a bayonet through your guts, scavengers come in after battle and help themselves to whatever they find. Rebel scavengers would be animals. From what I hear, they haven't eaten in a week."

"They're so hungry they'd eat your flesh."

"While you're still breathing and conscious."

Betsy almost smiled at the young men. Gruesome their suggestions might be, but they were doing their job, trying to dissuade civilians from taking a questionable route.

Tom's lips pinched. "I don't suppose we want to be caught in a retreat back to Log Town, either."

"Retreat?" The first soldier drew up in indignation. "Lord Cornwallis wouldn't retreat."

"No, sir, he didn't march out of here last night to retreat. He marched out to shove the war down the throats of seven thousand scummy rebels."

Tom's jaw hung slack. "*Seven* thousand?"

"Outnumbered three to one, and still he marched north. He's a lion." Pride glowed in the soldier's smile.

The three soldiers appeared to reconsider Cornwallis's odds, and then the first man leaned toward Tom. "You're right, sir, getting caught in a retreat wouldn't be jolly fun."

Tom exhaled. "We need to get to Charlotte Town."

"Wait a few days. Let all this settle down."

"Or take our chances on the Waxhaws Road today." Tom motioned Betsy closer. "This road connects with the road west."

She glanced from the soldiers to Tom, aware that the redcoats were attentive to their conversation, knowing that she and Tom had to make it sound convincing. "How much delay will we encounter on that route?"

"Perhaps an hour or two."

"Is that all?"

Tom shifted in his saddle. "Under ideal circumstances. As this fine soldier informed us, ideal circumstances probably don't lie ahead."

"If the rebels hold the ferry south of town, we cannot get past that way. Cousin Mary will be worried if we don't show." She rubbed her pregnant belly for emphasis.

"Let's head north, then. If it looks bad, we'll return to Camden and wait it out."

Or try to sneak west from one road to the other, perhaps, and skirt the action. Betsy flashed Tom a smile. "Very well, dear, let us try that course."

The soldiers stepped aside, their expressions doubtful. "Luck to you folks."

Tom tipped his cocked hat at the fellow in charge. "Thank you, gentlemen." He and Betsy clicked their tongues and headed the horses north at an easy trot. When they'd ridden a quarter mile, past several bends in the sandy road, he signaled for her to ride alongside him, his posture in the saddle conveying their need for wariness.

The eastern sky brightened over thinning pine barrens, and Betsy noticed the absence of birdsong and morning scamper from squirrels. About six o'clock, she sniffed the air. "Black powder and wood smoke."

"With that nose of yours, I'll take your word for it. Listen." Frowning, he signaled a halt. In the distance, they heard the report of a musket. "Three miles north, I'd estimate."

"Should we turn around?"

They listened again. After a quarter minute, they heard another musket shot. Tom stared north, pondering the source of the shots. "Too sporadic for a volley. It's the battle aftermath." Beyond a curve ahead, a horse snorted, and a harness jingled. Tom jerked his head toward the pine trees. "Let's get off the road."

They cleared it by twenty-five feet, sparse pines and dawn shadow offering concealment. Two-dozen begrimed redcoats on horseback trotted by with a litter. Betsy glimpsed a motionless, large man lying amid blood-soaked bandages. The litter hit a rut, jolting its unconscious occupant, and the commander of the party growled. "Damn your eyes, have a care with the general, or he shall never survive to reach Camden!" The party progressed southward and vanished beyond the road's curve.

Betsy followed Tom back out to the road. *The general.* She looked up at Tom. "The man in the litter wasn't Cornwallis."

"Must have been Continental." His forehead puckered in thought. "From what I saw of him, he fits the description I've heard of the Baron de Kalb."

Major-General Johannes de Kalb, fallen. Her gaze followed the road south. "If that's so — Tom, they weren't rushing as if in retreat."

He appeared just as amazed as she felt. "The redcoats must have triumphed. Otherwise they'd have fled to Camden — and far more of

them than were in that party. The only way they could get close
enough to inflict so many wounds on de Kalb and then remove him
from the battlefield is if Gates's army collapsed." He swiveled his
gaze north. "If the redcoats won, we aren't encountering more of them
because they're chasing the Continentals back to North Carolina."

"It *was* what you wished for the other night."

"So I did." As if reassessing the power of wishes, he expelled a
hard breath before gesturing north. "Let's go."

A quarter-hour later they forded a two-hundred-foot wide creek.
Above the burble of water on the other side, they heard faint shouts.

The horses trudged up a rise, the sulfur-stench of black powder
and the tang of wood smoke increasing as they continued north.
Sunlight flooded the area, unhindered by pine trees, and the sandy
terrain was free of underbrush except for weeds.

They came upon British supply wagons guarded by militia with a
few regulars in command. Off to the side, surgeons bandaged up
soldiers while wounded men sat waiting their attention. Women
tended fires, boiled water, and prepared bandages.

The two armies had fought at first light, with the entire battle
lasting an hour. Minutes after the forces engaged, Gates's entire left
wing, comprised of Stevens's Virginians and militia from North
Carolina, crumpled. Beset by disciplined redcoats in a bayonet charge,
the dysenteric rebels had flung down their muskets and fled in terror.
Most of Gates's grand army had followed suit and was being hunted
by the likes of Tarleton's Green Dragoons. General de Kalb, who'd
received numerous wounds in a valiant attempt to sustain Gates's right
flank, was being conveyed back to Camden for medical attention. As
for General Gates, he'd vanished from the battlefield after the first half
hour — turned coward and run, some boasted, like that dimwit
Abraham Buford at the Waxhaws back in May.

Betsy and Tom congratulated the men at the supply wagons on
the sound defeat of Gates, and, receiving permission to search the
battlefield for their missing Loyalist "brother," proceeded north. The
stink of human and animal sweat and the metallic stench of blood
greeted Betsy a hundred or so yards ahead, where they came upon
wagons being loaded with the wounded — some men quiet, many
moaning, a few thrashing about with inhuman agony tearing from their
throats. Horror wrenched her stomach, too recently filled with food.
She wanted to gallop Lady May past the face slashed open from a
saber wound, the bleached white of ribs gleaming in the sunlight, the

silver sheen of entrails; yet she found herself searching among the wounded militia for Clark's familiar face.

His expression taut, Tom rode back to her. "Good gods, what butchers. Clark isn't here. Let's move on."

Just ahead, the road bisected a clearing about a mile across. Muggy miasma hugged the earth in fetid layers. Betsy gagged on the stink of black powder and blood, feces, swamp putrefaction, sweat, scorched pines, and charred flesh.

Several dozen horses wandered trailing reins, picking their way around incinerated craters where cannonballs had gouged the earth. More horses sprawled in the weedy sand, a few of them torn in half by cannonfire, others twitching, disemboweled and still conscious, or thrashing their forelegs and unable to rise with broken spines.

While men hustled about with stretchers or secured the artillery pieces, other men and women drifted among the soldier and militia bodies in search of comrades or loved ones. And there were hundreds of fallen men out in the field — so many hundreds, dark and motionless against the pale sand, like the ravage of smallpox upon a giant face. A lone woman paused beside a body, sank to her knees, and wailed, lifting her hands to the sky. The miasma disembodied her keen as well as the screams, moans, and grunts of injured men and horses. Betsy swallowed, her mouth tasting of death.

Two privates strode past with a stretcher, headed for the wagons of injured, bearing between them a glassy-eyed soldier whose right leg below the knee was a shredded tangle of bloody breeches, magenta muscle, and pink bone. Betsy raised her kerchief to her mouth. Tom, his complexion green, whispered, "I say we try the west route. I've no great desire to press further through this carnage and discover how the Continentals fared."

She stuffed her kerchief away with trembling hands and grasped the reins. In turning Lady May back around, her gaze swept west where a horse stood still among scraggly pines at the perimeter of the battlefield, its head bowed. She gulped. "Tom, that's Clark's horse out there by the pines."

He squinted through layers of dust and fog. "It's almost half a mile away. You're certain of it?"

"Yes." She knew he could see, as she saw, a body lying near the horse. Tears smarted in her eyes. "I need to know," she whispered, blinking to clear her vision. "We both need to know."

"The gods help us, then." Although he appeared even closer to puking than she felt, he squared his shoulders. "Follow me."

CHAPTER FORTY-THREE

She kept her gaze on the tail of the packhorse ahead but couldn't shut out the stinks of blood-soaked sand, feces, and vomit. Nor could she block her ears from human and equine torment: a blend of whinnies, curses, supplications, and sobs.

Long before they reached the pines, she recognized the downed man as Clark. From the blood staining his shirt, and the fowler lying within his reach, his luck at receiving mere flesh wounds had run out. They knelt beside him. Blood seeped from the corner of his mouth. The wound to his chest was greater on the front. "Shot from behind," Tom whispered.

Tears smeared her vision again. "Ah, Clark," she murmured, and stroked his face.

His eyelids fluttered, and he focused on her. "Betsy, go — get away — safety," he whispered, and coughed bubbly blood.

A lung shot — beyond the skill of any physician to repair. Resolution steadied her gaze on Tom. "We cannot leave him like this. Find someone with a stretcher to help us."

Tom glanced over the battlefield. "I don't want to leave you out here. Looters have already started showing up."

She stood. "I've my musket and his fowler."

Tom rose also. "Very well, but I don't like this."

"No — both of you go —" Clark's speech curtailed with more coughing and bloody froth.

Betsy stamped her foot. "Be quiet, Clark."

Tom loaded Clark's fowler. Then, his expression dubious, he mounted his horse and headed back through carnage and chaos, the packhorse in tow. Betsy set the fowler within easy reach beside her musket. She stripped the saddle from Clark's horse and, ignoring his groans, propped him up against it.

The clench of pain in his face eased, and he spoke with less effort. "Go. They think you betrayed them. They'll kill you."

She knelt before him again. "Did they shoot you when you were trying to get away and warn me?"

"Yes. They may return."

"Let them come. I'll put a ball between the eyes of two of them, at least."

"Betsy, I never meant to hurt you."

A lump gripped her throat. She couldn't afford to break down just then, but later, later — "I know you didn't."

"Forgive me for leaving you."

She brushed fingers on his paling lips and swallowed. "Please, save your breath."

"I know you didn't betray me." She clenched her fist. Under no circumstances must he know. "Beware Adam Neville — Ambrose. He thinks you told the British about the furniture." He coughed flecks of blood. "And Fairfax knows I'm lying here —"

"Fairfax saw you and didn't kill you?"

A mirthless smile ghosted his lips. "Why bother? A fellow Patriot managed the task. I shan't see my child born."

"Oh, Clark —"

He coughed again. "Go somewhere safe and have the baby. Tom will help." He licked his lips. "I noticed in Augusta. The way he looked at you. He loves you. And he's still at your side through all this." A tear spilled over her lid and curved her cheek. She dashed it away with the back of her hand. He reached for her hand, his icy. "Darling, I should never have doubted your fidelity."

Her eyes widened, and she felt sickened by his words. Handwriting wasn't all Fairfax counterfeited. No wonder she'd been so easily lured to the cellar. If he planned to eliminate the spy ring, he might have left Clark alive as bait for any surviving members. The vigil with her husband could be a trap.

She sat up, alert, and swept her gaze over the battlefield. Tom was nowhere in sight, but she had the feeling of being watched. Clark's voice sounded gravelly, faded. "Behind you."

After seizing her musket, she sprang up. Grins on their faces, knives and tomahawks in their hands, the four of them charged from the swampy terrain concealed by nearby pines: Basilio, Francisco, and two other men she recognized from the meeting in the cellar. With no time to think, she cocked her musket, took aim, and fired.

Francisco dropped with a howl, clutching his stomach, but his companions continued their sprint for her. She heard the approach of a galloping horse from the north, even while she hauled up Clark's fowler and fired at Basilio. He shrieked and collapsed, blood spewing from his chest. The other two men had a second to reorient their attention and scream before a blur of scarlet and raised steel on horseback shot past Betsy and Clark and decapitated the men not fifteen feet from where she stood. Sunlight sparkled in twin geysers of crimson, and their headless bodies toppled over.

"Christ Jesus!" Still powered on adrenaline and survival instinct, she flung down Clark's fowler and reached for her musket, realized no one had reloaded it, and seized her cartridge box and bag of lead balls. Seconds later, she'd performed her quickest reload of a musket ever. She raised it to sight Lieutenant Fairfax, who trotted his gelding around for a more leisurely reconnaissance with the Sheridans, his carriage confident, his countenance enraptured and unearthly.

He reined back near where Basilio and Francisco moaned and thrashed, whipped out a rag, and wiped the blood from his saber. "Such gratitude, madam. I save your life for the second time, and you plan to thank me by blowing my brains out."

"I *will* blow your brains out if you don't gallop out of here. Now."

"Never underestimate a wounded opponent." He sheathed his saber and put away the rag. "These two rebels are still alive."

"Not for long."

"I agree." Before her heart hammered twice more, he whipped out a pistol from his saddle holster and shot Basilio in the head.

Clark gasped out "Oh, my god!" even as Fairfax dispatched Francisco with a shot from a second pistol.

Betsy stared down the muzzle of a third pistol. The lieutenant had moved so fast that she hadn't seen him swap out the weapons. Sweat slicked her hands and beaded between her thighs. The certainty rolled over her that his trigger finger was far quicker than hers, and even though they held each other at gunpoint, the disadvantage was hers, for he knew how to incapacitate without killing.

His smile softened. "Drop the musket, or shoot me. Your choice."

Men — *normal* men — used that tone to court women. She took several breaths and felt her entire expression, even her eyes, harden. If she didn't find a way to seize advantage, Fairfax would shoot her, or the noise they were making would attract soldiers to his aid. "Throw all your firearms on the ground." For seconds that stretched like centuries, he stared her down. She tightened her lips. "It appears you've given up believing I can lead you to my mother."

"Your mother — ah, bloody damn, now you've gone and called my bluff, you clever woman." With a sigh, he tossed the pistol, three others, and a musket on the ground near Clark and regarded her with an innocent expression.

She suspected he had another firearm hidden. "Keep your hands raised. Throw down the other firearm, the one you're planning to pull out as soon as you think I've dropped my guard." A surly expression enveloped his face. His right hand up, he plucked out a civilian pistol from near the holsters, tossed it down, and lifted his left hand again. "Good. Now head for the road."

"So you can shoot me in the back?"

"That's an excellent idea.

"Without hearing what I have to say?"

"I don't care what you have to say."

"Oh, I think you do, but I doubt your husband does."

Anger punctuated her composure. Clark hissed, "He isn't going to let you go. Give me your musket, and I'll keep him here long enough to let you get away."

"How poignant, sir."

Another lump formed in her throat at Clark's suggestion. She clamped down on grief and anger and glared at Fairfax. "Get moving. East."

He clicked his tongue, nudged the horse about with his knees, and smiled back at her. "Exhilarating, every moment of it — from the note you sent me about van Duser and the furniture two weeks ago to the kiss you gave me last night."

"Why, you son of a —"

"Betsy, watch out!"

Gambling on the distraction caused by her outrage, Fairfax reached for something else near his saddle, twisting at the same time she pulled the trigger. Her musket ball clipped his left upper arm, and he sprawled onto the ground.

"Give me one of his pistols!" Clark rasped. "I'll hold him off as long as I remain conscious. Go!" She looked at him through the haze of blackpowder smoke, her heart wrenching at the sight of his lips, now gray. He coughed blood. "Go!"

Fairfax, his back to them, had risen to his knees. Betsy shoved the pistols over to Clark, not knowing which were loaded, scrambled into Lady May's saddle with her empty musket gripped in one hand, and kicked the mare into motion. East across the cratered field of death she rode, the wind whipping tears from her eyes, the vision forever burned into her memory of Clark's final act as her rear guard, his face devoid of color, his lifeblood draining into his punctured lung.

Tom. She must find Tom. Clark had bought her that much. She paused at the road and scanned north, where hundreds of bodies cluttered road and field, and then south across the more ordered array of the British. Tom was nowhere in sight.

A glance behind blasted panic and grief through her. His left arm stiff, Fairfax was mounting his horse. Clark was either dead or unconscious. She galloped the mare southward, hoping to find Tom, hoping they could outrun Fairfax. He was, after all, injured. Maybe he'd lose blood in the chase and pass out.

Faces whizzed by her, none of them Tom. She passed wagons of injured men and supplies and headed downhill alone on the road. Gods, something must have happened to Tom. She'd have to press on to Camden by herself. She dared not pause even to load her musket. At least her mare was rested.

They slowed to ford the creek, and on the south side, Betsy glimpsed Fairfax cantering downhill toward her, seeming unfazed by his injured arm. *Never underestimate a wounded opponent.* She bent over to the horse's ear and stroked her neck. "Give me everything you can, my lady."

To her credit, Lady May held the gallop, but after a minute, Betsy could tell the gelding was gaining on them and knew she'd never make it back to Camden before Fairfax overtook her. Just as distressing: slow cramps had replaced the ache in her womb.

Around a bend, she spied a trail to the right, reined the mare onto it, and trotted her back thirty feet, where pines and undergrowth swallowed the trail. After wheeling the horse around, she seized her ammunition and began reloading her musket. Horse and rider thundered past on the road, and then the sound of the gallop ceased. Fairfax realized she'd left the road. Her breath drawn in gasps, Betsy fumbled a ball from her pouch, lost it on the ground, reached for another ball, and then dropped the entire bag out of fatigue and fear.

Through the foliage, the scarlet of his coat winked in and out of view. With no time to retrieve the pouch, she pulled up the musket and aimed at the entrance of the trail: Betsy Sheridan's brave, last stand. Seconds later, Fairfax walked his gelding down the trail, pistol held ready, and halted the horse about fifteen feet from her. "Ah, here we are again, darling. Shall we call it the second verse of the same song?"

CHAPTER FORTY-FOUR

Betsy jutted her jaw with confidence she didn't feel. "Move to the refrain, where I order you to drop your weapons."

Fairfax indicated the bag in the pine needles. "Were I a perfect gentleman, I'd invite you dismount and fetch a ball for your musket. I'm gambling that it isn't fully loaded, but you've no idea whether my pistol is." Midwinter built in his eyes. "Drop your musket, or I *will* take it by force."

Firing her musket — igniting the powder — might buy a moment's distraction, but she wouldn't get far when he had the faster horse, and he was beyond cerebral appreciation for heroic feints. Her game was over. Adrenaline ebbed from her blood, and fatigue poured into her arms. She cast down the musket.

"Dismount." His pistol was trained on her head. Legs and arms shaking, she complied and lowered her gaze. "Walk to me. Keep your hands where I can see them. That's far enough." He dismounted and walked a full circle around her before releasing the cock on the pistol and pushing it into his sash. "Look at me. How did you get out of the cellar?"

Though she felt certain Tom wouldn't be rescuing her, she saw no point in admitting she'd had an accomplice. "You left me plenty of time, so I gnawed my way out."

Perhaps her chafed wrists conferred credence. His mockery subsided into perplexity and metamorphosed into admiration and then sentiment hotter than admiration. Her skin crawled like a drove of caterpillars homing on spring-green leaves.

He lifted his left hand and caressed her cheek with his fingertips. Alas, the injury to his arm must have been minor, for no pain registered in his expression at the movement. His fingers wandered to her lips before stroking her chin and jaw, and she clenched her teeth against his scent. In one motion, he yanked her linen tucker out of her shift and jacket, leaving her shoulders and collarbone exposed. Steel glinted in his right hand. She flinched in anticipation of the blade on her throat. At least she wouldn't be flayed alive or hacked to pieces.

"Well, then, I shan't bind you with rope this time." The knife flashed, and fabric rent. He hauled her to a tree and pushed her back against it.

Through fatigue and numbness, she stared at Lady May while Fairfax bound her wrists behind the tree with shredded tucker. Then he blocked her view of the horse and traced his forefinger across her naked collarbone. "How wicked of the Fates to cast us as opponents, Widow Sheridan." He grinned at her wince of grief. "I hope you don't think *I* killed him? Thank his rebel allies for that. I have — all except for Adam Neville. I suspect he may prove useful in the near future. As for your husband, he expired on his own — but not before hearing my gratitude for your role in sparing Britons the rule of the Stadtholder. Since he was reluctant to believe me, I told him of our rendezvous in the cellar and how we witnessed his meeting. I even recounted portions of conversation. I'm not certain which concept upset him the more — imagining you'd betrayed his cause, or imagining you as my willing mistress." He spread his hands. "But he saw no reason to linger after that."

No one would have lingered after that. Fairfax had conferred harsh dignity upon Basilio and Francisco, shooting them and ending their agony, but he'd eviscerated Clark with a weapon that cut deeper than any spear or blade. "Go to hell."

"I've a better idea." He walked his fingers down the front closing of her jacket. "You tell me where to find your mother." His lips brushed her throat. "But you needn't hasten to arrive at the truth. We're both enjoying this."

Goosebumps emerged all over her body. "Take your hands off me. I didn't give you permission to touch me."

He chuckled and unfastened the top of her jacket. "Your permission is irrelevant. Let's start with your uncle. On July the eleventh, he paid you a quick visit on his way to Virginia or the Carolinas." She squirmed when he began toying with the drawstring of her shift. "He'd traveled with your mother north from East Florida?"

"I don't know. He didn't say."

"But she gave him a message to deliver to you. 'Don't worry, I'm all right, I'm hiding —'" He caressed the side of her mouth with his lips and whispered, "Hiding — where?"

She smelled blood on him — how many men's blood? Revolted, she jerked her head to the side. He forced her face back around to him while his other hand opened her drawstring. Primitive fear overcame her rational mind, and her knees knocked. "In the C — Carolinas or Virginia."

"Oh, she was more specific than that. She's your mother."

All Betsy wanted was to escape the smell, taste, sight, sound, and feel of death. "N — no, I swear it, and oh, g — gods, please just l - leave me alone! You've tortured me enough over my husband! Must you t — torture me over the mother and father I cannot find because — " She gulped back her words with renewed horror. Oh, no, she hadn't just said that, had she?

He dropped the drawstring in surprise. "*Father*? Then your father wasn't le Coeuvre?" Venom infiltrated his voice. "Why, he's that half-breed Creek bastard, isn't he? Ah, that makes much more sense." He bared his teeth, his face in her face, becoming her view of the universe. "*Savages.* I loathe the lying, traitorous lot of them. So where are Mother and Father, Betsy? Are they hiding with the Creek near Alton? Or with the Cherokee northwest of Ninety Six?"

Tom's voice bellowed through the clearing. "Maggot, unhand her!"

Drawing his pistol, Fairfax pivoted in a blur of movement faster than any human ought to be capable of moving and aimed for Tom, who stood a few feet ahead of his horse and the packhorse with his musket trained on the lieutenant. Aware of the accuracy of Fairfax's pistol, Betsy kicked his knee as he pulled the trigger, skewing the trajectory of the ball to the right.

The shots, simultaneous, loaded the clearing with smoke. Fairfax regained his balance from the kick and stepped away from her. Tom toppled to the ground, blood darkening the hair near his left temple, and lay still, supine. Betsy shrieked. "No! No! Oh, gods, no!"

His shoulders thrown back, Fairfax ambled over to his horse, granting Tom a cursory look on the way. He swapped his fired pistol for another, shoved the new one in his sash, and ambled back to Betsy without a second glance at Tom. "Pardon the interruption, darling. Where were we? Ah, yes, Mathias Hale —"

"God damn you to hell!"

He studied her a few seconds, no emotion in his eyes, before retrieving another strip of torn linen from the ground and gagging her with it. "I need your attention, and you've been talking too much and saying too little." He unfastened more of her jacket. "Such soft skin — You do know where your mother is hiding. Mothers tell daughters things like that." The remainder of the jacket opened. "She told you where to find her. Perhaps she communicated it to your uncle or sent you a letter. But you do know, and you will tell me."

Although he dominated much of her field of vision, she spotted movement over his shoulder — Tom swabbing the palm of his hand to his temple and bringing it away bloodied. She yanked her gaze away from a head wound that looked lethal enough to fool Fairfax, wondering how serious it actually was, hoping the lieutenant didn't notice where she'd looked. His attention was on the neckline of her shift, which he'd hooked with his forefinger and begun teasing open.

She allowed her body to slump, signaling acquiescence. Behind him, Tom rolled over, brought himself to his knees, and wiped away blood near his left eye with the back of his hand. If she hadn't kicked Fairfax's knee, the ball would have plugged Tom between the eyes instead of yielding that scrape to the side of his head. Tom blinked and spotted her, and she looked at Fairfax as pathetically as possible. Yes, yes, keep your attention on me. I'm surrendering. I'll tell you everything.

He registered the change in her and paused from tickling the skin on her upper chest. "Really? So soon? Damn. I thought you'd more resistance in you. Are you quite certain you're sincere? Perhaps we should play this out a bit longer, just to be sure."

She shook her head in misery, begging, tears filling her eyes — a more compelling actress than she'd ever dreamed she could be — and forced her gaze to hold his. In her peripheral vision, Tom found his footing, stole toward his horse, and reached for something. Surely he wouldn't try to reload his musket. Fairfax would hear him. She moaned. Two tears rolled down her cheeks, and she moaned again.

Fairfax stiffened, preternatural awareness alerting him to movement without sound behind him. When he spun around, Tom had sought partial concealment behind a pine tree, blood oozing down the left side of his face, a coil of rope in his hands. No mere coil of rope, Betsy realized with a zing of fear: a lasso. All right, so he'd chased down and lassoed one of their hounds the morning she and Clark left for Augusta, but Fairfax wasn't going to let himself be lassoed and tied down like a dog.

The lieutenant eyed her and moved out of kick range. "Are you challenging me with a *rope*, boy?"

Tom twirled the lasso. "Untie her and let her go."

"More than blood leaked from your head just now." Fairfax pulled out the pistol and took aim. "You have to my count of five to lay down the rope, or I shall put a ball between your eyes — and this time I won't miss."

Betsy's eyes bulged. He wouldn't count to five, but Tom might make the mistake of believing so. She stamped her foot three times. Focused on his opponent, Tom paid her no heed. She screamed through the gag and again stamped her foot three times.

"One."

She thrashed about, drawing Tom's eye for an instant, and stamped her foot three more times. Three. The faintest widening of his eyes told her he'd intuited her message.

Fairfax cocked the pistol. "Two."

With more nimbleness than she'd ever seen him exhibit, Tom pivoted from cover and flung the lasso. It hooked Fairfax's neck, fouling his pistol aim, sending the ball among the trees. When he tried to extricate his neck, Tom tightened the rope, creating a collar. The lieutenant charged him, slackening the rope. Tom dropped it, grabbed the tree for support, and jacked his knee just in time to catch Fairfax's groin.

Betsy heard the solid thud and then gaped. Fairfax hadn't dropped to the ground in agony the way a normal man would have done. The blow had only sent him into a crouch from which he began fumbling with the lasso, loosening it. His breath in gasps, Tom grabbed the rope and tightened it again, yanking the lieutenant up against the pine tree. Choking, Fairfax dropped the empty pistol and pushed off the tree. Tom hauled him back and kicked his knee from beneath him.

With a grunt, Fairfax tumbled to all fours, where Tom dispensed a kick to his kidney. Wandering the twilight between conscious and unconscious, Fairfax struggled to a sitting position. Tom ran the rope around the tree again and again, trussing him up against it. When he'd secured it and shoved the pistol beyond range, he staggered away, legs folding beneath him, head in his hands.

For excruciating seconds, Betsy expected him to pass out. Fairfax regained consciousness and began squirming to exploit a weakness in his bonds. Tom pulled a handkerchief from his vest pocket and mopped blood from his head and face. Stuffing the handkerchief away, he heaved to his feet and headed for her.

He cut her bonds and gag. They embraced, both a mass of muscle tremors from exhaustion and wracked nerves. Then, wordless, he stomped for his horse. She scurried after, puzzling over his stony expression, tightening the drawstring on her shift and fumbling her jacket closed. But when he snatched up his musket, she straightened her shoulders, understanding. So did Fairfax, who stopped squirming. With a derisive smile, he watched Tom load his musket.

The packhorse snorted. Betsy went to him and stroked his nose, her back turned. A metallic swish told her Tom had pulled the ramrod from the barrel of his loaded musket. The packhorse shifted around, frisky, as if smelling something good and familiar. All Betsy smelled was death, by then all too familiar.

Tom cocked the musket. "May the devil welcome his own."

"Lower your weapon, sir. We have you surrounded."

The packhorse's ears perked, and he whinnied in welcome. Betsy swung around in shock and watched four men emerge from the woods while Tom complied with their order: Josiah and Jeremiah Carter and two friends, all bearing muskets, all grimed with black powder. Cordiality filled Fairfax's voice. "Mr. Carter, how good of you to stay my execution. Please untie me and assist my apprehension of these rebel spies."

Carter looked from Fairfax to Tom and the wound on his head. Then he shifted his gaze to Betsy, who fluttered her hand across her naked collarbone. Her modesty supplied a summary of the scenario: violation and vengeance. Carter's gaze swept back to Fairfax. "Rebel spies? I'm certain you're mistaken, Lieutenant. I know this man and woman, and they aren't rebel spies."

"You stopped him from executing me just now."

Betsy saw determination root in Carter's expression. "We chanced upon you while pursuing bandits who raided my plantation. I think it likely this man and woman found you tied thusly and chased off your would-be executioner."

Fairfax's jaw bounced open. "What? He was aiming his musket right at me. Have you no eyes?"

"I've a good set of eyes, and I see a substantial injury to your arm, sir. You've had blood loss — maybe enough to affect your perceptions and memory. We'd best get you to a surgeon."

"I don't need a bloody surgeon! I need you to untie me!"

Carter cleared his throat. "Really, sir, perhaps we'd best leave you there until you calm down and we can make a thorough search of the area for the men who wounded you."

"Look no further. *She* shot me out on the battlefield!"

"Indeed, blood loss." Carter shook his head and walked to Betsy, motioning Tom to join him. Stroking the packhorse's neck, he said, low, "We can detain him an hour at most."

"Thank you," Tom whispered. "Do yourself a favor and kill him."

"You're as bad as he is, and no, I don't want to hear your grievances. I'm tired of fighting and killing. Madam." He looked at Betsy. "I'm grateful to you for exposing injustice that I myself was forbidden to bring to light. Seven of us will testify of the Branwells' criminal operations. I will be relieved if you left Camden this hour and reached the sanctuary you spoke of. And as you go, know that I shall hold your property for you until such day as you return for it."

She drew a ragged breath. "Thank you, Mr. Carter. Please don't let him see which way we go."

"Absolutely not. Now get on out of here."

CHAPTER FORTY-FIVE

Betsy awakened between a snoring Tom and cast iron pots, her face pressed to a blanket that had seen cleaner days, a wagon swaying beneath her. Her mouth tasted like a decomposed varmint, and her head ached as if it had been whacked against a tree. But the ominous cramping in her womb had stopped, and when she stroked her belly, the baby shifted about, happy to not be in flight down the Waxhaws Road or stupid with fatigue.

War might have ripped South Carolina apart, but people could still trust in the innate goodness of strangers — in her case, demonstrated by the Dean family, who had let them climb aboard their wagon at noon and ride west with them. The family had even offered to feed them supper and put them up for the night.

Her stomach growled, and she couldn't remember her last meal. She had a vague recollection of bandaging Tom's head after they'd been ferried across the Wateree by jubilant Loyalists. Yawning, she looked at Tom's bandage. Hair might cover the patch where the ball had scalped, but he'd bear the scar the rest of his days. Her eyelids drooped, and sleep again found her.

The Deans awakened them around six-thirty in the evening on the east bank of the Congaree River. After Betsy and Tom paid their own fare and contributed to that of the others, the entire party was ferried across. Their benefactors encouraged them to stay for supper at the home of a friend a quarter hour away and to also accept their hospitality for the night.

So after pork stew, cobbler, and coffee, Betsy, Tom, the Deans, and their friends watched moths flirt with the backyard bonfire, and Tom spun his tale: of traveling from Charlotte Town Tuesday afternoon, getting caught in a skirmish, being held prisoner all night, and escaping the battle. Children ensconced in mothers' laps listened with rapt eyes.

Much later, Betsy blew out a lantern and relaxed on her blanket in the barn, and when she regained sleep, dreams caught up with her at last. Around three in the morning, on the threshold between dreaming and waking, she gazed into the night to behold the specter of Clark turning his back on her and walking away a final time. Then she rolled on her side away from Tom and let the trickle of tears begin, let it gather momentum into the storm of reckoning she'd weather for a long while, clenching her teeth to silence her sobs.

She and Clark had never said goodbye — not in Augusta, nor in Log Town, nor on the battlefield — but every one of those moments had been a goodbye. The whole marriage had been a goodbye. Always he slipped away from her like mist clutched between fingers. When she searched her memories for laughter they'd shared in Augusta, it all receded before her, ungraspable.

Were it not for the child she carried, she'd have questioned whether Clark ever walked the earth, for he seemed imaginary. With a jolt, she realized that the man she'd married — the fellow of sensible politics who provided for her and lived a quiet shoemaker's life — wasn't Clark. The Clark she'd fallen in love with had never existed.

Even more astonishing was her insight that goodwife Betsy Sheridan who kept a tidy house and the books for her husband's business, the woman who'd settled down — she was imaginary, too. If the Augusta ladies knew she'd escaped a mass grave, emptied chamberpots in a whorehouse, exposed a blackmail scam, pulled a printing press, shot two men, and wounded a Horseman from the Apocalypse, they'd faint.

The straw beneath their blankets rustled, and Tom curled up to her backside, wrapping an arm around her. It was the same position they'd awakened in one morning at the Leaping Stag, except there was nothing sexual about it this time, and there was everything solid about it. For a month he'd been there, always a friend, always a partner the way Clark had never been. Not for a long while had Tom been the blushing, gangly apprentice from Augusta. Even that memory receded when she reached for it.

The Fates had granted her a brief reprieve. She lay safe on a blanket in a barn west of the Congaree with leisure at last to grieve. Miles northwest, refuge awaited her among people whose ways so differed from hers that a month earlier, she couldn't have envisioned herself living among them. During that month, however, her values and priorities had been stood upside down. That morning, Thursday, August seventeenth, her affirmation of her earlier decision to venture to Mulberry Creek and claim what was hers no longer seemed desperate and crazy, but just and wise.

***

Ninety Six was a piddle of artisans' shops, a courthouse, and a jail numbering perhaps a dozen buildings along the road. Even counting the surrounding flourmills and farmsteads, the village didn't seem worthy of the palisade around it — especially since the Cherokee hadn't been aggressive in years. She and Tom rode on through, minimal interaction with the inhabitants, just a couple of travelers headed somewhere, anywhere.

The way veered west, away from the sunlit sparkle of the Saluda River. They camped Saturday night among hills and hardwoods, and Betsy counted stars through verdant foliage. On the morrow, they'd cross Mulberry Creek.

How would her mother know she was there? How long would she and Tom have to wait? They had about ten days' rations and would need to move on by the twenty-fifth if Sophie didn't show. The problem was that Betsy didn't know where else to go. With all her proverbial eggs in one basket, it was a wretched time to mull over options.

A clever backup plan hadn't come to her by the time they set off Sunday. The terrain grew more mountainous, and they didn't reach the creek until the evening. No human had set foot on the ledges providing a view of the road in quite awhile, and it had been at least a week since another horse had traveled the road. Still, they couldn't be too careful, so after they picketed their horses above rhododendron and rocks, Tom sneaked an eighth of a mile back down the road and obscured their passage.

Monday and Tuesday they waited. Wednesday afternoon the twenty-third, a week after the battle of Camden, while Betsy sat beside Mulberry Creek and contemplated the water, she heard soft movement behind her and sprang up. Her alarm transcended into relief and joy. On the bank stood Standing Wolf.

With a grin, he helped her up the bank. She hugged him despite the stinky bear grease. "How did you find us?"

"Noisy. Birds for miles around chatter your location."

"Pshaw." She laughed, the first time she'd done so in too long. "It's so good to see you. Who else is here?" His smile grew mystical. "My mother? Oh, let's not tarry another moment!"

She earned kicks of annoyance from the baby for scrambling back up the hill. Joshua Hale spotted her next and pointed out a slender, dark-haired man approaching from the left, but she whirled Joshua about in a hug first.

The "man" turned out to be Sophie in a hunting shirt and trousers. "Mother, oh, Mother!" And then, because she couldn't help herself, because she'd doubted she'd see her mother again, Betsy began bawling as soon as she and Sophie embraced.

When she regained composure, she smiled through tears and fumbled a handkerchief to her face while her mother smiled through her own tears. It was indeed her mother holding her hands and stroking her face, though not Nagchoguh Hogdee, Paper Woman, so much as Mountain Woman, her face lightly tanned, her body toned and agile from riding a horse and sleeping beneath stars. But more than just color and activity contributed to her vitality. Sophie Barton looked content for the first time ever.

A wiry Indian approached them. Unlike Standing Wolf, he wore a hunting shirt and trousers, and his black hair, full and long, was plaited. Red man? White man?

Walk in Two Worlds: Ayukapeta Hokolen Econa. Memories stirred, placing his face among those she remembered from childhood in Alton, the incident a joke she'd overheard him share with Will and David. Wonder filled her voice. "Mathias Hale — why, I do know you!"

The obsidian of his eyes softened, and he touched her cheek with the back of his fingers, as if he couldn't believe she was real. "You I haven't seen in eight years."

"She looks just like Mama, doesn't she?" murmured Joshua. "Incredible."

"And look, here's one who escaped." Joshua pulled Tom over.

Tom made a stiff bow. "Pleased to meet you again, Mrs. Barton." He shook Mathias's hand. "Thomas Alexander, sir."

"Mathias Hale. Thank you for seeing our daughter to us."

Sophie glanced around. "Where's Clark?" Betsy lowered her gaze and cleared her throat, but Sophie spared her fumbling for words. "Oh, dear, I'm so sorry." Her mother embraced her again, and her voice emerged quiet, weary. "In that case, Mr. Alexander, we're very much in your debt for bringing Betsy safely to us." Sophie's gaze traveled to Tom's head wound. "I presume you put your own life in danger to do so."

Joshua clapped a hand on Tom's shoulder. "I told Betsy he'd be a good friend."

Mathias said to Tom, "Come back with us into the mountains. Wait for all this to blow over. The way isn't safe yet for you to return to Georgia."

Tom bowed his head. "Thank you, sir, madam." He turned a smile to Betsy. "I'd like that very much."

A crow cawed — no ordinary crow, Betsy knew when her kin stiffened to listen. "What now?" Mathias trotted for the ledge to get a view of the road. Standing Wolf accompanied him.

After more crow caws, Betsy and the others headed for the overlook. A Cherokee warrior sprinted from the brush, his hair, tattoos, and clothing similar to that of the Creek, but a more olive hue to his skin. He conversed with Mathias, gesturing south. Mathias nodded and turned to all of them. "Panther Leaping spotted a party of two dozen militiamen and several redcoats headed north on horseback. They'll pass beneath us within a minute. Mr. Alexander, are your horses secure behind those rocks?"

"Yes, sir."

"Good. Ideally the men pass by and never know we're here because there are too many to squabble with. All the same, ready weapons, choose cover, and don't fire unless I say so."

Shrouded in summer foliage, they scattered and crouched on the

ledge, Mathias, Standing Wolf, and Panther Leaping with arrows fitted
to bows, Betsy, Sophie, Tom, and Joshua with muskets ready.
Kneeling to the right of her mother, Betsy turned and caught her
glance of love. Then Sophie's gaze snagged on the road. Her eyes
stiffened, and she drew up her musket, sighting.

The hairs polarized on Betsy's neck, and her teeth bared. Riding
point for men on horseback was Lieutenant Fairfax, his predatory gaze
sweeping from side to side as the rocks rose around them. He halted
the party thirty feet away, and a man in a hunting shirt and trousers
rode forward: Adam Neville.

The Ranger was clearly not his prisoner. He studied the road
from his saddle and shook his head. "A quarter mile back, they left the
road."

"That's an excellent place for an ambush up there."

"Agreed."

Understanding crawled through Betsy. Fairfax was using Neville
without letting on that he knew he was a rebel. Like van Duser and
Branwell, Neville didn't comprehend the twists of Fairfax's mind. At
some point, his usefulness as scout and guide would expire. If he were
lucky he'd get his brains blown out or his throat slit. But she doubted
he'd be lucky.

"Savages." From Fairfax's sneer, there wasn't an Indian on the
earth he trusted. His gaze bored through foliage where Betsy and
Sophie crouched. Reins grasped in his left hand, he held his musket
ready in his right hand. "Follow me, men. Stay alert."

The party advanced north. Fairfax passed within ten feet of
Betsy, his head in her sights the entire time. She fought the urge to
squeeze the trigger until her stomach grew raw with it while entranced
with the thought of spattering his brains all over the road. Even after
the party pulled ahead, she followed them with her musket. Through
her trance, she heard Tom whisper, "Betsy, they're gone. Lower the
musket."

She let the barrel drop and saw her father's hand wrap about the
barrel of her mother's musket and push it gently down. His gaze
traveled between mother and daughter, and his black eyes filled with
understanding.

Another Cherokee emerged from the brush, as did Runs With
Horses. Mathias motioned them all to gather. The nine stood in
silence while forest noises around them resumed normalcy. Then
Mathias caught the gazes of the Cherokee. "You saw him, the redcoat

with hair like flame?" They nodded. "Lieutenant Fairfax is the one who murdered the Spaniard in Alton and made it appear the work of the people. We have the sworn word of one of his own, Lieutenant Stoddard, that it's so.

While Indians grumbled, Betsy drew in a breath of clarity, recalling the determination on Stoddard's face in Camden and the enmity between Stoddard and Fairfax in Alton. The British army wouldn't condemn Fairfax. It would hide him. Not the flavor of justice Stoddard craved.

Mathias threw back his shoulders. "Fairfax is also the enemy of my mother's house. He murdered her brother." Creek and Cherokee alike sucked in a breath of indignation, expressions toughening. "He laid violent hands on Nagchoguh Hogdee —" His gaze pierced Betsy, read her soul. " — and on her daughter.

"This moment was not ours. But someday soon, Creator may grant us our time. We will show Fairfax what it is to be a prisoner of war among the people, after the old ways." As one, the Indians bared their teeth in an expression unmistakable for a smile. "And then my mother's house will be avenged, and her brother's spirit will find peace." He released a war whoop, and the warriors joined him, altogether bloodcurdling, inhuman. They quieted, pleased to hear the forest ring with the summons.

Dread slithered through Betsy. Had her father known his opponent, he wouldn't have issued a challenge. After a lifetime of searching for him and finding him at last, after seeing her mother content at last, she couldn't let him fall into the trap. She gripped his arm. "At this distance, he will have heard you!"

The others, even her mother, remained silent, their attention on Betsy and her question of the warrior who walked in two worlds. Mathias looked from her hand on his arm to her eyes, and his tone was calm. "May he continue to hear us, even in his dreams. The gods have granted him foreknowledge of his doom."

Gods? Some gods granted victory to a champion who brought them trophies of human blood. "Mathias — Father — you still don't understand. He'll *appreciate* your warning!"

"I do understand." He removed her hand from his arm and clasped it. Love flowed from him, depth, shrewdness, courage. "His is an old spirit. I see him for what he is, creature of the lower world, and I will stop him."

A gust of relief emptied from her. Unlike Adam Neville, Mathias *did* know his opponent.

With his other hand, her father stroked her face. "Now let us move on. With each step you take west, leave behind the fear that brought you to this place." He smiled. "You have earned the right to do so, my daughter."

HISTORICAL AFTERWORD

History texts and fiction minimize the importance of the southern colonies during the American War of Independence. Many scholars now believe that more Revolutionary War battles were fought in South Carolina than in any other colony, even New York. Of the wars North Americans have fought, the death toll from this war exceeds all except the Civil War in terms of percentage of the population. And yet our "revolution" was but one conflict in a ravenous world war.

The impact of women during the American War, especially those on the frontier, has been minimized. Women during this time enjoyed freedoms denied them the previous two centuries and the following century. They educated themselves and ran businesses and plantations. They worked the fields and hunted. They defended their homes. They ministered their folk religion at gatherings. They fought on the battlefield. Although unable to vote, women did just about everything men did.

The Battle of Camden occurred on 16 August 1780 in South Carolina. The Continental Army was twice the size of the British Army, but it was annihilated because the commander, Horatio Gates, made severe errors in judgment — errors that cost the life of the gallant Major-General Johannes de Kalb. This battle came several months after another critical Continental defeat, the Battle of Charles Town. Those two battles, along with the Continental defeat at the Battle of Savannah (October 1779), might have meant total downfall for the Continental Army in the Southern Theater. But the British followed the Battle of Camden with their own series of military blunders, and soon they were headed up the road to their strategic encounter with the Continental Army in Yorktown, Virginia (October 1781).

Judging from his career in India after he left North America, Charles Brome, the Earl Cornwallis, was an excellent military strategist and an able and intelligent commander, not to mention being just a decent person. He didn't relish getting tough on colonists, pleading their case with Parliament before his wife died, leaving the harsher disciplinary measures to those of his subordinate officers who commanded mobile units throughout the Carolinas and Virginia, such as Lieutenant Colonel Banastre Tarleton. Frustrated in early 1781 by British setbacks and a lack of colonial submission, Cornwallis personally assumed the heavy-handed approach as he made his way to Yorktown.

British Colonel Francis Lord Rawdon is an unsung hero of the Camden Campaign. Combining courage and military common sense, he and his men protected the citizens of Camden in July and August of 1780 while delaying the approach of the Continentals, thus enabling Cornwallis's annihilation of the Continental Army in the Battle of Camden. Throughout the following year, he continued to distinguish himself in service to the king.

Loyalist Lieutenant Colonel Thomas Brown commanded the King's Carolina Rangers and was based for a short time in Augusta, Georgia, where he kept order in the city. While defending Augusta, he and some of his men were besieged for almost a week in the heat of summer (September 1780) by forces commanded by Elijah Clarke. When British reinforcements arrived and took prisoners, Brown promptly hanged thirteen of his besiegers. Historically Brown has gotten a bad rap for this action. However each of the thirteen hanged men had either broken parole (punishable by law with execution) or was from among a mob that had attacked, tortured, and maimed Brown in 1775 when he was trying peacefully and diplomatically to calm them down.

SELECTED BIBLIOGRAPHY

Dozens of websites, interviews with subject-matter experts, the following books and more:

Barefoot, Daniel W. *Touring South Carolina's Revolutionary War Sites*. Winston-Salem, North Carolina: John F. Blair Publisher, 1999.

Bass, Robert D. *The Green Dragoon*. Columbia, South Carolina: Sandlapper Press, Inc., 1973.

Boatner, Mark M. III. *Encyclopedia of the American Revolution*. Mechanicsburg, Pennsylvania: Stackpole Books, 1994.

Campbell, Colin, ed. *Journal of Lieutenant Colonel Archibald Campbell*. Darien, Georgia: The Ashantilly Press, 1981.

Cashin, Edward J., Jr. and Heard Robertson. *Augusta and the American Revolution: Events in the Georgia Back Country 1773-1783*. Darien, Georgia: The Ashantilly Press, 1975.

Cashin, Edward J., Jr. *The King's Ranger: Thomas Brown and the American Revolution on the Southern Frontier*. Athens, Georgia: The University of Georgia Press, 1989.

Dunkerly, Robert M. and Eric K. Williams. *Old Ninety Six: A History and Guide*. Charleston, South Carolina: The History Press, 2006.

Edgar, Walter. *Partisans and Redcoats: the Southern Conflict That Turned the Tide of the American Revolution*. New York: HarperCollins Publishers, Inc., 2001.

Gilgun, Beth. *Tidings from the Eighteenth Century*. Texarkana, Texas: Scurlock Publishing Co., Inc., 1993.

Hudson, Charles. *The Southeastern Indians*. Knoxville, Tennessee: The University of Tennessee Press, 1992.

Kirkland, Thomas J. and Robert M. Kennedy. *Historic Camden, Part One*. Columbia, SC: The R. L. Bryan Company, 1994.

Mackesy, Piers. *The War for America 1775-1783*. Cambridge, Massachusetts: Harvard University Press, 1964.

Mayer, Holly A. *Belonging to the Army: Camp Followers and Community During the American Revolution*. Columbia, South Carolina: University of South Carolina Press, 1996.

Morrill, Dan L. *Southern Campaigns of the American Revolution*. Mount Pleasant, South Carolina: The Nautical & Aviation Publishing Company of America, Inc., 1993.

Peckham, Howard H. *The Toll of Independence: Engagements and Battle Casualties of the American Revolution*. Chicago: The University of Chicago Press, 1974.

Scotti, Anthony J. *Brutal Virtue: the Myth and Reality of Banastre Tarleton*. Bowie, Maryland: Heritage Books, Inc., 2002.

Tunis, Edwin. *Colonial Craftsmen and the Beginnings of American Industry*. Baltimore: The Johns Hopkins University Press, 1999.

About the Author

S uzanne Adair is the *nom de plume* for Suzanne Williams, a native Floridian who currently lives with her family in North Carolina. In second grade, she wrote her first fiction for fun after the eye of a hurricane passed over her home, and she grew up intrigued by wild weather, stories of suspense and high adventure, Spanish St. Augustine, and the South's role in the Revolutionary War. She has traveled extensively and lived in England for half a year. After visiting the ruins of colonial-era Ft. Frederica on St. Simon's Island, Georgia, she began writing the first book in her series set in the American South during the Revolutionary War, *Paper Woman*. She enjoys participating in living history events from the Southern Theater of the Revolutionary War — a hobby that helps her depict colonial life in writing. For more information, visit **www.suzanneadair.com.**

Printed in the United States
111351LV00001B/8/A

ML